INQUEST

Paul Carson is a medical doctor and writer. He has published fifteen works (seven health books, two children's novels and, now with *Inquest*, six thrillers). His first thriller, *Scalpel* (1997), was an *Irish Times* number 1 bestseller and remained there for thirteen consecutive weeks. It stayed in the Top 5 Bestseller list for a total of thirty-three weeks. This was followed by *Cold Steel* (1998), *Final Duty* (2000), *Ambush* (2003) and *Betrayal* (2004). All were number 1 bestsellers in Ireland. His works have been translated into twenty languages.

Paul contributes to a wide range of publications, including the *Sunday Times*, the *Irish Times*, *Irish Independent*, *Medical Independent* and *Irish Medical News*. He is married and lives in south Dublin.

For more details, visit: www.paulcarson.ie

Also by Paul Carson

PAUL
CARSON
INQUEST

arrow books

Published by Arrow Books 2014

2 4 6 8 10 9 7 5 3 1

First published in Great Britain in 2013 by
Century
Random House, 20 Vauxhall Bridge Road,
London SW1V 2SA

www.randomhouse.co.uk

Addresses for companies within The Random House Group Limited can be found at:
www.randomhouse.co.uk

The Random House Group Limited Reg. No. 954009

A CIP catalogue record for this book
is available from the British Library

ISBN 9780099588771

The Random House Group Limited supports the Forest Stewardship
Council® (FSC®), the leading international forest-certification organisation. Our
books carrying the FSC label are printed on FSC®-certified paper. FSC is the only
forest-certification scheme supported by the leading environmental organisations,
including Greenpeace. Our paper procurement policy can be found at:
www.randomhouse.co.uk/environment

Typeset in Palatino (11.4/13.95pt) by Palimpsest Book Production Ltd,
Falkirk, Stirlingshire
Printed and bound by CPI Group (UK) Ltd, Croydon, CR0 4YY

To Jean, Emily and David

Acknowledgements

Dr Brian Farrell, the real Dublin City Coroner, advised on background to *Inquest*. The staff at the coroner's court also fielded my queries about court procedures.

Thanks to Simon Hess and Declan Heeney (Gill Hess Ltd) for supporting the novel and bringing it to Random House. Thanks also to Susan Sandon and Georgina Hawtrey-Woore at Random House.

A certain John Hobbs asked me to use his name. So I did. Here you go, Hobbsie.

Inquest is fiction based on a significant amount of fact. That said, there's a degree of writer's licence throughout the book. Blurring of procedures and the occasional factual error were necessary to move the story along.

Chapter 1

My work is death.

Homicide, suicide, death by misadventure, death by medical negligence, burns, drowning, drug overdose, electric shock, surgical shock, hit by a train, run over by a bus: I deal with them all. And a lot more besides.

I'm a doctor but my charges don't speak to me. None of them complain about stomach cramps, headaches, sore throats or dizzy spells. I don't check their blood pressure, inspect their skin and nails or examine their eyes. Yet I know more about them than they knew about themselves. I know more about them than their family and friends ever did. I know when and where they were born, how and where they lived. And how and when they died.

By day I learn of their lives and loves, marriages and offspring, occupations and social habits. By night I read their autopsy reports.

There are mornings I wake up with photographs scattered on the carpet at the side of my bed. Brutal and graphic pictures of crime scenes and post-mortem findings. They would have slipped out of my grasp the night before as I struggled against overwhelming tiredness. Sometimes these images haunt my dreams. Like ghosts.

On nights such as these I don't sleep well. I am banished to the guest room as Sarah, my wife, refuses to share the marriage bed. She finds the wretchedness of this work too distressing. It's not that she doesn't love me because she says she does and I believe her. And I love her more than I can ever express. But I have weighty responsibilities. My official title is Dr Michael Wilson, Dublin City Coroner.

I own the dead of Dublin.

I am their final voice.

Chapter 2

Patrick Dowling was found hanging in woodland on 30 November 2009. The police investigation into the twenty-eight-year-old man's death ended as soon as the autopsy result was announced. Suicide. They made a few inquiries, talked to close friends and family, but not with any real purpose. As far as they were concerned the case was closed. Then, tragic circumstances forced the inquest into my office, and after studying the file for some time I came to a very different conclusion. Dowling had been murdered.

My role as coroner is to investigate events like this. I inquire into unusual, unexplained, violent or unnatural deaths. I ask the who, when, where and how? And then I decide what happened. The state must have an understanding on strange fatalities, and families must have closure.

Once I decided Dowling had not died by his own hand I had to take on the state and prove it.

So at 1.45 p.m. on Thursday 3 June 2010, I started with Jack Matthews, the detective who'd discovered the body. We were in my office, or the 'room of sighs' as I call it, at the Dublin City Coroner's Court; sighs because that's mostly what staff hear from me there as I pore over paperwork. I've another name for the court itself: 'the chamber of ghosts'. I've a vivid imagination.

'When Dowling was found he'd been missing less than twenty-four hours.' I said it as if I was going over the inquest file for the first time. I looked across and Matthews nodded.

I arched my eyebrows. 'Why the sudden search? He was a grown man. He could've been anywhere. Shacked up with a friend. Sleeping off a hangover in his car. Got lucky with a girl. There could've been any number of explanations for his disappearance.'

'Dowling was a drug addict,' Matthews said. 'He was the son of Albert Dowling, government minister. He'd been in a brawl the day before with a notorious criminal. There was concern for his safety.'

Matthews was also the officer in charge of the search for Dowling. Mobile phone tracking technology had led his team to a deserted forest on the Dublin/Wicklow border.

I swivelled in my chair, then drummed my fingers on the desk in front of me. Matthews showed no emotion. Big, neutral face.

I pretended to accept this account. 'So that's why you moved so quickly.' I took a bite of a sandwich. It tasted lousy. I inspected the packaging: it was laced with enough additives to bring me out in a rash and give me heartburn. I pushed the snack to one side and flicked at another page from the dossier. Again, I made it look like I'd just come to it afresh. In fact, this was my third assessment. At the end of the first reading a number of things jarred. Suspicious bruising on the corpse. Conflict between toxicology results and Patrick Dowling's behaviour. An almost empty bottle of whiskey found in the deceased's car, with not as much as a smudged fingerprint on it. Why would a man hell-bent on killing himself take time to wipe down a bottle of whiskey? So I pored

4

over the paperwork again. This time I dissected it foren-sically. And since my training is in pathology I know how to do this methodically. I challenged the typed version, underscoring sections I was particularly unhappy about. By the end I was convinced someone was lying. Police, witnesses or family were the main suspects. Dowling had been murdered, I was sure of that.

I read aloud the toxicology findings. 'He'd traces of heroin, cocaine and amphetamines in his system.' I frowned so hard it almost hurt. 'That's quite a cocktail. I'm surprised he could tie his shoelaces let alone knot a rope.'

Matthews didn't answer. He shifted uneasily in his chair, rubbed at his nose and scratched his chin. He looked like he wished he was a million miles away. He was a tall and balding man in his early fifties, about six three and going to seed. His skin was pasty from too much deskwork and he'd developed a significant paunch. His fingernails were chewed to the quick. The crumpled suit he was wearing almost matched the creases on his face. Now a hint of uncertainty flickered there.

'When discovered there was a bar stool overturned beneath him.' I kept my voice monotone, boring. 'His muddy footprints were lifted from the surface. Conclusion: he placed the noose around his neck, stood on the stool and then kicked it away.' I darted another glance towards Matthews. 'Now how the hell did he manage to do all that?'

Matthews shrugged. His face was sombre, his eyes dull. I wondered briefly if the memory of the hanging and lifeless twenty-eight-year-old Dowling still haunted him. No one who comes across sudden death ever forgets the sight. 'Can't tell you, Dr Wilson,' he said. 'That's how we found him.'

5

He was giving nothing away. If he was lying, he was good at it. Then again, maybe he knew nothing. Or he actually believed the material in Dowling's file stacked up. If he did he was stupid. Or deluded. In my worst-case scenario Matthews was acutely aware the dossier was riddled with ambiguity. And deviously pretending ignorance. But I wouldn't reveal my suspicions. My immediate plan was to see if I could unsettle him. He thought he was here for a preliminary discussion on the inquest, not a cross-examination.

I slipped off my jacket and draped it over the back of my swivel chair. Then I opened the top button on my shirt and pulled my tie loose. Without a word I opened the dossier to reveal paperwork and photographs. Matthews watched my every move.

On the desk in front of me, I spread the police photographs of the hanging. Dowling's body was found in a clearing ten yards from the edge of a forest. The trees were clumped together, the setting dark and eerie. The photographer had captured fallen branches, broken branches and the debris of a recent storm: twigs, dead leaves and a chaos of foliage. Bark was peeling or torn from the trunks of thick pines. Then there was the body. FLASH. Upper torso, head resting on a neck twisted horribly forwards. FLASH. A different angle. Lifeless and swollen face. FLASH. Close-up of rope digging into Dowling's neck. This view caught Dowling's mouth, nose and blank eyes. I stared at the shot, turning it this way and that, as if the brutal image would offer some insight into the dead man's thoughts. Suicide is an act of despair. Most fight for life, even fight to the death to survive. Were you in the depths of despair that day, Patrick? Or did something else happen to you? Were you really alone as everyone believes? Or was someone with you? Did you take your own life? Or did someone kill you?

I switched to another section of the file. 'The autopsy concluded Dowling committed suicide and that's the state's position for the inquest.'

Matthews nodded again.

I sighed out loud. *Well,* I thought, *the state and I are definitely at odds on this.* 'I'm still surprised that he ended it all in woodland miles from home. Most suicides choose local territory.'

Matthews leaned forward. His breathing became heavy and laboured. He screwed his eyes up so tight all I saw were suspicious slits.

'Something's bugging you, Dr Wilson. What is it?'

I didn't answer. There was a lot bugging me. But I wanted to play my cards carefully. This might take time. I had time. Dead men don't rush their own inquests. I placed the police shots in three rows. The first highlighted the background and woods; the second collection of seven was of the hanging body. The last group showed a narrow trail leading past where Dowling was found. Outside a phone rang, stopped and then rang again. It rang out unanswered.

'Is that track used often?' I was so hungry I took another bite from my sandwich. To hell with rashes and indigestion, I had to eat.

Matthews inspected the back of his hands as if he'd written notes there. 'It's hard to say. It's not a major hiking trail but some hill walkers do follow it.' The suspicious eyes didn't relax.

'Where does it lead?'

'About a mile further on there's open ground leading to foothills. It's popular with cross-country runners in the summer months.'

'But in November?'

'Lemme put it this way, Dr Wilson. Dowling was hanging for almost twenty-four hours when we discovered his body. Nobody else came forward to say they'd spotted him.'

I sifted through the forest snaps, careful not to smudge the prints with greasy fingers. It didn't look inviting. Dark, hostile, spooky. I doubted many would venture there in winter.

'I can't get my head around the location,' I said. 'I read about this at the time. The papers said Dowling was a city boy, through and through. How'd he end up so far away?'

I wasn't expecting an answer and I didn't get one.

'I dunno.' I shook my head. 'I just dunno.' In the adjoining building site a heavy-duty digger started up. The windows rattled. My sandwich was wilting. So was my appetite.

Dowling's case was one of twenty that'd landed on my desk ten days earlier. His death happened in Dublin county territory and therefore the inquest should have been dealt with by Dr Harold Rafferty, the county coroner. But a month ago Rafferty was shot as he walked to his car. According to eyewitnesses, a hooded gunman calmly walked up behind him, called out his name and fired point blank into his face as he turned. Then, almost as unhurriedly, the assassin strode to a high-powered motorbike that'd pulled into the car park. He climbed onto the pillion seat and sped off. A passing motorist spotted him throwing the handgun into a river about a mile away. After that there were no sightings.

Rafferty was sixty-four and near retirement. His work was exemplary but not without controversy. He often challenged police evidence and forensic reports if he thought the work was shoddy. Famously he'd once taken on the might of the military during an inquest. A supposed accidental shooting turned out to be murder when Rafferty's probing from the bench exposed a web of deceit and cover up among senior officers. That day he became a hero in the law-enforcement community but loathed among army circles. Even so, there was no obvious motive to explain why he had been murdered in such a dispassionate and professional way.

Everyone, from judiciary to government, was stunned by his assassination. Then, in a scramble to complete pending inquests, Rafferty's backlog was dispersed. I'd been handed a significant bulk of his caseload. All seemed routine, except Dowling's. I was convinced Dowling hadn't killed himself. And if he hadn't, how did he end up hanging by the neck from a rope in deserted woodland? I decided someone was with him. Dowling hadn't died alone. Someone was contriving a cover up.

'Here's another thing I was surprised about.' I was like a dog at a bone. 'The hurry.'

Matthews couldn't strangle the groan. He coughed to hide it. 'What hurry?' Outside the digger's engine idled and the windows stopped rattling.

'He disappeared on the twenty-ninth, was discovered on the thirtieth and opened at autopsy within twenty-four hours. He was buried two days later.' I leaned back in my chair and stared at the detective. 'That seems like one helluva rush to me.'

'I investigated the Dowling death,' Matthews said sharply. He was scowling. 'We took about a dozen statements, including those from his closest friends. The family organised the burial, not me.'

I held up a hand. 'Once the pathologist decided he

committed suicide that pretty much was the end of the story, wasn't it?' This was the other man's get-out card.

'Yes.' Matthews' glower eased. He was off the hook. I'd deal with the pathologist later. He'd have a hard job persuading me his autopsy conclusion was correct.

I decided I wasn't going to get anything more useful from Matthews. He'd set his mind on the suicide theory and wouldn't budge. I'd come at him from another angle on another day. I closed the file and made a show of putting it at the top of a collection of other dossiers. I squared it neatly so it wouldn't fall off.

'Then that probably is the end of the story,' I lied. I needed more time. No way would this inquest be heard until my doubts were satisfied. I looked at my diary. 'I'll schedule it first thing on Monday, twenty-eighth of June. That's less than four weeks from now. I'll ask my secretary to notify the family. We need a jury verdict because of the circumstances. That means oral evidence from both you and the forensic team. Okay?'

Matthews looked anxious. 'Are you sure you can't start the inquest any earlier than this? His family obviously want to get this over with as soon as possible.'

I gestured towards my workload, a high pile of files. All were accounts of fatalities in strange or unusual circumstances. 'See these files?' I told Matthews. 'Each of them represents a man, woman or child. Each one died in strange or unusual circumstances. That's why they've ended up here, with me. No matter what their position in life, whether they're wealthy or the poorest of the poor, they all deserve my attention. They all deserve an explanation of what happened during their final moments of life. And they all deserve to have the truth written on their death certificates.'

Matthews shifted in his seat.

'If the minister is concerned about the date, tell him to come to me. But also tell him that I won't give in. In my court the dead wait in line, there are no queue jumpers. Money or influence does not grab an earlier slot.'

Matthews was on his feet. He couldn't get out of the room quick enough. 'Okay, okay, fine. Make sure you let the Dowling family know. They're very edgy about this inquest.'

I had heard of Albert Dowling, of course. He was the head of the family and a government minister. Any television footage I'd seen showed a tall, handsome sixty-year-old man with a fine head of steel-grey hair. He had a jutting chin with a dimple and narrow hawk-like eyes under bushy grey eyebrows that bristled when agitated. I didn't know him personally but was aware of his reputation as a bully who insisted on getting his own way. Gossip hinted at corruption. Need your land re-zoned from agricultural use to development? No problem, ask Albert. He knew how to buy votes at planning meetings. He knew which councillors could be bribed and for how much. He could force a motorway through medieval burial sites, switch EC grants to his own constituency to gather votes at election time. He was a crook in an administration plagued with crooks. But he stood out. He didn't give a damn what others thought about him. He was brazen and bold and intimidating. But the death of his eldest son Patrick had taken the fire out of his belly. Or so I'd been told by those who knew.

Matthews was at the door and halfway out.

'If there's a problem in the meantime,' I said, 'we can get in touch.'

He stopped, one hand gripping the door frame. 'What sort of problem?'

'I don't know,' I said, 'I'm speaking generally. Problems with availability of the pathologist, problems with court

11

time, problems with witness attendances.' Why was Matthews so edgy? He looked scared, as if there was a ghost behind my back, staring at him. 'Martians landing, floods, riots, tempests and pestilence. How do I know? I'm only using a turn of phrase: "any problem, get in touch". I'm not suggesting we're actually going to have a problem.' Yet.

Matthews offered a wintry smile. It didn't reassure me. There *was* something bothering him. His expression said it all. He wasn't confident with this case. He knew the evidence didn't stack up. He was going through the motions, hoping I'd get fed up asking questions and accept everything at face value. If I was right then Matthews was wrong. I don't do face values. I'm a specialist pathologist with a troubled background. I trust few. I didn't trust him. I didn't trust the autopsy findings. In fact I didn't trust anything in the dossier.

When he left the room I took the file from the pile and opened it. I glanced at my watch. I had thirty-five minutes before the lunch recess ended. Fresh hunger drove me to the final quarter of my snack. Within minutes acid spilled into my stomach and I reached for a packet of Rennies.

I sifted through the photographs until I found the one I wanted. It was in the group highlighting the woodland. I squinted at it from different angles, turning it to catch the light. Then I peered at it through a magnifying lens. An indistinct blur had caught my attention. No matter how much I looked it remained a shadow. A red-eyed shadow.

Chapter 3

I became Dublin City Coroner in February 2008, just as Ireland's Celtic Tiger was beginning to lose its roar. The property bubble, fuelled by cheap money, irresponsible bank lending and government incompetence, had been pricked. Air was whooshing out at a hundred miles an hour. Alarm bells were ringing in financial and administration circles. Estate agents were panicky, their sales pitches becoming more strident, desperate even. Property developers melted from sales rooms like snow on a ditch. Building firms found money drying up so fast they couldn't pay sub-contractors; sub-contractors couldn't pay their workers; the workers couldn't pay their mortgages. Banks moved in to repossess the workers' houses. Businesses around the country started pulling down shutters and not pulling them up again. East European immigrants, scorched by the sudden collapse, fled to their homelands. Stories abounded of cars abandoned at Dublin airport with house keys and property repossession orders left in the glove box. The sense of national gloom and dismay was palpable. Soon gloom turned to fury and the airwaves sizzled with rage against the government.

Out of the blue I got a telephone call from Damien Johnston, the Minister for Justice. At the time I was working as head pathologist in the halogen-lit basement of University Hospital, once the city's most prestigious medical facility. I'd just finished a post-mortem and was preparing for another.

'I'm looking to recruit a fearless, clear-headed and tough-talking coroner,' Johnston said, 'and I'm told you're the man for the job.' Flattery. Not usually the best tactic to use on me, but I was intrigued about the position nonetheless. He declined to visit my office to discuss the proposition. He confessed he felt uneasy in hospitals. I allowed him his weakness.

The UH pathology department wouldn't have been everyone's favourite meeting place, especially with bodies laid out on stainless-steel tables awaiting autopsy.

'Why me?' I waved directions to my assistant, a small, balding and morose man whose skin was as ashen as the corpses around us. I wanted a new set of dissection material for the next cadaver. Fresh scalpels. Fresh stainless-steel saws. Fresh heavy-duty plastic apron. Fresh eye protectors. Fresh latex gloves. I glanced at the clock. It was 3.35 on a Wednesday afternoon. We'd open the body at four sharp.

'Because you don't flinch from hard decisions,' Johnston said. 'You pull no punches and you've earned a lot of respect in that hospital. The place is riddled with professional jealousy.'

This was true. UH was plagued by dissent. Department heads fought like alley cats. The cancer division had been designated a centre of excellence but at the expense of other units. Cardiologists sniped at oncologists, the neurologists bitched about everybody, while the dermatologists staged a walk out. The hospital had become a sorry spectacle, decried for being disordered. When I took over the pathology unit I pushed through changes that triggered immediate controversy. First I dismissed an associate for shoddy clinical practice. Ten days later I insisted on the retirement of the longest-serving doctor after I tipped onto her desk a box of empty vodka bottles that had been discovered in her locker. Then, in an institution notorious for racism, I appointed two Asian pathologists.

'I take pride in my department,' I said to the minister. 'It's now the envy of the building. We have a real camaraderie here and I've overseen a significant improvement in standards. All that was needed was a leader.'

'But a leader with balls of steel.'

'Maybe I was just the right man in a bad place at the wrong time.' I played down my role. Johnston was patronising me and I don't like being patronised. I don't need it. My work speaks for itself.

The minister cut to the chase. 'I'd like you to be the next Dublin City Coroner. The pay is lousy; the workload is onerous and your office is in a Victorian building that should've been bulldozed years ago. You won't have enough staff and I don't have the money to provide more.' I could almost see him grinning. 'It's a wonderful opportunity for an ambitious man like you.'

I told him he'd taken me by surprise and I needed to think this over.

'I'll give you forty-eight hours. Today's Wednesday. Call me by five Friday afternoon.'

Later I spent an hour on the phone with Paul Crossan, the outgoing coroner and man I would replace. He was retiring early for health reasons after close on twenty years in the job. He outlined the challenges. 'Right now you're a hospital doctor,' he said. 'You do autopsies looking for cause of death or to learn more about disease progression or to better help your in-house colleagues understand why their treatments or operations didn't work.' Crossan's voice was gravel-edged; like he was a two-pack-a-day smoker.

'That's a fair assessment.'

'As a pathologist you know little about the person who inhabited the body you're dissecting. You're a scientist and not interested in the life lived beforehand.'

I nodded as I listened.

'But as coroner your objectivity ends. Now you get involved. Someone else will conduct the post-mortem and offer the findings. You assess this and all other factors. Finally, you decide a cause of death. You're going to be constantly involved with death. Indeed, you become an advocate for the dead.'

This took me completely by surprise. 'What do you mean by that?'

Crossan cleared his throat. 'Every inquest demands a final answer. And in that courtroom there is a ghost desperate to be understood. Why did he die? How did he die? If you want to be a coroner, you need to ask yourself whether you can reach out to that dead man and explain his sudden mortality. You need to be his voice.'

There was a silence at both ends as I tried to grasp the significance of these comments.

'If you take the job remember this.'

He paused again. I wondered what was coming.

'Your responsibility is to the dead of Dublin and no one else. Think of inquests as their final court of appeal. Never again will the deceased's final hours be so carefully examined.'

I thanked him and said goodbye. My hand was shaking as I put down the receiver. I hardly slept that night, tossing and turning as the responsibilities of the position flooded my imagination. Next morning I confided in my wife, Sarah. I'm forty-six years old and she's four years younger. We've been married seventeen years and I value her judgement greatly. She's a rock of common sense, level-headed and knowledgeable with a woman's instinctive intuition on matters of importance.

She listened carefully, only interrupting to clarify what she didn't understand. Finally she gave her opinion. 'You need a fresh challenge,' she said. 'You've turned the UH pathology unit around. What more can you do there?' She pecked me lightly on the cheek and gave me one of her teasing smiles. 'It's time to move on, Mike Wilson. There are bigger mountains to climb.'

I rang the Minister for Justice before his deadline expired. 'I'd like to be the next Dublin City Coroner.'

'Good man.' That's all he said.

The contract arrived within days. Pay, conditions of employment including holidays, sick leave and pension contributions. I studied it, put it aside and then re-evaluated it. Despite the minister's warnings, it was good. Good job, good pay, decent working provisions.

I started climbing the next big career mountain four months later. I thought it would be no more of a challenge than a hike in the foothills. I was wrong.

Chapter 4

I asked Joan, my secretary, to arrange for the group of forest background shots to be enlarged. That's not unusual. As coroner I occasionally ask for photos to be enlarged to better assess fatal incidents. It was while I was sorting through them that I discovered two were missing. On the back of each was a police stamp authentication, photo number and description. Shot 1 of body. Shot 2 of body. Shot 1 of forest glade. Et cetera. Separately there was a list of all material in the file. Witness statements that included names, addresses, contact numbers and exact total of pages in testimonies. The same went for police, forensic and toxicology paperwork. Everything was itemised and recorded. According to the inventory there should have been twenty photos in Patrick Dowling's dossier. I counted them again, placing each to one side so I wouldn't confuse myself. There were eighteen. Two were missing. Numbers eleven and twelve. Lost in transit? Misplaced while being collected for the inquest? Or stolen?

The desk clock warned I'd fifteen minutes before the first inquest of the afternoon. Still time, I decided, to push my questions in another direction. I dumped the remains of my sandwich in a bin. I almost threw in a few Rennies to stop it getting heartburn. Then I swallowed a mouthful of cold tea and started dialling. I wanted to check with the county coroner's office to see if the missing photographs were in the late Harold Rafferty's files. He'd had the Dowling dossier first. Maybe they were in his room somewhere.

My call was answered just as Joan double-checked which pictures I wanted enlarged. It'd be arranged through police HQ where the original digital images were stored.

'Andrew Styles here. What can I do for you, Dr Wilson?' Styles ran the county coroner's office. He'd been working there for at least a decade so he'd understand my concern. I'd met him once before at a coroners' conference in the Burlington Hotel. He was a tall, reedy man with an air of constant unease. First I offered my condolences on Harold Rafferty's death. I'd formally written to the county coroner's staff after the shooting expressing my shock, horror and outrage at his murder. I praised Rafferty's hard work and dedication to duty and expressed my hope that the killers would be brought to justice. His funeral turned out to be a major event, with a strong representation of police, judiciary and the serving administration. Every coroner I knew was there, all looking as sorrowful as I felt. The grey granite church in Rathfarnham was filled to overflowing. It was a blustery, unseasonably cold and damp May morning. Subdued and anxious conversations were held by sombre-faced mourners, ears cupped against the stiff breeze. Umbrellas blew inside out. Mascara ran as eyes welled with tears from both grief and the wind. During the service there were denunciations from the pulpit. The celebrant called for tougher sentences against criminals and condemned the revolving-door system of convict release in the state's prisons. Opposition deputies nodded approval. Government deputies looked more and more like the dummies they were: stiff and emotion-less. Rafferty's wife and two grown-up children appealed for help with the murder inquiry. The chief of police refused to comment on the investigation other than to say that it 'was progressing'. He made it sound like an update on some infectious disease. Nobody believed him.

The burial of Harold Rafferty marked a black day for the courts and coroners. But it was a good day for some politicians. The administration was already in melt-down from its handling of the economy. Rafferty's funeral captured the headlines and switched the electorate's attention from finance to crime. The Minister for Justice took the brunt of media wrath. By contrast, the Minister for Finance was removed from the glare of unwanted publicity. But his reprieve didn't last long. Within days yet another banking scandal surfaced and his face returned to the front page of every newspaper: scowling and anxious; defensive and vague. Explaining this, that and the other. The economy was sound. We'd turned a corner. Exports were buoyant. Unemployment was stabilising. Nobody believed him either.

I told Styles about the missing photographs. There was silence from the other end.

'Are you still there, Andrew?' I asked.

'Yes, Dr Wilson.'

'Is there a problem?'

'No, no.' Styles sounded anxious to reassure me. 'Not really. Nothing that can't be sorted.'

What the hell did that mean?

'Can't be sorted?' I echoed. 'What can't be sorted?'

'We're talking about the same file, aren't we? The Patrick Dowling inquest?'

'Yes.'

'If anything's missing it's probably with the police.'

'The police?' I couldn't contain my surprise.

'The team investigating Dr Rafferty's murder. They pored over every file he was dealing with in the six months leading to the shooting. They seemed particularly interested in the Dowling case.'

Alarm bells rang. My mind raced as fast as my pulse. 'Did they indeed?'

But my humming antennae were suddenly distracted. My secretary tapped on the door and looked in. 'Inquest ready to start,' she mouthed.

Joan was an attractive twenty-nine-year-old with superb organisational skills. Five foot eight with an hourglass figure, she had the deepest blue eyes I'd ever seen and a pout better than Angeline Jolie's. She styled her long dark hair to suit her mood: business-only mode was braided; off the shoulders hinted that she was hunting for a man; tied at the back and she became a shameless flirt. It was tied back now but she wasn't flirting. She scowled at me and I flashed five fingers. *I need more time.* She glared her disapproval. I gave her a fixed false smile. The glare worsened. I waved her away.

'Have you any idea why they were so interested in the Dowling case?' I made it sound an innocent query. Almost as if I was looking for a snippet of juicy gossip.

There was another worrying silence.

'Still there, Andrew?'

'I'm not allowed to say anything, Dr Wilson. I'm sworn to secrecy.' Styles now sounded cagey. Apprehensive, as if he'd spotted a gunman hanging around the court buildings.

'Oh, sorry,' I said. 'I didn't know I was compromising you.' I was about to end the call when I suddenly remembered why I'd rung in the first place. 'So the photographs I'm looking for are with the investigating team?'

'I'd try there first, Dr Wilson.'

Styles hung up on me so fast I knew I'd unnerved him. What the hell was going on? Why were the police so interested in the Dowling case? Had they reviewed their position on his death? Then the pennies began dropping, one by one. County Coroner Harold Rafferty was an astute and questioning man. He was known for his attention to detail. Few mistakes escaped his scrutiny. He must've spotted the same problems in the Dowling file that I did. Like me, I was sure Rafferty wouldn't have allowed the inquest to go ahead unless he'd satisfied himself on the conflicting issues. He'd have let his concerns be known. Is that why he was killed? Had Harold Rafferty probed too deep into Patrick Dowling's supposed suicide? Like I was doing? I leaned back in my chair and studied the ceiling. This was getting scary. I wanted to immediately call Jack Matthews, the officer in charge of the Dowling case. I wanted to grill him until he sweated. But time was against me. Instead I contacted a detective friend and asked him to find out who was in charge of the Harold Rafferty investigation and organise a meeting with him as soon as possible. I was promised a prompt response.

Now I had to forget about Patrick Dowling. I had to stop probing. I closed the top button on my shirt, straightened my tie and pulled on my jacket. I reverted to Dublin City Coroner mode.

The dead awaited me.

Chapter 5

The coroner's court is a three-storey Victorian red-brick building on Store Street, just north of the River Liffey in the inner-city area. A battered, scratched and worn dark-blue door links the outside pedestrian walkway with the inside porch. Tiled floors direct the visitor to the reception-cum-front office on the left. If you turn immediately right you're in the main courtroom, where inquests are heard. I dubbed this 'the chamber of ghosts' not long after getting a feel for my new workplace. Paul Crossan, the coroner I replaced, captured the atmosphere perfectly during our conversation: in that courtroom there is a ghost desperate to be understood. It's hard not to sense spirits in the chamber. These spirits are never hostile or threatening or frightening but always subdued, passive and resigned. Each one waiting the final answer to his or her cause of death. It's an illusion, yes, but a heartbreaking illusion nonetheless. The rest of the building includes a basement with files going back decades, restrooms, and upstairs office and storage facilities. It's over one hundred years old, sorely in need of refurbishment and I've never felt wholly at ease down there.

During inquests I sit on a high mahogany desk at the head of the room with full view of everyone. On the wall behind me is the Dublin City crest: three castle watch-towers, the grips of two swords and the Latin motto *obedientia civium urbis felicitas*: happy the city where citizens obey. This is a bit rich as a more contrary citizenship could hardly be found anywhere. The crest reminds all that this is the sole inquiry hall for the metropolitan area. It's also the oldest court in the land. To my left are jury pews, not unlike those in a church but without kneeling ledges. Here the wood is dark and worn. To the immediate right is the witness box, a narrow mahogany compartment with microphone so even subdued depositions can be heard. In the middle and directly below my bench is a wide and dark wooden desk with chairs for court staff and legal representatives. The walls are painted the white of a winter moon. Arched wooden beams prop up a high, peaked roof. Among their struts, plump spiders scuttle across webs, well fed from a steady diet of flying insects. At the rear of the chamber is a large glass window that allows natural light to flood even the darkest recesses. Beneath this window is the visitors' gallery, long tiered rows of worn, dark benches. The wood is highly polished from the ever-shifting backsides of families enduring public airings of their loved one's demise. If you chipped this wood it'd weep. If you took an axe to it there'd be enough tears shed to float Noah's ark. No other benches have witnessed such sadness and insufferable grief.

Only noises from outside lighten the overwhelming sense of wretchedness in the room. Seagulls squawking along the river. Curses, shouts and laughs from the street. The trilling of bells from Luas trams. The screech of brakes from train wheels in nearby Connolly Station. Car horns. The growl of bus engines from the central bus garage opposite. All human life and noises are here in Dublin's north inner city.

Two doors up is Store Street police station, the busiest

law-enforcement bureau in the country. Next door is a building site, once home to the main city morgue. It's been relocated to Marino, about four miles further north. A pity really. The ghosts now have a long trek from the mortuary to the coroner's court. Years ago they'd only to travel a few yards.

In the previous week I'd held twenty inquests. Two were murder victims, another two were suicides, while three were suspected accidental drug overdoses. The rest was a mixed bag of fatalities. Last night I'd totted the figures, and so had a reporter from the *Evening Herald*, Dublin's late-edition tabloid. Seven of the ten deaths were drug related, either in gangland killings, self-harm or overdoses.

HUGE SURGE IN DRUG DEATHS, the paper trumpeted.

As a father of two that concerned me a great deal. My eldest, Jennifer, is fifteen and the image of her mother. My son, Gregory, is eleven and a chip off the Wilson block if ever there was one. My wife calls him Mini-Mike. Gregory hates the term and yells at Sarah every time she uses it. Secretly I'm delighted he looks so much like me. My boy. I'm a family man through and through and fiercely protective of my wife and children. I was orphaned at the age of twelve and spent my formative years in a remote and desolate boarding school on the north Antrim coast. Winds howled and wailed through every season. If it wasn't raining it was threatening to rain. If it wasn't freezing it was only because it was raining. When it snowed it snowed longer and harder than anywhere else. The thaw took weeks. The sun begrudged us heat, always dodging behind dark cloud banks. In the height of summer it was usual to wear woollen jumpers or risk catching pneumonia. If you survived a north Antrim winter you could trek to the North Pole in jeans and T-shirt. And back again.

My upbringing means that I trust no one other than my wife, and it explains why I value my family so much.

And why some inquests break my heart more than others.

Today the first hearing of the afternoon was a harrowing account of a young fatality.

A twenty-year-old girl sobbed as she recalled being abruptly confronted with her sister's secret life. 'She was working the streets to buy drugs, Coroner. None of us knew. Not me, not me brothers, nor me ma or da. She was only seventeen. I'd an idea she was taking something, maybe cannabis or sniffing glue, something stupid like that. But not heroin. That night I forced open the bathroom door and there she was, slumped on the floor with a needle stuck in a vein. I stood there shaking like a leaf and crying me eyes out. She was me only sister, Coroner, and I loved her. I still do. I was trying to take it all in when her mobile rang. I dunno why I answered it but I did. There was some fella wanting to know how much she charged for a blow job. And her dead, as cold as the tiles she was lying on.'

When she finished I bottled up my emotions and thanked her for her deposition and honesty. I offered my sympathy to the family, a worn-out and despairing group in the visitors' gallery. They filed out slowly, sobbing and dabbing at their eyes with handkerchiefs not thick enough to soak their tears.

Seventeen. The dead girl was only seventeen. Two years older than my daughter. And I still consider her a child. I know she's almost a woman. But fathers don't like to see their girls grow up. At least, not this father.

My head pounded from the anguish I'd just heard. My

mind spun with images of teenagers shooting up in toilets and selling their bodies to pay for heroin. I fumed at the amount of illicit drugs swamping the country. I cursed the thugs who traded narcotics. I was working up a fair lather of resentment when my secretary set a scribbled note in front of me. 'DI Pamela Roche will speak with you when you're free.' A mobile phone number was at the bottom of the page. My detective friend had come through for me. So the officer in charge of Harold Rafferty's murder investigation was a she, not a he. And she was also especially interested in Patrick Dowling's file.

I suspected she already knew I was too. I had no doubt that Andrew Styles, the county coroner office manager, would have relayed our conversation to her. He might be sworn to secrecy but not loyalty.

Between inquests I called Pamela Roche. She sounded surprised at my request to meet. Was anything wrong? Paperwork missing? Police officers not cooperating? I told her it wasn't something I could discuss on the phone. Could we get together for coffee? After work today? We agreed on a nearby café. Bongos on the Quay. That's what it's called. You couldn't make it up.

Chapter 6

Detective Inspector Pamela Roche didn't look like any of the detectives I usually deal with. There was no bruised or scarred face. No haunted or pinched features from lack of sleep so common in the force. No scowl set underneath thickset suspicious eyes. No tobacco-stained fingers, chewed nails or straggling hair. I don't know what I was expecting but it definitely wasn't the redhead in tight denims and white linen blouse sitting opposite me. Three undone buttons exposed cleavage and lace bra. A pair of sunglasses rested in a breast pocket. I put her in her early thirties; cute rather than beautiful. She had good skin with little cosmetic camouflage, dimpled cheeks, a pert nose and narrow lips. There was a hint of perfume. She sipped on a cappuccino and toyed at a ridiculously indulgent piece of cake. Bongos was a single-storey terrace café along the quays. It had plate-glass windows on three sides with views along the street and river. I ordered a smoothie and inspected the traffic. Sun rippled on the Liffey, dazzling and then fading as a bank of fluffy white cloud passed overhead. Seagulls chased catch, without much luck as far as I could see. Fifty yards away a police motor boat circled a barge. Someone on the barge (it looked like a male in a wetsuit) was dragging a cable. A float with a red flag bobbed on the waves, slowly being drawn towards the barge. I hoped there wasn't a body in the water. I hoped this wasn't yet another river death. Yet another inquest, yet another ghost.

Across the table Roche sighed. The cake was pushed to one side. I grinned in sympathy. 'Too many calories?'

'Too much almond,' she murmured. Then she sipped on her coffee, dabbed at her lips and faced me. 'What's on your mind, Dr Wilson?' She flicked at her hair as if it was blocking her view. It was cut short at the front, long at the back and layered at the side. For some stupid reason it reminded me of a tea cosy.

I leaned into my chair, glancing around to make sure we couldn't be overheard. The nearest customers were two tables away, three teenage girls gossiping and texting. The whooshing of steam from a coffee machine drowned out most conversation. Outside a cement lorry trundled past and the wooden floor shuddered. It was okay to speak.

'Patrick Dowling,' I said.

I knew she knew this already. I suspected she knew that I knew that she knew. In any case, her expression didn't change.

'What about Patrick Dowling?' Real casual.

Now I had to be careful. My concerns about the Dowling file were still hunches. I answered her question with one of my own.

'Is his death linked to Harold Rafferty's murder?'

Another sip on the cappuccino. I matched her with a long draw on my smoothie. She frowned slightly. I couldn't be sure if this was from the taste of the coffee or the way the conversation was going.

'I can't comment on that, Dr Wilson. All I can say· is we're following a definite line of inquiry into Dr Rafferty's murder,' she said.

'Spare me the clichés,' I said, 'I've serious doubts about

the Dowling case. And I suspect Harold Rafferty had too. I'm worried he was killed exploring those uncertainties.' There it was, out in the open. Now wasn't the moment to hold back. 'I hear you've spent considerable time going over the same file.' I watched for any sign of surprise. There was none. She did know that I knew. 'His suicide is being reviewed by your team. And your team is also looking for Rafferty's killers. Dowling and Rafferty are linked.' I leaned back in my chair and studied her face. 'How's my logic so far?'

Roche unexpectedly took another forkful of cake. She munched on it thoughtfully, as if she was going to give me a rating on its texture. Sip of cappuccino to wash it down. Dab with napkin on lips. 'What in particular concerns you?' Her voice was soft and coaxing with a slight Munster brogue. It hinted at a thousand agendas, but none of them pleasant. I decided she'd wear down criminals with feminine guile rather than brute force and threats.

I offered a deal. 'I'll trade medical expertise and insights in return for your investigation progress.' I tugged at my shirtsleeves and turned a cufflink the right way round. Roche seemed to consider this. Then she nodded: go ahead. I cleared my throat. 'To begin with the file's riddled with inconsistencies. Testimonies don't add up, conclusions are ridiculous. Even the forensic report is at odds with his behaviour.'

Roche pushed the plate to one side. The cappuccino was drained.

'Do you want to expand on that?' She was looking straight at me, her eyes narrowed in concentration. She'd lost interest in the cake.

I ran my hands in front of me like I was checking for dirt. 'Here's one glaring issue, for example,' I said. Roche shifted forward in her chair so as not to miss a word. 'I studied the autopsy photos. I read the pathologist's report. Dowling's body was wasted; he'd hardly any body fat. He was malnourished and frail. He tested positive for Hepatitis B and C. His elbow creases showed intravenous drug use. There were thrombosed veins . . .'

'Explain, please.' Roche cut through.

'He'd injected himself so often the veins became infected and shut off. It's common with addicts. And it reflects desperation, a real hunger for the drug. They're so hooked they shove dirty needles into any blood vessel that'll carry the high.'

'What else did you learn from the autopsy?'

'Dowling wasn't a strong man. He was twenty-eight when he died, theoretically in the prime of his life. However, he was six two in height and weighed less than a hundred and twenty pounds. That's eight and a half stone. You'd agree that given his height that's very frail, yes? Yet it's concluded he drove his car to remote woodland, took out a bar stool and walked fifty yards up a side track, wrapped a rope around the branch of a tree and fashioned a noose. Then this same frail and drugged man climbed up on the stool, pulled the noose around his neck and kicked the stool away.' I pulled a face. 'That just doesn't make sense.'

'You don't think he could've done that?'

'Not on his own.' I looked for a hint of surprise. There was none. I knew then the police were working along similar assumptions to my own.

Roche was studying me closely. 'What do you mean, "not on his own"?'

I shrugged. 'I've absolutely nothing to support that theory. Just my interpretation of the file. I don't believe that wasted, emaciated and strung-out man found

31

hanging in that deserted woodland could've killed himself. It's not simply that he was weak. Killing oneself, well, it requires focus and determination. He had traces of heroin, cocaine and amphetamines in his system. It's a cocktail that doesn't lead to clear thought, not the sort of thought that would propel someone to get in a car and drive miles outside the city. It's just not logical. There had to be someone else involved.'

'Are you suggesting assisted suicide?'

'That's one possibility.' Indeed I had considered and dismissed that angle. So I told her what I really thought. 'Another is murder.'

Roche's features froze. The dimpled cheeks were sucked in, the narrow lips tightened. 'But wouldn't the pathologist have picked that up? The autopsy conclusion was pretty definite.'

'It's happened before. Not often, but it's happened. Suicides can be staged.'

Roche looked at me strangely, as if I was slightly unhinged. 'That's one helluva statement, Dr Wilson.'

'This is one helluva case.' I ignored the questioning look. 'Pathology is my speciality. I know how to unpick doubtful findings.' I let that sink in. 'The Dowling case is on my desk. I'm not just going to nod it through without challenging testimony. That includes testimony from the police, pathologist, family and friends. Someone's lying and I'm going to find out who's lying and why they're lying.'

Roche fished a handbag from around her ankles. It was black mesh with silver lining and bulging. She rummaged around inside, finally pulling out a notebook. She scribbled a memo to herself. Unexpectedly a beggar appeared at one of the windows. He was unkempt with a straggling and dirty beard that hid his features. Long coat, shoes tied with twine. He looked in and shook his head at the poor pickings. He shuffled further along the quay, cap in hand and being rejected left, right and centre.

'Anything else?'

'Harold Rafferty would've spotted this as well,' I said. 'He wouldn't have allowed the inquest to be heard until he'd satisfied his doubts.'

'He postponed it twice,' Roche said, 'despite pressure from the Dowling family.' At last something useful was being traded. I was about to pick up on this when three skinheads, all tattoos, ugly mugs and designer sunglasses, swaggered into the café. They eyed Roche up and down, muttered among themselves and retreated to a corner table. Coffees were ordered, the shades were removed. Mumbling started. I glanced at them and a hostile stare greeted me.

'Do they know you?' I asked.

Roche kept her attention on me. 'Probably. This is drug-dealing territory. The pushers smell police before they see them.'

There was a loud burst of leery laughter from the skinheads. A few whoops as a phone message was read aloud. Then they gathered into a subdued huddle. The teenage gossipers and texters paid no attention to the arrivals. They were too engrossed in their own company.

'The Dowling case does interest us,' Roche went on, 'although not in the way you're suggesting. This is the first time anyone's questioned the autopsy report. We're looking at a link to Rafferty's murder. But boy, are we having difficulties pulling this together.'

'What do you mean?'

Roche sighed. She lifted the spoon from the saucer and ran it along the remaining froth of her coffee cup. Almost absent-mindedly she plopped it into her mouth.

The door opened and a man walked inside. He was wearing sunglasses. His overcoat, made of a heavy grey tweed, was buttoned to the neck despite the warmth of the late afternoon. I noticed he was in blue denims and white sneakers under the coat. The formality of the coat, combined with the informality of the jeans and trainers, struck me as odd but then we were in an odd part of the city. If someone sauntered in wearing a Roman gladiator's outfit, complete with helmet, no one would pay the slightest attention. This was a live-and-let-live district.

The stranger scanned the empty tables and singled one out. It was three from where we sat, two from the skinheads and next to the teenagers. Neither group looked up. Roche had her back to him so I was the only curious onlooker. The newcomer had a laptop case hanging over his left shoulder. He placed it carefully on the floor beside him and studied the menu. I could just about make out his face. There was a deep scar running from his left ear to neck. His fair hair was streaked with blond highlights. Big ears with studs. High brow. Jutting chin. I couldn't see his eyes behind the shades but sensed they were darting from side to side, as if surveying the terrain. He made me uneasy.

'Dowling was linked to organised crime.' Roche's comment immediately distracted me. 'He'd close contacts with a major drug dealer called Jonathan Redmond. Redmond controls most of the middle-class market here. He shifts only cocaine and amphetamines, doesn't handle heroin. Says it's beneath him and dangerous. He believes heroin is only for the dregs of society. And he wants to stay alive. Most drug killings involve heroin.'

Never were truer words spoken. The number of heroin-related homicide inquests had doubled in the past two

34

years. I knew that for law-enforcement officers throughout the city it was a worrying trend.

'The day Patrick Dowling hanged himself,' Roche paused, '*if* he hanged himself—'

'Indeed, *if*,' I wanted to reinforce my position.

'He brawled with a thug called Noel Carty.'

'How big is Carty?' I asked.

'Over six feet, broad-shouldered and very strong. He uses steroids to bulk his muscles. Last time he was arrested it took four officers to hold him down.'

I snorted my derision. 'So the emaciated and wasted Patrick Dowling battled it out with the equivalent of Attila the Hun. Now why would he have done that? He might've been spaced out but he must've known he wouldn't win.'

'We wondered that ourselves, Dr Wilson. I'm merely recounting the sequence of events. Dowling and Carty had a fist fight. Next day Dowling was found dead, apparently after taking his own life. There was a significant police investigation.' Roche leaned towards me conspiratorially. 'After all, he was the son of a senior government minister. So someone had to make a fuss. But as soon as the pathologist concluded suicide, the file was closed and the investigation called off.'

I mulled this over briefly. 'Do you know much about Carty?'

'He's Redmond's right-hand man.'

That brought me up sharply. 'The same Redmond that Dowling was close to?'

'Yes. Redmond spends most of his time in Marbella arranging drug deals and shipments. Carty handles the raw materials when they reach Ireland. He looks after Redmond's interests here.'

The man in the overcoat was still studying the menu.

I looked at it myself. There weren't many choices. Coffee (four varieties: cappuccino, regular, espresso, Americano) and tea (hot or iced). Three flavours of smoothie. Miscellaneous biscuits and cakes. Soft drinks. Gourmet dining this was not. Choosing a refreshment shouldn't take long. But the stranger was studying the options like he was learning them off by heart. I noticed him lean down and adjust the laptop case; he turned it awkwardly so that it rested between his feet. Then he looked towards the skinheads. They ignored him. He risked a sideways glance at the teenagers. He was still off their radar. Then he looked towards the sole assistant, a chubby black girl with a mass of curly hair. She was bursting out of a navy-blue trouser suit with yellow logo. As I glanced at her, she was drying cups and staring into the distance, miles away in a world of her own. The stranger now focused on our table and I cursed the dark glasses. I couldn't see his eyes. I didn't like him, whoever he was. He was making me more uneasy by the second. *For Christ's sake, order something.*

'Do you've any idea what Dowling and Carty were fighting about?'

'No. Carty denies any involvement with Dowling. He claims he was on the far side of the city all that day. And he's got witnesses to prove it.'

'Reliable witnesses?'

Roche looked at me as if I was a simpleton. 'Reliable liars.'

'So how do you know there was a row?'

'One of Dowling's friends called Harry Malone was with him. We've his testimony. And so have you.'

I made a mental note to re-read that section of the file: Harry Malone's deposition. Now I sensed an impasse, and I couldn't figure out how to get around it. I squinted into the busy street, deep in thought, and wishing I'd brought sunglasses to protect against the glare. *What's the link? How can I connect Dowling's hanging with Rafferty's murder?* There was one question demanding an answer. 'Why did Redmond, a major drug dealer from what you're telling me, have such close links with a two-bit wasted addict?' I kept one eye on the stranger. The waitress was moving towards him, smiling and humming some tune.

Roche was looking at me appraisingly. I sensed that there was something she was holding back from me. 'Dunno, Dr Wilson,' she said. 'If I knew that maybe we'd understand why Rafferty was shot.'

'What's stopping you connecting the dots?'

Roche leaned closer. I could see her eyes, speckled and grey. And deadly serious. 'Someone doesn't want us to make this association. Someone's going to a lot of effort to frustrate the investigation.'

I leaned back in my chair and mulled this over. The coffee machine whooshed. From the skinhead's table I overheard the end of some smutty story. The gang erupted with howls of delight. The stranger had his head buried in his hands, as if trying to shut out the words.

'Files have gone missing,' Roche was expanding on her problems, 'witness statements have been retracted, and memories are becoming forgetful. All of a sudden. I suspect Redmond has a mole in our camp.'

That shocked me. 'But what's being covered up?' I was struggling to grasp all I was hearing.

Roche shrugged another 'dunno'. Then her eyes suddenly narrowed. She flicked at her hair and eased back into her seat. She eyeballed me with an intensity that was almost scary. 'You're keen to get to the bottom of this, aren't you?'

37

It was an odd question and I sensed an agenda surfacing.

'Yes, of course I am,' I said. 'I'm the coroner in charge. The death is in the strange, unusual or violent category. My job is to find the truth.'

Roche leaned across the table. 'How far will you go to help?' She whispered the words as if we were starting our own conspiracy. 'Harold Rafferty was your colleague. You owe it to him and his family.'

I looked at Roche, surprised by her bald attempt at emotional blackmail. 'You don't need to remind me of my obligations,' I said. 'Just tell me what's on your mind.'

She sat back in her chair and fixed on me. 'The coroner's court is your territory. Everyone there plays by your rules. If the Dowling file's botched you can challenge everything from the bench during the inquest.'

'I've already told you. That's what I plan to do.'

Roche's features hardened. 'The Dowlings have been pushing for an early inquest. Rafferty refused. Why don't you hold it as soon as possible? Let's see if we can catch the bastards off guard.'

I was so engrossed in her enthusiasm I almost missed the overcoated stranger hurrying out. I only saw a blur of grey tweed, the flash of blue denim and white sneakers. He seemed in a real hurry to leave.

Roche leaned both elbows on the table and rested her chin on upturned palms. Her eyes never left mine. Piercing. Like bullets. 'Think about it. The police investigation is stymied. We've come at this from every angle but still the shutters stay down. Harold Rafferty hit the same obstacles.'

'How do you know?'

'His staff told us. It's no secret he had doubts about the file. And it's no secret he had problems sorting it out.'

'Who brushed him off?'

'The family, mainly. They kept hounding him to get on with the inquest. They clammed up when he asked questions. "Our son's dead," they'd say. "Nothing will bring him back. Stop annoying us. Hold the inquest and let us have an end to our misery. Isn't it enough that we lost Patrick?"'

'And Rafferty didn't believe them?'

'I suspect not. What's strange is that he bypassed official channels to get information. It's as if he didn't trust us.' Rafferty sounded a lot like me. Neither of us trusted strangers.

'Was he right?'

'The answer has to be yes. Why else was he shot? He was digging too deep for some people's liking.'

I slipped off my jacket. The café was becoming oppressively warm and I felt sweat trickle under my armpits. For a split second I wondered why the stranger in the tweed overcoat had it buttoned to his neck. Wouldn't he have been sweltering? Or – and even in the heat of the café this realisation chilled me – was he concealing something?

My mind switched to the moment. It was swirling with questions that needed answers. I wanted to know why Roche had held back photos eleven and twelve – I hadn't had the chance to ask her yet. I also wanted to know what she thought of Jack Matthews, the detective in charge of the Dowling case. Was he trustworthy? Could he be in on the cover up? Had she studied the autopsy photos? Had she noticed the red-eye blur that was puzzling me? I checked my watch. It was close on six o'clock. 'Maybe,' I offered, 'it centres on Dowling's link with the drug dealer?'

Roche's mobile shrilled and she cut it to mute. She

pursed her lips and rolled the phone back and forth. For the first time I noticed she had the long, delicate fingers of a piano player. No rings, no arm jewellery, just a slimline gold watch on a black leather strap around her left wrist. She dragged at her hair again. Then she checked the café. The skinheads were in deep conversation. The three teenage girls were still gossiping and texting. I sensed she was going to say something important but was weighing up the wisdom of sharing it with me. Her eyes clouded with inner conflict. She glanced left and right. She pulled at the buttons on her blouse nervously. The wooden floor beneath us shuddered again.

'More coffee?' The waitress was beside us.

'No thanks,' Roche replied.

'A smoothie for you?'

'No,' I said. 'I'll be leaving soon.'

The waitress started dragging chairs together and cleaning table tops. When she was out of earshot Roche sat upright, put the palms of her hands on the table and looked at me. 'What I say now stays here. Got that?'

'Of course.'

A flick of her hair and she was off.

'Dowling's father is a government minister.'

'I know.' Albert Dowling was Minister for Economic Development in a country sorely in need of any sort of development, economic or otherwise.

'Albert Dowling is linked to Jonathan Redmond, the drug dealer.'

Now she had my full attention. I opened the top buttons on my shirt and fanned at my neck with the menu.

'We don't know what the connection is but something's going on. Redmond rarely leaves Marbella. But last year he was spotted in Dublin speaking with Patrick Dowling regularly. Right up to the time of his death. Redmond doesn't handle goods so Dowling couldn't have been buying drugs. Anyway, Dowling's favourite hit was heroin.'

'And Redmond doesn't sell heroin,' I reminded myself out loud.

'Exactly.'

'So why was he so buddy-buddy with Redmond?'

'Albert Dowling couldn't be seen in the gangster's company. But his son was an addict and mixed freely in those circles. Maybe he was a go-between? Maybe he told his father what Redmond wanted him to hear and passed the reply back. It cuts out any phone or paper trail.'

Roche's argument made sense. I was about to add something when her mobile sounded again. She excused herself to take the call. She moved to a corner of the café, muttering and nodding.

I was left to my own thoughts. Harold Rafferty had spotted inconsistencies in the Dowling file. Did he think Dowling had been murdered? One way or another, searching for the truth had cost him his life. The police investigation was running into sand and now the head investigator wanted me to take the pack of lies on in my court. Which I planned to do, but maybe not in the way she was suggesting. The coroner's court is not a court of law. No one is charged with offences, tried and convicted there. It's a forum for the truth. The dead wait in line to hear the final and accurate account of their last hours.

But the more I thought about it the more I realised that I could do what Roche wanted me to. I'd need more information but it was very possible. If liars came to my chamber and I exposed their deceit, the mystery behind Dowling's death would finally unravel. After that it was up to the police to follow any link to Harold Rafferty's murder. I liked it. I liked it a lot. I was already working on an inquest date when I spotted the man in the grey overcoat. His forehead was pressed against a side window of the café. His shades were off and he was squinting inside. He looked anxious. I turned around. One of the skinheads had also noticed him. And a sudden agitated scowl swamped his features. Then, almost in slow motion, I looked towards the table where the man in the overcoat had sat earlier. The laptop case was still there. I spun back to see him staring straight at me. Our eyes locked for maybe two seconds, and his expression unnerved me. Then he turned and ran. And as he ran he dragged off the overcoat, abandoning it where it fell. Now I could see his real attire: white T-shirt, blue denims and white sneakers. Perfect for a quick getaway.

Oh Christ, no. I had the equivalent of a volcanic eruption in my brain. *He's left a bomb.*

'Get out!' I shouted. I was on my feet and lurching towards Roche. She spun around, phone still clamped to her ear. She looked at me as if I'd lost my mind. I stumbled sideways to the group of teenagers, grabbed one and threw her towards the door. 'Get out!' I roared frantically at the others. 'There's a bomb!'

There was a chaotic uproar. The skinheads scrambled over one another to make for the door. The chubby-faced assistant stood rooted to the spot, cup in one hand and tea cloth in the other. Her face was a mask of confusion. 'Get out, get out!' I bellowed again. My heart was pounding in my chest. 'For Christ's sake, get out!'

It was too late.

There was a muffled blast and suddenly the laptop

case burst into flames. I jumped on Roche and forced her to the floor. Her head banged off the wood and I heard a grunt of pain. Her mobile fell from her hand and skidded under a table. 'Get down, get down!' I was shouting like a madman.

One second later the glass walls shattered as a larger explosion filled the room. I went suddenly deaf, then heard a loud ringing in both ears. I felt shards of glass and bricks fall around my head. Roche flinched as rubble hit off her. She swore and tried to wriggle free but I held on tight. I heard screams: muffled, stifled screams. My ears hummed and rang. I buried my face in the soft bosom of DI Pamela Roche, and wondered how I'd explain that to my wife later. If there was a later. More wreckage fell to the floor, showering me with cement dust. Horns blared in the street; I thought I heard an ambulance klaxon. Maybe it was just wishful thinking because it ceased very quickly.

After what seemed like an eternity I heard sobs and groans, and risked looking up. A stranger peered at me. Rough hands grabbed me under the armpits and dragged me out of the ruined coffee house. Roche was being hauled beside me on the footpath. I saw mouths move, I think I heard someone ask if I was okay. I nodded and pointed back to the shell. 'There's a girl in there behind the counter.' My mouth was full of dust and the words came out like some foreign language. Dazed, shaken and stunned, I crawled to a sitting position. One of the skin-heads was lying in an unconscious bloody heap. The others were nowhere to be seen. The teenage girls were in a shocked and terrified cluster, surrounded by helpers. They didn't seem badly hurt. I shook my head free and suddenly bright red blood dripped onto my shirt. *This is a new shirt. I only bought it last week.* In my muddled thinking that was the first thing that crossed my mind. I felt my scalp gingerly. There was a graze oozing fresh blood. Then I saw Roche. She was propped against the side of a car, anxious strangers surrounding her. Her clothes were torn and covered in dust and glass splinters. Her hair was matted down with grime and dirt and wetness of some kind. Her denims were ripped with bare flesh exposed. Pale but undamaged. She'd a jagged cut on her forehead and blood on her left cheek. Some of the rubble must have clipped her. Through a criss-cross of legs I caught her eye. She was looking at me, stunned and disbelieving. And I knew what she was thinking.

Was that bomb meant for us?

Chapter 7

The media said no.

'GANGLAND FEUD HITS NEW LOW'; 'IT'S WAR!'; 'TURF-WAR EXPLOSION'.

The tabloids made their minds up overnight. The target, they decided, was the bunch of skinheads. Reports claimed the trio was a well-known inner-city criminal gang fighting with a rival mob to control the heroin trade in downtown Dublin. Two managed to flee the scene, despite being covered in blood. The third sustained significant head and limb injuries and was taken to hospital. The teenage girls got out with nothing more than shock, glass fragment skin cuts and lost mobile phones. They were distraught. The waitress escaped with cuts and superficial burns from hot water from the coffee machine spilling on to her legs.

DI Roche was also lucky. The blast and collapsing debris caused a jagged gash to her forehead and a few grazes. The wound required stitches, the rest no more than antiseptic and Band-aids. Her sunglasses were smashed and her mobile phone was missing. Her clothes were ruined, her hairstyle dishevelled and she was psychologically shaken. She had a swelling on the back of her head as big as a golf ball from my heroics, and bruising on her chest too from my weight. I learned these details from a police source later that night. He promised that the bit about me with my nose stuck in Roche's cleavage would go no further. Especially not to my wife. Nor to Roche's lover, a Polish doctor called Danuta, who was, according to his account, 'stunningly beautiful'. I immediately revised my stereotypes of the Irish police force.

I survived with grazes and ringing eardrums. My suit was peppered with glass shards and beyond repair. My shirt was too blood- and grime-stained to wash and ended up in the recycling bin. My mobile phone survived.

Sarah was aghast when I arrived home in a police car, completely unaware I'd been caught up in the explosion. Bongos wasn't a usual watering hole for me. I'd called earlier to say I'd be late but didn't elaborate. I also didn't say who I was talking with or why. I didn't want to alarm her more than necessary and have her worrying about my safety. I stood at the front door with a silly grin on my face, covered in builder's dust and bloodied shirt. But I was alive and talking (not that I made much sense) and moving all limbs.

There could've been worse outcomes, I hinted. 'I was just in the wrong place at the wrong time when Dublin's underworld decided to extend their battle zone.' I said that and a lot more to allay her fears and eventually she calmed down. My police minders hung around, bored and itching to flee. Their brief was 'see the coroner home, make sure he's settled and his wife reassured'. They quit after eight o'clock, leaving me and Sarah staring at one another in the kitchen.

I consider myself a strong individual. I don't mean the muscular bar-room brawler type who can't walk away from a taunt and ends all arguments with an uppercut to the chin. Definitely not that sort. I consider myself to be more intellectually tough and emotionally solid. I can handle most situations. I've had to since I was left to fend for myself at an early age.

Early in March 1976, when I was a twelve-year-old child, I packed every possession I owned into three suitcases and four cardboard boxes. Books, games, football jerseys and boots, shirts, trousers, vests and underwear, shoes and socks. Photographs of my mother holding me as a child, pushing me on a garden swing, sitting with me in a dodgem car in a fairground. Photographs of me playing rugby. Seaside shots of me splashing water into my father's face. Memories of better times.

I'd grown up along the border between Southern and Northern Ireland during terrorist years. Two IRA hit men, twenty-nine-year-old Dermot McKeever and thirty-year-old Morgan Cusack, waged a campaign of ethnic cleansing on Protestant farmers in the area. My father slept with a shotgun and a handgun at the side of his bed, and I had a Glock underneath my pillow. I'd like to say I was the only twelve-year-old in the area who did, but I doubt it. Our house was attacked twice without success. But at dawn on the last day of January 1976, the terrorists finally got lucky. They unleashed a barrage of armoured piercing bullets that ripped through the brick and mortar walls of our homestead. My mother was killed instantly. The British Army discovered me an hour later in the master bedroom cradling her bloodied and unrecognisable face, sobbing and moaning, unable to comprehend the nightmare I'd been plunged into.

My father succumbed to his head wounds a week later.

Twice in the first weeks of February 1976, I stood beside an open grave as a coffin was lowered. Twice my mind screamed horror. Twice I froze my emotions and held back my tears as each parent was buried. My father had left instructions in the event of his death. The farm was to be sold and the proceeds put into a trust to pay for my education. Existing savings could be used for expenses during my upbringing. Close relatives were nominated as guardians, but they were elderly and not confident they could rear a growing and active boy on the brink of his teenage years. So I was parcelled off to boarding school. I can still remember the battered Ford Cortina driving away, fumes belching from its rusted exhaust pipe. As it disappeared from view I felt my childhood fall apart. Within days what remained of it was blown away by bitterly cold east winds, stinging rain and a sense of intense loneliness.

At school I was instructed in mathematics and sciences, taught languages and literature. I learned to be my own man, be independent and look out for my friends. I learned to stand up to bullies and not to cower in the face of intimidation. Isolated by circumstances beyond my influence, I soon understood the importance of being in control of your own destiny. I clung to two basic beliefs: always look after yourself and don't ever trust anyone else who offers to do that for you.

Hospital colleagues teased me about this: 'you're a control freak'. And they were right. I had to be on top of every situation and usually succeeded. Except in affairs of the heart. From the moment I met my wife my emotional control collapsed. I fell like a ninepin. And it happened so unexpectedly. During (of all things) a Medico–Legal convention in the spring of 1993.

I spotted her gossiping with friends around a coffee urn in the conference auditorium. Medics and solicitors milled, making polite chat, exchanging business cards, networking, the usual set-up when professions gather. She seemed vague and vulnerable but so very pretty at a distance. I revised that to beautiful after I'd pushed through the crowd to get a closer look. Her name tag said Sarah Ross. We engaged in small talk. Lecture and lecturers: we both agreed they were boring. Doctors versus lawyers: that sparked a lively debate.

We were summoned to the next session. 'Why don't we skip this and get into the sun?' I said. My heart was beating so loudly I was sure everyone must hear it. I was awkward and shy, nervous about holding her attention without making a gaffe. Initially Sarah was hesitant and looked around the reception area. The crowd was heading back to the lecture theatre. She caught the eye of one of her colleagues and pointed at me. A wink acknowledged the call. She placed her cup on a side table and dabbed a tissue at her lips. Then she slung a bag over her shoulder and eyeballed me. 'If you give any trouble I'll make you suffer.' I gestured my immediate surrender. Minutes later we were strolling the city quays, discussing likes and dislikes. She was a U2 fan; I couldn't stand them. She loved the theatre while I preferred the cinema. That took up another twenty minutes of mutual assessment.

Unexpectedly she switched subject. 'What speciality are you studying?'

'Pathology.' We sat on a bench close to the River Liffey, Dublin's main waterway.

'Why pathology?'

I stretched my legs and flicked non-existent fluff from my trousers. 'That's where the truth lies. Detective work is done in the hospital wards. When they fail it's up to me to find the killer.'

'That's a strange way of putting it,' she said.

I offered a clumsy grin. 'Unfortunately, that's me. Not good with words.'

'But a thinker and a doer,' she offered.

'It's the way I was raised. Words can mean anything, depending on the speaker. If you want to know the truth, watch the man and his actions.' I shrugged. 'That's what my father used to say.'

I could sense Sarah analysing her sudden companion, his accent, his ill-at-ease manner.

'You're very beautiful,' I blurted. I was immediately embarrassed and turned to hide my discomfort.

She kissed me on the cheek and entwined an arm through mine. 'We better go,' she said, 'before someone comes looking for us.'

We held hands all the way back. Neither of us spoke. For me it was a special moment. Was it love? It couldn't have been. Not that quick. But if it wasn't love then, love certainly followed like an express train. We were married almost a year to the day after we met. Jennifer came along in 1995, then Gregory, four years later.

Over subsequent years my feelings for Sarah became so intense they frightened me. Childhood insecurity often flooded my imagination and I panicked whenever I thought of what would happen if she left me or got killed in some horrific road accident. In those appalling fantasies I saw myself comforting Jennifer and Gregory, trying to explain our loss. I always ended up asking myself: how will I cope? How will I raise these children? How could we live without their mother? Always, thankfully, I managed to force these images from my mind. But each time I was left drained and worn. And each time afterwards I looked at her afresh, as if we were meeting for the first time.

That's how it felt again. Seventeen years later, in the hallway of our house I was consumed with the same emotions for the beautiful woman looking at me with such puzzled eyes. She was wearing a loose cotton T-shirt and figure-hugging denims that made her look much younger. Her long blonde hair was pulled back to reveal her features. High cheekbones, perky face and full lips. Only the hint of forehead wrinkles and crow's feet. I'm six foot three in bare feet and close on two hundred pounds. Female news reporters have described me as 'ruggedly handsome' (though one spiteful witch added 'more rugged than handsome'). Sarah is forty-two, five nine and slender. Despite two pregnancies she's kept her figure. She has bumps where I like bumps, and curves that take my breath away. And my breath was taken away now. Maybe the brush with death heightened every sensation. Whatever, I wanted to sweep her off her feet and straight into bed, and ravish her until dawn. But my belly rumbled.

'I'm starving,' I said.

Sarah reached up and brushed fingers through my cement-dusted hair. I kissed her fingertips. Then her gaze explored my face, her hazel eyes searching for some explanation to a conundrum that was troubling her. Her brow was furrowed, her lower lip quivering. She looked frightened, like I'd never seen before. 'Mike Wilson,' her voice was trembling. 'Don't ever come home to me dead.'

I was about to reassure her when she silenced my words with a lingering and wet kiss that seemed to go on for ever. When we broke for air she slipped out of my embrace and headed to the kitchen. 'We'll eat,' she called over her shoulder. 'The kids are with friends so we have the house to ourselves. You could get lucky later.'

Nothing is better than getting lucky with Sarah. Our lovemaking is slow, passionate and explosive. She can make my head spin, my eyes see rainbow colours. My heart races, my hair drenches with the sweat of desire.

51

But that night I fell asleep as fast as my head hit the pillow. So there was no head spin, no rainbow eyes and no palpitations. And me on a promise, and all.

Jennifer and Gregory heard about the blast next morning when they returned home. Sarah had contrived a pact of silence with their friends' parents so as not to worry them. By then I was clean and refreshed and my grazes covered. I didn't even get a crumb of sympathy. Strange and confused looks, yes. Sympathy, no.

I took that day off to recover and get my thoughts together. Fridays are often slow in the office. It's mainly taken up with paperwork, chasing up laboratory, police and forensic reports; hounding hospital doctors to explain their treatments and advising family doctors on court protocol when giving evidence. I contacted Joan and arranged for a bunch of files to be sent out by courier. I specifically asked for the Dowling dossier. 'I'll work at home until I can show my face in public again,' I explained. I thanked her and the rest of the staff for their calls of support and sympathy. Even a bunch of flowers had been delivered. 'I'll be ready by Monday. Just give me the weekend to recover.' And that's all I thought of it. Friday, Saturday and Sunday should see me rested and refreshed. I'd renew company with the ghosts of the coroner's court on Monday.

When I studied the morning papers I shook my head in amazement. Photographs showed the café with a partially collapsed roof and shattered glass windows. Technical experts described the device as small. I decided if that was the result of a small device I'd skip refreshments along the quay for the foreseeable future. The bomber wasn't identified, despite my detailed description. The skinhead admitted to hospital was named, his two buddies described only as 'accomplices'. The teenage girls were named and two even gave quotes: Ciara from Drumcondra: *'Ohmigod it was so scary. All I remember was this man, like screaming. The place went mental.'* And Sorcha from Clontarf described how they escaped injury: *'The table toppled over and we hid behind it. All the glass hit off it. We could've been killed. Will I be on TV?'*

The waitress was identified as a young Nigerian who'd only arrived in Ireland six weeks earlier. It was reported she'd fled Nigeria to escape tribal violence. There's bad luck and there's bad luck, but to flee one country because of bloodshed and then find yourself at the sharp end of gangland rivalry somewhere else? Well, that's just being jinxed.

Neither DI Pamela Roche nor I were identified. We were described only as 'two other innocent customers'. I suspected the heavy hand of police HQ at work. The chief of police wouldn't have wanted our names in the public domain.

All accounts portrayed the incident as an escalation of tactics in a brutal turf war. When Roche rang around eleven that morning to confirm this I heaved a sigh of relief. From the moment I saw the bomber's eyes lock onto mine I'd feared Harold Rafferty's assassins had me in their sights. So the detective's words were reassuring. To a point. But something niggled at me; something made me question this explanation. Sure, it looked like a turf-war attack. Sure, it was staged like a turf-war attack. And sure, everyone believed it was a turf-war attack. Even crime correspondents, always good for thinking outside the box, believed it was turf-war violence. So why wasn't I wholly convinced? Because Harold Rafferty had been murdered for asking pretty much the same questions I was now asking. Someone hadn't wanted Rafferty prying where he shouldn't have been prying. And he was shot. *If this was the same gang, I argued silently, they wouldn't use the same tactics without drawing attention to themselves. So, I continued to argue, they'd try a different strategy to take me out.*

I didn't say this to Roche. I politely asked about the bump on the back of her head ('Sore but healing') and drew her quickly back to our conversation in Bongos. The Dowling case was still on my mind. Despite the shock of yesterday it tormented my imagination and challenged my pathologist's brain. How did he really die? Was someone else with him that day? So when Roche called I insisted we focus on her early inquest idea. I told her I needed more information. 'Why'd you hold on to photographs eleven and twelve?'

'They're shots of the forest,' she said. Her voice wasn't as strong as I remembered. The distress of the bomb must have traumatised her. Sure as hell it traumatised me but maybe not as much. I'm used to bombs. A no-warning bomb was the IRA's favourite stun tactic. 'We wanted a crime-scene investigator to look at them.'

That caught me by surprise. 'Why? You told me yesterday Dowling's autopsy conclusion wasn't in doubt.'

'There were doubts about the first investigation. It ended too abruptly for my liking.'

So I was right. I wasn't the only one unhappy about Matthews' handling of the case.

'I wanted to see if anything had been missed.'

'What'd he conclude?' Or maybe it was a she? The forensic unit was almost seventy per cent female.

'He couldn't find anything to force a review of the autopsy findings.'

'Can I see them?' I was determined to review the images myself. There was a lot of technical material I was unhappy about. This could be one more to add to the list.

'Sure. I'll email them to your home PC.'

I passed on the address. 'Great. There's two others I'm interested in.' I didn't elaborate. I still didn't know what the red-eye blur was, and until I did I was keeping it to myself. 'Once I've studied them I'll let you know if I'm any the wiser.'

Chapter 8

The Dowling file was couriered to me that afternoon. The police photographs numbered eleven and twelve came by email attachments shortly afterwards, along with spam offering products to enlarge my penis by four inches and a personal message from a girl I'd never met who called herself Lil: *'Let me introduce myself. I am a nice lady with a big and tender heart. I am looking for my prince to give him joy and happiness and to share my life with. I think you can be the one I am looking for. I am attractive and kind, joyful and open-minded.'*

At least it made me smile. Not something that happens a lot in my line of business. Yet I've a good sense of humour; I just don't get to use it that often. The dead aren't a great audience. I don't get guffaws and back-slapping when I come out with some cracking one-liners. No ghost doubles up, chuckling and gasping, 'Stop, you're killing me.' In the days when I worked in the pathology unit at University Hospital I used every opportunity to lighten the sombre mood in the tile-floored basement. A favourite pastime was to study patients' charts. The deceased would arrive for autopsy complete with a thick folder of medical notes, and inside would be some gem written by junior staff in the wards above. Two of my favourites were: 'The patient refused an autopsy and demanded to be treated' and 'The patient experienced chest pain while having sex. This continued in the emergency room.'

Dr Jaival Chande, one of my Asian recruits, a small, wiry and fiercely intelligent pathologist, gleefully mocked how Irish journalists reported on homicide investigations. 'They say,' he used to regale me with his latest observation, brown eyes twinkling with mischief, 'police are conducting a *full* murder investigation. What other type is there? Do they do half-full investigations? Quarter full?' Here his voice would rise with exaggerated concern. '"Look boys,"' and his attempt at an Irish accent was usually very good, '"there's a big match on the telly at eight. Don't drag this out. Arrest someone, anyone, I don't care who, before six and let's get down to the pub for the kick-off."'

The banter eased our workload, shortened the day. It took the edge off being surrounded by death.

But now, in the study of my house, I was back to the riddle of one particular and suspicious death.

I opened Roche's digital images on my PC. Number eleven showed the forest glade where Patrick Dowling's body was discovered. It was a long shot from about twenty feet back. Hanging corpse, rope wrapped around a solid branch, end tied tight to trunk of tree. How the hell could he've done that? For the umpteenth time my pathologist's brain challenged that riddle. Dowling had a mixture of drugs in his blood that day. He must've been confused, addled. Surely he wouldn't have had the mental agility to put together such a suicide apparatus? It didn't make sense. I scanned the rest of the image. There was a police officer at the edge, on his hunkers and inspecting the ground. His head was bowed, exposing a bald pate. He was wearing oilskins, rubber boots and surgical gloves. There was mud on the boots

57

and gloves. He clutched an evidence bag in his left hand. It was mudstained too. The rest of the picture showed nothing new. Trees, broken boughs, peeling bark: nothing I hadn't seen in the other shots. Nothing of note, anyway.

Number twelve was a closer shot. For some reason the photographer had angled his (her? forensics again: seventy per cent female) camera to capture the ground immediately below the dangling feet. At the top of the photo two brown brogues pointed downwards. They were heavily mudstained. Muck clung to the heel of one. A bar stool, wood, tripod style with supporting struts, lay where you would expect if Dowling had stood on it and pushed it away to kill himself. In other words, directly to the side of the body. Leaves, twigs, pine cones were in the frame. No matter what way I zoomed and turned the image no footprint became obvious. Why had Roche singled these two out for particular attention? I recalled our earlier telephone conversation. 'There were doubts about the first investigation. It ended too abruptly for my liking.'

Then she'd added, 'I wanted to see if anything had been missed.'

My chance to interrogate Roche in more detail ended with the Bongos' bomb. It kinda killed that conversation stone dead. But I realised now she'd been looking at Dowling's death from a different angle than the one I was viewing it from. She'd assumed the autopsy was correct: Dowling had committed suicide. She wasn't looking for a killer; she was probably trying to connect the dead man to Noel Carty in some way. Carty was the thug Dowling had confronted the same day he died. Carty was drug dealer Jonathan Redmond's right-hand man. And, according to Roche, Redmond and Patrick's father, the government minister Albert Dowling, were linked. But how? And how was it interwoven with his son's death? Was the Minister for Economic Development involved in organised crime? Was that the dot-to-dot puzzle Roche was struggling to complete?

Now I understood why my allegation of murder had taken her by surprise. She suspected a rat; I suspected a rat. But my rat was a different type of rat to hers. My suspicions would've thrown her investigation into even more difficult territory. And now I grasped why she was so keen to get me on board and do the detective work through the coroner's court. She recognised my medical expertise and questioning brain could expose whatever cover up had been contrived. But no matter her agenda, I'd my own reasons to find the truth. Now that I was the overseeing coroner, Patrick Dowling's inquest was my responsibility. It was in my territory, and no botched investigation would go through my office without challenge.

Sarah had taken Gregory to soccer training. He'd a big match tomorrow when it'd be my turn to ferry him to and from the playing fields. I'd stay to watch and cheer him on, like other dads do on Saturdays. Jennifer had gone to the movies with a group of friends. I was left alone, poring over death files (as usual). But this time with more than the usual amount of thoroughness. The Dowling file had possible links to a major drug dealer. And I hate drug dealers. If I could find something to connect Jonathan Redmond to Patrick Dowling's death I'd move heaven and earth to get there.

It was closing in on five o'clock. Afternoon shade was creeping into the garden, along with a ginger cat. Sarah's roses, her pride and joy, were still in bud, pink and white blooms scenting the early evening air. Pink and white petals lay where they'd fallen. The grass needed

59

cutting. I'd offer five euros to Gregory to do that tomorrow if he was up to it after the game. I opened a side window and breathed deeply, savouring the garden smells. I heard a distant lawnmower, far-off traffic rumbling, birds chirping. The ginger cat was prowling close to a dividing hedge. Next door was a mongrel that never stopped yapping when it sensed anything, animal or human, stir in our plot. I waited for the inevitable growl. The ginger cat pawed at the earth. Then the yelping began. I grinned as I watched the tabby flee like a bat out of hell. But I had to close the window to drown out the dog's barking. There were days when I harboured murderous thoughts about that animal.

I inspected photographs eleven and twelve more closely, repeatedly using the enlargement facility on my PC to get a clearer view of the setting. But, like Roche's crime-scene investigator colleague, I couldn't for the life of me see anything to suggest there was evidence of more than one person with Dowling. Not in these shots and not in any of the other shots I'd studied. That didn't sway my opinion that the twenty-eight-year-old man hadn't died alone. I still believed someone had killed him. But the photographs in front of me didn't support that assertion. Mind you, they were taken the day after Dowling died. Anything could have happened to the terrain in that time. So I went into Met Éireann, the Irish weather bureau website, and did a search of weather conditions on 29 November 2009; the day Patrick Dowling died. Records showed that night a storm driven by westerly currents, strong winds and heavy rain took close on two hours to pass over the eastern counties and clear into the Irish Sea. Enough to confuse any clues left in the forest clearing where Patrick Dowling was hanging. Maybe even wash away footprints.

I switched to the separate enlargements Joan had arranged for me. These had been shot with flash photography, creating an eerie image. When flash bounces off the retina it produces a red-eye result. I'd any number of family shots spoiled by this effect.

I studied photograph ten closely. It captured the reflective eyes of a woodland animal. Low down, medium-size dog or fox, two pin-point red retinas stared at the camera. They were close together, separated by a slight snout. I decided it was a fox. That fitted in with the terrain, distance from the ground and narrow shape of the eyes. The fox, wild dog, or whatever it was, was about twelve feet from the hanging body, deep in the surrounding undergrowth.

Photograph twenty captured a more distant glow. I couldn't be sure but it had the look of yet another red-eye shot. One eye only. And it was firmly in the middle of an indistinct blur. That, I speculated, might be a head on shoulders. And if so, it was the height of a reasonably tall man. I examined a number of the other photographs where policemen were included. I argued that the height of an average policeman is around six foot. Then I aligned one officer with the tree behind him. The top of his head reached approximately the eighth branch from the ground. Using that yardstick I counted the number of branches off the ground of the indistinct 'red-eye' image. Nine. If this really was an eye it had to be in a person who was around six feet tall. No forest animal matched that. There were no Yetis in the Dublin/Wicklow woodlands. So if my suspicions were correct someone was hiding among the trees and squinting at the search party the day *after* Patrick Dowling took his own life, a conclusion I still didn't accept. But this didn't make sense. Who would possibly have been in that wood at that time of day and at that unseasonable time of the year? Especially with so many police prowling the area? I wondered was it just my imagination on overdrive. I scanned the other pictures. None of them showed the same indistinct shadow.

I squinted at the photo again and again from different angles. I turned on the desk light to see it better. Then I peered at it through a magnifying lens. I calculated the shape was about thirty yards from the hanging body. It was indistinct, the glowing eye possibly an optical illusion of some kind, or an artefact. But it was unusual. And no one had commented on it in the police files. It wasn't one that Roche or her crime-scene colleagues had paid special attention to.

I leaned back in my chair and yawned. My right ear was slightly muffled from the blast and began to hum. My back ached. I felt suddenly physically exhausted and mentally drained. The Dowling file was getting to me. The mystery was taking over my life. I picked up one of the enlargements and studied it one more time. Someone was in the woods that day. I just knew it. Someone, someone, someone. But who? And why?

Chapter 9

I heard the phone ring in my sleep. One long persisting and demanding drone. It stopped. I turned to one side and dragged a pillow under my head. Beside me Sarah stirred. I hadn't brought any death files with me tonight so I was allowed to share the bed. She mumbled something, and then kicked out a leg for more space. In my half-awake state I edged nearer and draped an arm around her waist. She pushed it away and shifted to the safety of the other side. She started snoring. I drifted back to sleep.

Sometime later, I don't know how long, the phone rang again. It was the landline, it's like an old-fashioned fire alarm bell. The landline connects to two mobile handsets. In our house it's a battle to keep them in their rightful place: one *should* be in the kitchen; the other *should* be in the master bedroom. Jennifer usually has both. In fact, Jennifer has so many communication devices her room reminds me of NASA headquarters. It's not unusual to look there for the landline and find both handsets, a mobile phone and computer on the go. She'll be lying on her bed, back against headboard, and working the keys on her laptop. She can email, update her Facebook page, text *and* carry on a conversation with the landline set to speaker mode. I know women pride themselves on multitasking but Jennifer manages to take this to an extraordinary level. So, as I drifted in and out of my doze, I felt sure the ringing would waken her. I wanted to get up, answer the call and spare her broken sleep. But I was so exhausted my limbs refused the effort. I waited, convinced it would stop. A bleary eye checked the bedside digital clock. 4.20 a.m. Anyway, who the hell was calling? The line was ex-directory and only a select group knew how to contact me. Police, coroner's office, hospitals, close friends. Rarely would I be disturbed at such an early hour. The drone continued. *Dring, dring. Dring, dring. Dring, dring.* I turned so that my good ear could listen. The bomb-muffled side was still dull. I realised the ringing was coming from downstairs, not Jennifer's room. At least it wouldn't waken her. Gregory slept so heavily an earthquake wouldn't bother him. I could hear the slow and gentle breathing of my wife. She was fast asleep. Still the phone droned, demanding attention. *Dring, dring. Dring, dring. Dring, dring.* I put one foot to the floor to get up when it stopped. I breathed a sigh of relief and slumped back onto the pillows. Half-awake now, I risked a glance at Sarah. Her long blonde hair was mussed and straggling. Her lips pursed in a soft snore. I leaned across and kissed her softly on the forehead. She didn't stir. I made myself comfortable on my side. I drifted off to sleep again.

I was dreaming of ice cream when the phone rang again. Don't ask me why but I was back in my childhood, sitting on the stone wall that surrounded the family home and eating an ice cream. My mouth moved to the movements. My tongue tingled and relished the soft texture of ice-cold milk, whipped egg and sugar. It was home made to my mother's recipe. I was looking towards the farmstead with its two front bay windows, granite lintels and white plaster frontage. I could see my mother, her greying hair swept back to reveal a high brow, small nose and wide smile as she watched me. I waved my free hand and she waved back. I was about to call out when the bloody phone broke through.

I sat up, dazed and bemused. My dream was still vivid and I choked back tears. There was a lump in my throat. For years after my parents were killed dreams like this haunted me. Terrifying images of my mother's blood-stained head cradled in my arms, my tears falling among the gore. Flashbacks of my body convulsing with sobs that matched the death throes of her body as it struggled to survive. Then another of me, shielding my eyes from an open grave, afraid a skeletal grin would greet me. Often I dreamed I heard the angry laments and curses of relatives demanding justice. I even heard the delighted whoops of terrorists celebrating two successful killings. Gradually these faded. But every now and then, usually under great stress, they returned. I had a burst of nightmare activity around university exam times. Then another cluster as I moved up the career ladder of medicine. It was as if I was looking for reassurance. *It's all right, Michael, it's all right.* I could almost hear my mother's comforting voice. It was light and gentle with the soft country lilt of south Derry where she lived until moving to Tyrone with my father. *You know you can do this. Dad and I will always be there for you.* But they weren't. They were in the same plot in a village graveyard.

When the dreams first started they scared me. I often awoke, anxious and disturbed, in a lather of sweat. Tearful, despite my adult years. Later they troubled me less, even becoming comforting. It was as if I sensed my parents looking out for me. But I hadn't had one as intense as this for years.

Now, as I sat in bed, heart pounding, eyes moist and swallowing hard to shift the lump in my throat, the phone kept ringing. *Dring, dring. Dring, dring. Dring, dring.* The fire alarm bell burrowed into my brain. I checked the digital clock. It was 5.10 a.m. I had to get up. Somebody somewhere wanted me. I decided it had to be a hospital doctor, probably looking for advice on some strange, sudden death. Wearing only night shorts I padded across the carpeted floor, careful not to disturb Sarah. It was warm and the soft glow of an early dawn caressed the curtains. *Dring, dring. Dring, dring. Dring, dring.* I glanced at the dressing mirror. The graze on my cheek from yesterday's bomb looked pink. There were pinkish scratches on my arms. They'd heal. I tiptoed down the stairs so as not to waken the kids. The phone was ringing in the kitchen. *Dring, dring. Dring, dring. Dring, dring.* I imagined some bedraggled and exhausted junior medic in one of Dublin's emergency rooms urging me to answer. *'Dr Wilson, I'm so sorry to call you at night but we have a sudden death in one of our units and I need advice on how to deal with it.'* Those were the usual opening lines. And I'd listen, trying to suppress yawns and tiredness and pass on whatever instruction was needed. This usually involved a post-mortem, clinical notes assessment and discussion with the most senior doctor in charge.

I finally found the handset, tucked into the side of a cushion on a wicker chair. I flicked the answer button. 'Hello.' I sensed a sharp intake of breath, then silence. The line went dead. Puzzled, I stared at the receiver for maybe thirty seconds. Then I pressed the recall button and waited. I got an engaged tone. It was possible that whoever rang was trying another line. I scrolled through the call register to check if the other two calls were from the same number. NUMBER WITHHELD came up twice. It meant nothing. It could mean anything. But right then, in the kitchen with an early dawn throwing shadows, I felt suddenly very cold. I started shivering. I knew it was warm outside, I could see the patio temperature gauge. Closing in on 6 a.m. it was already fourteen degrees. Why was I shivering? NUMBER WITHHELD meant nothing. I said it out loud to reassure myself. But did I really hear a sharp intake of breath or was that my imagination? Maybe it was only my own exhausted breathing? But why did the line suddenly go dead? I was torturing myself and I knew it. *It means nothing. Go back to bed.*

I didn't.

I sat in the wicker chair and stared into the distance. *Use common sense and logic, Mike. Don't indulge your paranoia. That call came from some hospital doctor or police unit dealing with a sudden death and needing advice.* But paranoia hinted something else: Harold Rafferty's killers closing in on me. Then I remembered my dream. I licked my lips as if I might recall the sweetness of the ice cream but I tasted only bitterness and fear. Was the dream an omen, a portent of something to come? Were my dead parents reaching from the grave to warn me of danger? I realised my brain was in overload, my musings moving from reason past paranoia and into a vortex of unreasonable dread. I rested my head in my hands and stared at my toes. I counted the moles on my legs, rubbing at a few to make sure they weren't changing into skin cancers. I inspected the grazes on my arms. Then I clasped my arms tight against my chest, held my breath and tried counting to forty before exhaling. I only got as far as twenty-two. I was trying to distract my mind but my mind was not for distracting. Patrick Dowling's death had me in its grip.

I went into my study and opened the dead man's file. I flicked through the different sections until I found Harry Malone's statement. Malone was a close friend of Dowling and with him on the day he died. Malone was also there when Dowling sparred with Noel Carty, drug dealer Redmond's henchman. I read the deposition, gradually realising I hadn't paid much attention to it before. Indeed, I'd skimmed the section, focusing more on the forensic evidence. That's what suited my inquiring pathologist's brain. On page fifty-five, Malone described driving Dowling to a pub in Stepaside, a suburb on Dublin's south side. In the car park an altercation broke out. I tried to imagine the wasted and emaciated Dowling squaring up to Carty, described by DI Roche as over six feet tall, broad-shouldered and so strong it took four police officers to arrest him. Malone added a few comments and details but the testimony was limited. Even as I read it I sensed hesitation. It was as if he was holding something back. I turned the page. The narrative was interrupted abruptly. I realised I'd skipped a page. Fifty-six and fifty-seven were stuck together. When I teased them apart I found a scrawl on the margin.

'Malone's lying.'

There was the late Harold Rafferty's spidery handwriting. I'd pored over a bunch of his inquest files and immediately recognised the county coroner's distinct scrawl. So Rafferty hadn't believed Malone. Had he pursued a separate interrogation? What might he have learned?

I was pondering this and a hundred other issues when I realised Sarah was standing in the doorway, staring at me. Her hazel eyes were wide with astonishment, her long blonde hair still messy from bed. She was in a loose white cotton nightie that barely hid her nakedness underneath. One strap was hanging off at the shoulder exposing more flesh than was good for a man of my age.

'What're you doing down here at this hour?' She made to grab the file but I caught her in time, tumbling her onto my lap. Her nightie rode up, exposing her wonderfully long legs. And black panties. My hands found her breasts, my mouth found hers. We kissed hungrily, tongues exploring, wetness shared. 'You said I'd get lucky the other night.' My voice was husky with desire.

Sarah tried to resist but her struggle soon collapsed. 'But you were *soooo* tired,' she teased. Then the questions spilled: 'Why're you here so early? Are you reading those ghastly files?' But I silenced her with even more intense and passionate kisses. The struggles weakened. 'Okay, tell me later.'

I lifted her in both arms and she ran a hand through my hair, playing at the roots with little tugs. She stroked my grazed cheek. Slowly I inched upstairs, shifting my weight to make sure she didn't slip. Sarah nibbled at my neck. 'I haven't said I will,' she murmured playfully. Underneath her words I sensed lust.

'No,' I whispered, 'and you haven't said you won't.'

I darted a quick glance into Jennifer's room. Fast asleep. Then into Gregory's. He was curled in a ball, his chest rising and falling with each breath. A floorboard creaked. 'Ssshhh,' Sarah giggled. I pushed our bedroom door closed with my heel.

I laid Sarah on the bed and allowed my gaze to drift over her. She undid both shoulder straps and tugged her nightie off. She feigned shame but with a come-on smile that made me groan with anticipated pleasure.

'Mike Wilson,' her voice was husky. 'Get in here quick before the kids wake up.'

I lay beside her, stroking her hair, running a finger along her lips. Her hands reached down and found me ready.

'Slowly,' she whispered, 'and quietly.'

Chapter 10

'Pass the ball, Anto. Pass the ball. Ah, for fuck's sake, would ya look at that. Anto, Anto. First touch, rememmer wha I said? First touch football. Jesus wept.'

There's nothing like under-twelve soccer matches to bring out the worst in some coaches. I stood on the sideline of a pitch in Ballybrack in south Dublin, cheering Gregory and his team. It'd just gone 1 p.m. and there wasn't a cloud in the sky. A light coastal breeze offered some relief but the air was humid. Unusually for Dublin, the city and suburbs were enjoying warm, sunny summer. The weather bureau was even predicting a prolonged settled spell and it was still only the beginning of June. Unheard of conditions for this country. Still, some people had already started complaining, the usual suspects who are never pleased. For them it was either too warm or not warm enough. The garden could do with rain; the garden's water-logged. That sun would take the skin off the back of yer neck; wouldn't it be nice to get clear blue skies for a change?

On field the playing surface was lush green, the ground hard underneath. Supporters clustered in groups. Littering the sidelines were kit bags that spilled towels, spare socks, shorts and shirts. Those cheering Gregory's side, Glasthule United, were throwing water bottles to the players, despite the referee's instructions not to. Shouts

mingled with curses and fierce criticism. A dog threatened to invade the pitch and was shooed away with
threats and flailing kicks into the air. It barked to a safe
distance and then snapped at any small child coming
near. Somebody finally sent it hightailing with the swish
of a walking stick. The opposition, Shankill Rovers,
looked taller and stronger than our lads. They spurned
all offers of liquid with an air of contempt: 'Water's for
wimps.' Yet the game was finely balanced, two goals
apiece with ten minutes to play. It was an important
match too. Not exactly a World Cup final but promotion
to a higher league was at stake. If Glasthule won they
moved up a division. Shankill were guaranteed advance-
ment as long as they didn't lose. A draw was good
enough for them, whereas Glasthule needed all three
points. And if they got them, they'd pip Shankill. So there
was a needle to the exchanges. Some tackles were near
leg-breakers. The referee was getting a hard time from
both sets of supporters. 'You're a bollox,' was one of the
less offensive jibes. Others questioned his social standing
and eyesight and whether his mother was married when
she gave birth to him. Something to that effect. Pretty
average youth soccer parents' banter, really.

Gregory had been pulled to midfield after one of the
squad twisted an ankle. He was the team's star striker,
averaging a goal a game throughout the season. Indeed,
he was having a fantastic run. Two nights a week and
each Saturday morning he was ferried to and from
venues. I tried to help as much as I could but more often
than not it was Sarah who shouted from the sideline. I
sat at home reading depositions on death. Today, Saturday
and almost forty-eight hours after my near-miss bomb
experience, it was my turn to cheer him on.

I don't know where Gregory gets his skills, for it

certainly isn't from his Wilson side. I couldn't kick a ball to save my life while at school. Sarah played hockey to provincial level and made sure Jennifer joined both school and club teams. Secretly she was trying to protect her from the teenage social circuit where there was too much binge-drinking and loose morals. Many young girls in Dublin were using oral contraceptives to help with 'period cramps'. It was strange how 'period cramps' seemed to surface around summer holidays or major music festivals. Few doctors believed them. It isn't easy rearing teenage children. It never was, even before the boom years. But during that crazed decade Ireland's social mores nose-dived. Church scandals and revelations about paedophile priests, or priests fathering children, undermined the foundation of people's religious beliefs, which in turn undermined basic decent conduct. Then sexual promiscuity, combined with illicit drugs, produced an explosive cocktail of out-of-control behaviour. Therapists reported large increases in those seeking help with addiction, and clinics that dealt with sexually transmitted infections were run off their feet. Some children who turned up there were as young as twelve. More for parents to worry about.

I scuffed my heels and gossiped with fellow supporters. On the other side of the city Sarah was watching Jennifer in a club side out-of-season tournament.

The Glasthule United coach was a stocky man with balding grey hair and a face like thunder. I worried about his blood pressure. Dressed in a green tracksuit he prowled the touchline like a wild beast stalking prey, shouting instructions and abuse in equal measure. Every now and then he'd stop to scribble some vital observation on a pad, using an upturned knee for support. He was also Anto's dad (God help Anto) and fiercely competitive. Every match was played with a fiery intensity, each result analysed with chalk and blackboard in the changing room afterwards. He was a mixture of Genghis Khan, Mike Tyson and Roy Keane: combative, fearsome, seething and foul-mouthed.

Gregory was in the away strip of blue top, white shorts and blue socks. Woodies, a local hardware store, had given financial assistance to the club. Their logo was prominently displayed on each young chest. I cheered and shouted encouragement, even having the good manners to clap when the opposition played well. This didn't go down well with the sparky trainer so I stayed quiet, now only roaring when the blues were on the ball. I was pleased with the company, relieved with the distraction. I made small talk with other parents, laughing at the intensity of the coach and admitting I'd be the last to challenge him. 'Sure if it makes him happy and the kids enjoy it, what's the harm?' That was the resigned air. I soon forgot about Patrick Dowling. And Harry Malone. And Harold Rafferty's scribbled note, *'Malone's lying.'* Basking in the early afternoon sunshine and cheering on my boy distracted me from everything. Including Thursday's bomb, even though my grazed cheek and arms reminded me of that particular skirmish. The early morning telephone calls also slipped out of my mind.

Gregory, socks rolled down, puny legs pumping like pistons, intercepted a wayward Shankill pass and headed for the opposition goal. A lad the size of a house lunged at him but he skipped the tackle, holding on to the ball.

'Support him, Glasthule! For Chrissake, support him!' Anto's dad had worked himself up to a frenzy. He could sense promotion.

A pale-faced fullback, long and gangly with a tight crew

cut, bore down upon him. Gregory feinted to pass to the right but rolled the ball to the left. A lunging tackle almost took his feet from under him and he stumbled. I jumped up and down with excitement. 'Come on, Glasthule. Come on. You can do it.' Gregory managed to stay upright and keep control.

'Pass it, Grego, pass it now.' The coach looked as if he was about to have a stroke.

Gregory eased the most perfect ball to a runner coming alongside. It was nipped back to him immediately. First touch passing. The coach was delighted. Now Gregory had only the goalkeeper to beat, and the keeper was dwarfed by regulation nets: the space to shoot at seemed as big as a barn door.

'Shoot, Grego, shoot!' The coach's face was blazing red; his fists pumping the air. The Glasthule parents shouted and roared. 'Shoot, shoot!'

The ball went so far over the bar it disappeared down an incline and out of sight. The effing and blinding that followed it could be heard for miles.

I held my head in my hands and swore softly. I inspected the ground, and then checked the disappointed faces along the sideline. Rueful grins were exchanged. Silent curses mouthed. When the final whistle sounded I couldn't wait to escape. The star striker had misfired; Gregory had missed an open goal. There'd be no promotion this season. Glasthule United was devastated; Shankill Rovers elated. *Olé, olé, olé, olé.* Gregory was crushed and I didn't know what to say to ease his pain. So, like most dads, I said nothing. It's often the wisest policy.

Our return trip involved a pit stop at a McDonald's where Gregory wolfed down a Big Mac and fries, washed down with two chocolate milkshakes. I nursed a coffee.

We made small talk. School, summer holidays, friends. I noticed him staring at my grazed face but said nothing. There was no point worrying the boy unnecessarily. And now I had time to look at him properly. Usually we were like lodgers in the same house, me rushing to work and him heading for school. If I came home late he'd often be preoccupied with sports training, Xbox games or homework. He was growing but slowly, and at eleven stood just over five feet. He had mousy, untidy and curly hair that he gelled when he remembered. There was hardly a pick of fat on him and clothes hung off him. When he smiled he reminded me of his mother. When he frowned I could see myself. He'd a petite nose, wide blue eyes and unusually long eyelashes for a boy. In the middle of his forehead was a fading birthmark that still glowed when he was angry or sprinting. His favourite non-school attire was a Chelsea soccer shirt over tracksuit bottoms. He'd four pairs of 'sensible' shoes but rarely wore them, preferring his Adidas trainers.

He was in better form after he'd eaten. We chatted more on the way home, like old buddies. I pulled up in the driveway of our house around 4 p.m. Sarah and Jennifer were there already. Jennifer and three from her team sat on wooden benches around a barbecue table in the garden. They hadn't changed out of their club colours of white tops over olive-green skirts. Olive-green socks were rolled to the ankles, hockey shoes kicked off. Teenage hands flailed the air as some juicy gossip was recounted. There were laughs and giggles and heads came together to better hear.

I spotted Sarah dead-heading roses. She was wandering about the garden with a wicker basket that overflowed with weeds and spent blooms. I admired her from the distance. She was in white shorts and navy top, white pop socks in white sneakers. Long legs, tanned and taut. The final effect was spoiled only by a very un-sexy pair of gardening gloves. Gregory, still in his sweat-stained and grubby Glasthule United gear, sidled over to her. He muttered something. Sarah ruffled his hair and then leaned down and pecked him on the cheek. He made off again. I sensed that a deal had just been struck on cutting the lawn. He was off the hook until tomorrow. That'd give him time to get over the earlier disappointment.

'Someone rang just now,' Sarah said as I came beside her. I shielded my eyes from the sun's glare.

'Oh, who?' I assumed it was the early morning caller finally getting through.

'He didn't say,' she said. 'Just told me to pass on his regards to Coroner Wilson.'

'Must be somebody I know then.' Next door's dog started barking and I muttered a series of threats under my breath. That mutt would definitely have to go.

'It was a strange voice.' Gregory was hovering in the background and Sarah whispered to make sure she couldn't be overheard. Jennifer and her friends had moved indoors.

'Strange in what way?' I swatted away a bluebottle, wondering what the concern was. Sarah's eyes were her giveaway. All her emotions poured through them.

'I don't really know. It was a man with a sort of educated south Dublin accent.' She mentioned the brogue of one of our acquaintances as an example. 'But he wasn't pleasant. He sounded intimidating.'

I stood back to see her more clearly. 'What?'

She shrugged, as if trying to dismiss the notion. 'Maybe it's my imagination. Since Harold Rafferty's murder and that bomb I've got really nervous.' She smiled but there was no warmth there, only tension. 'You'll look after yourself, Mike, won't you?'

I felt as if I'd been pushed into an icy shower. Sarah didn't do anxiety. She was a well-adjusted and level-headed woman. Few things frazzled her. But I knew by her troubled expression the call had unnerved her.

I held her tight. 'Don't worry, Sarah,' I said. 'Nothing's going to happen to me.'

But her stiff embrace warned me that Sarah was far from convinced.

I started wondering who'd called. And why would an unidentified male pass on his regards as 'Say hello to Coroner Wilson'? And who *was* ringing during the night?

Chapter 11

I had to get to the bottom of this.

It *was* an unusual parting shot: 'say hello to Coroner Wilson'. What friend, neighbour, work colleague or casual acquaintance would ring to leave such a message without engaging in conversation with Sarah first? The answer was no one. Was the caller letting us know he knew how to contact us? That he knew where I lived? And how the hell did he know my telephone number?

My first instinct was to ring DI Roche and I was furiously scrawling through my contacts list when I remembered she'd lost her phone in the chaos of the explosion at Bongos. So I called the local police station and explained the predicament. I apologised, saying, 'I'm probably being over-cautious. But after what happened to the county coroner and Thursday's bomb I want to play it safe. I hope you understand.' They did. Fifteen minutes later a superintendent at police headquarters rang me. He insisted on hearing everything I'd told the first officer. Then he made me repeat it, word for word. He grilled me about security and burglar alarm codes and panic buttons.

'I'll send a squad car around immediately, Dr Wilson,' he said, 'and I'll make sure your house is watched over the weekend. We need to assess your personal safety. I'll speak to a few people about that and get back to you.'

I thanked him. I was hoping he'd have laughed and said I was completely overreacting. I thought that he might have made nonsense of any link with the other assassination and my family. But he didn't. His response to arrange surveillance was reassuring. That he felt it necessary wasn't.

'I'll also change your home number and put a trace on that call,' he finished.

'Thanks,' I mumbled. But I was rattled. He was taking this seriously.

I decided to keep the family close to base. Until I was sure of the situation I wouldn't share my unease with the children. I didn't want a house of fear. Not unexpectedly the first challenge came from Jennifer. Her friends had left but arrangements had been made for later that evening. She announced she wanted to stay overnight with one of the group. That might be safe to her but not to me. I now saw danger in every shadow. So I told a not-so-white lie about not seeing my daughter enough, that she was always on the phone gossiping and hadn't time any more for her dad.

'I'm only going to Juliet's house,' she complained. 'I could walk there in ten minutes.' She wore a black T-shirt, black cotton shorts and canvas sneakers. Jennifer was now very much a young woman. An inch taller than Sarah she'd the same hazel eyes but her ash-blonde hair was close cropped. Her skin was clear apart from a few teenage spots, her figure filling out. She'd be as beautiful as her mother in time. And she confided in Sarah rather than me. I knew no secrets.

'In a couple of years you'll be planning to go to university.' I laid it on in spades. 'And when you're there we'll rarely see you.' I palmed her protests silent. 'And you're not coming with us on the family holiday this year. You prefer to be with your school friends on a trip to France.'

I pulled a face of exaggerated loss. 'You're growing up so fast you're a stranger to me.'

Jennifer saw through this immediately. She curled up on a sofa and eyeballed me, both arms folded defiantly against her chest. At that moment she looked the image of her mother. This broke my heart. If anything happened to her because of my work . . . I had to force away such thoughts.

'Dad,' she said. Her body language screamed exasperation. 'First of all *you're* never home. And when you *are* at home you're stuck in that study with your nose in those horrible files. With the door locked.'

This was true, I did lock the door. The files were so gruesome I didn't want them falling into the hands of inquisitive teenagers. Some crime-scene images would strike terror into even the most mature and hardened mind.

Sarah listened, an amused smile playing on her lips. I guessed by her expression this was a lecture she'd wanted to give for some time. She was enjoying hearing it come from our eldest child. Gregory had a hand over his mouth to hide a grin. He sidled up to Sarah and squeezed beside her. His eyes glinted with delight. His dad was at the sharp end of a popular scolding.

'I'm fifteen in case you hadn't realised. And I'm past the stage of sitting in with my parents on a Saturday night, playing Scrabble or Monopoly.'

I looked to Sarah for help but didn't get any. She'd one arm around Gregory's shoulder, pulling him to her. They looked like co-conspirators.

'Just this weekend,' I pleaded. 'The weather's so nice we can barbecue tonight and then go to the beach tomorrow. I'm working long hours next week so you can spend all that time with Juliet.'

'Juliet's away next week.'

'Well, what about Danielle?'

Jennifer's eyes rolled in her head. 'Danielle doesn't live in Dublin any more. Her family moved to London six months ago.'

Ouch, I thought. *Caught out on that one.*

'I bet you don't know the names of half my friends.'

I didn't, and I wasn't going to be trapped. I tried switching the subject to hockey. Still the argument ping-ponged. I turned the screw with the 'neglected daddy' routine, Jennifer responding with her 'I've moved on. Maybe you should too'.

Sarah kept her neutral umpire's posture through it all but Gregory delighted in the squabble. I gradually realised this was the longest conversation we'd had together as a family, even if it was a minor spat, for some time. Jennifer socialised so much that our paths sometimes only crossed late in the evening. In the end she relented. She gave me a big hug. 'Still, it's true what I said, Dad. You're the stranger in this house, not me. Sometimes when you come out of that study it's like I see ghosts following you.'

This was an extraordinarily perceptive comment. Especially because it's what I sometimes felt. Work followed me home, around the house and up the stairs to my bedroom. Jennifer was right. There were nights I slept with ghosts.

'Nonsense.' I was still holding her in a massive bear hug that threatened to squeeze the breath out of her lungs. 'I think you've inherited my imagination.'

Jennifer pulled a face in reply.

Then her mobile sounded and she was gone. I was relieved. Her insights were too incisive for comfort.

That evening we barbecued in the back garden. Sarah allowed Jennifer and Gregory to do most of the cooking.

She watched on, offering suggestions and fine-tuning the turning of the steaks. A bottle of red wine sat on the table with two glasses. I sipped on the same measure throughout, careful to keep my wits about me. Sarah drank iced water. Twice our eyes met and twice I offered a reassuring smile. It didn't work either time.

Then I played frisbee with Gregory against a soundtrack of next door's yapping dog. We chased each other round the garden in bare feet. When it got dark we moved inside. I tried watching a girly movie with Jennifer and Sarah. Sandra Bullock was in it so I left pretty soon. In the next room Gregory was playing computer games. He didn't want to be disturbed so I excused myself and inspected the locks on every window of the house. I squinted out at the road, noting vehicles and pedestrians. I couldn't see any squad car but assumed there was one in the area.

When we finally turned in for the night, Sarah held me tight. For reassurance.

'Michael,' she whispered. My heart sank. Throughout our courtship and married years Sarah always called me Mike. Casual conversations, among friends, in front of the children: it was always Mike. It was especially Mike during lovemaking. Michael was reserved for arguments, serious disagreements and important discussions. This was a Michael moment: serious discussion coming up.

'Yes?'

'You're worried about that call, aren't you?'

I took a deep breath and let it out slowly. 'Yes, I am. Maybe we're both overreacting but it was a bit unusual, wasn't it?'

'Do you think Harold Rafferty's murder is the beginning of some campaign?' Sarah propped herself up by her elbow and leaned her head on a hand. Fortunately in the gloom she couldn't see my troubled expression. And I couldn't see hers. 'I can't understand why gangsters would target coroners. It's not as if any of you are judges or detectives trying to put them behind bars.'

I pulled her to my chest and she nestled into me. 'Police are poring over his inquest in case there's an answer there,' I whispered.

What I didn't add was that I'd been asking the same hard questions as the county coroner that had triggered his hit. I wanted to get through the night. But tomorrow I'd have to be honest and explain the background, scary as that might be. I explained my conversation with the local police station, hoping that would reassure her. Instead it sparked a mini-crisis.

Sarah wrestled free and sat upright. She turned on a bedside light so she could see me better. 'Why'd you call them?'

'To be on the safe side.'

'What'd they say?' She was staring straight at me, her eyes pricked with worry.

'They've sent a squad car to keep an eye on the house. And police HQ want to review security on Monday.'

'Then they're taking this seriously.'

'They're playing safe, that's all.' I tried to calm her concern. It was, after all, only a strange telephone call. No threats were made, no veiled warnings suggested. Everything about the exchanges was vague. 'We've a police unit watching us all weekend. So we're safe. Why don't you turn out that light and go to sleep? I want to go to the beach tomorrow.'

'Well,' yawned Sarah. The light was killed. 'I hope they get this sorted out soon. I don't want to have to worry about your security. And I don't want strangers ringing my house and scaring us.' She kissed me lightly on the cheek and then turned on her side away from me. 'Try and get some rest, Mike. You look worn out recently. That job's getting to you.'

I leaned across and kissed the nape of her neck. Soon I felt her body jerk and her limbs twitch as sleep took over. But sleep eluded me. I tossed and turned, slipping downstairs almost every half hour to check for intruders. I spotted a squad car drive past on one occasion. It stopped and two officers got out. They spent some time assessing the area. When the car drove off one remained. He lit a cigarette and huddled into the shadows. I watched the butt glow to an ember.

I went back to bed and stared at the ceiling. I had to protect my wife and children. Sarah was more than partner, passionate lover and mother of my children, she was my best friend and confidant. Jennifer was an impish and clever teenager who was growing more like her mother every day. And she'd an extraordinarily insightful mind, as I'd learned earlier. By contrast, Gregory was only eleven years old. And like most boys he was maturing at a slower rate than his sister. Mentally and physically. He doted on his mother and she fussed over him more than he needed. But he was our youngest and I suspected Sarah was frightened at losing him. Too soon he'd be a teenager and away from us, socialising with his mates and hanging around the locker room after school, eyeing up girls.

Thinking about my family under threat reminded me of my dreadful past. By the age of twelve I was used to sleeping with a loaded Glock pistol under my pillow. I'd been taught how to use it. I'd been told when to use it.

Right now I wished I had it back again.

Chapter 12

Early light filled the bedroom. It was around five the next morning. I'd been dozing but was now awake. Already the room was clammy and sweat stuck to my chest and armpits. Sarah had been restless all night, throwing back the duvet for comfort. I opened a quarter panel on the windows, yawning and scratching as I inspected the road. The surveillance team was nowhere to be seen. Perhaps with daylight the squad considered us less at risk. I walked across the first-floor landing, darting a glance into the kids' bedrooms. Jennifer's area faced south-west and caught the last of the sun. She was curled up, head resting on an open palm. Her bedding was in a crumpled heap on the floor. A smile flickered on her face and she mumbled in her sleep. Pleasant dreams. I kissed her on the cheek and opened a quarter panel to allow in the morning air. Somewhere in the distance a car engine backfired. Then all was quiet again.

Gregory's room was unpleasantly stuffy. The walls were covered in Chelsea soccer posters. Over his head Didier Drogba scowled down. I wouldn't have fancied that sullen face looking over me all night. The floor was a mess of discarded clothes, socks and soccer magazines. There was a smell of unwashed feet. The room overlooked the next garden and when I looked I spotted the yapping dog. It was hunched, its jowls on its front paws and drowsy-looking. There was a bowl of water close by. Usually it stayed in a kennel but this morning was slumped on the lawn. The heat was probably getting to it as well. I teased open a gap in Gregory's window, careful not to waken him or the mongrel. Gregory often complained the barking kept him awake. I checked our grounds. Small birds were hopping across the rose beds and a black cat prowled the side hedge. I prayed it wouldn't stir the dog and start a scrap. If that happened none of us would sleep.

Downstairs the windows were shut tight behind drawn curtains. I moved from room to room, testing the locks on the front, side and back doors. They were secure. The digits on the kitchen clock flicked to 5.16 as I climbed the stairs again. I eased myself beside Sarah and draped an arm over my eyes to block out the light. Exhaustion dulled my brain. *Just another couple of hours' sleep*, I thought. *That'd make such a difference.* I was almost there when a hand shook my shoulder.

'Dad, Dad. Wake up. There's a man outside.'

I was out of bed in a heartbeat. Gregory stood there, duvet wrapped around his shoulders. Although the room was warm, he was shivering. He was frowning the way I frowned when something worried me. Then I heard next door's dog barking. I'd never heard it barking so early in the morning.

'Where, Gregory? Where'd you see the man?' I pulled on a T-shirt.

'In the garden.' Even in the gloom I could see Gregory was pale and anxious. This'd never happened before.

I couldn't stop myself. I grabbed him by the shoulders and shook him. 'Where in the garden, Gregory? It's important.'

Sarah was awake, struggling to take in the commotion. 'What's going on?' she said.

I shushed her furiously, adding to Gregory's concern. 'What's wrong, Dad? Why are you so angry?' His voice was cracking.

My pulse was racing, my mind in overdrive, yet I forced myself to regain my self-control. 'I'm not angry, Gregory,' I whispered loudly. 'I need to know where you saw this man.'

'What man?' Now Sarah was out of the bed and scrambling into a dressing gown.

Gregory turned to his mother, teeth chattering. 'Next door's dog woke me and I looked out the window. I saw a man in our garden.'

'Oh my God,' Sarah clutched at her throat. Our eyes met and I flashed a warning: *don't say anything*.

'Stay here, both of you,' I warned. 'I'm going to check.'

I was at the door and glanced back. Sarah was comforting Gregory, holding him tightly. 'Are you sure you saw a man?' she asked.

'Yes, Mum. I definitely saw someone.'

'Did he see you?'

'I don't think so. He was wearing some sort of mask.'

My insides somersaulted.

I stumbled barefoot down the stairs. I missed the last two steps, stubbed a toe and swore loudly. My mouth was dry, my chest thudding. My hands shook as I searched for a weapon. I found a baseball bat in a cupboard and rushed to the doors.

Another old and violent memory flashed. The second terrorist attack on our farmhouse. That night our watchdog warned of an assault. The Alsatian's snarls woke my parents. My mother dragged me out of bed, half asleep and mumbling. I heard the dog growling with menace. Seconds later there was a single gunshot. The snarls turned to a desperate yelp, then whimpers of pain.

Silence. Followed by a salvo of heavy-duty machine-gun rounds.

Now, so many years later, that fear returned. This time I'd no weapon other than a baseball bat. If armed men were in our plot that wouldn't protect me or my family. Especially if it was the same two killers who'd murdered Harold Rafferty. I ran from front to side to back door, bat swirling above my head. There was no forced entry. I eased a gap on the drawn curtains in the living room. The front entrance was quiet. Two cars parked on gravel, pot plants with trailing geraniums in bloom. Black wrought-iron railings that separated our residence from the road. The gate was shut. I hurried to the next room and risked a glance out the window. Here was a space to store wheelie bins. Nothing. Now the study with good views of the garden. I crawled on hands and knees to the window, squirmed to the furthest corner where I knew I'd get a better lookout. My back spasmed and my toe throbbed as I angled my tall frame to a safe position. I risked a quick glance. Nothing. The lawn was deserted; the barbecue table and chairs exactly as we'd left them. I slumped onto my backside and stared at my feet. My mind was racing. Maybe Gregory had a nightmare and there wasn't anyone in the garden. That'd happened before with a high fever. Then he saw monsters and spiders. My fears began to ease. *That's it*, I thought, *the heat's got to him again*. I was no sooner reassured when I remembered the barking dog. That wasn't hallucination, I heard it too. Then I realised the dog had stopped barking. My gut knotted so tightly I thought I would scream.

'Dad, what are you doing on the floor?'

Jennifer was at the door in her nightdress. She was barefoot and looked totally confused. 'And why is Gregory crying?' She started walking towards me. 'And why did Mum shout at me not to come downstairs?'

'Go to your room immediately,' I snapped. 'You shouldn't be here.'

Then I heard the sound of breaking glass. Somewhere on the ground-floor level. I was on my feet, soaked with sweat and consumed with dread. I lifted her in one swoop and dumped her at the bottom of the stairs. I looked up to see Sarah, distraught and shaking. She was beckoning Jennifer. I heard glass break again and the sound of a handle being tried. I was in the kitchen, frantically dragging at drawers. I found a steak knife. I held it in my left hand while I swirled the baseball bat in my right. The sounds were coming from behind the curtains of the room where Gregory kept his Xbox. When I stopped at the door the curtains shifted slightly. My mouth was bone dry, my chest thudding. I desperately wanted to pee. Then leather-gloved fingers appeared, teasing an opening. Now every action I made was from the experience of years before. What I'd been warned to do if confronted with IRA intruders.

I held the baseball bat high above my head with my right hand. The gloved fingers behind the curtains were slowly drawing at the opening. Whoever was there was trying to see into the room. I squeezed myself well back. With my left hand I gently gathered folds of curtain. I waited until the fingers moved again. Then I took a deep breath and yanked the curtains open. The double-glazed window had been breached using a glass cutter. Two men wearing balaclavas stood outside. One had his hand through the gap. The other was immediately behind, gun in hand. An instant calculation put one around six foot, the other a few inches shorter. In the fraction of a second I saw startled eyes through slits in their face masks. Then with all my strength I crashed the baseball bat onto the exposed limb. There was a sickening sound of bones breaking and a howl of pain.

I dropped the bat and grabbed the gloved hand, pulling it towards me. Broken bones grated. Now came a scream of excruciating pain, then a string of oaths. I kept my body between the injured man and his buddy. He was trying to get a shot at me. I bobbed and weaved, using the first intruder as a shield. Then I plunged the steak knife into his shoulder. I felt it slide between flesh and hit off bone. When the steel could go no deeper I hauled backwards. Blood sprayed against the window pane. I rolled out of sight. Shots were fired. Bullets punctured glass and skimmed the plaster walls. Powder flaked the floor. I heard screams from upstairs and the panic alarm sounded. The noise was deafening. I grabbed the baseball bat and swung it against the window. I knew this would shatter the double glazing but not break it. If I obscured the gunman's view he'd nothing to aim at. There was shouting and angry roars.

More bullets peppered the room and I curled into a ball. With the lull in shooting I rolled along the ground until I reached the door. The alarm shrilled, bouncing off internal walls. I still had the baseball bat. Irrational anger drove me to unbolt the front door and run barefoot outside. For a moment I stood at the side of the house panting and sweating and raging. Then I heard the screech of tyres, car doors opening and angry shouts. I risked a glance round the corner gable. One man was being dragged into the back seat of a car. A trail of blood followed him. He was moaning and cursing. The other masked man was edging backwards, trying to make his escape. Suddenly he stopped. Then, very deliberately, he clasped his gun in both hands and pointed upwards.

And the room he was aiming at was where Sarah and the children were sheltering. Had one of them looked out? I didn't wait. With a frenzied roar I tore across the ground, baseball bat swirling. The gunman spun towards me. I caught him with a swipe across the side of the head and he staggered backwards. Just as quickly another from the getaway car appeared, gun drawn and leaning on the car roof for support. I recognised him immediately. The Bongos bomber. Scar from ear to neck. Fair hair with blond highlights. High brow and jutting chin. He was right here on my street. That bomb *was* meant for me. I dived to one side as the first rounds pinged.

This was no time to be a hero. I skipped over a small hedge and zigzagged my way back to the house. More gunfire filled the morning quiet. I heard screams from the master bedroom and raced upstairs. *Please don't let them have hit my family.* I found Sarah, Jennifer and Gregory on the floor. They were alive and unhurt but terrified. There were four holes in the windows. Two rounds had stuck in wooden cupboards while the others had skimmed ceiling plasterwork. White dust covered the floor and Jennifer's hair. Through the din of the alarm came the sound of an engine revving. Gregory and Jennifer looked up, trembling with shock. I darted a glimpse outside. The getaway car had disappeared.

'It's okay,' I mouthed. 'They've gone.'

Sarah stared at me. She was ashen with fear, her eyes wide and disbelieving.

Chapter 13

Help arrived within minutes. A squad car with two unarmed officers pulled up in an agitated scramble around 6.10 a.m. One tall and bulky man with a bushy moustache immediately contacted headquarters to arrange road blocks and stop-and-search strategies. He sweated as he rushed around, mobile phone to his ear, struggling to take in what was going on. Barefoot and wearing only boxer shorts and a blood-spattered T-shirt, I paced the pavement. I was shaking with fury and hungry for revenge. I listened to the moustached man bark instructions. Each time I tried to interrupt I was angrily waved away. As soon as the house was cordoned off I blasted him: 'Who pulled the surveillance unit? Why wasn't somebody here all night?'

'It seems there was an incident that drew them away,' he mumbled. 'Sorry about that.'

'Sorry about that?' I roared. 'Could it have been possible that the "incident" might have been a diversion? What is the point of a surveillance unit if they're so easily called away?'

There was no response.

We were gathered into the kitchen and a second officer with the name tag Maurice Harte hit us with a rush of questions. He was in regulation uniform of navy trousers, blue shirt and a dark-blue tie that hung loose at the neck.

His face was scarred from acne, his brogue thick and demanding. What happened? How many were there? Who saw them? Gregory was very brave as he stammered through the first sighting. How tall or small or fat or thin were they? Did they all wear masks? Did you see the car? Make and model? Registration plates? I babbled how I'd recognised one of the attackers as the Bongos bomber. That stopped him immediately.

'Stay here.' Harte suddenly looked very worried. 'There's another squad on its way.'

He pulled his mobile free and began dialling furiously. Hand cupped over mouthpiece he began the first of many calls.

Despite the morning warmth I couldn't stop shivering. Was this just a bad dream? Would I wake up, laugh and excitedly recall a terrible nightmare where our house was attacked by armed and masked men? But no matter how often I shook my head to rid the images, the dreadful truth was in front of me. Jennifer and Gregory clung to their mother for reassurance, their faces drained of colour, eyes wide with terror and disbelief. This was not a bad dream. It was a horrible reality.

The day was becoming brighter and muggier and neighbours in dressing gowns were on the road. The gunfire and shouts must have been heard throughout the area. They huddled in groups, pointing and muttering and shaking their heads.

By the time the second law-enforcement team arrived I was soaked in sweat. Jennifer and Gregory were much the same, their night clothes sticking to their skin. They were pale and drawn. Sarah had a hand towel against her neck, dabbing away beads of perspiration. Her questioning glare followed me everywhere. *What's going on? What's happening?* I couldn't talk to her until I'd all the facts. But I knew the explanation would change our lives for ever.

DI Pamela Roche arrived soon after. Now it wasn't the red-hair in tight-fitting denims and white linen blouse I'd met two days before. The relaxed detective lingering over coffee and complaining about her choice of cake was gone. She was in baggy navy-blue tracksuit with POLICE on the back. A handgun was clipped to her waist. Her hair was swept back severely in a wet mess, as if she'd thrown a bucket of water over herself to waken up, then hurriedly dressed and sped here. And there'd obviously been no time for make-up. The laceration over her left eye looked bruised and ugly, held together with black suture. There were lesser grazes on her chin and neck. But there wasn't a hint of lost sleep on her face. She was sharp, alert and focused, her eyes darting in narrow slits as she took in the chaos. Her elegant fingers clutched a mobile phone and notepad.

I led her from room to room, explaining the chain of events and pointing out gunfire and window damage. We were like total strangers, no hint that three days before we'd discussed an inquest file and its link to Harold Rafferty's murder. Especially no hint that I'd forced her to the ground to try and shield her from falling glass and masonry. And that maybe she'd have had a lot more scars if I hadn't. This was professional policing. Name, address, date of birth? Where were you on the night of the twenty-first? That type of attitude. I found it reassuring. Especially since I wasn't yet functioning properly, my mind confused and agitated, and enraged how my family had been so brutally traumatised. The men who'd murdered Harold Rafferty were trying to kill me. And it seemed they didn't care about hurting innocent bystanders. The Bongos bomb was obviously meant for me and not the skinheads. This morning the same gang came with guns and shot up the room where my family crouched in fear. So this was their second unsuccessful attempt. They'd try again, I was sure of that.

Still clutching his duvet Gregory was taken to the room where he played computer games. His teeth chattered nervously, his hands shook. He tried to respond to the gentle queries posed by a sympathetic and smiling police-woman, also dressed in a navy police-issue tracksuit, who was shadowing Roche. I stood at the door to encourage his memory. But his eyes kept drifting to the smashed and heavily bloodstained window and bullet holes in the walls. When he broke down and started crying the interview was halted. I held my son in my arms, stroking his hair and kissing his head and murmuring words of comfort. His body convulsed and I asked Sarah to console him. His distress reminded me so much of my own ordeal many years before. There was a lump in my throat as big as a golf ball.

Finally Roche asked to speak with me alone. I ushered her into the study and dragged two chairs together.

'As from now,' she said, 'I'm in charge of your security.' There was determination in her voice. A clear 'I'm in control' statement. *You may be coroner*, was her underlying message, *but you've strayed into my territory.*

I eyeballed her. 'It's not my security I'm worried about. It's my wife and children who need to be protected.'

'Do you have relatives they could stay with?'

I thought this over quickly. I was an only child so all blood relations were on Sarah's side. There was Sarah's older brother, fifty-three-year-old Trevor, an IT consultant based in New York. Then her younger sister Carol, a forty-year-old unmarried banker who doted on Jennifer and Gregory. Auntie Carol, as the kids called her, lived close by in Blackrock village. She and Sarah got on famously. I was sure she'd offer an immediate safe house until we worked this through. I mentioned this to Roche and she jotted it down in her notepad. The pages were filling quickly.

'What happened last night? Why did you contact the station?'

I explained the message Sarah had fielded: 'Say hello to Coroner Wilson.'

Roche flicked through her notepad. 'That came from a public telephone box.' She hitched at her baggy trousers revealing grubby sneakers. 'Did your wife recognise the voice?'

'No. But she said the caller had an educated south Dublin drawl. It reminded her of one of my friends.'

Roche's mouth twisted, as if she'd tasted something nasty and wanted to spit. Suddenly I noticed the blood spots on my T-shirt and ripped it off. I was about to throw it to the floor when Roche grabbed it. Minutes later it was bagged and sealed and I was in a fresh cotton top.

Roche leaned back in her chair, pulled out a mobile phone and started dialling. Her free fingers dabbed at her head wound. I took the opportunity to check on Sarah and the children. They were in the kitchen, sombre-faced and munching on tea and toast. I spotted special treats laid out. Chocolate spreads reserved for cheer-me-up occasions. Soft drinks that were limited to afternoon treats. Sarah was trying to distract Jennifer and Gregory with sugary indulgences. They looked up when I glanced in. But my frown told its own tale and they returned their gazes to the table.

'Our guessing game's over,' said Roche when I

returned. 'The man your wife spoke to was Jonathan Redmond. His accent's very distinct.'

Now it was my turn to hang off Roche's every word. In Bongos she'd listened closely as I set out my concerns about the Dowling file. I'd shocked her with my claim the government minister's son had not committed suicide but been murdered. The laptop bomb killed that conversation, leaving me with many unanswered questions. I'd a feeling I was going to hear what might have come out then. And I didn't think I was going to like it.

'He's behind both attacks,' Roche informed me.

That much I had worked out for myself. I recognised the bomber as he leaned on the roof of the getaway car, taking aim to shoot. It had to be the same mob.

'And he's changed tactics. Normally, Redmond avoids violence. He rarely uses muscle to get his way. He knows it's a two-way street. Start shooting and sooner or later someone shoots back.'

Outside a forensic team dusted windows for fingerprints and bagged pieces of cloth snagged on rose thorns.

My mind raced as I struggled to take in Roche's words. Jonathan Redmond, the drug dealer with possible links to government minister Albert Dowling, was determined to kill me. Redmond was almost certainly behind the murder of county coroner Harold Rafferty. And both of us were targeted by Redmond because of an inquest file. Rafferty was no longer a threat. But Redmond must've learned I was asking the same questions about Patrick Dowling's death.

'How'd he get my telephone number? How'd he find out where I live?'

Roche was back as fast as the words left my mouth. 'Somebody you know told him.'

I stared at her for almost thirty seconds. It was only

then that I realised she was trying to warn me how serious this had become. Redmond was determined. He'd bribe or bully anyone to get his way. No one could be trusted. Friends, work colleagues, even the police. And even though suspicion is a basic instinct for me I suddenly felt very alone. And vulnerable.

Two thoughts dominated right then. My family. Their safety.

Chapter 14

Around 11 a.m. I watched on while Jennifer and Gregory stuffed clothes and personal items into suitcases. I tried to comfort them as their tears poured but they ignored me. Sarah fussed over them, pulling out what wasn't necessary, insisting on putting in what she knew was important. Every attempt to help I offered was dismissed.

Thirty minutes earlier I'd gathered them into the study and outlined the situation. Sarah sat in the same chair Roche had occupied. She was in a white towelling dressing gown pulled tight at the front. Her hair was held tightly in a clasp at the back, a stray wisp trailing over her forehead. She looked at me anxiously, trying to hold my eye. *Explain, Mike, explain. What's going on?* Jennifer and Gregory hunched on the floor, staring at me with astonishment and fear as my words spilled out.

'An inquest file has been passed to me,' I started. 'It was being checked by another coroner called Harold Rafferty.'

'I've already told them that,' Sarah cut through. 'You said last night police were going over Rafferty's files. What we want to know is what's going on now? Why is someone trying to kill you?'

So I spent the next fifteen minutes outlining Patrick Dowling's death. I kept the gory and technical bits to myself, for there was enough fear in the room without adding to it. The expressions on each face changed as the background unravelled. Surprise that the county coroner had uncovered the same irregularities in the Dowling file that were troubling me. Horror that he'd been murdered trying to find the truth behind the cover up. Shock and disbelief that I was now the target for the same killers, which quickly changed to alarm as one by one, Sarah, Jennifer and Gregory realised their lives were also in danger while I chased the truth.

'The men who attacked us want to stop me finding out what really happened to Dowling,' I ended. Sarah was stunned; the blood had drained from her face. She mouthed words that refused to come out. She looked as if she might collapse but when I stood to help she waved me away.

'What really happened to him?' Unexpectedly Gregory was first with questions.

'I don't know.'

'If you don't know how can you be sure that's why you were attacked?' Jennifer was still in her pyjamas. Confusion had replaced the earlier fearfulness on her face.

I sighed. I searched the floor for help. There was none. I inspected the ceiling for inspiration. There was none. I chewed the side of my cheek until I drew blood. 'The file's a cover up. And that cover up is protecting some very important people.'

'Protecting them from what?' Jennifer again.

'I don't know.'

'Dad,' Gregory interrupted, 'why don't you get another job? If you weren't coroner would these men be after you?' He had his duvet clutched tight around his shoulders. He was scowling. The Wilson concerned scowl.

It's often the simple challenges that are the most difficult to handle. My explanations weren't enough to help
my family understand what was happening to them. I
didn't know what truth I was supposed to be chasing
or what treachery I had to uncover. And while I strongly
believed Patrick Dowling had been murdered I still didn't
know the circumstances behind that. And I couldn't find
the words to explain all this. Including why I wouldn't
quit as coroner. How do you defend stubbornness and
a refusal to be intimidated to an eleven-year-old who
has just seen his house attacked, his bolt-hole of security
violated? How do you explain that to an innocent boy
who has just dodged gunfire? I didn't want to offload
my ruined childhood on Jennifer and Gregory.

'It's not as easy as that,' I said.

'Why not?' Now it was Sarah's turn to interrogate me.

'Because . . .' I struggled to find the right words. '. . .
because they know I'm going to challenge that file. So
even if I quit I carry those doubts with me. Running
away won't stop them chasing me.'

I looked at my family, hoping to see understanding
and sympathy. I didn't. Sarah was pale and drawn, her
expression a mixture of fear and incredulity. Jennifer
looked stunned. She shook her head from side to side,
as if trying to get rid of my words from her head.
Gregory's eyes were brimming with tears. 'They'll kill
you, Dad.'

That was like a kick in the stomach.

'They won't. But I need to move you and Jennifer.
Once I know you're safe I can plan how to deal with
this.'

That's when the discussion went downhill.

'Why can't you give the file to another coroner?'

'You're a coroner, not a detective.'

'What's wrong with you, Dad? What is it about you that makes you keep fighting?'

That uppercut from Jennifer almost sank me. I didn't answer. I couldn't handle my family's shocked and bewildered faces, their pleading questions and their dismay at my answers.

'This'll only be for a short time,' I hedged.

'How do you know?' Jennifer, yet again challenging my uncertainty.

I didn't speak until I had gathered the mental strength. 'Because I won't allow my family to become strangers.'

Gregory started to say something but Sarah silenced him with a shush. 'Let's get packing,' she said. 'Auntie Carol is getting your rooms ready.' Carol had immediately agreed to shelter Jennifer and Gregory as soon as she heard about the attack. Her home would come under police surveillance while they stayed there.

I was left on my own in the study. The first tears came from Gregory when he was less than halfway up the stairs. Jennifer's room was directly overhead. I heard her moving about, pulling drawers open and dragging a case across the floor. There was a short silence. Then muffled sobs broke through. My heart ached and tears smarted my eyes. I stared out the window, barely noticing the armed policemen patrolling the garden.

Finally, I bottled my emotions. I'm good at that. It's something I learned at the graveside of my parents, and in cold, deserted boarding-school dormitories. I went upstairs to help with the packing but was shooed away. Sarah's expression reflected her disbelief and intense loss at the security her home once offered. That disbelief was something we were all sharing. *How could this be happening to us?* The loss was profound. Our family unit was fractured, our normal and ordinary lives completely ruined. My children were being moved to safety. I looked around, half dazed. Police officers were muttering into mobile phones, forensic experts in white paper suits were tracking bullets and spent cartridges. DI Pamela Roche, the grim-faced woman now in charge of my security, was stalking the ground floor. I went back to my study to clear my head.

I needed space to think.

Chapter 15

'Tell me more about Redmond.'

I targeted Roche at the front gate just as Jennifer's suitcases were being loaded into a squad car. The street was busy with uniformed officers. Out the corner of my eye, I could see curtains move as neighbours looked on. A small group was still gathered at the far end of the road, gossiping and complaining about traffic restrictions. The thoroughfare had been sealed off while police decided on their strategy. I suspected telephone lines would be humming as news spread of the attack. Tabloid photographers and reporters had already turned up. The security barricade was extended another fifty yards to keep them at bay.

Roche finished a conversation on her mobile and nudged me to one side. 'He's from a respectable family and well educated.' She paused to oversee Gregory's belongings transferred to the car. 'He started as a high-school cannabis user and soon discovered he could make a lot of money by supplying. At university he focused on his middle-class mates and their hangers-on. He knew not to cross the bigger players. Despite a first-class honours degree his proper career was drug dealing. His parents and friends disowned him.'

She reached into the boot of a car and hauled out a briefcase. She sifted through her paperwork and finally handed over a glossy photograph with INTERPOL stamped on a corner. 'That's him.'

I wiped sweat from my brow with the front of my T-shirt and studied the picture. Redmond looked in his thirties, raffish and handsome, wearing a linen jacket over an open-necked navy striped shirt. His V-shaped face was tanned. His hair was receding at the front. He had strong cheekbones and a dimpled chin. I couldn't see his eyes behind wrap-around shades. But there was something familiar about him and I struggled to think what.

'Lock that face in your memory,' said Roche.

'Done.'

'Redmond moved to Marbella about eight years ago. He'd a girlfriend called Orlagh Bressan. She was a dumb socialite in her twenties who liked being seen in the right places with the right people. She was beautiful but naive and immature. Redmond was tall and charming and flush with money. He dressed well and had an accent that suggested good breeding. He turned many young women's heads. Bressan fell for the Redmond image and stuck with him.'

Jennifer and Gregory appeared at the front door, Sarah shepherding them from behind. Gregory was in his Chelsea top, tracksuit bottoms and trainers. He sobbed as he struggled to carry his Xbox and collection of video games. Jennifer had dragged on a T-shirt and denims. Her body trembled as she fought back tears. Sarah was pale and distraught. I'd never seen her so upset. Her eyes were red, her features distorted with distress. Her hands shook and she was unsteady, leaning on Jennifer for support. I stopped Gregory, took the Xbox and videos from him and passed them to a policeman. Then I wrapped my arms around his shivering body. I could feel his heart pound. I kissed him on the top of his head and whispered, 'Don't worry, Gregory. Everything'll be all right. Auntie Carol will keep a close eye on you until we get back together.'

He pulled away from me and looked up into my face. His lower lip quivered, his fists were clenched. He blinked away tears. 'Why won't you come with us?'

I held him by the shoulders and looked straight at him. 'It's too dangerous. I'll talk to your mum later and we'll work out something between us.'

He wiped his nose on the edge of a sleeve and pushed past me. I turned to Jennifer. She started to say something but I shushed her. 'Keep an eye on Gregory for me,' I said. 'You're his big sister and he needs you now more than ever before. I promise I'll sort this out.'

Jennifer's expression hardened. I knew she didn't believe me. 'Dad, you spend too much time with the dead. Someday you'll wise up and realise that the living are important too.'

Thankfully, Sarah came to the rescue. 'That's not fair, Jennifer. Your dad's going through enough. We'll see this through together as a family. Let's get you and Gregory settled first.'

Two burly policemen squeezed into a squad car beside Jennifer and Gregory. Sarah sat in the front. The engine was gunned alive and the vehicle eased away from the sidewalk. I kept it in sight until it rounded the corner and out of sight. It broke my heart that not one of my family looked back to see how I was. The lump returned to my throat and I clenched my teeth for control. I wanted to run after them and wrap my arms around them and bring them back to the safety of the house. But I knew I couldn't. No, while a mobster had me in his sights our home was no longer safe for my family.

I beckoned Roche inside and we sat again in my study. 'What else should I know?' The heart-piercing unhappiness at watching my family taken from me was replaced by anger. *By God*, I vowed, *I'll see this bastard down if it's the last thing I do.*

'Redmond and his girlfriend moved around the south of Spain. He made contacts with local gangsters and they introduced him to bigger players. His confident manner impressed everyone. He could take a Moroccan hashish dealer and a Colombian cocaine trader to the best restaurants and make them fit in as if they were successful businessmen. Unlike most crooks with money, he ordered good wines, not the most expensive. He dressed fashionably and ingratiated himself into ex-pat social circles.' Roche struggled for the right words. 'He was a class act.'

I heard next door's dog barking. It hadn't been shot. 'Redmond flooded Ireland and Irish communities in Britain with cocaine and amphetamines. By 2006 he'd become a major player. He ordered cocaine from Colombia and amphetamines from Amsterdam. He shipped supplies to North Africa and then arranged for it to be delivered in smaller packages along the south coast of Spain. He bribed police and judges. He was untouchable.'

'How so?'

'By staying distant from the action. He'd so many contacts it was impossible to know where he was or what he was up to. He'd a string of luxury apartments and rarely stayed in one place for more than a day or two. He kept his distance from the usual gangsters. If he needed muscle he hired professional hit men. He never dealt with them directly, always using a middleman to recruit and pay. He never saw any of them face to face. I doubt if any of them knew what he looked like.'

Suddenly images flashed in my mind. Leather-gloved

fingers pushing through curtains to allow its owner to get a better view of the room. The sickening crunch of my baseball bat breaking bones. The sound of gunfire. The sight of my family cowering with fear in a corner of the master bedroom.

Now a wave of uncontrollable shivering coursed through my body and I gripped the sides of the chair to steady my shaking limbs.

Roche's voice broke through my thoughts. 'But he made one serious error.'

I looked across. Roche had made a steeple with her piano-slim fingers and was playing them against her chin.

'He tipped off police about a shipment of cocaine arriving for a rival called Oliver Rooney. When Rooney came to collect he was grabbed.'

'What was the error?'

'The revenge factor. Rooney raged behind bars. Frustrated and infuriated he put a contract on Bressan. He knew he'd never get close to Redmond.'

I wasn't sure I wanted to hear what was coming.

'She was killed in a staged hit-and-run accident.'

I held a hand up for a break, trying to absorb all I'd heard. But Roche continued. 'Sources say this changed Redmond completely. It made him realise how vulnerable he was. He decided to get out of drug dealing and use his cash empire to move into legitimate businesses. That's why we've been following his links with Albert Dowling so closely. Is the government minister helping him buy respectability?'

'And I'm just an obstacle he has to crush?' I wondered out loud.

Roche didn't answer. But I knew that's what she was thinking.

I realised then I was in the Dublin version of a David

versus Goliath battle. But I was a David without a sling.

'I'll need to carry a gun,' I said.

Roche frowned.

'Get me a Glock handgun. I've used one before.'

Roche leaned back in her chair and inspected me closely. I could almost hear her thoughts. *How come this doctor knows how to use a Glock?* I ignored her and reached for the telephone. I had to call Sarah's sister to make sure Jennifer and Gregory had arrived safely. As I punched the keypad Roche was on her mobile again. I overheard 'Glock 17'. Then 'immediately', followed by 'live ammunition' and 'target practice'. Finally she asked for my security file.

While I waited for Carol to answer I planned strategy. Redmond was in Dublin, not his usual Marbella hideout. His attacks had failed and that would anger him greatly. I could not confront him in the equivalent of a fist fight. There had to be another way.

'Hi, Carol, it's Mike. How are the kids?'

Carol reassured me that everyone was beginning to calm down. She told me how shocked she'd been at the state of agitation when they arrived. But composure was creeping in. Not a lot, but some.

'Thanks, Carol,' I said, 'you're a star. Can I have a quick word with Sarah?'

Then a thought struck me. The insider leaking information had to be Jack Matthews, the detective who'd investigated Patrick Dowling's death. He'd dealt first with Harold Rafferty and then moved to my jurisdiction with the file transfer. Only he and Roche knew my doubts about the case.

Chapter 16

Later that afternoon, a Glock 17 handgun in composite holster was handed to me for personal protection. It had a seventeen-round capacity with a double column box magazine. The gun was metallic black, scratched and worn. It looked like it'd been used before and often. It also came with a spare magazine clip. Roche arranged weapon familiarity and target practice at police HQ. As she drove me there I shared my suspicions about Jack Matthews.

'We're following him,' she told me, 'and we've been following him since Rafferty's murder. Personally, I think he's secure. But he's still being checked.' I took comfort from that.

The journey was through light traffic in a sun-baked afternoon. It seemed as if almost everyone had fled to the seaside. Jealously I watched the rest of Dublin's citizens go about their leisure time. Lazing outside restaurants and enjoying lunch; sitting outside pubs sipping on beer and wine; kicking ball in public parks; strolling along waterways. Young mums pushing buggies, toddlers trailing behind. Normal, everyday activities that I wondered if I would ever enjoy again.

In a thick-walled basement at the command centre I surprised my handlers by displaying familiarity with firearms. I didn't tell them I'd been shooting live rounds from handguns as a twelve-year-old. The Glock fitted into my right hand like a glove. The surprising lightness of the weapon, the recoil when discharged and the smell of cordite brought back memories. None of them good. Then I puzzled the group when I told them I loathed guns. 'I'm a pathologist by training,' I said. 'I've performed autopsies on dozens of gunshot deaths. I know all about bullet wounds.' I deliberately kept back the account of how my parents died. The audience was impressed and however dubious they had been when I arrived at the training centre, I sensed that they were now on my side. I didn't want them to think I might be an unstable gun-on-the-loose revenge freak.

Next I was introduced to my bodyguard. 'This is Tony Reilly,' Roche said as we shook hands. Reilly was an inch shorter than me, wiry with wrinkled face and suspicious eyes. His grey hair was cut in a tight crew cut. He was in denims and an open-neck shirt.

We were an unusual trio. Roche was still in baggy navy-blue tracksuit with POLICE on the back. At least it hid her dirty runners. Her dishevelled state was becoming more obvious by the hour. She kept touching her head wound to make sure it was dry. The black sutures looked good to me; scabbing as would be expected, but clean. I was in casual trousers and sweat-stained T-shirt; grazed and unshaven. To the casual observer we must have looked right misfits.

'Hi,' I said.

Reilly said nothing.

'He knows about the Dowling inquest. He knows your suspicions. And he knows about the separate inquiry we're following. From now on he follows you everywhere. He'll collect you in the morning and drive you to work. He'll stay in the coroner's court all day and take you home each evening. We're recruiting a night and weekend shift.'

'I coach a rugby club,' Reilly explained. 'I'm all over the city on Saturday and Sunday.'

There was an awkward pause as I wondered how to respond. I soon realised his tough exterior was deceiving as Reilly opened up to tell me about his wife and family (four children, all boys ranging in ages from eight to eighteen). He was a regular guy with no hidden agendas.

'That's great,' I muttered. I couldn't think of anything better to say.

'Reilly has direct contact with HQ command and can order support immediately.' Roche handed over a bullet-proof vest and I tried it on for size. It wasn't a great fit but then it wasn't supposed to be evening wear. 'He's used to protection work.'

I smiled weakly. 'I hope I won't need your expertise for long.'

Reilly glanced at Roche and her eyes flickered a 'be careful' hint.

'I hope so too,' said Reilly.

We made small talk on the trip back to Glasthule.

'You're from north of the border, aren't you, Dr Wilson?'

My accent was a giveaway. 'Yes.'

'Your family died during an IRA attack.' He swivelled in his seat to catch my eye.

'How'd you know that?' This was something I kept quiet about. It was something I didn't like discussing.

'Roche told me. I insist on detailed background briefings of the people I look after. Personal habits, vices and addictions. I once looked after an ambassador with a weakness for hookers. I had to wait outside brothels for hours.' We were cruising along Merrion Road and stopped at lights beside the Four Seasons Hotel. A group of Japanese tourists were posing and taking photographs.

'You won't have to worry about that with me,' I said.

'I should hope not.'

The lights changed and we moved forward. 'So how did a northern Baptist with such a tragic history move to Dublin?' he asked. 'Is this not enemy territory?'

I looked out the window. The grand red bricks of south Dublin flashed by. Now St Vincent's Hospital came into view on the right.

'I met a girl.' There was no point offering any other angle. I'd come to Dublin for a short study period. I met Sarah. I fell in love. The rest was history.

'I'm told she's very pretty.' Reilly's voice dropped an octave. This was conversation for conversation's sake. He was tracking a car in his side mirror. He slowed and edged to the left to allow it to pass. Then he stopped for a few seconds to follow its progress. Satisfied he changed gear and pressed the accelerator.

'Yes, she is,' I said. 'I'm very lucky.'

The car picked up speed. 'Let's hope you stay lucky.'

There wasn't another word spoken until he dropped me at my front door. And he didn't leave until the next surveillance team took over.

I shuffled into the empty house wearing a bullet-proof vest and handgun strapped to my waist. I was exhausted and heartbroken. I wandered from empty room to empty room, lifting the pillows my children's heads slept on. I buried my face in their softness and held back tears. Then I slumped on the side of the bed in the master bedroom, wishing Sarah was there to console me. I held her nightdress and ran its silk through my fingers. Would our lives ever be the same again?

Then Sarah rang. She told me she was going to stay with Jennifer and Gregory overnight to calm their fears and help them adjust to the new and appalling circumstances.

'Michael,' she said at the end. I hated when she called me Michael. 'I'm not going to spend my life looking over my shoulder wondering if a gunman is following me. I won't have our children frightened to a state of hysteria. And I can't live with the constant fear that some gangster will kill you. I'm too young to be a widow. We have to talk this over on our own. And soon.' She hung up, leaving me staring at the handpiece.

I made a supper of scrambled eggs on toast and ate it in the kitchen. I watched the evening light fade, the garden fall into shadows, the shrubbery lose its colour. My mind was addled, a confusion of loss, grief and anger. And still troubled by the mystery surrounding Patrick Dowling's death.

It was late and I didn't want to get involved in his paperwork. But I found myself drawn to the file. Soon I had pictures strewn on the floor in my study: autopsy shots and report; police and witness statements. I scruti-nised the death-scene photographs again and again. Then I dissected the dossier into what was offered as truth and what I believed to be fiction. I scribbled my thoughts on A4 sheets, ringing the most important, scoring out what was probably irrelevant. An hour after midnight I had a clearer picture, and a plan organised. At the inquest I'd target the following:

Toxicology result vs Dowling's strength to carry a bar stool.
Bruising on Dowling's fists.
Clean-as-a-whistle bottle of whiskey.
Why did Jack Matthews cordon off the area? Did he suspect someone else was with Dowling?
Bloody fingerprint on Dowling's BMW dashboard.
Harry Malone's dodgy deposition.

I sent a text to DI Roche. DOWLING INQUEST THIS FRIDAY.

Chapter 17

The week starting Monday 7 June was both hectic and hell.

I slept fitfully Sunday night, stumbled out of bed at six and made breakfast. Then I pored over the Dowling file yet again.

I rang Sarah to check if everything was okay. It was. Jennifer and Gregory were slowly coming to terms with their changed circumstances. But they were pining to come home and Sarah was struggling to make them understand that wasn't possible for some time. We agreed we'd have to rely on our security advisors. They'd decide when it might be safe to try and pick up the pieces of whatever would be a normal life after yesterday's attack. Sarah sounded wary and uneasy, repeatedly challenging what I knew.

'How much have you been holding from me?'

'Nothing,' I said. 'This all came to a head last Thursday. I quizzed the inquest investigator about the Dowling file and then arranged a meeting with Roche to discuss it further. Neither of us knew then that bomb was meant for me. I'm still trying to grasp everything that's happened. I'm as shocked as you.' I wasn't exaggerating.

We agreed to park our differences and focus on making the children safe. Sarah would stay with them until she felt confident to leave. Reilly turned up to collect me, dressed like a banker. Charcoal pinstriped suit, starched white shirt and sober tie. 'Gotta blend in with the commuters,' he explained. He made it sound like a joke but he wasn't smiling. Nor was I. Instead of going from A to B he diverted the car along side roads and back alleys. Any attempt on my life would be thwarted by varying the journey. His eyes were focused on traffic and suspicious overtaking and he rarely spoke. That suited me. I was juggling a lot of balls and needed head space.

When we arrived at the coroner's court there was a scramble of journalists and photographers. The morning papers carried banner headlines about the attack with any amount of motives offered. Someone found out I was in Bongos when the bomb exploded so that was added to the melting pot of speculation. A link between Harold Rafferty's assassination was analysed in detail. The airwaves sparked with security correspondents. Each offered their own theory, each had an opinion.

I gathered the staff for a briefing.

The court had three front-of-house secretaries. Aoife: small, chubby and dark-haired; Eleanor: medium height and painfully thin with a pinched nose you could cut yourself on, her hair colour varies week by week; Mary: elegant and quietly spoken with a cherubic face, and a collection of swear words that would make a sailor blush. They were all in their twenties, chatty and engaging. They brightened the drabness of the facility. Jury recruitment was the territory of Arthur O'Leary, a tall and seriously overweight thirty-year-old with a marked nasal twang, and an eye problem that meant he couldn't see his shoe-laces. He was forever leaving crumbs and dirty footprints in the corridors. But his poor short sight was compensated by excellent long sight. Then there was my PA, Joan Costello, the pouting man-hunter. Finally there was Larry

117

Naughton, the paunchy, weary and wrinkled night watchman. Larry rarely appears in the building during the day.

'You know my house was attacked yesterday,' I started. All looked on, aghast and stunned. Criminal offensives on coroners were unheard of. To have two in such a short time was stretching everyone's credulity. Throw in the bomb at Bongos and the overwhelming reaction was one of total disbelief.

'The police are dealing with this and I've full confidence in them.' I sounded like a politician. 'In the meantime it's business as usual. Inquests continue as always. We live in a civilised society and how we treat the dead is as important as how we care for the living. No thug will unsettle the work of this office.' I scanned the audience. I couldn't spot a traitor. If the informer was among them, then he or she was bloody good at shielding guilt.

I dismissed them, asking Joan to remain behind. 'Contact the Dowling family. I'm fast-tracking the inquest to this Friday.' Joan looked startled. 'Pass that on to the police and forensics involved. The state is offering a verdict of suicide and no one is challenging it. It could be over in an hour.'

Joan was scribbling furiously on a notepad. She glanced up at me. 'Anything else?'

'No,' I said.

'Are you feeling okay?'

I sighed. 'All things considered, I'm good. Let's get on with the day's business.'

She was about to leave when I stopped her. 'I'll not be in this Thursday morning. But I'll handle whatever is outstanding in the afternoon.'

'Anything important?' she asked.

'Nah,' I forced a dismissive tone. 'I just need time out, that's all.'

She rested a hand on my forearm and gripped it slightly. 'I'm sure you do, Dr Wilson. This must be hell for you.'

'It is,' I mumbled, 'it sure is.'

Then we went to work.

For the rest of that week Reilly escorted me to and from chambers. He never took the same route. He never relaxed. He dressed impeccably, a different suit each day. He concealed an Uzi sub-machine gun while I carried a Glock handgun in my briefcase.

Each morning in the chamber of ghosts I conducted inquests. I worked through lunch break in the room of sighs. I read depositions, signed off on death certificates and held pre-inquest discussions. I ear-bashed community doctors or hospital medics when important information was missing. I spotted worrying trends in a nursing home. The establishment was owned and overseen by a well-known physician. I was suspicious at the number of elderly folk dying from heart failure within months of their arrival. I worried if he was playing God and helping some into the next world with drug overdoses. I arranged for a health inspector review.

My desk overflowed with folders of death. Suicide, fatal traffic accidents, workplace fatalities, bar-room brawl killings, murderous knife attacks, shotgun casualties, hospital tragedies. I'd all that and a lot more. But I was the final voice for the dead. Without me they had no keeper, no one to persevere in trying to understand their final moments.

On Tuesday one particular deposition captured the effects of the economic recession and Ireland's boom-to-bust crisis.

'He was bankrupt, coroner. Hadn't a cent to his name. At the height of the boom he was worth up to three hundred million. He had developments in Dublin, Cork and Waterford. The banks wined and dined him. They took him on golf trips and big sporting events. When the bubble burst he had about five sites on the go. Then everything dried up. Nobody was buying, everyone was trying to sell. He laid off workers left, right and centre. He hadn't the money to pay them. And then the banks started hounding him for repayments. Even though they knew he had nothing. This was the same crowd who couldn't give him enough when things were going well. But as soon as they got a sniff of his financial difficulties they turned on him. They'd ring him four, five, even six times a day. "Where's our money?" He was walking along Howth pier when the repossession men took his car. He asked them how he'd get home and they pointed to the nearest bus stop. He walked to the end of the pier and jumped in. The tide carried his body out to sea.'

I heard this sort of story on an all-too-regular basis.

After that first Sunday evening apart, Sarah had returned to the wreckage of our house and that week set about turning it back into a home, throwing out anything that had been destroyed by gunfire and hiring plasterers and decorators to patch up the bullet holes in the walls, and glaziers to replace the glass. Each evening Sarah and I called on Jennifer and Gregory. The meetings were fraught with tension and distress as the kids pleaded to be allowed to return home. I was uptight and seething at my impotence. Sarah shielded them from our worst fears but urged they stay away until it was safe again. The return journeys to Glasthule were in stony silence, neither of us able to speak. Sarah would go straight to bed. And I'd hear her cry herself to sleep.

Chapter 18

On Thursday morning, 10 June, a heavy mist enveloped Dublin city and county. Sky and sun were hidden behind a grey, wet blanket. Temperatures dropped so much it felt cool. Traffic was slow, fog lights vainly trying to pick out landmarks.

'I'm not going to the office,' I told Reilly. We were in the hallway of my house in Glasthule.

His eyes narrowed and he ran a hand across his crew cut, as if checking it was still there. 'What's up?' he said.

'Something's bothering me.'

Until now I hadn't told anyone about the 'red-eye' figure in the woodland pictures. Not Roche, not Reilly. No one. There was a traitor in the police and maybe another in my office. I didn't want any plans scuppered before they got off the ground.

'What's bothering you?'

'Too much to talk about,' I said.

'What are you planning?'

'A trip to the countryside.'

'You're going nowhere unless I'm with you.'

'That's good,' I said. 'I may need your help.'

Reilly's unease increased. 'What's that mean?'

'I'm not sure.' I was being honest. 'It depends on what happens.'

'What happens where?'

I pulled the Dowling file from my briefcase. 'Where this man was found hanging.'

Reilly swore softly. Then he pulled out his mobile phone and started dialling.

'We're only going off radar for a few hours,' I said. 'Don't start calling the army in.'

We pulled away from Glasthule towards central Dublin but cut left through side roads in Monkstown until we found Newtownpark Avenue. The traffic was bumper-to-bumper in the opposite direction. We made good time despite poor visibility, crossing Leopardstown Heights and hitting the hamlet of Aikens Village just after nine. Here the mist was in pockets. One minute we could see daylight, then twenty yards further we were smothered in fog. Reilly shifted to third gear and crawled. There was little traffic, just occasional trucks and tractors with dazzling lights. Each corner was taken cautiously. It needed only one fool overtaking against us and we'd all be dead. Soon we were on the R117 to Enniskerry. This bustling community was across the county border in Wicklow. Patrick Dowling was found hanging in woods north of the town.

In the back seat I studied the area map. 'There's a forest on the right about a mile ahead,' I said, 'with a trail running alongside it into foothills.'

Reilly grunted. His hands gripped the steering wheel and he leaned forward for a better view.

I re-read the account of Dowling's discovery. A search party found his locked BMW nudged into a gateway beside a cornfield. It was parked awkwardly, as if abandoned in a hurry. Inside was the detritus of drug abuse: needles and syringes, foil packets of heroin and opened packets of cocaine. A bottle of Jameson's whiskey, one-quarter full, was jammed into the glove compartment;

later this was found to be as clean as the day it came off the production line. There wasn't a single fingerprint or smudge on the glass. The upholstery stank of spilled spirits. The car keys were lying in a culvert close to the vehicle, as if dropped in a hurry.

Less than an hour later the searchers came upon the missing man. His body was hanging by the neck from a rope around the branch of a tree in a clearing. The glade was no more than ten yards in from a hiking trail. He'd been dead at least twenty-four hours. Lying to the side of the dangling feet was a bar stool. His footprints were later lifted from the seat. He was wearing casual clothes: a heavy-knit sweater over shirt, denims and brown brogues.

That November was cold and blustery. Strong winds and heavy showers had denuded many trees. On the day, conditions were poor, the air damp with heavy cloud cover. The terrain was covered in fallen leaves and twigs.

When the forensic team arrived their assessment was that Patrick Dowling had hanged himself. This was confirmed at autopsy. From that point the case was closed. Dowling was buried and his file passed to Harold Rafferty. In the usual course of events the county coroner would've held an inquest. He'd confirm the state's findings and issue a death certificate. Except the usual course of events didn't occur. With Rafferty's assassination, all hell broke loose, leaving me with a mystery to solve.

'Stop,' I said. Reilly let the car cruise to a halt. I squinted through the mist. There was dense woodland to the right. I grabbed my briefcase and got out. 'Park somewhere safe. I'll look for the track and wait until you catch up.'

I stood on a ditch and watched the tail lights disappear into the gloom. The road was deserted. Behind me I heard a dog bark, then sheep bleating. Someone whistled and the dog growled. The rumble of a heavy engine warned of an approaching lorry and I squeezed backwards until it passed. It chewed up grit in its wake. I skirted the road until I found the track. I was anxious to go ahead but knew this would drive Reilly crazy. Roche's instructions were clear: 'Don't let Wilson out of your sight.' I waited until I saw him hurrying towards me.

'What're we doing now?'

'I want to find where Dowling's body was discovered.'

'Why?'

'Because I don't think he was on his own.'

If this was news to Reilly he didn't show it. He stroked his crew cut. 'What the hell are you expecting to find after all this time?'

'I dunno. But I'm looking anyway.'

'Jesus,' he muttered. 'I need this like a hole in the head.'

He followed me. He complained, but he followed.

The track was hard. It hadn't rained for two weeks and sun had dried the earth. Each step jarred the bones. After a few minutes I stopped to check our bearings. The woodland was dense with mist drifting in and out of trees. There was little daylight, just a glimmer through fog. Somewhere a wood pigeon cooed. The undergrowth rustled with small animals. It was even spookier than in the death-scene pictures.

We kept going. As we hiked I considered some of the issues in the inquest depositions that troubled me. Investigators showed that the bar stool could be fitted into the BMW. So it was feasible that Dowling drove here with it in the back seat. I wondered for the hundredth time how the twenty-eight-year-old wasted addict carried that stool up this incline. And why he picked this isolated spot. If he'd wanted to kill himself why didn't he do it at home? It wasn't steep but already the backs of my thighs were aching. Reilly was puffing and panting and he was fit.

'How much further?' he asked.

We stopped on a level. I pulled the enlargements from my briefcase. 'We're trying to find this spot,' I said. We both squinted into the darkness, but the trees were shrouded in mist. And it was seven months since Dowling had taken this path. Rain, wind and seasonal growth had changed the foliage. I became disheartened but didn't dare admit it.

'Gimme another fifteen minutes,' I said.

Reilly grunted and went on ahead. I waited behind, scanning the wooded area for anything that bore a resemblance to the photographs.

We trudged for another few minutes. Then I called a halt. 'I think we've gone too far.'

Reilly didn't say anything. His expression said it all. *I'm pissed off.*

I went down on my hunkers and spread the pictures on the ground. In one shot a tree had a distinctive forked branch with its left bough partially snapped. The stump looked like a giant tuft of toothpicks. 'Keep an eye out for that.'

We retraced our steps. We looked an odd couple. Neither of us was wearing hiking gear. Reilly was in navy trousers, linen jacket with blue striped shirt and suede loafers. Despite his wiry frame and wrinkled face he looked a million dollars. I was dressed for the office in suit, shirt, tie and black leather shoes. And I was carrying a briefcase. Who the hell goes to the woods carrying a briefcase?

The mist lifted and swirled in gentle breezes, then

descended again. Sun was burning off cloud cover to our right and that warmed the air. We skirted the edge of the forest. We saw nothing that resembled a broken forked branch. Now the only sounds were our laboured breathing and heavy steps.

At one point the woodland seemed to want to drag us in. Branches sagged from the weight of their leaves and trailed onto the path. I recalled Dowling's body was found in a clearing. There had to be some brightness somewhere. But we were hindered by swirling fog. Each puff of wind dispersed it. In some patches it clung to treetops, in others it drifted above undergrowth.

Then I smelled something that was out of place in a forest.

'Wait,' I whispered. I grabbed Reilly's arm. I sniffed the air. 'I smell smoke.'

He sniffed the air. 'You're right.'

We stood on the same spot for maybe three minutes. 'It's up higher,' I whispered. I don't know why I was whispering. I didn't want to frighten anyone. And I didn't want to disturb anyone. I just wanted to see where the smoke was coming from.

We trekked further. Our steps were slower, our eyes trained into the undergrowth. Reilly stopped. He sniffed again. 'I smell cooking.'

I could smell it too.

Reilly looked at me. 'Could be campers.'

'Why so far into the forest?'

Reilly didn't answer. He was moving ahead. His pace had quickened. I hurried to follow. Fifty yards further we spotted a trail of wood smoke curling through trees. It was thicker and whiter than the drifting mist. Now the smell of cooking was stronger. There was the faint sound of tin against tin. Then a mumbling voice. Reilly drew a handgun. He was obviously taking no chances. I was unarmed; I'd left my Glock behind, not expecting trouble. We moved deeper into the shadows, clambering over fallen branches and snagging our clothes on brambles. The further we went the darker it became. The darker it became the more the mist swirled. Now the smell of wood smoke was strong, a wisp curling into the air maybe ten trees ahead. But the sound of tin against tin had stopped. And so had the mumbling voice. Reilly fanned to the right. I veered to the left. Cobwebs wrapped themselves across my face. A bug flew into my eye making it twitch and water. I rubbed it away and when I could see again Reilly had disappeared. I heard his boots snapping twigs but I couldn't see where he was. I stopped. I was sweating and my heart was pounding. I was nervous without any reason. *It can only be campers,* I said to myself. *And Reilly has a gun.* Two more paces and suddenly I saw the same blur I'd noticed in the photographs. Maybe five thick trees straight ahead. I stared at it. I was sure I could see half a face and a staring eye. The blur disappeared. I put one long step in front of the other. More cobwebs. More bugs. I swatted them away. Dead wood crunched under my size eleven shoes. I swore silently. I stopped and listened. Now I couldn't hear Reilly and couldn't see him. I felt vulnerable. This wasn't such a good idea after all. I wiped sweat from my brow. I put my briefcase on the ground and took out the enlargements. I darted glances left, right, forward and behind. This was not the territory I was looking for. I checked the tree where the blur had appeared. Nothing. No blur now, no noise, no movement. I had a sense of being watched and that made me nervous. *Why didn't I bring the gun?* I picked up my briefcase and took another step. There was rustling and I spun the quickest 180 degrees

I'd ever done in my life. Nothing. No small animal, no shaking leaves, no flapping wings. The fog was low in the trees and disorientating. My mouth was parched and my hands shook. I licked my lips for moisture. *Where the hell's Reilly?* I cleared my throat to shout. The fog shifted again. I sensed movement. I suddenly felt an impending sense of doom. Someone was ready to strike. I held a hand up to save my face from any blow. I looked right and left. Nothing. When I looked ahead again my heart seized and I yelled with fright.

'The last time somewan came here carryin' a briefcase he ended up gettin' hisself killed.' The voice was deep and guttural and rasping and angry. 'Waddye want?'

A few paces from me stood a man who looked one hundred years old and counting. He was around the same height as me, over six feet, with long, straggling and mangy hair. His thick beard was streaked with grey. He wore a heavy coat that even at a distance reeked of smoke, cigarettes and beer. His fingers were stained with nicotine, his hands dirty. His shoes were worn and held together with twine. He was a typical vagrant but not in typical vagrant territory. And, unlike most down-and-outs, his eyes glinted. He was watching me with an unsettling intensity.

I wanted to run but stood my ground. 'Who're you?'

The vagrant didn't answer. He kept staring at me. I felt stupid. In my office dress code I probably looked like a salesman desperate to make a pitch.

He scratched his nose and then hoisted his trousers. He deliberately looked to his left, as if listening. Then he turned back to me.

'Usually all I seen here are squirrels n' foxes n' birds n' moles n' badgers.' He chomped his gums. 'Then agin,' he rasped, 'I seen rats. Not jus' the furry kind with four legs n' a tail.'

Out the corner of my eye I spotted Reilly. He was tight against a tree about five metres away. He'd hung his fancy linen jacket over a branch. He'd his handgun trained on the vagrant.

'Tell him to put that fuckin' gun down,' the vagrant said.

Chapter 19

His name was John Hobbs. He wasn't a hundred years and counting. He was a sixty-three-year-old ex-serviceman who'd fallen on hard times. Once Reilly showed his ID, Hobbs's suspicions eased and he opened up. He told us he'd served his country in Kosovo, Chad and Lebanon. He'd been shot at, mugged and survived a mortar bomb attack. But he found his most dangerous enemies were at home. 'Bent politicians n' fuckin' crooked bankers.' That was the first group. This was followed by an angry tirade against police, lawyers, social workers and priests. 'Useless bastards. I wanted food n' they told me to pray.' Reilly and I listened without interrupting. Not that we'd have got a word in. Hobbs was in a vicious mood.

His anger spent, we trekked towards the wood smoke and found a hideaway. Hobbs had put it together using steel rods and waterproof canvas. Inside was a camper bed with sleeping bag. There were wooden boxes and a beer barrel to sit on and an oilcloth ground sheet. He'd a gas-fired cooker for food and wood burner for heat. Both were on the go. The set-up was deep inside the forest and out of sight from the trail.

'I don' like people aroun' me,' he said.

A few yards from the hut was a bundle of newspapers and clothes protected with tarpaulin. There was also a significant collection of empty beer cans, whiskey and vodka bottles. A latrine, sensibly distant, had also been dug. Hobbs had carefully isolated himself from the world. And we'd disturbed his breakfast. He had a pan with sausages cooking, bread rolls wrapped in paper and a pot of tea with dirty mug. 'There's not enough for yiz as well,' he said. 'I wasn' expectin' visitors.'

We murmured our disappointment.

He flicked the heat up on the gas fire until the sausages sizzled. Slowly and lovingly he turned them until they were a crisp brown. Satisfied he forked them onto a tin plate, pulled out an empty beer barrel and sat on it. He blew on the meat until it was cool enough to risk a bite. Then he chewed contentedly, like a man without a care. Reilly and I had our jackets and ties off, shirts open at the collar. Our faces were streaked with sweat and grime and dead midges. I wanted to ask Hobbs a hundred questions but didn't know where to start. Was he in these woods when Patrick Dowling died? Was his face the blur I'd spotted on the death-scene photographs? Had he looked on as police and forensic investigators assessed the body before removing for autopsy? And had he seen Dowling hang himself?

Hobbs wrapped a bread roll around two cooked sausages, added ketchup and squeezed. The ketchup trickled out the ends of the roll and fell onto his coat. He ignored the mess. The pong off the coat was over-powering. He mopped at grease in the pan with crusts of bread. Then he wiped his fingers on his coat and sipped on his tea. His table manners wouldn't have gone down well in better restaurants. He ignored us, as if we weren't there. He stared into the gloom, whistling tune-lessly. I glanced at Reilly and he shrugged.

Finally, Hobbs broke the silence. 'Waddye doin' here?'

131

I ignored his question. 'You said somebody else came here?'

'That's righ'.' Hobbs nodded. He took another mouthful of tea and gestured towards the collection of newspapers. 'Then wan day I read the poor bastard was shot.'

This had to be Harold Rafferty, the county coroner.

'He was a tall man,' he looked towards Reilly. 'Maybe an inch more than ye. Beefy, with it, like a rugby player. Mebbe mid-sixties. He was carryin' a briefcase just like ye.' This time he looked at me.

He had just described Rafferty to a tee. The county coroner had trekked this same path. Like me, his suspicions about Patrick Dowling carried him back to the death scene. And he'd paid for that with his life.

'What was he doing here?' I asked. I knew, but wanted to hear what Hobbs might say.

'Dunno,' he mumbled. 'I just kep' an eye on him.'

'Where'd he go?'

Hobbs looked up at me and smiled. A row of dirty teeth appeared. 'The same place I guess yiz are headin'.'

Reilly took an angry step closer. 'Cut the crap. We haven't all day.'

Hobbs threw out the dregs of his tea. He switched off the gas and tossed a couple of logs onto the wood fire. It sparked and crackled and soon flames licked the dry tinder. Fresh smoke drifted towards the treetops. 'When I read abou' the shootin' I realised he was a coroner. I didn' know tha' when he was here. But he wasn' out for a stroll. Not carryin' a briefcase and map. And sure enough I followed him to where Paddy was found hangin'.'

I looked at Reilly and saw him looking at me. I knew we were thinking the same thing. How did Hobbs know the name? And the use of the informal 'Paddy' tag suggested familiarity.

'Did you know Dowling?' I asked.

Hobbs looked at me. 'Yeah.'

My insides knotted. Was I finally going to hear the answer behind the mystery?

'How?' Hobbs was considerably older than Dowling, and they'd hardly have mixed in the same social circles.

Hobbs's eyes glinted, this time with anger. 'Wance upon a time, mister, I looked after meself. I washed n' wore clean clothes.' He blew snot from his nose, one nostril at a time. Then he wiped the residue on his coat. It was taking quite a hammering. 'But with the buildin' crash I couldn' get work. I'd nothin' comin' in. I gambled every fuckin' penny and lost a packet. I couldn' afford anywhere to live and ended up sleepin' rough. Then I took to the bottle. Anythin' I could get me hands on. Beer, vodka, gin: I drank it. Anythin' to block the misery. Then I met Paddy. We were both in the gutter only he wasn' comin' out. We'd sit under Baggot Street Bridge talkin' about this and that. Paddy would be shootin' up n' I'd be knockin' back cheap wine. Paddy said things he shouldna said.'

He spat into the fire. 'Look at me now.' Hobbs's hide-away wasn't a bad effort, but it wasn't the Ritz Carlton either. 'I haven' a fuckin' penny to me name. I hustle for money; I beg and steal.' He lurched towards me and I could smell his breath: last night's drink and this morning's sausages. 'I knew wan day Paddy's loose tongue would cause trouble. And it did. That's why I'm hidin' here n' he's in the grave.'

'What'd he tell you?' I asked.

Hobbs became suddenly subdued. He ducked inside his hut and rumbled around, finally emerging with a pouch of loose tobacco and cigarette paper. He rolled one, lit it and blew smoke rings into the air. Then he

133

studied his nails, scratched the back of his hands and massaged his temples.

'I can' say.'

'Why?'

More smoke rings. 'I wanna stay alive. I heard stuff I shouldna heard. I saw people I'm tryin' ta forget.'

Then he turned the tables on me. 'Who're ye anyway?'

'I'm a friend of the man with the briefcase.' I fudged the reply. He'd learn soon enough who I was.

Hobbs sucked hungrily on his cigarette butt and then flicked it into the air. The ember arced and disappeared. 'Be careful,' he said. 'Yer dealin' with fuckin' dangerous bastards.'

'Who are they?' Reilly broke his silence.

Hobbs turned to look at him. 'Ye'll have to find that ou' yerself. I'm not gettin' involved.'

I sensed Hobbs was going to clam up. What he'd revealed so far made sense. Vagrants don't hide in remote woodland; like foxes they prowl urban areas. I'd a feeling the more we pushed the harder it would be to get real answers. And he could spin us a line to get us off his back. I tried a different angle. 'Do you think he was telling the truth? Or was he just another lying addict?'

'He wasn' lyin'.' Hobbs was emphatic. 'If he was I wouldn' be here.'

'Where'd he get money for drugs?'

'I dunno.' Hobbs spat into the fire again and it sizzled. 'But he was never short.'

'Did his family bankroll him?' I offered.

Hobbs snorted. 'Mebbe.' I knew by his tone he wasn't buying into that.

'Did he sell himself as some rent boy for money?' I was clutching at straws.

Hobbs looked at me with utter contempt. 'Yer way off track.' He stood and shook his coat and a million fleas were dislodged.

We were being dismissed. I'd a final question. 'Did you see Dowling hang himself?'

Hobbs sat on the beer keg and stared into the distance. He worked at the side of his mouth with his tongue. Then he buried his head in his hands. When he spoke again his voice was muffled.

'I seen wha' happened,' he said. 'That's all I'm tellin' yiz. Ye find out why he ended up here and then come back. I'll fill in the missin' pieces.'

'We'll be back,' I said.

Hobbs looked up and held my gaze. I sensed a man anxious to tell all. But I could see he was worried where that would lead him. He knew the county coroner had come this way. And he knew what'd happened to him.

'This isn' abou' drugs,' he said. He glanced towards Reilly, then back to me. 'Anywan tells ye that's lyin'.'

He crept back inside his hut, slumped onto the camper bed and turned his back on us. 'This is all abou' money,' he called out. 'Forget abou' drugs, follow the money.' Reilly nodded, signalling that we should leave. 'Go back onta the trail,' Hobbs was mumbling now, his words hard to hear. 'Go road-ways for fifty yards and then cut in. That's where Paddy died.'

We found the track again. I gripped my briefcase so tightly my knuckles ached. *Forget about drugs, follow the money*. What was Hobbs suggesting? There were as many questions as answers. Reilly was counting his steps. 'Thirty-eight, thirty-nine, forty.' Pause. 'Forty-eight, forty-nine, fifty.' We stopped. The forest was dense and dark and still. Fog clung to the treetops. The mist cleared and a beam of light picked out a clearing. We stepped into the woodland.

'There it is.' I spotted the forked branch with toothpick tuft.

We pushed further, kicking away branches, stepping over brambles. A swarm of midges attacked my skin and I swatted at them. They disappeared. More fallen branches were kicked away. It suddenly seemed wrong to be going to this place of death. But I knew I had to see it for myself. We entered the clearing. The forked tree was at the edge. I identified the bough from which Patrick Dowling was found hanging. I circled the glade, crunching dead wood underfoot and squinting into the gloom. This time there was no blur behind a tree. There was nothing but silent woodland.

My instincts had been right. Dowling didn't die alone. Hobbs had looked on. His must have been the staring eye blur on the police photographs. And he was no stranger to hostilities. In uniform he'd been shot at, mugged and bombed. He wasn't the type to be easily intimidated. Someone else *had* been here that day. Someone Hobbs was so scared of he didn't dare get involved. I closed my eyes and listened. I heard forest sounds: rustling leaves, cooing wood pigeons, creaking trees. But my imagination heard shouts; angry, vicious and violent shouts.

Chapter 20

'Do you believe him?' I asked Reilly when we were back in the car.

'I do. There's nothing in this for him. He's no reason to lie.'

'Still, it seems a helluva coincidence he knew Dowling.' I was challenging my misgivings. 'And that he was in those woods when Dowling died.' I had to be sure of my position. It was one thing for me to accept Hobbs, it was something else to persuade others. One look at the vagrant and credibility would disappear.

'I watched him closely,' said Reilly. He gunned the engine alive and we edged out onto the road. Sun had burned off the mist and the day was now warm and bright. In the distance the Wicklow hills glimmered in a purple haze. 'He wasn't to know we'd turn up out of the blue. Suddenly we're crowding him and firing questions. If he was lying he'd have hummed and hawed, mumbled and backtracked. Instead he was convincing.' He threw me a quick look. 'What I'm trying to get my head round is how you thought someone would be there.'

I outlined my concerns from the first time I read the Dowling file, and elaborated how those doubts increased with each reading. And why I'd kept the forest blur puzzle to myself until now.

We drove towards Dublin. It was 12.30 p.m. and my first inquest was due to start at two o'clock.

'I'm surprised he spoke to us at all.' Reilly overtook a tractor with a black-and-white sheepdog sitting on the driver's lap. He hailed our beeped salute.

I agreed. Hobbs's bolt-hole had been exposed, his solitude disturbed.

'He's ex-army,' I said. 'We should check his service record.'

We left the R117 and headed towards the M50 Dublin ring road. Sunlight was making me squint. Traffic was heavy and Reilly kept to the slow lane. His eyes darted from the motorway ahead to rear and side mirrors. 'I'll get someone to follow that up,' he said.

'Someone reliable,' I emphasised.

Which was a big ask.

We exited onto the N81 Tallaght Road and cut through the suburbs of Templeogue, Rathgar and Harold's Cross. A street protest about government cutbacks delayed us for twenty minutes. It was a bad-tempered rally with the crowd angrily chanting 'OUT, OUT, OUT'. Many carried caricatures of state ministers. I craned my neck to see if there was one of Albert Dowling. If there was one, it was so poor to be unrecognisable. Reilly zigzagged and diverted off the main route to confuse any possible followers. Neither of us spoke, each to our own thoughts. I sensed Hobbs had unnerved Reilly. Like me, he'd be wondering who was with Dowling the day he died. And why was Hobbs so scared? What'd he seen that forced him to flee to the countryside? Admittedly, he'd picked a good spot to hide. Out on the road was a public transport link to central Dublin. He could be back in his usual city haunts within an hour. And he was within walking distance of Enniskerry village. This was a well-to-do town with a token police presence. It'd offer half-decent pickings.

We drove along the quays, crossed O'Connell Street and lane-hopped until we were outside the Victorian red-bricked coroner's court. Reilly shadowed me to the safety of the tiled entrance.

DI Pamela Roche, now in denims and navy-blue cotton crew neck under linen jacket, was waiting. Her scarred forehead was camouflaged with make-up. The bruising was fading. Strange to think that only a week had passed since the bomb. So much had happened since then.

She motioned us to a corner and we huddled out of earshot. 'Things are hotting up. The head of Standard and Chartered Bank, Dan Thornton, has been arrested. He's being questioned about money laundering, crooked accounting and falsifying bank records.'

I looked blank.

'Thornton has close ties to Albert Dowling, our Minister for Economic Development.'

'And father of the late Patrick,' I added, 'whose inquest is scheduled for tomorrow.'

'Exactly.'

'Has Thornton incriminated Dowling? Has he connected him to Redmond?'

'Not yet. He's surrounded himself with lawyers and is refusing to answer questions.'

Joan hovered in the background, trying to catch my attention. I mouthed a 'what?' She mouthed a 'need to talk'. I mouthed back, 'gimme five'. She nodded. But she didn't move away. I checked the time. It was closing on two o'clock and the first inquest of the day. And I hadn't eaten. My belly grumbled with hunger.

'When I've anything new I'll let you know.' Roche glanced towards Joan, and there was something unsettling about the look. Did she think Joan was the traitor in my office? I wanted to check for Joan's reaction but held tight. I'd keep an eye on her myself. 'In the meantime,' said Roche, 'keep your head down and trust no one.'

She left me and Reilly staring at one another. I hadn't had time to tell her about John Hobbs and his revelations.

I collected myself and forced a neutral expression on my face. I beckoned Joan forwards. 'What's up?'

'Mary Dowling, the mother of the late Patrick Dowling, rang and thanked you for bringing the hearing forward. She'll be here tomorrow with her family.'

'Good.'

'She's hired a lawyer.'

I didn't want that. But I'd no choice. 'That's her call. The state is working towards a suicide verdict and will not have legal representation.' I didn't add I was planning a blitz on the evidence that had been brought before me. I prayed the Dowling lawyer was inexperienced.

Joan pointed at her watch. 'Your first hearing is ready.'

I grimaced. 'I'll go straight in.' I'd have to miss lunch.

'I think you should freshen up first.' Joan was inspecting me from head to toe.

I realised that my hands were grimy and sweat stuck to my shirt. 'Gimme another five minutes.'

I hurried to the washroom.

Finally I took my place at the bench in the chamber of ghosts. In the visitors' gallery sat a group of five. They were pale, their features drawn with worry. I had no way of knowing if they were family or friends or a mix of both. They were dressed, as most relatives did when they turned up to the inquest of their loved one, in the equivalent of their Sunday best. Two men in ill-fitting suits and shirts that couldn't contain their bulging necks and waistlines. Two middle-aged women in shabby dresses while the third was in a black trouser suit with black blouse. She wouldn't have looked out of place in a funeral home. I put her in her late thirties, perhaps early forties. I settled myself, arranged paperwork and prepared to listen. Soon another account of a wretched young life and tragic death was recalled.

'Her husband never sent her a penny, coroner. He walked out and left her with three kids under ten years to rear. So she sold herself for sex. How else was she gonna put food on the table? She only did tricks on weekdays, while the children were at school. She turned to heroin to dull her brain. It helped her do what she had to do for the clients. Know worra mean? Some of the things they asked were only brutal. Disgustin', they were. I dunno how she kept goin', coroner, if ye ask me. I just dunno. I'm not surprised that she jumped in front of that train. I'd a done it meself if I was in her shoes, God rest her soul.'

The deceased was a week shy of her thirty-first birthday when she took her life. The woman in the black suit sobbed throughout. They all listened to the deposition, then one of the men confirmed it was correct. No one wanted to hear the post-mortem findings. I glanced at photographs of the mangled body on the rail track. One leg was separated from the torso. The head was partly severed at the neck. There was blood everywhere. *Dammit,* I thought. *What was going through your mind? Your children's faces? Your husband's face? Or just blackness and despair? Your life was hell but was it so bad you couldn't go on another day?* No one would ever know. Autopsies reveal cause of death, but there's no such thing as a psychological post-mortem. No matter how carefully the pathologist inspects, slices and dices the brain, he'll never discover what the deceased was thinking at the time of death.

I snacked on cheap sandwiches and bottled water during lulls in the rest of that day's hearings. By six I'd heartburn and a headache. I was exhausted from all that'd happened and willed an early night. Bed and a sound night's sleep were so appealing. I needed to face the Dowling inquest with a clear head.

Reilly drove me home and Sarah was waiting. She was dressed in a white cotton T-shirt and denims. Her hair was swept back, showing off her high cheekbones. Her smile was welcoming but her eyes weren't. She seemed uneasy, troubled almost. She'd made a supper of breaded chicken wings, salad and cheesy potato slices. I wolfed it down. I declined wine and sipped on iced water. We made conversation, strained and overly polite. Eye contact was minimal. The children were fine but unhappy. The weather was hot and clammy. The garden needed rain. The government was in a mess, but then when had it ever been different? Finally we moved to the main topic: our lives. Now we had to engage.

'Michael, what's happening to you?' There was no warmth in her voice, only concern.

'What do you mean?'

'You've changed,' she said. She reached across the table and found my right hand. She squeezed it. 'You're not the man I used to know. Where's the fun Mike Wilson? The man who could make me laugh with the twinkle of an eye and then bed me minutes later? Your sense of humour is now as bleak as those reports you read.'

I sat bolt upright, completely surprised. 'I don't understand. None of us can ever be who we were before. Too much has happened. There's nothing to laugh about.'

But Sarah hadn't finished. 'You're totally caught up in this inquest. Your mind's distracted. You wander around in a daze half of the time. You're losing touch with me and the children. When we visit them you can't wait to get away.'

'That's ridiculous.' Jennifer and Gregory were my whole life. I lived for those children. The accusation cut to the bone.

'No, it's not.' Sarah's face was hard, her eyes burning with barely contained fury.

I sensed another row and I was in no mood for one. So I backed down. 'If you say that's so then it must be true.' I stared at our clasped hands. 'But I can't turn the clock back. This inquest is my responsibility. The gang chasing me must have something very big to hide. If I cave in it only passes to the next coroner in line. Then they'll target him. It'll keep going until only the strongest is left standing.'

'And will you be the one left standing, Michael Wilson?' She took her hand away, leaned back in her chair and eyeballed me. 'And if you're not, how do you think we'll remember you? With love and affection? Or as some stubborn Northerner carrying so much baggage he couldn't see the woods for the trees? Like most of that crowd up there.' This was the first time I'd ever heard Sarah describe my kinfolk as 'that crowd'.

'Sarah.' I took a deep breath to calm myself. 'I had to run from killers once and it destroyed my childhood. I won't allow that to happ—'

Sarah's fury exploded. 'That was then, Michael Wilson.' She slapped the table so hard the cutlery rattled. I'd never seen her so distressed. I wasn't sure how to handle the situation. We were in new and very unpleasant terri-tory. 'This is now. Your childhood's over. Jennifer and Gregory are only in the middle of theirs. Are you going to make them suffer because of some cursed inquest? That man Dowling's dead, Michael. Can't you understand

143

that? He's dead and no matter what happens from here on nothing will bring him back.' Her hands shook with rage. 'Do you want to join him in the grave because of some warped sense of pride? Is this just typical Northern stubbornness that brings no good to anything or anybody?'

I got up from the table and left the room. I heard Sarah sobbing but I couldn't go back. Not while she was in this mood. We'd get no good out of one another. I put the plates in the dishwasher and tidied up the kitchen. Sarah stayed put. And even though my heart was breaking I wanted to keep that distance. I couldn't handle any more unpleasantness between us. After a while I edged towards the study for a final check of the Dowling file. Tomorrow would be my last chance to chip away at the state's case.

Sarah came in. She'd calmed down but her chest still heaved. She deliberately stood over me, reached down and shut the file.

'Michael,' she said, 'you have to put your family before your work.'

I stood and held her tight in my arms and kissed the nape of her neck. 'This will be over soon.' How I longed for us to be back together and happy. With Jennifer and Gregory.

Sarah pulled back and her eyes searched my face. She was crying and I kissed away her tears. 'I'm desperate for that to be true,' she sobbed.

Chapter 21

I didn't sleep well. Sarah clung to me from the moment we hit the sheets. I finally sensed her body ease around midnight. I waited a few minutes until I was sure she'd settled, then slipped to the spare room. There I tossed and turned for hours. Close to four I fell into a deep slumber. I dreamed of dead bodies and ghosts, of hangings and shootings and knifings and car accidents and drownings and children falling out of trees onto concrete. My heart was racing and I was drenched in sweat when the alarm shrilled. I sought the comfort of the shower.

At eight o'clock Reilly was waiting for me in the hallway, and I knew immediately something was wrong. He held his Uzi sub-machine gun at the ready. That wasn't usual. He rarely carried his hardware openly. His tight crew cut was growing out and looked jagged. He was unshaven. That was strange also. Reilly was careful about his appearance. Gone too were the smart clothes. Today he was wearing a white T-shirt and bullet-proof vest under a casual jacket. A handgun bulged in a shoulder holster. When I looked at him he avoided eye contact.

'Have you got the Glock?' His voice was strained.

I slipped the pistol out of my briefcase. Then I made a grand gesture of showing how quickly I could un-holster it. He was unimpressed.

'Bullet-proof vest on?'

I nodded. It was underneath my jacket.

'Why the interrogation?' I asked.

Reilly looked very uptight. He started to answer but was momentarily distracted.

Sarah was in the hallway, ashen grey with fear and worry. Her face was aged beyond her years. She squinted against the morning sunlight that streamed through the stained-glass windows in our porch.

'Keep it at the ready.' Reilly was using Sarah to avoid my question. 'There's a change in routine.'

I sensed Sarah freeze. But I didn't look. I couldn't bear her to see my worry.

'There's a black Ford Mondeo outside. There's also a silver Lexus. Nobody knows which car you're going to be in, so here's the plan. There's a support crew in the Lexus. You and I get into the Mondeo. The driver's waiting, engine running. He'll start to move off, stop briefly, and then cruise forward about a hundred yards. He'll stop again and then everyone except the drivers swap cars. We transfer to the Lexus, the others switch to the Mondeo.'

I nodded. I could see the sense in varying the routine but this seemed overly elaborate. More worryingly, Reilly was sweating. And it wasn't that warm.

'If anything happens, no matter how simple it seems to you, get your head down and keep it down. Whether it's a kid fallen off his bike on the way to school, a flat tyre being fixed and stalling the traffic, whatever.' He eyeballed me. *Listen to what I'm saying. This is deadly serious.* 'You keep your head well outta sight.' This was not Reilly the buddy minder, this was Reilly the profes-sional bodyguard.

I nodded again. This was the most intense briefing

146

ever. *What the hell's going on? Has something happened overnight?* I wanted to quiz Reilly but not while Sarah was listening. 'The Lexus is bullet proof but not bomb proof so we're not one hundred per cent safe.'

The protective vest was making me sweat and I could feel the back of my neck itch. 'Can we go?'

I forced the image of an explosion out of my mind. Gunshots were bad enough, bombs something else altogether. I'd once conducted an inquest into three deaths caused by a terrorist bomb. Not all body parts had been recovered.

Reilly grunted something unintelligible and then tapped on the keypad of his mobile phone. There was a short conversation, barely ten words on his side. Then he gripped the Uzi firmly in both hands and eased the door open with the tip of his boot. He'd never done that before. Sunlight streamed inside the hallway and I could just about glimpse a hint of blue sky. For the citizens of Dublin this was going to be a beautiful day.

Reilly stood on the front steps and shaded his eyes from the sun. He took some time to assess the street. There was a steady trail of commuters rushing towards the main road link for buses, taxis and trains. To my untrained eye it seemed like any other day, the people ordinary and unthreatening.

'The support team will stay one car behind us.' We had reached the Mondeo and I squeezed into the back. I double-checked that the Dowling dossier was inside my briefcase.

'Hiya, Doc. Havin' a nice day?' The Mondeo driver was inspecting me via the rear-view mirror.

I dismissed his clumsy attempt at familiarity and waited until Reilly was inside before I lied through my teeth. 'Yeah, never better.'

'That's great.'

The Mondeo pulled out, the driver first checking the road was safe. Then he accelerated slightly before sharply applying the brakes. We hadn't moved more than fifty feet. Reilly sat upright, anxiously scanning the road ahead and behind. He held his Uzi sub-machine gun out of sight. He tapped the driver on the elbow and the Mondeo edged forward. Ahead a silver Lexus waited.

'Away ye go, Doc.'

I opened the right rear door. As soon as my feet hit the ground the passenger door of the Lexus opened and a shadowy figure moved swiftly from one car to the other.

Reilly took the briefcase from my hand, waited until I was settled in the back seat of the Lexus and then pointedly forced it onto my lap. He patted the side where he knew I kept the Glock. 'I didn't want to say this in front of your wife but I've a bad feeling about today.' My stomach lurched. He put a finger to his lips and whispered, 'Someone may not want you to get to work.' Before I could say a word he slammed the door and climbed into the front. He briefly introduced our driver, a thickset man called Devlin. He was dressed in a navy tracksuit zipped up at the front. Devlin mumbled hello and I mumbled hello back.

The Lexus pulled out and quickly gathered speed. A group of teenagers were playing ball in the middle of the road. They scattered as the car revved towards them. One of the boys mouthed obscenities at me. I ignored the gesture. I'd other things on my mind. I checked out the rear window, relieved to see the Mondeo following. My mouth was dry and I licked at my lips to stop them chapping. I chewed on the inside of my cheek until I tasted blood. 'The traffic's bad all the way in, Coroner.'

Devlin was courteous and respectful and that suited me. I was so on edge I couldn't have attempted conversation. I checked the time. It was 8.20 a.m. With a few breaks in traffic and decent luck with stoplights we could reach the coroner's court in Store Street by 9 a.m. The Dowling inquest was due to start at nine thirty. Right now the Dowling family would also be making their way towards the court. I doubted they'd be troubled by fears of assassination.

Ten minutes travelling and we'd reached the end of the Blackrock bypass. The road was crowded: buses, taxis, cars, vans and trucks vying for space with cyclists and motorbikes.

Then Reilly's mobile phone shrilled.

'What?' Ominously his left hand reached for the Uzi.

'How many?' He twisted in his seat and looked out the rear window. His eyes darted towards me and I sensed fear.

'Anything wrong?' I asked. I noticed Devlin's knuckles whiten on the steering wheel.

Reilly snapped his phone shut. 'There's a motorbike on our tail.'

I swivelled in time to see a flash of red and black as a motorcycle swerved past on the left. There was a driver and pillion passenger in black leathers with tinted visor crash helmets. The pillion passenger pointedly turned to stare into the Lexus. In a second they were a blur disappearing around a corner as we entered Ballsbridge. I looked behind but could see no sign of the Mondeo, and a significant gap was opening up after about five cars behind.

'What happened to the backup?'

'Dunno,' muttered Devlin, eyes darting from rear-view mirror to the road ahead. 'Maybe they got caught at the last set of lights.'

149

I wasn't reassured. The sudden change in traffic flow concerned me more than the motorbike. Reilly had said the backup crew would tail us. How could they've been cut off? I felt patches of sweat underneath my armpits and loosened my tie. It was now warm and the Lexus was like an oven. Reilly's comment echoed. *'I've a bad feeling about today.'* Yet perhaps there was a perfectly innocent explanation for the motorcycle duo. Were they just commuters on their way to work? Instinct warned no. This was how Harold Rafferty had been attacked.

The Lexus swerved into a bus-only lane and accelerated at high speed. I tumbled around the back seat, grabbing at the headrest in front for support. Paperwork scattered to my feet. From somewhere inside the bonnet a siren started wailing.

The car sped along the set-aside lane, forcing its way back into the traffic queue if anything blocked. The horn blared, demanding a way through. We overtook buses and taxi cabs, heads turning to follow our progress. My chest pounded, my mouth dried and then I tasted blood again as I chewed my cheek. Reilly half turned in his seat. 'Something's wrong. I don't like this. I don't like this one bit.'

His face was white, his eyes narrowed to slits.

Chapter 22

'Put your foot to the board.' Reilly was working the buttons on his mobile phone. He picked up the conversation.

'Where are they now?'

Pause.

'How many d'ye think?'

Pause.

'Where's our support?'

Pause.

'Fuck.'

He scanned the area. 'We're turning into Shelbourne Road. Do we detour?'

Pause.

'Got it.'

He waved at me to duck out of sight. I grabbed the Glock. If they were coming I wanted to be ready. My brain flooded with images of the last attack. I heard the screams of my family as bullets peppered the master bedroom. The stench of sweat and fear filled the car. I jammed the Dowling file deeper into my briefcase and kicked it under the front seat as far as it would go.

Reilly pulled himself forward in his seat. He searched the streets for signs of danger. 'Turn right.' The Lexus swerved up a one-way street. We zigzagged in a drunken line for about seventy yards.

'Right again.' Reilly had his window down and the

morning air rushed past, offering relief from the heat and smell of the cabin.

Ahead a refuse truck was idling as the collectors dragged wheelie bins across the road. The noise of the siren distracted them. Sensing danger they ran for safety. The Lexus mounted the pavement, glanced off a container and narrowly missed the lorry. Rubbish littered the street. I heard angry shouts.

Three minutes later Reilly slapped the dashboard. 'Pull over.' We were in a side road somewhere in Ringsend. Despite Reilly's warning, I couldn't lie down in the backseat, I had to see what was going on. I raised my head and peered out of the window. Two elderly women wearing headscarves stood at the front door of a terraced house. Reilly jumped outside and squatted on the pavement, ears strained for any noise. The women became edgy, uncertain at the strangers in their street. I saw one point at Devlin, now holding a revolver in full view. They almost fell over one another to flee inside. Seconds later the same faces appeared at a side window.

'I think we've lost them.' Reilly was on his mobile phone again. He checked the road. 'Let's go.' The Lexus roared off and soon we were leaving Ringsend. The siren drove us forward, forcing a path through traffic. Five minutes later, after right, left and left turns we crossed Grand Canal Quay at the end of Ringsend Road. Ahead was Pearse Street. We were no more than ten minutes from my base on Store Street and safety.

Then the danger of the situation struck me. Whatever detours we'd taken we were always going to end up on the last third of Pearse Street as it ran alongside Trinity College. It was about 400 yards of road. We'd then swing right onto Tara Street and cross the River Liffey at Butt Bridge. After that we'd be less than three minutes from the coroner's office. In the adjoining building was the busiest law-enforcement station in the city. The police presence was so significant that no criminal, no matter how deranged or desperate, would attempt an attack there.

However, a really clever plan would be to first stall and separate the Mondeo. A second group would then focus on this short and crowded stretch of road. It was closing on 9.15 a.m. and traffic was excruciatingly slow. There could be no sudden diversions whether our siren blared or not.

The Lexus was now stuck in the middle lane, offering no give left or right. It was one way only towards the city. As we edged forward my nerve endings were stretched to snapping. Reilly had his back to the front door, Uzi just out of sight but at the ready. His eyes searched the area. Every pedestrian was a potential killer. Mark Street, a side road to our right, became a threat until safely bypassed. So too Moss Street. The silence inside the car was ominous. My heart pounded in my ears. Devlin glanced at me in the rear-view mirror, beads of sweat heavy on his brow. The stoplights seemed to take for ever and I fumed in the back seat, silently urging us on. I gripped my handgun.

Then the traffic stopped. About ten cars ahead a blue Ford transit van had stalled, the driver was out on the road and urging drivers to slip past. He was a wiry and edgy-looking youth in a blue boiler suit that should've been buttoned up at the front but gaped slightly. He repeatedly glanced towards our Lexus, now less than twenty feet away.

'If he puts his hand inside his tunic get outta the car and lie face down on the road.' Reilly opened the side door. 'I'm checking this.'

Then the blue boiler suit drew a weapon.

'Drop the gun,' I heard Reilly roar. 'Put the fucking gun down or I'll blow your head off.'

I was out of the back seat in seconds, squeezing between traffic. There was a blur of shocked, then horrified faces as chaos unfolded. The rear door of the Ford transit burst open and two other men in blue boiler suits jumped out. They were carrying handguns and one ran towards me while the other trained his gun on Reilly. I heard men cursing and children screaming hysterically.

The first shots came from Reilly. A short salvo from his Uzi. More terrified shouts filled the air. Car doors opened and then slammed shut, drivers shunted one another in a desperate attempt to escape. The first blue suit was almost upon me, but got wedged between two cars. He stopped and pointed his handgun; I ducked and swung my briefcase wildly in the air, but he discharged at least three rounds. I heard a pistol shot to my left and felt a round scorch my forehead. I spun in time to see a twisted and hate-filled face, a gun gripped in two fists directed at me. I swung the Glock in an arc and pressed the trigger but the damned thing jammed. Then the face was peppered in blood.

'Armed police, drop your weapons.' From behind came warning commands. 'Drop the fucking guns.'

Suddenly the air crackled with gunfire.

By the time the shooting was over there were two bodies on Pearse Street. One lay in a heap on the road while the other was hunched against the Ford transit, as if inspecting the bodywork. The third assassin was being handcuffed by Reilly. He was covered in gore but protesting. Reilly kicked him in the groin and the protests stopped. Devlin was sitting on the bonnet of an abandoned car, shouting into a mobile phone. He seemed unhurt. I dabbed at my forehead and inspected the blood, then kept pressure on it to stem the ooze. 'It's okay, Dr Wilson,' a detective in battle fatigues said. I was surrounded in a huddle of bodyguards. 'We've got you. We were waiting for this. We've been tailing them for the past hour.' He was holding a Heckler & Koch sub-machine gun.

He moved to disperse onlookers. I noticed small groups of spectators, shocked and stunned by the carnage. They whispered, pointed, looked away and then looked back again. Faces crowded at office and shop windows, inquisitive children were ushered out of sight. The thoroughfare was a confusion of stalled vehicles, some up on the pavement, others skewed sideways across traffic lanes. Car alarms shrilled. Paramedics in green tunics were rushing towards us. In the distance a cacophony of sirens came closer. I suddenly started shivering and faced the sun for heat. Overhead an aircraft trailed across a clear blue sky, oblivious to the drama below.

I pulled my mobile phone out and started dialling. 'Sarah? Hi, it's me.' I glanced at my watch. It was 9.37 a.m. 'There's been another incident but I'm okay.' I heard a gasp. 'In fact we're all okay and that's all that matters.'

Chapter 23

After the shootings I was rushed to the coroner's court. A mob of journalists crowded the footpath, jostling for position and spilling onto the road. They'd turned up for an inquest but now had an overflow of drama. Questions were barked from all sides as lenses were pushed into my face. The whirr of shutters was matched only by the glare of TV lights. Out of the corner of my eye I spotted office workers huddling at the windows of an adjoining block, drawn by the excitement below. Then I was gathered into a blur of black tunics as court security forced a path into the building.

Joan was waiting for me, coffee in shaking hands. 'Dr Wilson.' She was struggling to hold back tears. 'Are you all right?' She couldn't stop staring at my forehead, which had been bandaged by a paramedic at the side of the street.

I swallowed the coffee in two gulps, placed a hand on her shoulder and forced a smile onto my face. 'I'm fine and we're going ahead as planned.' I felt a slight wetness on my forehead and dabbed a fingertip at my wound. It was seeping. 'A fresh dressing and another coffee would help a lot though.' She hurried to the kitchen.

Minutes later DI Roche was on the line. How was I? Did I need medical attention? She reassured me about my family. Jennifer and Gregory had been taken home to Sarah. All were now under armed guard. 'Can you go ahead with this inquest?'

'I have to,' I said. 'There's too much at stake.' The bravado might have sounded impressive, but inside I was quaking.

'I'll be in the back row listening to every word,' she said.

'Good.' I felt weak and wanted to end the call.

But Roche hadn't finished. 'We have to meet tonight. Significant new information has come out and you need to hear it.'

I mumbled an okay. I pressed the off button and stared into space. Then delayed shock kicked in. I felt faint and sat down. My hands shook and my belly heaved. I made the toilet that adjoined my office just in time. I emptied my guts into the bowl until there was nothing more to give up. I dry retched for another few minutes. When I finally made it back to my desk I was clammy and sweating. There was a knock on the door but I called out for privacy. I studied the faded and worn photographs of previous coroners. *Did any of you go through anything like this?* There was no response. In the room of sighs the only noise was my laboured breathing.

Five minutes before the inquest began Charles McGrath, the Dowling lawyer, came into my office. He was a small man, tubby and slightly balding. Underneath a three-piece suit he wore a striped blue shirt and faded tartan bow tie.

He introduced himself and then launched into a wave of sympathy. 'I can't tell you how shocked I am.'

He was about to swamp me with compassion before I cut him short. 'Let's just get on with the inquest.'

'Whatever you say.' He looked at me as if I'd two heads.

157

I finally took my place on the bench at the head of the court at 11.30 a.m. I scanned the room. Seated to my right was Jack Matthews, the detective involved in the investigation. He was in a better-looking suit than the first time I'd met him and his pasty face had some colour in it. Probably more than mine at that moment. He glanced towards me but our eyes didn't meet. He seemed uneasy, like he didn't want to be there. To the left, sitting in the dark-wood pew-like benches, was the jury, four men and five women ranging in age from early twenties to late sixties. Some were leaning back, others hunched forward. Two were reading newspapers. All turned to look at me as I sat down. Puzzled looks were exchanged. Clearly, none of them expected to see a coroner with a dressing covering a head wound. In the well of the court waited Charles McGrath. He had the table reserved for legal representatives to himself. He'd managed to squeeze his tubby frame into one of the chairs beside it. In the visitors' gallery at the back of the chamber, on the shiny wooden benches, waited a crowd of journalists and the Dowling family. I recognised Albert Dowling at once. What I recalled from TV footage was a tall, handsome man with steel-grey hair swept into a duck tail. I studied him closely. He was slumped, as if bored or unaware of what was going on. He appeared much older than sixty. He'd obviously lost weight as his expensive shirt was loose around his neck and his jacket hung off him. His left arm was linked around his wife's right elbow. But it was clear she was supporting him rather than the other way round. Beside him his wife, Mary, fingered a pair of rosary beads. All I could see was a Botox-taut face, cosmetically darkened eyebrows and lashes, and tight, severe lips, heavy with red gloss. I knew from media reports she was fifty-five but from this distance she might have passed for early forties. The wonders of plastic surgery.

The two of them were squeezed into a corner by a rag-bag collection of journalists from print and broadcast media. There was a mix of men and women, ratio possibly three males to one female. Most wore casual clothes, denim and T-shirts, which immediately set them apart from the grieving families who were usually in my court. I spotted DI Roche, squashed into a corner and dabbing at her neck with a handkerchief. We avoided eye contact. The room was already so warm many people were flapping loose pages at their faces for relief. Sleeves wiped sweaty brows. Notepads, cassette recorders and mobile phones were at the ready. Depositions would be documented and noteworthy snippets sent by text to editors. But all eyes were on me. There was no mistaking the atmosphere of disbelief that filled the courtroom after the events of this morning. But that had to be put to one side. I set the agenda immediately.

'We're here to decide the cause of death of the late Patrick Anthony Dowling.' I shuffled paperwork to stop my hands shaking and took a sip of water. I addressed the jury. 'Your role is to decide how he died. Then I can authorise a death certificate.' But it was more than Patrick Dowling's day. It was my day as well. My chance at last to expose the state's case for what it was. A pack of lies.

I nodded to the staff. Let proceedings commence.

Charles McGrath stood and cocked his thumbs in his waistcoat. My plan was to allow him free rein. I wanted to see how he'd approach proceedings. I'd no doubt Albert and Mary Dowling were desperate for a quick suicide verdict. McGrath was there to get that result.

Gerard Canny was the forensic pathologist who'd conducted the autopsy. He was a regular visitor to my court. A tall man in his mid-forties with a fine head of dark hair, his appearance was spoiled somewhat by a narrow and pockmarked face. He was in trousers and open-neck shirt. His post-mortem result was one of my targets for attack.

McGrath took Canny through his testimony. 'Is there any doubt in your mind that Patrick Dowling committed suicide?' The lawyer's tone suggested there could be no other interpretation.

Canny answered carefully. 'Forensic pathology is not an exact science. Autopsy results are open to challenge. But on the basis of how the body was found, the setting and suicide paraphernalia combined with post-mortem findings, I believe that Patrick Dowling took his own life.'

'You know there was no suicide note?'

'Yes. But not every suicide warns of his intentions or leaves a note of explanation.'

'Indeed.' McGrath was practically beaming. Then he put on his sober, reflective face. 'Might there be another interpretation?'

'If there is the deceased isn't here to explain it.'

'Thank you, Dr Canny,' said McGrath. He'd done his bit. If the pathologist wasn't for turning he wasn't going to push him. He sat down, slumped in his seat and threw his short legs out for comfort. Then he clasped his hands on his ample belly and waited for the inquest to end. Outside a car horn sounded angrily, and then blared again. The gentler trilling of a Luas tram was followed by rumbling as a light rail train made its way into nearby Connolly Station.

Canny made to leave the witness box. I gestured to him to stay there. It was time to start probing. 'Dr Canny, was there evidence of drug use in the deceased?'

Canny inspected his report. 'There were needle tracks in both ante-cubital fossae. Dowling also had a perforation of the nasal septum consistent with habitual cocaine use. Toxicology showed a significant level of heroin with traces of amphetamines and cocaine.'

I flicked through the Dowling dossier. 'What was his blood alcohol concentration?'

'Zero point zero three per cent.'

'Is that excessively high?'

'No.'

'Might the combination of drugs and alcohol have clouded his judgement?'

'That's possible.'

'Could it have rendered him incapable of simple actions, such as driving a car?' *Come on*, I nearly shouted. *Of course he couldn't have driven a bloody car. He could hardly have opened the boot!*

Charles McGrath unclasped his hands from his belly. He furiously sifted through paperwork. As the pages turned he threw questioning glances in my direction.

'Not necessarily.' Canny was unruffled. 'Cocaine causes euphoria. The user may feel more alert and have increased energy, enhanced self-esteem and feelings of invincibility.'

'I understand that.' I wasn't going to give in easily. 'But considering Dowling had taken such a cocktail of drugs, can you be certain that he was alert enough to commit suicide?'

'I can only form a conclusion of reasonable probability.'

'Well,' I pressed the point, 'if this combination of drugs didn't sedate him, wouldn't it at least have disorientated him?'

'It would certainly have disorientated me,' said Canny. There were a few grins at the back of the chamber.

'However, in the chronic drug user, tolerance is a factor. More drugs are needed to achieve a high.'

I had the next question ready. 'But could he have made his way from his car, walked up a narrow path carrying a bar stool, thrown a rope around a branch, fixed it to the tree trunk, tied a perfectly good knot and pulled the noose around his neck?' I glanced towards McGrath. He was staring at me with complete astonishment. The jury foreman was leaning forward to catch every word.

'I regularly conduct autopsies on addicts,' said Canny. 'Cocaine can trigger acts of unnatural strength and determination. In drug abuse every variation of human activity surfaces.'

And with that comment Canny completely undermined my questioning. I decided to allow this for the moment. I was conducting an inquest, not a criminal trial. I had to walk a fine line between looking for the truth and straying into adversarial mode. I'd return to this when the time was right. I'd more material. I passed a set of autopsy photographs to Canny. He sifted through them.

'There was bruising on Dowling's knuckles, wasn't there?' I asked.

'Bruising and abrasions.' Out the corner of my eye I noticed DI Roche sit forward, focused and intense.

'Would you explain the difference?'

'An abrasion is like a graze.' Now Canny seemed wary. He'd never been interrogated like this in the coroner's court. In a court of law it's commonplace for expert witnesses to challenge one another's findings. But not during what was supposed to be a routine inquest. 'It's a superficial skin injury. If a closed fist, knuckles first, hits a solid object like a bony chin, the skin of the knuckles can become abraded.' Here he closed a fist and threw a punch for effect. 'Bruising suggests trauma to deeper skin levels.'

'So what do abrasions and bruising on the same knuckles suggest?'

'Repeated blows. I understand the deceased was involved in a fracas that day.'

'Is it possible,' I asked in a most innocent voice, 'that there were two fights, separated by hours?'

Canny considered this. 'That's possible. Offering time scales to bruising is not easy. In forensic autopsies the pathologist may look for deep-seated bruising hours and even days after initial inspection.'

'Indeed,' I murmured. 'I'm a pathologist so I do recognise the problem.'

Canny blushed and for a split second I almost felt sorry for him.

Charles McGrath now had his back to me, head tilted upwards as if facing some imaginary audience. I could see folds of excess flesh roll over his blue shirt collar, leaving sweat stains. I sensed he was trying to grab the attention of Albert Dowling. But Dowling sat stone-faced. Beside him his wife clasped her rosary beads in both hands. Her lips moved in silent prayer. The room was now so uncomfortable one of the jurors fanned her neck with the pages of a pocket diary. DI Roche looked up at me from her corner, eyes wide with surprise. I was taking her and the court into territory they weren't expecting.

'There were bruises on the upper arm and under his armpits as well?'

Canny inspected his notes. 'Yes.'

'How would you interpret those?'

'My feeling is that Dowling was lifted or dragged by

someone gripping him under the armpits. This type of bruising is often seen in brawls where one side is dragged away or forcibly restrained.'

'Might there be another explanation? Could he have been forcibly subdued, lifted to the noose and then dropped.'

There was a shocked gasp in the room. Canny seemed completely bewildered. It was almost as if he'd forgotten where he was and needed directions. Charles McGrath started to say something but I asked him to wait until I'd heard the answer. In the visitors' gallery, Albert Dowling slumped backwards. His wife was whispering furiously into his left ear. He brushed her away with an angry flick of his wrist. DI Roche's surprise was becoming more obvious with each question. Beside her journalists exchanged puzzled looks. One in particular was focused on me. He was squashed into the top row at the very back. A press pass was draped around his neck but I didn't recognise him. I massaged my neck and then checked my bandage. It was dry. When I glanced back he was still staring at me. I sipped on a glass of water, then scribbled a note and dropped it to Aoife in the row below. She read it, looked towards the area, frowned and slipped out of the court.

Canny regained his composure. 'In murder-by-assault, Coroner, the victim fights to save his life. Flailing arms, legs, hands and feet are used to defend against attackers. The forehead might be used to butt. Fingernails would be broken. These are known as defensive injuries. The bruises, abrasions, cuts and scrapes in the battle for survival. Dowling had none of these.'

The room had become so uncomfortable staff were opening windows. Street noises, shouts and loud replies momentarily distracted me.

I looked again to the mystery man at the back. Now he was smirking, as if he knew something no one else did. Aoife returned with a piece of paper.

'He's using the press pass of Stephen Brady of the *Evening Herald*. But he doesn't look like Stephen Brady.'

I looked up and studied the stranger at the rear of the court. *No*, I thought, *you don't look a bit like Stephen Brady.*

I called a recess.

Chapter 24

The mystery man carrying Stephen Brady's press pass didn't return after the recess. That allowed me to focus on the matters to hand without distraction. Jack Matthews, the detective who'd investigated Patrick Dowling's death, was in the witness box. The Dowling lawyer, Charles McGrath, questioned him slowly and carefully. McGrath was a changed man. Even when Matthews' answers suited his argument he repeated the query. He seemed desperate to make up lost ground from the earlier session. After a while I rebuked him for wasting time. 'Get to the point.' He glared at me. I ignored him. He finished with a few simple clarifications.

Now it was my turn to quiz the detective. He looked apprehensive. After the grilling I'd given the forensic pathologist he'd good reason. 'Since this was considered a suicide why did you seal off the area?'

Matthews coughed into a closed fist to hide his uncertainty. 'We were dealing with the son of a senior government minister. I knew this'd be a high-profile inquiry.'

'But,' I feigned puzzlement, 'the pathologist decided he'd committed suicide.'

'Yes.'

'So why investigate further?'

Matthews gripped the side of the witness box to steady himself. 'When the deceased has obviously committed suicide the circumstances are noted, the scene photographed and witness questions recorded for the subsequent inquest. It's not standard practice to conduct a detailed analysis of vehicles, clothing et cetera.'

'But you personally ordered that. Why?'

'As I said, I knew this would be a high—'

'I know that. But it was more than just covering your back.'

'I'm not sure what you're suggesting.' Matthews gave me a withering look.

'I'm suggesting you had doubts. You weren't convinced Dowling committed suicide. Especially since you were aware of the earlier fracas.'

Matthews didn't respond. I could almost hear his brain ticking over as he searched for the right reply.

I prodded him along. 'Dowling was involved in at least one fist fight on the day he died, isn't that correct?'

'Yes.'

'The other person had a criminal record, didn't he?'

'Yes.'

'And,' I persisted, 'you knew he wasn't the sort to take a beating without revenge.'

'Yes.'

'So, is it fair to say that raised doubts?'

'It made me consider other explanations.'

'There can only be two interpretations: either Patrick Dowling committed suicide or he was murdered.'

There was a stunned silence. Pens hovered over pads, jaws dropped. Even from the bench I could see DI Roche had gone pale. Albert Dowling buried his head in his hands while his wife prayed like a woman possessed.

Matthews's response was almost a plea for help. 'Coroner, the post-mortem was conclusive. Dr Canny's findings—'

My simmering exasperation broke through. 'I've read Dr Canny's findings a number of times. I know that report inside out. What I'm trying to find out is whether Patrick Dowling hanged himself or was hanged.'

The room fell silent again. I shifted paperwork from one side of the bench to the other. Out the corner of my eye I could see the jury. Doubt, disbelief and upset were etched on many faces. The others seemed totally at sea. This was supposed to be a routine inquest. The verdict of suicide was a given. Now proceedings were shaping up like a criminal trial. And I'd told them that wouldn't be the case.

'Let me explore another concern,' I said. Matthews's shoulders sagged. I held up a sheet of paper. 'In addition to the trappings of drug abuse found in Dowling's car there was a bottle of Jameson's whiskey in the glove compartment. It was about a quarter full. Am I correct?'

'Yes.'

'And Dowling's blood alcohol concentration was only zero point zero three per cent.'

Matthews said nothing.

'If Dowling was on his own and drank three-quarters of a bottle of whiskey, surely his blood alcohol level would have been much higher?'

'A considerable amount had tipped onto the carpet and upholstery,' Matthews came back. 'It's impossible to estimate how much was there at the beginning or how much he might have taken.'

'That I understand.' I was now the reasonable man, apparently understanding the difficulties of this complex inquiry. 'But something puzzles me.'

If Matthews could have groaned I knew he would have. *Leave me alone*, his body language screamed.

'The bottle was clean. There were no finger- or hand-prints on the glass. Isn't that strange?'

'That's correct. The bottle had been wiped clean.'

'Does that sound like the action of a man so mentally disturbed he was about to take his own life? In fact, if he was going to take his own life, why would he bother wiping down the bottle at all?'

Matthews didn't answer. His brow furrowed and he nervously adjusted his shirt cuffs.

McGrath interjected. 'Coroner, may I say something?'

'Of course.' I couldn't have been more accommodating.

'When you spoke with Dr Canny you more or less asked the same question.'

He called for a transcript. '"Cocaine can propel young men into acts of unnatural strength and determination. In drug abuse every variation of human activity surfaces." Do you think it fair to ask Detective Matthews to decide on Patrick Dowling's mental state?'

I wasn't going to be put off. 'I do. Why would Dowling, a man hell-bent on committing suicide, stop to wipe clean a bottle of whiskey?' I frowned so deeply my scar throbbed. 'It doesn't make sense.'

Matthews visibly wilted under the weight of my unreasonableness. 'I can't explain it,' he said finally.

'I can,' I said. Everyone in the chamber strained to hear. 'I don't believe Dowling was alone.' Now Roche was almost on her feet, craning her neck lest she miss a word.

Matthews asked for a glass of water, a delaying tactic to collect his wits. Finally he spoke. 'There could have been someone else in the car.'

There was a frisson of excitement in the court. One reporter couldn't resist dialling up his editor and I immediately directed security to him. The mobile was shut off and he stared sheepishly at the floor.

'I've read the list of material discovered in the car.' I

flapped a page in the air. 'There were fingerprints other than his lifted from the dashboard and steering wheel.'

Matthews confirmed this. 'There were many different prints found. It was three years old. There might have been any number of passengers in and out over that time.'

'But,' I cut through, 'was there one particular fingerprint?'

'There was a bloodstained print.'

'So,' I mused out loud, 'while you might never know when or how the others came to be in the car, you'd a reasonable explanation of when the bloodstained print got there.'

'Yes.'

'And would you share that?'

'It belonged to the man Dowling fought with earlier that day.' *Noel Carty, Redmond's henchman.*

'How could you've been so sure?'

'His fingerprint's on record. Forensics showed the blood was fresh, contemporaneous with the day of Dowling's death.' There was another ripple of surprise. The jury foreman produced a notebook and scribbled something into it. McGrath loosened the buttons on his shirt and dragged his bow tie free.

So much for Carty's assertion he was on the far side of the city all that day with witnesses to prove it, as DI Roche told me during our first meeting, I thought.

'Detective Matthews,' I was like a dog at a bone. 'You agree there might have been someone else in the car with Dowling the day he died.'

'It's a possibility,' said Matthews. He looked like a man who wished he was a million miles away. He'd boxed himself into a corner and knew it.

Now was the time to ask the crunch question. I said it slowly, clearly and loud enough so no one could miss it. 'Do you really believe Patrick Dowling committed suicide?'

The chamber fell suddenly quiet, with only the background hum of traffic breaking through. McGrath had his back to the bench, no doubt observing the husband and wife team who'd hired him. DI Roche was staring at the ceiling, as if frightened to hear what was coming.

Matthews's brow furrowed, he pursed his lips, took a deep breath and exhaled slowly. Then he clenched and unclenched his fists.

The answer, when it came, was decisive. 'No.'

McGrath spun around, totally stunned. One of the female jurors instinctively put a protective hand to her throat. Her eyes widened with disbelief. Albert Dowling kept his head in his hands. His wife Mary stared straight ahead, as if she'd missed the exchange. There was an excited babble of conversation among the reporters. I appealed for silence.

'What *do* you think happened that night?' I was leaning so far over the bench I was almost on top of Matthews. The tension in the room was almost unbearable, a mixture of nervous anticipation and incredulity.

Matthews massaged his temples. Sweat beaded on his brow and he dabbed at it with a sleeve cuff. 'I don't know.'

Yes, I thought, *the only one who knows what happened that night is Patrick Dowling. Is his the ghost in the corner, waiting for the truth to come out?*

'If you didn't believe Dowling committed suicide,' I said, 'why did you allow that decision to go forward?'

'It didn't go uncontested. Our team spent many hours looking at this case from every angle. We'd a meeting with the pathologist. The final decision to was based on post-mortem findings. I investigate to the limit of my powers, Coroner. Then I evaluate all evidence: forensic, autopsy, circumstantial, witness statements et cetera. But the cause of death is always determined at autopsy.'

This was the first I'd heard of a more detailed investigation into Dowling's death. Up to this point I'd been told the post-mortem result forced a halt to everything. So, despite concerns that Dowling might not have committed suicide, someone closed the case. I wondered who that might have been.

'Was there disagreement?'

'Yes. But the pathologist wouldn't budge on his report. Patrick Dowling hanged himself. Full stop, end of story.'

'That simple?'

Matthews stiffened, then bit hard on his lower lip to contain his anger. 'I resent that comment, Coroner. There's nothing simple about suicide.' It was a perfect retort and I immediately apologised to both Matthews and the Dowlings.

I checked the time. It was closing in on 1.30 p.m. and I wanted to clear time for the jury to have lunch. Then Aoife slipped me a message. And I knew by her expression she wasn't bringing good news.

I scanned the text, my heart quickening as I grasped its significance.

Chapter 25

I announced an end to the hearing and told the journalists the inquest wouldn't continue that day. I warned there might be considerable delay and instructed the jury likewise. There was consternation, questions and dismay all round. But events were out of my control. I explained that I was not at liberty to clarify the circumstances. There'd be a press release later. I called DI Roche and told her what'd happened.

'I've just heard myself.' She sounded as stunned as I felt. 'We'll discuss this tonight.'

Then I summoned Albert and Mary Dowling, with their lawyer, to my chambers.

While I waited I considered how my life was going from bad to worse. Last night I'd held Sarah in my arms and kissed away her tears of fear. I'd said this would all be over soon, and meant it. I'd looked into her eyes and saw the desperate hunger for that to be true. Instead, there'd been a third attempt on my life. And if that wasn't bad enough, Jonathan Redmond had orchestrated a backup plan to collapse the inquest. He was outwitting me left, right and centre. And my wits were my strength. I couldn't take this man on in any other way. He had weapons, hit men and a ton of money. He could drag out this campaign for years. How was I going to explain this to Sarah, Jennifer and Gregory? My dejection was interrupted as Charles McGrath introduced Albert and Mary Dowling.

For days I'd deliberated how to handle any meeting with the Dowlings. When we first met DI Roche told me how they'd harassed county coroner Harold Rafferty: *'They kept hounding him to get on with the inquest. They clammed up when he asked questions. "Our son's dead," they said. "Nothing will bring him back. Stop annoying us. Hold the inquest and let us have an end to our misery. Isn't it enough that we lost Patrick?"'*

I'd asked if she thought Rafferty trusted the Dowlings. She believed not.

Then I'd learned Albert Dowling was somehow linked to Jonathan Redmond. And that his deceased son had regular contact with Redmond. So, I wondered, was Mary Dowling also involved? Did she know of any links between her husband and the major drug dealer? Did she know of her late son's meetings? Or was she an innocent mother and wife, caught up in a side show of deceit, intrigue and corruption.

Now was a good time to try and find out.

Albert Dowling, the once tall and handsome sixty-year-old with steel-grey hair, looked disorientated and unsure. The strong face I'd seen on television was a mask of uncertainty. His dark-blue shirt was loose at the collar, red-striped tie pulled free and hanging mid-chest. His blazer looked two sizes too big. My initial impression was of a man in deep shock.

By contrast Mary Dowling looked younger, stronger and spoiling for a fight. Her eyes followed me from behind a thick layer of eyeshadow. While powder and blusher did cover a decade of years, the giveaway was her hands. They were wrinkled and dotted with liver spots. But Restalyn, Botox and layers of L'Oréal could not disguise her mood. Her mascara was untouched by tears, her pumped-up cheeks and tight lips holding up well despite the tension. She sat before me, clutching a Gucci handbag like a shield. She seemed calculating, as if trying to decide how to stay on top of this encounter. Charles McGrath had his bow tie off. 'What's happening?' he asked as he sat down.

'One of our witnesses is missing.'

I glanced from face to face and noticed a vacancy about Albert Dowling. It was as if his mind was elsewhere. I looked away and then observed him out of the corner of my eye.

'Patrick's friend Harry Malone was due to give his deposition this morning.' And according to that deposition Malone had dragged Patrick Dowling from a fist fight on the day he died. Then he'd shadowed him, concerned for his safety. Malone knew the reputation of Noel Carty, the gangster involved in the brawl. When Dowling's body was discovered, Malone spent hours with police piecing together his final hours. He'd agreed to attend the inquest, give evidence and then sign the deposition. I'd planned to challenge it in open court, knowing that County Coroner Harold Rafferty didn't believe it. Redmond had outwitted me yet again.

'Missing?' McGrath looked as if he couldn't take many more shocks.

'He left the house this morning and hasn't been seen since. He's not answering his mobile and none of his friends know where he is.'

The lawyer's face collapsed in disbelief.

'And there's worse,' I added for good measure. 'One of the journalists was bogus. He was carrying the press pass of Stephen Brady, crime correspondent of the *Evening Herald*.'

I couldn't decide if the anxiety in Mary Dowling's eyes was exaggerated for my benefit.

'The real Stephen Brady was found dead an hour ago. He'd been murdered.'

Albert Dowling's features went blank, lifeless almost. His lips moved but nothing came out.

Mary Dowling blessed herself and rummaged in her Gucci bag, producing her rosary beads.

McGrath was taken aback. 'This is outrageous.' He was agitated, nervously buttoning and unbuttoning his waistcoat. His pudgy face was a confusion of emotions.

'Police are searching for Malone,' I added. 'They'll decide when to reveal this to the media.'

McGrath fastened the straps on his briefcase. 'There's nothing more I can do here.' He ran his fingers around the collar of his shirt and walked out. He was so addled leaving he didn't even acknowledge his clients.

Mary Dowling spoke a few words into her mobile phone. She snapped it shut and turned to her husband. 'Albert, leave me with Dr Wilson. I think you could do with a rest, you look exhausted.'

Albert Dowling started to protest but was waved quiet.

'I've a car waiting. Go straight home. I'll be with you in an hour.'

I was left alone with Mary Dowling. Innocent spouse and mother, or witch? My immediate impression was that behind the cosmetic facade was a lady of iron resolve.

'My husband is losing his mind,' she said. 'He's refused to have a medical assessment but he's showing signs of Alzheimer's.'

'Why do you think that?'

'It started with little things,' she explained. 'He'd claim he'd lost his keys and all the time they were in his pocket.

He'd turn up at meetings in the wrong building and not even remember his advisors' names.'

I listened. But I wasn't convinced.

'One day I knew it was more than forgetfulness. He asked what time his mother would be home.' Mary Dowling dabbed at her eyes. 'And she's been dead ten years.'

'How can he possibly function?' I decided to run with the conversation to see where it led. 'He's a government minister.'

'Civil servants are doing most of the work.' Her voice reflected her age. A slow, suspicious female growl. 'They want him out.'

Then she reached into her handbag and produced a clutch of photographs. 'That's Albert holding Patrick when he was six months old. Look at the pride on his face.'

Now it was my turn to be taken aback. Why'd she brought family photographs with her? I set aside my doubts as I studied the photo. Albert Dowling would have been about thirty-seven when the snap was taken. His face was lean and taut, his eyes sparkling with delight. The baby was so wrapped up that I could barely see him.

'He loved that child.' Mary Dowling took the photo back and handed me more. 'There's the two of them at Patrick's first day at school.' There was a rear shot of Albert Dowling holding his son's hand. They were at the side of a building, bathed in sunshine. 'And there he is comforting Patrick when he ran out of the classroom.' This time the lens snapped a small boy clinging tightly to his father.

Mary Dowling handed another two. 'That one,' she pointed, 'is Patrick on his first day at university.'

Patrick Dowling was about eighteen at the time and had grown into his father's likeness. He'd dark, wavy hair and a stud in his left ear. His brow was broad, his chin strong and dimpled. He'd high cheekbones. He grinned at the camera, showing a row of perfect teeth.

'That's about a month before he died.'

Now I was shocked. When Patrick Dowling was found hanging he was twenty-eight. Comparing the confident, handsome and strong eighteen-year-old with the gaunt, hollow-cheeked and sunken-eyed older version was disturbing. Gone was the vitality, the sense of a life on the threshold of excitement and adventure. In the most recent photo was a stranger in terminal decline.

Mary Dowling looked at me. 'He wanted to die, Dr Wilson. He told me that more than once.' She gathered up the photographs into her handbag. 'I don't know how you can think he was murdered,' she said. Her voice was thick with emotion. 'To suggest that is outrageous.' She was struggling to maintain her composure. 'He took his own life. He wasn't living; he existed. He staggered from one fix to the next, like a zombie. I can't remember how often police found him slumped in back alleys.' The Gucci bag was snapped shut. 'Patrick broke Albert's heart. His addiction destroyed my husband and I'm sure it's brought on his mental deterioration.'

You're either totally deluded, I thought, *or this is an Oscar performance in deception.*

Mary Dowling looked straight at me, her gaze fixed and determined. 'My son was a useless addict who mixed with the scum of the earth. He'd few friends but no enemies. I know he'd a row with that drug dealer but I can't believe the same man would've dragged Patrick to the woods to hang him. I don't know what agenda you're pursuing but it's wicked. All you're doing is heaping

178

more pain on my family. And we don't deserve that. We don't deserve that at all.'

I heard footsteps in the outside corridor, voices, then doors opening and being shut. 'Let me explain my role as coroner, Mrs Dowling,' I said. I decided to lay down the ground rules. Mary Dowling could rant all she wanted but I'd still pursue the truth behind her son's death. Whether she wanted that or not.

I pressed the intercom and asked for refreshments. When we'd the room to ourselves I took a quick sip on my coffee, grimaced and added a spoonful of sugar. Dowling didn't touch her cup.

'A year ago,' I began, 'a twelve-year-old girl was knocked down and killed in the middle of the road. The driver of the car insisted she'd run out in front of him. He was a middle-aged man with a clean licence and free from drink and drugs when checked on the day of the accident. There were no witnesses. It was the driver's word against the dead girl's.'

I paused. Mary Dowling offered a sullen nod: *get on with it.*

'At the inquest there was something about the driver's attitude that worried me. He was evasive and hesitant in the witness box. So I made an excuse to defer the hearing and ordered mobile phone analysis.'

Dowling's glower didn't lift. So I went on. There'd be a point to this story at the end.

'The dead girl also had a mobile that was crushed in the accident. But technicians were able to get the exact time of impact. It differed by six minutes from the driver's account. And the phone clocks synchronised.'

I sipped on my coffee and gestured to Mary Dowling's untouched cup. 'No thanks,' she said.

'It turned out the driver was on his phone to a friend

at the exact time of impact. The police tracked the friend down. He'd been keeping his head down and saying nothing. He was in significant debt to the other man and didn't want to attend the inquest. When he was threatened with criminal charges of withholding evidence he caved in and made a statement. It was read out in court. "In the middle of our conversation there was a shout and then 'oh Christ, I think I've hit someone.'" With that, the driver's story was exposed as a pack of lies.'

'What happened?'

'I postponed the inquest again. It was now a police investigation.'

She pretended to look impressed. 'Your dedication to duty is admirable.'

'It wasn't dedication to duty.' I put my cup down and made sure I had Mrs Dowling's full attention. 'I was doing my job. That girl was screaming for the truth from the grave.'

There was silence in the room.

Mary Dowling leaned both elbows on the desk and eyeballed me. 'What are you trying to tell me?'

'Today's hearing has thrown up many uncertainties.'

Her hand went up for silence.

'What if Patrick didn't commit suicide? Nothing will bring him back. He's dead, at peace at last. I've lost him and now I'm losing my husband. That only leaves me with my two sons. I don't want to lose them too.'

I listened. I didn't like what I was hearing but I listened.

'Patrick mixed with criminals. When I buried him I prayed that link would end.' The Gucci handbag was shoved under her arm. 'My son committed suicide because he'd no future. Our family's better off without him.'

Mary Dowling's words hung in the air long after she'd left. And I puzzled how to interpret them.

She could've been telling the truth. Drug addicts are like wrecking balls in family units. They set sibling against sibling, siblings against parents and mother against father. They trigger grief, hardship, heartache and despair. They cheat and lie and steal to feed their habit. They drain savings and then sell whatever's left to buy drugs. Mary Dowling wouldn't be the first mother to wish her addicted son dead. And she wouldn't be the last to be unconcerned how he died.

Or . . .

She was lying through her teeth. She'd dismissed her husband because she didn't trust his judgement under pressure. Then she'd hung back to create a smokescreen of deceit.

The Alzheimer's facade might be only that, a facade. A construct put up to confuse anyone checking Albert Dowling's activities. I might learn more when DI Roche briefed me later.

I was erring on the side of believing Mary Dowling when something struck me. John Hobbs's words as Reilly and I were leaving his woodland hideaway. *'Forget about drugs, follow the money.'*

If Hobbs was right then Mary Dowling was lying. And somehow I trusted Hobbs more than the politician's wife.

But why would she lie? There was only one logical answer: to cover up how her son really died. And why would she want to cover up her son's death? Because that would expose the connection between her husband and Jonathan Redmond.

And whoever the imposter was at the back of the court, he must've been involved. How could he have got the press pass of the murdered Stephen Brady? Was he the killer? Certainly his fixed stare and final smirk suggested complicity.

I was exhausted, drained of energy and emotion. My big day in court had been sabotaged. My chance to find the truth behind Patrick Dowling's death had been frustrated yet again. Redmond had pulled off another brutal stunt to derail the inquest. I wanted to go home and make peace in my own house. And turn up looking half respectable. I went to the washroom and inspected my face. I groaned at the reflection in the mirror. The scar on my hairline was almost as ugly as that on Roche's forehead. We'd look a right pair together. I stuck a fresh dressing on and checked the result. There was considerable bruising along the bullet wound but the raw track was covered. I sighed, a wave of dejection sweeping over me: *this is what you're going to look like when you cross the front door. Not a pretty sight.* I arranged a car and bodyguard.

Chapter 26

'Daddy!'

Jennifer, my beautiful, wonderful fifteen-year-old daughter, was in my arms and hugging me tightly. Her bear-like grip made me catch my breath but she wouldn't let go and I didn't want her to. I smelled shampoo off her hair, felt the softness of her skin against my stubble. I held her like there was no tomorrow.

In the hallway, eleven-year-old Gregory looked on. I could sense he was unsure of himself; like most boys he was shy to express affection. It was always easier for him to hug Sarah than me. I winked and gave him a thumbs-up. He offered a half grin of acknowledgement. Then instinctively he linked arms with Sarah and drew her closer. The gesture told a million tales: a boy, on the cusp of becoming a man, protecting his mother.

Sarah was in denims and a clinging blouse that showed off her figure. Her hair was drawn back from her face. She was trying hard to offer a welcoming smile but I could see it was forced. And that broke my heart. I teased Jennifer's arms away. 'I have to say hello to Greg and your mum.' Slowly and reluctantly Jennifer let go. When I looked down and could at last see her face, she was crying.

'I was told you were dead,' she sobbed. 'Everyone was saying that, even the reporters.'

A surge of anger made me stiffen and I had to hold my temper. Yet why wouldn't they say I was dead? Hadn't I come within an inch of a bullet to the skull?

'Well, here I am.' I put as much power into my voice as I could muster. But I was close to cracking. Jennifer's distress and the distance I sensed from my son and wife was overwhelming. I forced Gregory to give me a hug but he was tense in my arms and quickly pushed me away. Then he watched on as I wrapped my arms around Sarah and held her. I kissed her hair and forehead and coiled my arms around her waist. I wanted to kiss her lips, feel her tongue in my mouth, but such intimacies shouldn't take place in front of the children.

'Hi,' was all I could say.

'Hi.' She stood back and inspected me, her eyes searching my face. There were questions I knew she wanted to ask but dare not at that moment. She tipped a finger off my scarred hairline. 'That must hurt.'

'It does,' I said.

'Let's have something to eat.' Sarah led me by the hand, like a child. 'If you lose any more weight your clothes will fall off you.'

The evening was warm, sunshine bathing the back patio. It was closing on six o'clock. I dreaded having to announce this, but I was due to meet DI Pamela Roche at nine. I sat with Jennifer squashed on my knee and didn't want to leave the house. It was the first time we'd been together as a family in five days.

Sarah had decided to dine in the garden and set the table with cutlery and fresh napkins. In the middle was a small bouquet of pansies and sweet peas. Their aroma lifted my spirits. A bottle of chilled Sauvignon Blanc was uncorked and a liberal glass poured. Sarah kissed me on the side of the cheek as she passed by to light the barbecue. I couldn't take my eyes off her. Somehow my brush with death had heightened my sensitivities and I looked at everything through different eyes. I admired the gentle curves of Sarah's figure and delighted at her gestures of affection with Gregory. She was bringing calm and happiness to the household again. But then the shadow of a Special Branch officer passed along the hedge and the moment was lost. I was back to being Dr Michael Wilson, Dublin City Coroner and under police protection.

Sarah set down a green salad on the table. Gregory brought bread rolls from the oven. He was nibbling on one, all the time staying close to his mother while I made small talk with Jennifer. 'How was your day, apart from the horrible wrong news?' 'Are you keeping up with your hockey?' 'Any good movies to see?'

The smell of steaks grilling made my stomach rumble. Jennifer prodded me in the midriff. 'Dad,' she whispered, 'Mum says you're losing weight so the bad guys won't have anything to shoot at.' We both laughed at that. But the humour was forced. My vulnerability had become a household joke.

Boiled potatoes with a knob of butter and a sprinkling of parsley were passed from plate to plate and I couldn't resist taking the largest portion. Gregory complained, accusing me of being a glutton. I puffed out my cheeks in response. 'Don't care,' I said, 'I need to fatten up.'

Gregory smothered his steak with ketchup and cut a slice and started eating. Out the corner of his eye he studied my wound. I'd removed the Band-aid to allow the air at the bullet track. 'Will that leave a scar?'

I forked a potato into my mouth, and then sipped on my wine. 'Yeah, but it'll make my face more interesting.'

Gregory poured a glass of Coca-Cola and took a deep

gulp. He started to say something but a warning glare from Sarah stopped him. He cut more steak.

We made small talk, family talk: who was doing what and plans for the rest of the summer. It was a strain but we all made an effort to ignore the shadowy presence of the security team.

I looked across the table. Gregory had filled out a little. Auntie Carol must have been indulging his sweet tooth. I risked a glance at Jennifer, now running a spoon along a bowl of raspberries. I was suddenly conscious of how much I'd lost touch with my family lately. I toyed with my wine glass, pinging my nail against the stem. I was playing for time, desperate to collect my thoughts.

Sarah reached across and squeezed my hand. Our eyes met and I knew immediately that she knew what I was thinking. 'Jennifer and Gregory are home for good,' she announced, 'and they're not going away again.'

I didn't say anything, my mind a chaos of emotions: guilt, loss, fear and angry resentment. But mainly guilt.

Jennifer brought me back to earth. 'We're not children any more, Dad. We know what's going on and we're not scared. We're not leaving you and Mum alone. All you do is argue.'

Maybe it was the wine or maybe it was the final straw of a day of too much drama, but Jennifer's comments made me feel totally inadequate. I made an excuse and left the table.

Chapter 27

I sat in a chair in the master bedroom and stared out the window. It was 7.30 p.m. and the sun was low, throwing long shadows on the road. A copper beech in full leaf caught the last rays, shimmering in a gentle breeze. A grey squirrel leapt from branch to branch, and then stopped. It nibbled on something, dropped it and continued on its onward skip-hop. Across the road an elderly gentleman was cutting his front lawn, slow and careful turns of the motor mower producing a cricket-pitch perfect result. How I envied his freedom and trouble-free existence. Parked outside my house were three police cars, one holding an urgent response team that I knew had enough fire power to start a revolution. I sighed and dropped my head onto my upturned palms and tried to think.

I heard the door open. I looked up to find Sarah.

'I told the kids I wanted to speak to you on my own.'

I shouldn't have done it but instinctively I glanced at my watch.

'I know about the security meeting,' she said. 'Reilly rang to confirm it. I know you have to leave soon.'

I concealed my relief. I didn't know how I was going to break that news.

'You look dreadful,' she said after yet another moment of intense scrutiny. 'Your shirt has stains on it,' I glanced

187

down and started rubbing at a coffee mark, 'your trousers are hanging off you and your belt is a notch tighter.' I felt as if I was a school child being reprimanded for breaking the uniform code.

'It's been a difficult day,' I started.

'No, Michael,' Sarah interrupted. 'It's not just today.'

Dammit, I thought, *not another Michael moment.* I waited for the onslaught.

'Today was certainly appalling.' She brushed hair from her face so she could see me better. 'I spent the morning listening to the radio. RTÉ dropped their usual schedule to bring eyewitness accounts. It was so frightening. Then the police brought Jennifer and Gregory home. Can you imagine what that must have been like? Being driven by officers carrying guns?' Her voice raised an octave, the censure even more strident and piercing. 'They don't deserve this.'

'Sarah,' I said, 'it's not that I don't know what's going on around us. It's just that—'

Sarah was waiting. 'What?' She folded her arms and eyeballed me angrily. 'What is more important than your family, Michael Wilson?' Her voice was shrill and I made a shushing movement. She went to the door and listened, then quickly opened it. The corridor was deserted. She shut the door. She was back in interrogator mode. 'They know not to disturb us,' she said, 'but they're looking for answers too, Michael.'

I shrugged. 'What can I say? I'll know more after this meeting.' But last night I'd said almost the same thing.

'Do you really think your police buddies can protect our family for ever? What planet do you live on?'

I was on the ropes and punch drunk. I could take on every crook and gangster in the country but I couldn't lock horns with my wife two days in a row when she was in this mood. There was no way I'd come out on top. I took the easy route. I didn't throw in the towel. I pleaded the equivalent of a cut eye to give myself time to think.

'When I've heard what Roche has to say we can discuss this. There's no point arguing without all the facts.'

'And when you have these facts?'

'We'll talk through our options.'

'Does that include resigning?'

'If that's what I have to do.'

Sarah eyed me warily. I could sense what she was thinking: *is he telling me what he wants me to hear? Or is this the truth?* She started to say something but I waved a hand to stop her words.

'Please leave it like this. This is appalling for us all and has to end. I know that. But let's park the cross-examination.' I massaged my temples, and then tentatively touched off my wound to make sure it was dry. It was. Maybe that gesture brought sense to the situation for when I looked up Sarah was crying. Her features reflected a bubbling cauldron of sadness and despair, love and rage, fear and defiance. Her eyes brimmed with tears. She unwrapped her arms from their tense, self-protected posture as a tidal wave of emotion swept over. She came to me and held me, pushing my face into the softness of her belly. She ran her hands through my hair. Then we kissed. Slow, soft, lip-on-lip kisses. Her tongue sought mine and we tasted each other. I stood and we wrapped our arms around one another. I felt her relax in my embrace.

'Look at me, Mike Wilson,' she said. The affectionate and loving Mike had returned. Sarah cradled the side of my head in her left hand, fingers splayed to caress and stroke. She ran a fingertip along my lips. With her right hand she slowly undid the buttons on her blouse.

'Keep looking, Mike Wilson,' she whispered huskily. I couldn't take my eyes off her. Now the blouse was fully unbuttoned and the white lace of a very sexy bra was exposed. I started undoing the zip of the front of her denims and brushed my fingers along the top of her panties. She murmured softly and pushed herself against me. The denims were at her ankles and my hands caressed her buttocks. She moved with my movements, pushing against my hardness. Our eyes met. 'I love you, Mike Wilson.'

It was what I wanted to hear and my heart skipped. 'And I love you too, Sarah Ross.'

I lifted her, one hand sweeping her from her feet, the other cradling her back as I lay her down on the bed.

She gazed up at me with unashamed lust. 'Prove it.'

We didn't leave the bed until the front doorbell rang.

My bodyguard Tony Reilly was waiting to collect me, dressed in casual trousers and white open-neck shirt. No bullet-proof vest this time, which was reassuring. But he hadn't the decency to stop smirking. 'Your fly's open.'

I hurriedly zipped myself up.

'And there's lipstick on your neck.'

I blushed. He pushed me out the front door to a waiting car.

'I wouldn't like to think you were enjoying yourself.'

I slumped into the back seat of yet another unmarked car. Reilly climbed in beside me.

'I couldn't give a fuck what you think.'

Chapter 28

'Stephen Brady was shot in the head and chest.'

That's how DI Pamela Roche began the security briefing. It was 9.30 p.m. and we were in a small room at police HQ lit by a single hundred-watt bulb that hung by an electrical cord from the ceiling. The room was too warm and reeked of stale cigarette smoke. In the middle was a circular Formica table. It was chipped and scratched. Chairs were drawn up. I sat in one, Reilly took another. Wearing denim jeans and a Munster rugby jersey, Roche squeezed her petite frame into the third. Like me she'd a Band-aid over her scar. We did look a right pair. She introduced a fourth man.

'This is Brendan McHugh.' We shook hands. 'He's with the Criminal Assets Bureau and involved in our investigation.'

The Criminal Assets Bureau was the state's answer to organised crime. It identified gains from illegal activities and arranged court orders to seize goods, cash and properties. The organisation was also vital in gathering intelligence.

McHugh rummaged through his briefcase. He looked like a younger and taller but overweight Al Pacino: dark hair, swarthy looks and an annoying edginess. He was wearing jeans and short-sleeve shirt. He ran his knuckles along the table twice before sitting down.

'Brady was planning a major exposé on Patrick Dowling,' continued Roche. 'It's believed he was waiting for the inquest verdict before going public. When his apartment was searched his notebooks and laptop were missing.'

This had everyone's attention.

'His desk at the *Herald* is full of scribbled notes, telephone numbers, et cetera.' Now she looked straight at me. 'There was also a letter addressed to your office.'

I managed to concentrate, despite my overwhelming tiredness.

'He wanted this file.' Roche passed across a request for information under the Coroner's Act. Included was ID number, name of deceased – Timothy Cunningham – and date of inquest.

I put it to one side. 'I can't think why he'd have asked for that. Nothing comes to mind immediately, anyway.'

'There were signs of a violent struggle in his flat,' Roche went on. 'Chairs and table overturned, glasses broken. Blood spattered everywhere. It was an awful mess.'

Then she looked straight at me.

'The good news is that Harry Malone's turned up alive and well.'

I almost cheered. I suspected Malone knew a lot more about Patrick Dowling's death than he'd hinted at in his deposition.

'He made contact through a solicitor called Fred Hodgins.' Roche couldn't conceal her contempt. 'Hodgins says Malone's reconsidered his position.'

I groaned.

'He got it all wrong and apologises for misleading.'

I swore softly.

'He's made a fresh statement.'

'What's in it?' I knew it'd be full of lies.

'He contradicts everything. He was with Dowling for a short time, not the whole afternoon. He didn't see any fist fight. He's never heard of Noel Carty.'

'He's been got at,' I said.

'That's a given.'

Chins were scratched, eyes rubbed. McHugh did a knuckle roll.

'Malone claims Dowling did talk about ending his life. He was so sick he said he'd prefer to be dead.' Roche leaned back to invite a response.

So I related my conversation with Mary Dowling: '"My son committed suicide because he had no future. Our family is better off without him." I don't trust her.'

Roche's glower told its own tale. She didn't trust her either.

'Carty has an alibi that puts him on the far side of Dublin that day,' Roche added.

'What about his fingerprint in the car?' I asked.

'His story is Dowling called on him for help with gearbox problems. Carty's a mechanic and does cash repairs. He gashed himself on the engine casing and may have left a bloody print.'

I stared at the table, as if admiring its false grain. *Where will this end? How will it end?*

'Over to you.' Roche nodded to McHugh.

McHugh opened his briefcase. He set four photographs on the middle of the table. 'That's Jonathan Redmond, Albert and Patrick Dowling.' His finger jabbed at the last one. 'And that's Dan Thornton, head of Standard and Chartered Bank.' I studied the head and shoulder images. The one in front of me was a different snap of Redmond, probably recent. He looked raffish still, designer stubble, stylishly long hair and confident face. He was in a yellow crew neck over a navy-blue shirt. He looked wealthy. Old-money wealth too, rather than drug-baron flash. The more I looked the more I was sure I'd seen him before. But I was so exhausted I just passed the photograph to Reilly. Albert Dowling had more weight on him than when I saw him earlier in the day. Patrick Dowling was gaunt and haggard. I guessed it was taken within the last year of his life. I passed them on. Then I inspected Dan Thornton's photograph. I put him in his late fifties. He had frontal baldness, thin grey side locks and tight lips. Joe Average. 'Thornton's been moving a lot of money in and out of that bank. Not hundreds of thousands, not millions, but billions of euros. He showed healthy end-of-year reserves by taking billions in inter-bank loans, keeping it for audit, then shifting it back. He lied to the auditors and monetary regulator. He lied to a state commission on banking.'

No big deal there, I thought. Ireland's economic crisis had opened a Pandora's Box of fiscal malpractice. Those at the top conspired to maintain a facade of normality. Behind the scenes the financial industry was crumbling from overexposure to property lending during the boom years.

'But,' McHugh continued, 'Thornton mixed funny money with these transfers. Sometimes a billion would go in and out but often there was an extra million, or half a million, or a quarter million added on. This was retained for thirty days before being shifted off books to an account in Jersey. This is a holding facility for Redmond. We've identified three shelf companies he uses to launder drug profits.'

It was 10.30 p.m. and I was emotionally drained. Roche had hinted there'd be significant new intelligence. It was coming by the bucketful. I stretched and massaged my neck muscles.

'Redmond has such a high turnover from drug trafficking he has to move money constantly. He's bought cash-rich businesses such as taxi companies, restaurants, pubs and betting shops. He owns a fleet of limousines in Marbella and declares healthy earnings, pays taxes and the capital enters the banking system legitimately. This is moved to his holding companies for investment.'

'And,' I gestured to the photo, 'Thornton's helping him?'

'We suspect Thornton used Redmond's money to prop up a number of ailing investments. This allowed him to show healthier cash flows. It balanced the books and kept the regulator off his back.' McHugh shifted his paperwork. 'If we're right, then Thornton has created a vehicle for Redmond to shift money into the banking system. He could distance himself from drugs by moving into legitimate commerce.'

'How's Redmond linked to Albert Dowling?' I asked. I was finding it difficult to keep up.

McHugh abandoned another knuckle roll. 'I don't know. There's a connection but we're not making it. Both Redmond and Dowling have been careful to cover their tracks. Dowling has a long history of flirting with crooked practices. He's never been charged but he's always been considered dodgy. He's in a political party that's used to plundering state coffers. The word corrupt doesn't do justice to what some of them have been involved in for years.'

I interrupted. 'Mary Dowling claims her husband has Alzheimer's disease.'

Roche couldn't hide her contempt. 'She's lying.'

If so, I thought, *she's in on this as well. Why else would she contrive such a story? And how is her husband keeping up the charade? He is, after all, Minister for Economic Development.*

'Where does Patrick Dowling fit in?'

'We still don't know,' Roche conceded. 'As I said on the first day we met, maybe he was the go-between for Redmond and Albert Dowling.'

John Hobbs's comment echoed through my mind: *'Forget about drugs, follow the money.'* His words were being proven true.

I suddenly realised both Roche and McHugh were staring at me.

'Pulling this together is being compromised by leaked information,' said Roche. Her hair was a mess, unkempt and straggling. But that was probably the least of her worries. 'Redmond has infiltrated police and financial security services. Thornton knew the fraud squad was coming. He was waiting with an army of lawyers. It may prove difficult to show he's linked to organised crime. Any court case could drag on for years. We need to come at this from a different angle.'

'Meaning?' I don't know why I asked.

'Through this inquest,' said Roche. 'What you uncovered today was astounding. It puts that investigation into serious doubt. But we'll need a lot more to close the circle.'

I made an immediate decision. I would not reveal John Hobbs's existence. If traitors were undermining the investigation I didn't want my star witness targeted.

Roche summed up the situation. 'We're in a recession. Banks aren't lending and need state support to survive. Cash is king. Redmond has more cash than he can handle. For him it's an ideal coincidence of circumstances. He wants to move from drug dealing to respectability. With his university education, charm and confident manner that progress could be smooth.

To start this transition he's bought into a corrupt and wasted banking house. Now he can divert money to legitimate trading institutions. There'll never be a better time for him to cut and run.'

She let this sink in.

'Redmond knows narcotics has a high turnover of bodies. He lost his girlfriend in a staged hit-and-run. He's moving on and wants to put a lot of distance between him and his past. Stephen Brady must have been killed because whatever he was writing about must have incriminated Redmond.'

Roche reiterated her concerns about Albert Dowling and Redmond. A connection was suspected but not understood. The two had so far managed to keep their dealings secretive. The supposed impaired mental health of Albert Dowling was a smokescreen.

Rounding the circle of deceit, intrigue, corruption and criminality ultimately fell to me.

I outlined my strategy. If I could catch one of the Dowlings off guard something might be revealed. 'Let's start with baby steps,' I said. 'This will be unpicked slowly, not by some sudden revelation.'

The meeting broke up. Silently I considered John Hobbs's words. *'Yer way off track.'* He'd seen Patrick Dowling die. *'Ye find out why he ended up here and then come back. I'll fill in the missin' pieces.'* If I could get Hobbs to reveal all in the coroner's court the floodgates would open. Roche's suspects would be named and shamed. And I could get on with my life.

As we walked along the gravel path at police HQ Roche spoke with me.

'Jack Matthews is not in Redmond's pocket. We've done a thorough security check on him and he's good.'

Matthews was the policeman in charge of the Patrick Dowling inquiry. He'd wilted in face of my inquisitorial onslaught.

'Good.' I was pleased he wasn't involved. 'He hinted the investigation was halted abruptly. Do you know who gave that order?'

Overhead a shooting star soared and disappeared; under our feet gravel crunched.

'A man called Alan Hutchins,' said Roche. 'He's a divisional chief who moves around a lot. From what I heard he asked for the autopsy result to be faxed to him as soon as it came in. Then he pulled the plug.'

'Do you trust him?'

'Right now I trust no one.'

Which was pretty much how I felt.

Then Roche checked we couldn't be overheard. She beckoned me closer. 'If we get sight of Redmond we'll try and detain him.'

'What do you mean "try"?'

'We won't be too careful. A gun could go off by mistake.' There was an awkward pause. 'He won't go into custody handcuffed. I can't see him hiding his face to avoid paparazzi. He'll go down rather than be humiliated. Nobody's preparing for a dog fight. If he's spotted he'll meet with an accident.'

Reilly had me in the back of the car before I could draw breath.

I checked my mobile phone for messages. There was a voicemail from Joan. 'Hi, Dr Wilson. I've prepared a press release postponing the Dowling inquest until further notice. Bye.' Then a short text from Sarah. 'I'll keep the bed warm for you.'

I flicked off the phone.

We were on O'Connell Street, lit up and gaudy, like a

whore offering her wares. Crowds were spilling out of night clubs and bars and gathering along the sidewalks. Rows of taxis queued, their signs flashing for fares. Someone's stag party was reaching a crescendo with fire-crackers and shouts. No one was sober. I smiled at the frivolity but in the mirror I noticed Reilly's taut and anxious face. This was no territory for a high-profile target.

'Why'd you say you had a bad feeling about today?'

Reilly let a minicab overtake. 'Roche suspected Redmond was using local manpower. She'd ordered a tail on a particular gang. They were spotted moving guns early this morning and were followed.'

I wasn't sure if I was relieved or disturbed. They'd come within inches of killing me.

'I don't want anyone to know about Hobbs.'

Reilly glanced at me in the rear-view mirror. 'Okay. We'll sit on it for a few days.'

To distract myself I went through the paperwork from the meeting. Redmond's photograph was the first thing to hand. I squinted at it under the glare of street lights. *There is something familiar about that face,* I thought. *Where have I seen him before?* Then I checked the inquest file request made by reporter Stephen Brady. The ID number didn't mean anything, nor did the name Timothy Cunningham. The inquiry was dated January of this year. Did something unusual or dramatic come to public scru-tiny that month? I couldn't recall. But then I was so dead on my feet my brain wasn't functioning properly. *January? Wasn't there a question over another post-mortem?* I tortured my memory, urging it to focus. Then, out from the depths of my mind, a name, an angry family and controversy surfaced. Cunningham had committed suicide, according to the verdict. But his brother accused me of rushing the inquiry. At the time there were frequent complaints about delays and the backlog of cases. Then something suddenly jogged my memory. It made the hairs on the back of my neck stand up.

I leaned across the seat. 'Take me to the coroner's court.'

'Now?'

'Yes.'

'It'll be locked up.'

'There's a night watchman.'

Reilly pulled over to the pavement and let the engine idle. He turned and looked at me. 'Are you feeling all right?'

'I've a reason.'

Chapter 29

If Larry Naughton, the paunchy night watchman, was surprised to see me he didn't show it. He unbolted each of the three locks on the front door. 'Will you be staying long?' Naughton had a face like the lion in *The Wizard of Oz*, wrinkled with heavy jowls and bushy eyebrows, and the tired look of a man with a thousand worries. He was in the court uniform of navy jacket and trousers over white shirt and tie emblazoned with the Dublin City logo. The tie was pulled loose.

'No,' I said. 'I left something behind.'

Reilly sat in reception and picked up the evening paper. 'Don't hang about. This place gives me the creeps.'

'Fifteen minutes and we're gone.'

I went to the rear of the building and flicked the light on in my PA's office. Joan kept keys to all locked rooms and I found them under a diary. Security in the coroner's office was not considered important. There was nothing to steal apart from computers and printers. No cash or valuables. Only ghosts and their life stories.

I made my way to the basement. Here documents were moved up and down regularly. It was an eerie and dimly lit vault, accessed by three rows of stone steps. I felt my way down, one step at a time. The air was stale and musty and cold. It made me cough. Now came an iron-studded door, over a hundred years old. The keys turned the well-oiled bolts and it unlocked silently. I reached a hand round the corner and groped for the power switch. A low-watt bulb glimmered and flickered. It threw shadows and dark shapes and confused me momentarily. I moved further inside, cursing the gloom. I wished I'd brought a torch. It was even colder than the stairwell and smelled of mildew. I shivered as I traced my way along its twists and turns. I found the large steel cabinets I was looking for jammed against the walls.

Each held paperwork relating to bombings, fire disasters, brutal murders, suicides, accidents and medical misadventures. They held the files of men, women and children fished out of the River Liffey, some who had jumped, others who were pushed. There were files on men, women and children who stepped in front of trucks and trains. Or were pushed in front of them. The material went back decades.

Plans were afoot to transfer old files to another stronghold. These had been hauled to the front for easy retrieval. So the most recent inquests were located at the least accessible part of the passageway. Directly opposite, and obscured from view, was the last wall. Unlike the rest of the red-brick structure, this was built from granite. A lintel shouldered boulders to the ceiling. Underneath was a heavy oak door studded with metal. It hadn't been opened in years. This was the final link to the old city mortuary, now the rubble-strewn building site adjacent to the court. In past times the forensic pathologist could walk from the mortuary to the coroner's court using this underground connection. He'd give his evidence and return without going onto the street. This saved time and spared Dublin's citizens the sight of a man in a bloodstained apron trudging from one building to the other.

In the gloom I saw names and ID numbers: BOMBINGS ON PARNELL STREET, TALBOT STREET AND SOUTH LEINSTER STREET 1974. Then, in another section: STARDUST FIRE 1981. There was row upon row of harrowing and dramatic inquiries into the dead of Dublin.

I found the subdivision I was looking for and searched through the index cards. My fingers smudged and sweated and I dropped a bundle onto the floor. I swore silently and almost put my back out gathering them up. Finally I had the cabinet and file numbers I was looking for.

I rummaged through the keys, cursing the poor light. I retraced my steps until I was directly under the bulb and studied the ID tags for each unit. At last I found the right one. I couldn't contain my sense of dread, even though I argued I was being totally irrational. Blood again in my mouth. The side of my cheek was taking serious pressure. For some reason I stood in front of the metal box, almost frightened to open it. I smelled the air. It was clammy and heavy and stale. It tasted of death. I slid the key into the lock. I glanced up and down as if waiting for a ghost to appear. My hands were shaking and I gripped them tightly.

Even though it was cold I found sweat and grime when I wiped my brow. I moistened my lips where they'd gone dry. I pulled the door, suddenly realising I hadn't turned the key. The cabinet was unlocked. *Oh no.* All storage units were kept locked. That was standard procedure.

And when I checked, the inquest documentation on Timothy Cunningham was gone. I double-checked, feverishly cross-referencing the dossier number with its compartment tag. I pulled folders out, laying them under the light so I was sure I wasn't missing something.

Very soon I realised it hadn't been put in another section by mistake.

The final account on the birth, life and death of Timothy Cunningham had been removed from the security and sanctity of the Dublin City Coroner's Office.

Only court personnel had access to the basement.

Now I knew one of my staff was working against me.

One, or maybe more than one, was working for someone else. Jonathan Redmond.

And what was so important about Cunningham's dossier?

What information was Stephen Brady looking for?

My brain was a fever of questions, suspicions and fears.

I shut the door and locked the cabinet. I slid to my hunkers and took deep breaths. Then I heard footsteps. Soft, deliberate and careful. Someone was coming downstairs. My rib cage pounded and my heart strained to cope with the adrenalin surge. I scrambled to my feet and the footsteps stopped. I wanted to call out but didn't. Then the footsteps retreated, slowly and deliberately. I was left an inch short of a heart attack. I felt bile in my mouth and almost gagged with fear. There was only Reilly and the night watchman in the building. Or had someone else come in? I was almost too scared to go upstairs. But I did. I stopped at every step to listen. Nothing. Now I was in front of the studded door again. It was half open, as I'd left it.

Reilly was sipping on tea and chatting to Naughton. I sneaked past them, hiding in the shadows. I went into the court chamber and sat at the rear, where family and friends of the deceased wait during inquests.

There were six employees in the coroner's court. All had access to the basement. Documents were shifted up and down daily. Files were placed, files were retrieved. Each staff member had legitimate reasons to be there.

Their faces flashed: the front-of-house secretaries, Aoife, Eleanor and Mary. Occasionally temps came and left if illness or social engagements meant days off. That increased the list but I dismissed the idea one of them might be involved. Jury recruiter Arthur O'Leary was nearly as blind as a bat. Then my PA, Joan. There was nothing in her demeanour to suggest she'd been got at. But Roche's unsettling look hinted she might have suspicions about her. I'd have to be extra-cautious from now on. Finally, there was the night watchman. Naughton was sixty-three and had been with us for nine months. Made redundant with little notice he'd walked in one day and asked for work. He was desperate. His redundancy package was a pittance, eaten away by investments gone wrong. He needed money to put food on the table. He took the job as soon as it was offered.

In recessionary Ireland everyone needed money. Some more than others. And some would go to extremes to get money. Naughton needed money. He hadn't been working in the chambers that long to have formed a bond of loyalty with the staff or the office. He was my main suspect.

I sat in the darkened chamber trying to decide how to deal with this. Reilly was still talking with Naughton. I could hear their mumbled conversation. I sat on, wrapped in the silence of the court. Not even the outside traffic and street noises disturbed me.

I was on the well-worn and uncomfortable benches at the rear of the room. Ahead, to my right, were the jury pews. To my left was the mahogany witness box. In the middle was a desk and chairs reserved for lawyers.

At the very top, and higher than the rest, was the

coroner's bench. There, during proceedings, I had full view of everyone. It felt strange to be sitting opposite my usual chair. I'd never been in the visitors' gallery before and wondered how I must look to the public. Wise and caring? Comforting and compassionate? Or cold and detached? Was I a good coroner or not? I was a doctor with many clients, all of them dead. None ever came back to thank me for giving them justice.

I recalled talking to a cancer specialist who developed cancer. He told me how unnerving it was to be on the wrong side of the examination couch and how frightening it was to watch another doctor study his lab results. If his colleague frowned did it mean bad news? If he seemed upbeat did that suggest the treatment was working?

Is that how families in this gallery look on me? I wondered. *Do they hang on my every word, trying to decide what verdict will be delivered?*

A strong beam of light flashed across the chamber. The grumbling of a truck rattled the window. The room lit up, and then just as quickly darkened. The glare was dazzling and I rubbed at my tired eyes. A wave of exhaustion swept over me and I dropped my head in my hands.

I sensed movement. Out from the shadows I saw a ghost approach, then another, then more and more as my charges turned up for their day in court. I didn't move. I stared into space. Ash-grey fingers pointed at me as they glided beside me into the gallery. They whispered as they jostled for position. I felt the chill from their breath and smelled the decay of their shrouds. I followed them out of the corner of my eye. Their fleshless faces showed neither grief nor sorrow; glee nor joy. Merely resignation. They were soulless ghouls; murmuring and sighing.

These were my comrades, my unseen and nameless followers. They knew I was their sole defender. They had come to support me.

I felt at ease, relieved almost. I wasn't without friends. I had the dead of Dublin behind me. Who could defeat me?

I yawned, massaged my neck, closed my eyes and kept them closed. When I opened them again the chamber was empty, the ghosts no more than the hallucinations of an exhausted mind and tired body.

I gradually became aware of a figure standing close to me. I looked up to find the night watchman.

'You look like a man waiting to hear his own inquest.'

Chapter 30

'Have you a copy of Cunningham's inquest?'

'Everything's saved on the office hard drive. The system's encrypted and never been breached.'

Reilly and I discussed the stolen file. We were parked on my street in Glasthule. The area was quiet, the heavy police presence gone. There were no lights on in my house. Considering it was close to 2.30 a.m. that wasn't surprising.

Reilly pressed a button and the windows glided down. The hum of traffic competed with a house alarm. Somewhere a dog barked, whined, then stopped.

I explained my concern about staff and how any one of them could have gained access to the basement, located and removed the file.

'From now on, don't trust any of them,' Reilly said. 'If you ask where the file is it'll trigger a cover up.'

That was something I'd thought about. 'The investigating police would have a copy. You could check this out without drawing attention.'

'I'll get on to it.'

Reilly opened the door, stood and stretched.

'Why don't you go to bed?' He was looking at me through the open window. 'You look whacked. It's been a helluva day.'

I started shoving paperwork into my briefcase.

'We've taken over the house opposite. The owner's a

retired judge and he's happy to let us use it. Your family will be under twenty-four-hour watch and there's a rapid response unit.' I climbed out of the back seat and inhaled. The salty tang off the nearby sea freshened my nostrils. I took a few more breaths to clear my lungs.

'While I was in the basement did anyone else come into the building?'

Reilly was scrolling through the text messages on his phone. 'No.'

'Did Naughton leave you at any stage while I was down there?'

'No.'

'Did you come down looking for me?'

Reilly stopped scrolling. 'What the hell are you getting at?'

'I heard footsteps,' I said. 'While I was down there I heard footsteps. They came halfway down the granite steps and stopped. Then the same footsteps went back up again.'

Reilly ran a hand over his crew cut and inspected me in the gloom. 'This is taking too much out of you. You're overtired. Next you'll tell me you saw ghosts down there.'

I didn't answer. I hadn't seen ghosts in the basement. But I did see ghosts in the court chamber. They were visual hallucinations. Maybe the footsteps were auditory hallucinations. Maybe it was time I saw a psychiatrist. Maybe it was time I had a decent night's sleep.

Reilly waited until I was safely inside the front door before driving off.

I dumped what I was wearing and showered in the bathroom downstairs. I lathered myself with soap suds, forcing the spray to rid my body of sweat, grime, ghosts, decay and death. I found Jennifer's scented shampoo and washed and rinsed my hair three times.

I towelled myself dry and inspected the final result in

the mirror. I looked gaunt. I had stubble. My eyes were sunken in my head, red-rimmed and bleary. Flecks of grey that had been slowly invading my hair seemed more obvious. As well as a bullet track above my forehead I even had a pimple on my chin.

I put both hands on my belly and checked how much flesh I could pinch. There wasn't a lot.

What must Sarah think of me? Then I remembered her text: 'I'll keep the bed warm for you.' This wasn't a night to sleep alone.

I crept upstairs, careful to avoid creaking steps and loose floorboards. I looked in on Jennifer, fast asleep and tousled curls covering the pillow. She was clutching her favourite teddy bear. Fifteen years old and still needing that comfort. I put it down to recent events.

I kissed her lightly on the cheek and pulled the duvet cover higher. But the night was warm and she turned and kicked it away. I stepped backwards out of the room and shut the door.

Then I checked Gregory. Didier Drogba still scowling down on him. There was a new poster beside that, a new sporting hero. Brian O'Driscoll, the Leinster and Ireland rugby captain, in full flight despite the attention of three England tacklers. *Good on ye, Dricco*, I gave a silent hurrah. I stepped over the usual mess of abandoned clothes and damp towels and stroked his hair. He didn't stir, dead to the world.

Sarah was fast asleep. I studied her in the darkness, desperate to caress her but unwilling to wake her up. I climbed in beside her, pulled a pillow to one side and settled down. My brain was still teeming but fatigue took over and I felt myself drift. My body jerked as the first wave of sleep washed over me. My eyes opened slightly, and then closed. I fell asleep.

Chapter 31

I woke up to the smell of grilled bacon and sausages. Then I heard voices. Sarah was talking with someone downstairs. I checked the time. It had just gone 11 a.m. The bedroom was in shade with the curtains closed. I pulled them open to discover another beautiful summer's day. In the front garden a ginger cat chased a blackbird. It was out of luck. The bird flew away and perched on a branch of a silver birch tree. The cat sat on its hunkers and stared. Then it padded off in search of more adventure. I looked up and down the street. It was deserted apart from two police officers leaning against a patrol car. One of them waved. I didn't know what else to do so I waved back. Then I realised I was naked and retreated.

I pulled on a dressing gown. Breakfast was on the go. Heaps of bacon with a plateful of sausages and tomatoes were spread on a serving dish. Toast was popping, tea was brewing.

I slumped into a chair, dragged the dressing gown around my legs and tried to get my thoughts together.

'Get dressed, Mike,' said Sarah. She was in white cotton shorts, Nike trainers and a floppy navy cotton top. 'You're like a lost soul.'

That's pretty much how I felt.

'Reilly's outside in the garden. Why don't you join him?'

She dropped a pile of newspapers in front of me. 'And you've made all the headlines. Top story in every one.' I pushed them away. I couldn't bear to read about yesterday.

'Where's Jennifer and Gregory?'

'With friends. I drove them there under police escort. They're being watched until we collect them. I promised a day at the beach, despite all this carry on.' She leaned down and kissed me on the left cheek. 'Let's stop arguing and see this through together.'

I caught her hand and squeezed it. 'Thanks,' I said. That's all I could say. We'd made peace. That was good enough for me.

I went back upstairs, dragged on a shirt and jeans and combed my hair into order. I checked the bullet scar. It was healing well. Even the pimple on my chin was less angry-looking. I found Reilly sitting at the barbecue table. He was in black tracksuit bottoms and black T-shirt. He was wearing dark shades.

'Isn't Saturday a rest day?'

'I'm stuck with you and you're stuck with me till this is over.' He pushed his sunglasses back on his head. 'Have your breakfast and let's get working.'

The sun was warm; the skies clear with only an occasional fluffy cloud. A magpie strutted along next door's roof. There were no noises from the dog. Maybe its owners moved it to safety. Maybe they'd all moved? Why wouldn't they? Their neighbours, the Wilsons, were a health hazard.

I wolfed down everything Sarah put in front of me. I devoured a rack of toast. Sarah watched with faint amusement, sipping on a cup of coffee. I kept eating. I wanted to enjoy the moment. The night's rest had worked wonders. I felt refreshed and ready to take on the world.

Then Reilly slipped Timothy Cunningham's file onto the table.

Sarah took the hint. 'I'll leave you to it. But I want Mike to have time with the children later.' At least it was Mike and not Michael. I wasn't in the bad books.

I drank a mug of tea and admired the garden. There were petunias in a riot of colours, blue lobelias, orange pansies and trailing geraniums. Sarah's treasured rose patch was producing yellows and reds and whites. Their scent drifted in the morning air.

'Timothy Cunningham was thirty-eight when he died,' Reilly began. 'I spoke with the investigating officer. He traced this incident file.'

He opened it up.

'His body was pulled out of the Royal Canal near Blanchardstown last July.'

The inquest came back in snapshots. 'I remember his brother claiming he didn't commit suicide.'

'Correct.' Reilly swatted at a fly.

'There were heated exchanges in court.'

Reilly tapped the dossier. 'It's all here.'

More memories spilled into my mind. Timothy Cunningham's elderly mother had sobbed throughout the hearing. She kept returning to his fear of water, citing some childhood incident where he'd fallen into a river. Since then he'd had a phobia of deep water. No, she protested, if her son was going to kill himself he'd have found another way.

Reilly flicked to another page. 'Here's a statement from a work colleague: "Tim was depressed."' He found another section. 'A witness said he walked out of a nearby pub as if he was going to press the self-destruct button. Do you remember what you asked her?'

'Why didn't you stop him?'

Reilly read out the answer: '"It was none of me business. He'd been acting real strange and I didn't wanna get involved. I'd enough goin' on in me own life."'

There was a third deposition from a bystander claiming to have seen Cunningham walking along the towpath. He said Cunningham stopped, stared into the water for a long time and then jumped in. At autopsy there were no signs of a struggle. Toxicology revealed low levels of alcohol. There were no other drugs in his body. The conclusion was death by drowning. Pulling together witness statements and circumstantial evidence there were two possibilities: accidental death or suicide while of unstable mind. I decided Cunningham took his own life. The dead man's family was adamant: Timothy did not jump into the canal.

'His brother was the most vocal,' I said. 'He said Timothy had everything going for him. Good job, steady girlfriend and an apartment in a decent location.' I racked my brains trying to recall the exchanges. I tapped the dossier. 'Does it say what he worked at?'

Reilly didn't answer immediately. He squashed a bug scuttling across the table. Finally he looked up. 'Standard and Chartered Bank. He looked after their wealthy clients.'

Our eyes locked. Standard and Chartered was suddenly becoming an important part of this mystery. 'Forget about drugs, this is about money.' I reminded Reilly of Hobbs's words.

Reilly ran a hand through his crew cut. It was growing into an untidy mess but I doubted he'd get time to see a barber. 'Everything he said now sounds very believable.'

'When we've enough information,' I said, 'we'll go back. He said he'd fill in the missing pieces.'

Then my mind went into another tailspin. A sudden recall. The photo of Jonathan Redmond. I darted inside for my briefcase, almost tripping in the haste. I hurried back, ignoring Sarah's startled look. I started pulling out documents and files. Finally I found the picture Roche had given me.

'I *have* seen him before.' I was almost shouting.

Reilly looked at me. 'Where?'

'He was at that inquest.'

'What?'

'He stood out in his sharp suit, expensive shirt and tie. He never said a word, just listened. When the verdict was announced he left.'

Reilly was astounded. 'What the hell was he doing there?'

Chapter 32

Reilly stood and stretched and walked around. He dead-headed roses and squashed greenfly. I struggled with this new twist to the link between Jonathan Redmond and my court.

'We're screening all court employees.' Reilly was dialling up on his mobile.

'Good.' My mind was elsewhere. Was Redmond one of Cunningham's wealthy clients? Could the assets management employee have uncovered shady dealings in Standard and Chartered involving the drug dealer? Had he confronted Redmond not realising how much danger that would have put him in?

Reilly was deep in conversation. His features clouded, his hands flailed as he fought to get his point across. Then he was on his hunkers, phone held downwards so no one could overhear. He glanced towards me but his face was expressionless. He was back to walking around, mumbling and listening. His black T-shirt stuck out the back of his tracksuit. Now he looked like a tradesman pricing a job.

'What's usually in an inquest file?' He sat down at the table.

'Depositions, witness statements, details of the police investigation.'

'Like what?'

'A body is found in the canal and the police are called. The officer who comes on the scene explains what he saw, the background and setting. He arranges transfer to the state mortuary and awaits formal identification. That sort of stuff.'

'Okay, what else?'

'Statements from family confirming body ID. Police confirmation there's been a positive ID.'

He nodded me to go on.

'Autopsy report, autopsy pictures, lab and toxicology findings.'

Reilly dismissed these with a wave of the hand. 'Not important.'

'What are you getting at?'

'I'm trying to figure out what Stephen Brady was looking for. And why Redmond wanted it.'

'Names and addresses,' I said. 'Brady must have wanted to interview the witnesses. One claimed Cunningham was depressed. Another said she thought he went out to press the self-destruct button. Then someone saw him jump into the canal. He must've had doubts about those statements.'

From the next garden came the commotion of a violent cat fight. There was mewling and screeching. Seconds later a large black cat scampered through the hedge, zigzagged along the rose bed and then bolted to freedom.

Reilly drummed his fingers on the table. 'What links Cunningham and Patrick Dowling?'

'Through Standard and Chartered,' I said. 'We know Cunningham worked there. We need to know if Dowling also had contacts.'

'Redmond bribed one of your staff to take the Cunningham file. He wanted names and addresses of witnesses. He's checking statements. Mebbe one in particular. Something was going on in that bank he needed to know about.' He fixed on me. 'Is that how you read it?'

'It's the most logical explanation.' I heard Sarah calling from inside. I looked but couldn't see her. 'Who were you talking with?'

'The officer in charge of the case. I want to find out where Cunningham's brother lives. He didn't believe Timothy killed himself. He must have reasons for his doubts. And did he know that a major drug dealer was sitting beside him in the visitors' gallery?'

Sarah marched out holding my mobile phone in the air. 'This has rung out three times in the last five minutes.'

I took the phone and checked the call register. The number wasn't in my contacts list. 'I'll ring back now.'

Sarah stood over me, hands folded defiantly across her chest. 'And when you're finished, let's go. I've made a picnic and spoken with the kids. They're waiting to be collected.'

'Five minutes,' I promised. I pressed the recall button and listened to the dialling tone.

'Dr Wilson,' a voice answered. 'It's Alex Johnston. How are you?'

It took me a couple of seconds to remember the name. Alex Johnston was one of the latest pathology recruits at University Hospital.

'You're all over today's papers,' Johnston said.

'That's not something I wanted, Alex.' I knew Johnston from the pathology circuit. Nick-named 'Dumbo', he was a podgy man with a receding hairline and floppy ears. We weren't buddies but occasional companions at medical meetings.

'I bet not.'

'What can I do for you?'

'There are four corpses in this mortuary.'

The bodies he was referring to could have been in-house mortalities, ambulance cases or sudden deaths through the emergency department. I didn't think he was contacting me about a routine fatality.

'And?'

'One of them is a thirty-three-year-old male. Story is he fell from the top balcony of a high-rise apartment block. He was brought here by ambulance DOA. I've just posted him. He's multiple limb, pelvis and skull fractures with severe brain contusion.'

'And?'

'His name is Noel Carty. Police tell me he's linked somehow to yesterday's inquest.'

I took a deep breath and let it out slowly. 'You're sure it's him?'

'The officer's emphatic.'

I made a quick decision. 'Check again for signs of external bruising. Carty is connected to that inquest. This sounds like more than an accident.'

'That's pretty much what I was thinking. But so far I haven't found signs of a struggle.'

'Look again.'

'You're the coroner. I'll do it.'

I hung up, deep in thought. My scar began to throb.

'Another problem?' asked Reilly.

I told him about Carty.

He shook his head. 'He had that coming. Did he jump or was he pushed?'

'We'll know that later.'

'Sooner the better.'

'Let's take a break,' I suggested. 'We're getting bogged down in detail. We need to clear our heads. I'll go to the beach and you take time out. I'll call you later if I hear anything new.'

Chapter 33

We made the beach.

Reilly contacted two different police stations and agreed a strategy to allow the Wilson family to have time to themselves.

Sarah and I made ourselves comfortable on Killiney strand, further along the coast from Glasthule. It was 3 p.m. and the blue skies didn't hold a threat of cloud. In the bay, yachts struggled to find a breeze to carry them from Dunlaoghaire on the south side towards Howth on the north. White sails drooped, speedboats ruled. In the waves Jennifer and Gregory swam and cavorted, shouting at one another, splashing one another, arguing with one another. Because it was mid-afternoon on a Saturday, the stretch was busy. There were clusters of young mothers with babies and toddlers. Sandcastles were being built, buckets and spades worked overtime. The air was warm, the sun still shining directly onto the shoreline.

Sarah wore a black-and-white striped swimsuit that hugged her curves. She rubbed suntan cream onto her legs and arms. I was in shorts and T-shirt and wearing flip-flops. My pale bony legs stuck out and I hugged my knees self-consciously.

In a basket were sandwiches, a flask of coffee, crisps and soft drinks. But underneath paper napkins rested my handgun. I was taking no chances, despite Sarah's disapproving look when we packed.

'Reilly's a real gentleman,' Sarah said.

'Yeah. He's solid and dependable.'

'He's got four children, he told me. All boys.'

'That's right. And all rugby fanatics.' Reilly's sole escape from work was rugby. Like Sarah he believed in the distraction of sport to keep his growing children away from harm.

Sarah turned onto her belly and stretched out. 'Would you do my back?'

Jennifer was running up and down the beach, trying to keep up with Gregory. On days like this she indulged Gregory's sporting appetite. She'd kick a ball or play rounders or allow Gregory to take shots at her while tending goal between two shoes. She was that type of sister. She adored her brother but fought like an alley cat to defend her territory if he encroached upon it.

I squeezed cream onto my fingertips and slowly rubbed it onto Sarah's skin. I took my time, turning the exercise into an erotic massage. 'Careful,' she murmured, 'your new bodyguard's watching.' Reilly had organised an experienced recruit from special protection to shadow me. He was a tall and thin thirty-something, dressed in shorts and a V-neck cotton top. His left wrist was in plaster from a recent fall. 'Don't start something we can't finish.'

I eased up. I was becoming frisky and knew I couldn't move comfortably if suddenly called on.

'What else did he say?'

'Not much. I'm sure he kept a lot back not to worry me.'

I didn't respond.

Sarah rolled slightly to one side to keep an eye on the

strand. Jennifer and Gregory had strayed further down the beach. Their heads were close together, deep in conversation. Close by children played, running in and out of the water, screeching with a mixture of delight and shock at the cold. A stunning brunette in a skimpy bikini flaunted her wares in the near distance.

'You haven't told me what happened last night.'

I wasn't listening. 'Just a minute.' I'd spotted someone close in on Jennifer and Gregory. A squat, broad-shouldered and long-haired youngish-looking male. They were about three hundred yards further along the beach, chasing one another. Gregory was running in and out of the sea, kicking water at Jennifer. She was throwing sand at him.

The stranger appeared from behind a tall concrete bunker, used as a viewpoint for life-savers at the height of the season. It was impossible to see what he was carrying but there was something in his right hand. And it looked like a gun. My heart jumped.

I grabbed the Glock from the basket, upturning our afternoon snack. Sandwiches and crisp bags fell onto the pebbles. I stumbled across stones and pebbles until I hit hard sand.

'Stop!' I shouted. I ran towards the children. 'Jennifer, Gregory. Stop, come back.'

My voice was frantic. In the distance they paused and turned towards me. So did the stranger. I stubbed my toe on a rock and swore out loud but kept going. Behind I could hear frightened yells from Sarah. I ran like a man possessed. 'Stop!' I bellowed.

There was a scramble for shelter. Women and children screamed in terror. Bathers hauled their kids from the sea to safety. Out the corner of my eye I sensed panic ripple along the strip.

The stranger was now beside Gregory and Jennifer and fixed on me as I closed in on him. His right hand pointed in my direction. *Oh Christ, he's got a gun. He'll shoot before I get to them.* I put on a spurt, roaring and waving. My heart pounded in my chest from effort and fear. *Please don't kill my children. Take me, they're innocents.* A well-built young man moved to close in on me but I pointed the Glock at him and he froze.

Jennifer grabbed Gregory's right hand and dragged him towards me. Even in the blur I could see astonishment and shock on his face. 'Quick!' I shouted. 'This way!' I beckoned them towards me.

Seconds later they were in my arms, Jennifer distraught and sobbing, Gregory shaking and white with fear. Sarah was almost upon us, running faster than I'd ever seen in my life. And hot on our heels was my bodyguard, struggling across the pebbles, desperate not to fall again. He only had one working hand. In it he gripped his service revolver.

The stranger stood rock still, completely astonished. He looked no more than eighteen. His arms were tattooed, his ears and lips speckled with metal studs. In his right hand was a plastic water pistol. 'Jesus, man.' He finally found his voice. 'What's got into your fucking head?' I spotted boxes of beach novelties lying to the side of the lookout tower. Sun umbrellas, buckets and spades, softballs, windmills on sticks. And plastic water pistols.

I swore silently. The killer was no more than a sand-boy salesman.

I'd made a fool of myself.

I'd ruined the first decent day we'd had together as a family.

I'd seriously screwed up.

And Sarah's face was as dark as thunder.

'Let's go.' She took Jennifer and Gregory by the hand and frogmarched them towards our picnic spot, past suspicious and frightened onlookers. Groups were huddling to watch, pointing and waving and gabbling. Mobile phones were burning hot as the spectacle was relayed across the city. Jennifer turned to stare at me and in her eyes I saw distress. Yet again.

'Sorry,' I said to the sand-boy.

'Get a life.' He was inspecting my scar. It probably made me look like a thug. 'You're way outta line running up and down with a gun. There's women and children here, y'know.'

I handed the Glock to my bodyguard. He shook his head at my embarrassment. I started walking back. I looked neither left nor right.

You idiot, I called myself. *You stupid, fucking idiot.*

Chapter 34

Minister for Justice
Government Buildings
Upper Merrion Street
Dublin 2
12 June 2010

Dear Minister,

It is with deep regret that I inform you of my decision to resign as coroner to Dublin City.

You are aware of recent circumstances. This has had a profound effect on me and my family.

I believe it is both unwise and selfish to continue in this position. It puts my life and the lives of my wife and children at risk. That is unacceptable.

To comply with severance terms and conditions and to protect pension entitlements, I will continue as coroner for four (4) more weeks. This should allow you time to approach and interview a suitable replacement.

Thank you for the honour of allowing me to serve as Dublin City Coroner. In better times I would have preferred to continue the work I so enjoy.

Yours sincerely,
Dr Michael Wilson.

'Sign it.' Sarah was standing over me, pen in hand. She'd typed the letter herself, in a rage so violent I thought the keyboard would melt.

I put my scrawl to the bottom of the page. Sarah snatched it from me. She scanned it and sealed it in an envelope. There was a courier waiting in the front lounge. He inspected the address, listened to the instructions and glanced at me. I grimaced and he grinned. Then he was off. I listened to his motorbike until the growl of the engine disappeared. A dog chased after it.

Jennifer and Gregory were watching television. Gregory was munching on crisps he should have enjoyed at the beach. That vanished with my dramatic overreaction to a water pistol.

In many ways it was the breaking point for us all. Something had to give. The pressure was too intense. Sarah had made the decision.

'It's me and the children or your job, Michael Wilson.' She tongue-lashed me all the way from Killiney. Michael this, Michael that. It was back to the mind-numbing Michael. Over Vico Road and along the coastline into Dalkey I endured an outpouring of pent-up emotion and anger. I'd never heard Michael used in such an abusive, angry and frustrated manner before. Michael: I was beginning to hate the sound of my own name. This was reinforced from the back seat.

'It's not fair, Dad,' complained Gregory as we rounded a bend on Sorrento Road. 'I was scared stiff. And it wasn't the sand-boy who frightened me. It was you. I thought you'd gone mad.' That didn't help my morale.

'He's right.' Jennifer added to the mountain of unhappiness. 'We were having a great time until you started shouting and ranting. And all those people looking on.

I think I know one of them. It'll be weeks before I can show my face again.'

For Sarah it was the last straw.

We called the kids and asked them to sit at the kitchen table while I explained our future plans. Sarah read out a copy of the letter she'd just sent.

'Four weeks.' Gregory's dismay broke through. His lower lip trembled and he fought back tears. 'Not another four weeks like this.' He rushed from the table and ran up the stairs. Seconds later his bedroom door slammed shut.

Jennifer remained seated, head down and fiddling with her watch strap.

'I'm sorry, Jennifer,' I said, 'but no one just walks out of an important government job. I have to allow them time to find a replacement.'

She didn't look at me. 'Is it okay, Mum, if I go up to Gregory? He's very upset.'

Sarah nodded and we were left alone. There was silence. Neither of us knew what to say. I was struck dumb. I couldn't recall a worse moment in my life. No exam failure, no botched clinical decision, no medical misdiagnosis compared to the wretchedness I now felt. I was a failure in my wife and children's eyes. Even worse, I was a risk to their well-being. Possibly they even considered me mentally unstable.

'That's the last we'll say about this, Michael. You've four weeks to stay alive; I've four weeks to protect my children. After that I'm sure you'll pick up a pathology post somewhere. If we have to go abroad, so be it. I've heard there's a vacancy coming up in the Mater Hospital in August. If you get your CV in soon you'll be in a strong position. Maybe you could get one of your security cronies to put a word in for you.'

That stung more than a slap on the face. But I held

my temper. The situation was my own doing and I could fault no one else for where I found myself. These were desperate times in Ireland. Economically, politically and on the security front. Others might squabble and fret over money, divorce, unemployment and addiction. In our house the challenge was physical survival.

But by signing the letter of resignation I'd set in motion a chain of events that would change my life for ever.

In four weeks, if I was still alive and my wife and children unharmed, I'd no longer be coroner to Dublin City. I'd revert to Dr Michael Wilson, MD; MRCPI; FRC Path.

I'd find a position in pathology. Once installed I'd conduct autopsies looking for cause of death, classifying medical mistakes or pinpointing evidence of surgery gone wrong. I'd study tissue slides under microscopes, searching for malignant cells, infective cells and cells in places they shouldn't be. I'd carry buckets filled with formalin preservative, and inside those buckets would be body parts: liver, kidney, brain, bone, ovary, testicle et cetera. Wherever there was a body part that could be damaged or diseased I'd dissect it, fix it in formalin, slice it wafer thin and examine it for signs of abnormality. Or confirm normality.

But I didn't want to return to hospital practice. I enjoyed the challenge as final voice for the dead. With sudden loss of life relatives need to know what happened. While each inquest was different and testing, my final words were usually the same. 'I'm sorry to learn of the death of your brother/sister/child/mother/father/grandmother/uncle/friend or loved one. Please convey my sincerest sympathies to the rest of your family. I hope that with this decision you can find closure.'

On occasions no one would turn up. There was no one to represent the deceased, who was, in those cases, usually a vagrant found in some back alley. And the autopsy might read: heart failure, lung failure, liver failure, kidney failure. Every organ had failed, as if they decided just to give up. To stop supporting the wasted body surrounding them.

At the end of each inquiry slowly, almost reluctantly, the bereaved would file out of the hall, occasionally mouthing a thank you. And always, without fail, I would sense a separate and final going away. A ghost would wait until the room emptied. Then that spirit would shuffle from the chamber, never to return. It'd had its day in court. But before this apparition disappeared, it would turn towards me and nod. It was an acknowledgement from the grave. Thank you, Coroner.

I was an ordinary man entrusted with an extraordinary responsibility. I searched for the truth, even when it seemed impossibly elusive.

As with Patrick Dowling's death: if I completed that inquiry and brought a rightful verdict I believed the murder campaign would end.

Something very unusual had happened to Dowling. Something so strange, secretive and dangerous that it was worth killing to conceal.

I rang Reilly. 'I want to meet Albert and Mary Dowling. Tomorrow if possible.' I told him of the scare at the beach. He'd heard about it already. Bad news travels fast. I told him I'd resigned as coroner.

'This is a big day for resignations. Albert Dowling announced his retirement an hour ago.'

'I don't give a damn about Albert Dowling.' I couldn't contain my bitterness. 'And I want you to set up a meeting with Timothy Cunningham's brother. I need to know why Redmond was at that inquest.'

Chapter 35

On Sunday 13 June, Reilly drove me to the Dowling residence. He was dressed in neatly pressed trousers, crisp white shirt and blue striped tie. I was wearing casual slacks and a short-sleeved shirt. The city skyline was cloudy that morning but now the sun was breaking through. It was warm and humid and I wished I was doing something else more enjoyable. But I was stuck with my lot: the Dowling inquest and the truth behind it.

Before I left I spoke with Sarah and discussed our exit strategy. As a family we'd another four weeks of police protection. After that we were on our own. I'd decided not to seek an appointment locally. I suggested we sell the house and leave the country. We'd homeschool the kids for a year until we got our heads around our long-term plans. It was fortunate that my medical expertise would be highly sought. I'd get work anywhere in the world. Australia, New Zealand or Canada seemed attractive options. I'd have to prove myself – that wouldn't be difficult – but it would mean building new contacts, networking and integrating all over again. But at least no one would be shooting at me. We'd never return to Dublin – or anywhere else in Ireland – and considering the state the country was in that might be no bad thing. We'd rear our children where their futures wouldn't be weighed down by inherited debt and religious bigotry. Where employment and promotion was based on merit rather than which school you went to or which rugby club you played for.

'In the meantime,' I emphasised, 'I'm still coroner with a job to do.'

The discussion was, as politicians say, full and frank. Sarah didn't want to leave the country for ever. But, like many others, she was worn down by the constant drip-drip of bad news. According to pundits the country was bankrupt. The IMF would have to be called in. Every day the airwaves filled with tragically sad tales of families losing their loved ones to emigration. While neither of us said it, quietly we were both thinking the same thing. Would Jennifer and Gregory still be with us in ten or fifteen years? Or would they have sought a better life elsewhere? In the end we reached a compromise. Sarah would look after the children and keep them busy while I tied up loose ends before my final day at the coroner's court. Conditions reluctantly agreed, I left for a head to head with the Dowlings. Sarah said she'd distract herself with another day at the seaside. Jennifer and Gregory would go with her. They couldn't be left on their own, no matter how grown up Jennifer felt herself to be.

On the way over, Reilly told me he'd had difficulty setting up the appointment. There'd been stonewalling from the other side. Since Albert Dowling announced his retirement the family was in no mood for hostile visitors. He soothed their concerns by explaining this was my way of bringing the inquest to an end.

'I said you'd be in and out in an hour.'

Further obstacles were offered including Albert Dowling's poor health and Mary Dowling's religious obligations. In the end they relented and I was asked to turn up after early mass. We delayed our arrival until 11 a.m. 'In case there's a long sermon,' Reilly smirked.

The Dowlings owned a grand Edwardian red-brick in the suburb of Dartry. This was a well-to-do neighbourhood with quiet, tree-lined streets and generous pavements. It was genteel Dublin, affluent and stylish, with expensive cars on gravel driveways.

Reilly parked his unmarked car on the road and let me out. 'Good luck.'

The street I stood in was quiet. To protect the Dowlings' security, police crews were refusing entry to all but residents. A young boy in white shorts and green soccer jersey kicked a ball aimlessly against a wall, checking up and down for traffic. He looked bored. He sat on the ball and waited for me to pass. 'Hiya, mister.'

'Hiya.' I didn't have time to say anything else.

The front door was opened by a man I didn't recognise. 'Dr Wilson?'

'Yes. I'm here to speak with Albert and Mary Dowling.'

'I know.' A hand went out and I shook it. The grip was firm but unwelcoming. 'I'm Richard. The second in the family.'

I struggled to match the face with what I'd seen of the Dowling brood. The earlier photos of Patrick showed a handsome man, very like his father. Richard was small and bulky, maybe four inches off six feet and weighing about two hundred pounds. He had coarse features, a big nose and pockmarked skin. He was wearing denim jeans and white crew-neck T-shirt. He pulled the door only slightly open, forcing me to squeeze past. Then it was shut with a bang. 'Dad's fast asleep.'

'Is he okay?'

'He's just tired.'

'Indeed.' We still hadn't moved from the porch. Dowling was making little effort to hide his dislike of me. 'Then I'll talk to your mother. I won't keep her long.'

He inspected me from head to toe, as if sizing me up for a suit. 'She told me about your conversation.' There was no comment on my scar. 'She's still very upset.'

'I'm sorry to hear that.' Out of the corner of my eye I could see a grand hallway with a large gilt-edged mirror. I pushed my way past him. To the right was a drawing room. 'Will I wait there?'

'No, we'll go to the kitchen.'

Mary Dowling was waiting in a hard-backed chair at a long, wooden table. This time there was no attempt at cosmetic camouflage. She was in a tracksuit bottoms with a loose tennis shirt. Her eyes had dark rings around them, the whites bloodshot. I sensed she might have been crying. I also sensed nervousness. And I doubted she'd been to mass. Not in that attire.

'Sorry to interrupt you on a Sunday.'

'What do you want, Dr Wilson?' She looked directly at me. 'I thought we'd said all that needed to be said.'

I sat down at the table. I had a list of issues in my head. I decided to start with what I considered a simple opener. 'Tell me more about Patrick.' As I pulled my chair in tight I smelled whiskey off her breath.

Richard cut through. 'I'll deal with this, Mum. Why don't you sit in the garden for a while and I'll take Dr Wilson to Patrick's room. We can talk there.'

I glanced out the kitchen window at the manicured lawn and shrubbery. On a small terrace an umbrella and sun lounger were ready. A pot of coffee with cup and saucer and milk jug were arranged on a small table.

I knew immediately this was a set-up. Albert Dowling

233

was fast asleep and no way was I going to be allowed to question his wife.

'I'd prefer to speak with your mother.'

Richard offered a concerned frown. 'She's too distressed. First Patrick's death, then all the unpleasantness at the inquest. Now my father's resignation. It's taking its toll on her.'

A wet sniff confirmed Mary Dowling's insufferable grief.

I made a quick decision. I wasn't going to get anywhere with this approach. I'd speak with Richard. 'That's fine by me.' It wasn't but I'd try and think of ways to wheedle information out of him.

He led me upstairs. On the stairwell were photos of the family in better times. I pointed at one. 'Who's that?'

'That's my younger brother, Seamus.'

'Where's he now?' Seamus was definitely from his father's side of the family. He'd dark, wavy hair, high forehead and cheekbones, strong chin with even teeth.

'In London looking for a place to live. I think he's moving into an apartment this week. He didn't want to be in Dublin during the inquest.'

He opened a door. 'This was Patrick's room.'

The word 'basic' sprang to mind. The room was large with bay windows overlooking the garden. There was a well-worn carpet. A single bed was pushed into one corner and stripped down to the mattress. There wasn't even a pillow at the head. Built-in wardrobes were shut. There was a desk at the window, swivel light and basic office-type chair. The desk top was free of clutter. There wasn't a picture on the walls. Neither a trophy nor memento remained of Patrick Dowling. It looked to me as if a deliberate attempt had been made to erase the dead man's existence.

I glanced around. 'Do you have photos of Patrick?'

Dowling searched my face. 'Why?'

'I'm trying to understand a bit more about your brother.'

'Why?' The pockmarked features now became ugly and challenging.

I was pissed off by his attitude. 'Are you going to help or not? I'll hang around here all day if I have to.'

Dowling held my angry stare. 'I'll tell you all you need to know. Patrick was a drug addict with no future. Committing suicide was his only act of kindness. It spared our family more misery and distress.'

'Weren't you upset when you learned he'd hanged himself?' A hint of regret, no matter how insincere, would have been appropriate.

'I didn't give a damn.'

The hatred and loathing Dowling felt for me was obvious. But I couldn't grasp why. What'd I done to him or his family? But I also sensed fear. And that I couldn't understand.

I stood my ground. Minutes later I sat at his late brother's desk, sifting through a photograph album that I had found in one of the drawers. Along the corridor I heard heavy snoring. I looked at my watch: it was 12.30 p.m. The retired politician was having a long lie-in.

'Patrick lived on the edge.' Dowling watched as I examined the snaps. 'Everything was done to extremes.'

I inspected an old school photo. It was taken in the grounds of Mountbrook College, an expensive institution run by Jesuits.

'How'd he get on at Mountbrook?'

'He was in the top five of his class every year. He was on the team that won the rugby senior cup. You can imagine how proud Dad was that day.'

Among Dublin schools, winning the rugby senior cup was a pinnacle of sporting achievement. Grown men boasted of the triumph years later, and parents basked in the reflective glory.

'Do you play games?'

'No.'

I decided that wouldn't have gone down well with his father. I now knew that at one time Patrick was a talented sportsman and academic scholar. So his decline to wasted addict was more dramatic and tragic than I'd first understood. I wondered what triggered his drug use.

'What about Seamus?'

'He's more aesthete than athlete. He's a gifted pianist and plays the cello. He's trying to pursue an acting career.'

I thought through this information. In his prime Albert Dowling was a bully-boy politician with a reputation as a bruiser. He'd a notorious bad temper and didn't suffer fools gladly. He was a man's man and would've delighted in Patrick's successes. Possibly he'd have found the other boys harder to rear. Richard was unattractive and un-athletic. Seamus was handsome but artistic. That could've sparked friction.

I looked out the bay window onto the garden. Mary Dowling was pacing up and down. She looked uneasy, worried even. She was fingering her rosary beads.

'What do you mean Patrick lived on the edge?' My mobile phone rang. I checked the incoming call. It was Reilly. I let it cut to voicemail.

'He never believed in taking a drink. He only knew drunkenness.' Dowling's voice was a drone, as if he had rehearsed his lines well. 'He relished challenges but didn't care how he won. He had to come out on top.' He looked across at me. 'My dad thought this was wonderful. "You'll make a great politician," he said to him once.' A sneer flickered. 'But we'll never know that now, will we?'

'How did he get involved in drugs?'

'Like I said, Patrick only did extremes. Why drink without getting drunk? Why use cannabis when there's heroin? Why compromise? Dad'll pick up the pieces.'

His tone was pure acid.

'Do you know who supplied him with drugs?'

'No.'

A photo caught my eye and I used it to switch the subject. 'Who's that?' I pointed to a snap of Patrick in T-shirt and shorts at a beach bar. In the background a tropical-green sea washed against white sand. Beside him was a young woman in bikini top. She'd long, jet-black hair pulled into a tress across her left shoulder. She was nursing a cocktail.

'Niamh Shanahan.' No more was offered. Dowling stood as if to leave but I got in quickly.

'Was she a girlfriend?' I pressed. 'Did they date?'

'They were friends. That's all I know.'

Dowling's attitude had suddenly changed. He was evasive and uncomfortable.

'Do you know how I could get in touch with her?'

'She used to live near Ranelagh but she's gone abroad. I don't know where.'

'Why did she go away?' I sensed Dowling knew more than what he was telling me.

Dowling sat on the bed. 'I'm not completely sure.' He shrugged at the uncertainty. 'But I was told Patrick was in difficulties with a drug pusher. Niamh may have left because there was a threat to harm her if he didn't pay his debts.'

I pushed myself from side to side in the swivel chair.

I studied the ceiling. From along the corridor came more snoring. It was 1.15 p.m.

'Does your father often sleep this long?'

Dowling offered what sounded like a laugh. It came across more like a croak. 'Only if he's been up most of the night.'

'And was he up last night?'

'He walked the floors till three. This resignation's crushed him. He eats, sleeps and drinks politics. He has nothing to live for now.' He stared at the threadbare carpet as if trying to decide whether to replace it.

I found another photo. In it Patrick and Richard were posing. Between them was Niamh Shanahan: her hair was combed back and held in place with a red ribbon tied in an extravagant bow. She was wearing an off-the-shoulder cocktail dress. I'd have fallen for her myself. And so had Richard Dowling, going by his expression. Patrick and Niamh were staring at the camera. Richard, shorter by some inches than the girl, had an arm around her waist. He was looking up at the young woman. His eyes gave him away. *I want you, Niamh.*

I coughed to distract and pretended to check my mobile phone for messages. Then I slipped the picture into a side pocket.

'Have you spoken to Niamh since she left?'

Dowling shook his head. 'No. Her father asked us to leave her alone.'

'Why?'

Dowling frowned more uncertainty. 'Maybe he heard of the threat.'

'How did your brother finance his drug habit?'

'He borrowed from family and friends. He stole from family and friends. He sold whatever belongings he had, then whatever belongings we had that he could get hold of.' Dowling looked straight at me. 'Do you want me to go on?'

'I get the drift.' I tried to say thank you, but the words stuck in my throat.

Dowling's mobile phone pinged a text. He studied the message, frowning. Then, with his left heel he pushed the door almost closed.

Outside, on the landing, I heard a floorboard creak.

I stood up, stretched and forced a smile. 'Time for me to go.'

Dowling confronted me as I tried to leave. 'Now will you leave us alone?' My immediate thought was how ugly he looked, and that when he was angry his ugliness made him look like an oaf. An uncouth and unpleasant yob.

'Yes,' I said. *The hell I will,* I thought.

I finally managed to squeeze past him. Yet again. He had a thing about stopping me in doorways until it suited him to let me through.

We were near the bottom of the stairs when I realised I'd left my mobile phone in the room. I made an excuse to go back up to collect it and use the first-floor bathroom. Dowling waited at the foot of the stairs, following my every move.

I'd barely made the top step when I heard an angry shush. Then I sensed a hint of whiskey breath. Albert Dowling's bedroom door clicked shut. I studied the daylight underneath the door frame. The shadow wasn't distinct, but I was sure someone was edging backwards.

I had a pee and then washed my hands. In front of me a mirrored cabinet was slightly ajar. There was a grubby fingerprint on the bottom right-hand corner. I eased it open and looked inside.

Chapter 36

'Albert Dowling's ill-health is a load of crap. They're hiding something, I just know it.'

Reilly listened carefully. He was leaning on the bonnet of the car. His shirt was open, his tie undone. There was sweat on his face. He pushed his shades onto his head to see me better. 'Waddye mean?'

I told him about the heavy snoring, the door click when I went back up the stairs, the smell of whiskey breath. I was sure Mary Dowling had sneaked upstairs and clumsily raided the medicine cabinet – but she'd left behind a grimy fingerprint. It was as if she'd hurried from the garden, desperate to clear the cabinet in case I looked there. But she'd left one item behind and, according to the label, Albert Dowling was on tranquillisers strong enough to sedate a horse. Never used in Alzheimer's disease.

'I want a list of all drugs Dowling takes,' I said. 'I'll need a court order but that'll take weeks. Can one of your IT men hack into the pharmacy computer?' I scribbled the name of the chemist shop I'd seen on the prescription bottle.

'It's illegal but they'll do it.'

'Great.'

We climbed into the car. Reilly reported in to HQ and advised we were on the move again. An armed response team would shadow us.

'Richard claimed his father had a bad night. Then we couldn't use the front room because he was sleeping above it. That didn't stop him banging the door.' I was getting more annoyed as I thought this through. 'He delayed me as long as he could.'

'Why?' Reilly slowed at a checkpoint. He flashed his badge and we were waved through.

'To warn his mother.'

'They're concerned about you. You ask too many questions.'

I suddenly recalled DI Roche's comment at the security briefing. Then I'd mentioned Mary Dowling's claim that her husband had Alzheimer's disease. *She's lying.* Roche had been pretty emphatic about that. She was right.

With my eyes, I followed a stray dog that mooched its way from lamp post to lamp post. Then another thought struck me. 'Their reaction to Patrick's suicide is bizarre.'

'What do you mean?' Another corner and another squad car. Reilly tipped his fingers from the steering wheel at the officers. They tipped back.

'I've spent many hours talking with relations of suicide victims. They're always devastated.'

'What do you say to them?'

'Suicide is like a brain tornado. It's a final scream: "I won't take any more." That can leave an immense amount of pain in the people who are left behind. There are no words that can take that pain away.'

'And there's not enough pain for Patrick's final scream?'

'There's no pain. No pain at all. It's like they're relieved he's gone.'

We were driving along the Grand Canal, heading towards the east of the city. The traffic was light, most people taking advantage of the warm June sunshine to head to the seaside. Sarah had driven Jennifer and Gregory to Brittas Bay, a beachfront along the Wicklow coast. She'd also arranged friends to accompany them. I was out of the equation so everyone could relax. Sarah had refused to have armed protection. Reilly arranged protection anyway.

When the traffic idled I showed Reilly the photo I'd slipped into my pocket. I identified the faces and explained the background. I drew his attention to Richard Dowling and Niamh Shanahan.

'What's that expression suggest?'

'He has the hots for the girl.' He beeped the horn to speed up an L-driver chugging slowly at stoplights. 'And he said she's left the country?'

'Yes.'

I checked my watch. It was 3.30 p.m. 'Can we trace the Shanahans? I'd be interested to hear their side of the story.'

'Any idea where they live? Address, area code, anything?'

'Near Ranelagh,' I offered weakly.

'That's a big help.' Reilly negotiated traffic at a roundabout. A large white van was threatening to topple as it swerved. 'That only narrows it down to forty to fifty thousand people.' He found space to pull over and dialled HQ. There was a long discussion about street directories and names. The officer at the other end said he'd call back.

'Why'd you ring me earlier?' I asked.

'Something was passed on while I kicked my heels.'

'What?'

'Noel Carty was probably thrown off that balcony. Someone heard shouts before he was seen spinning through the air.'

I sucked air.

Then a thought struck me. Harry Malone was with Patrick Dowling the day before he was found dead. He'd changed his deposition under duress. And the man most likely to have forced that was Noel Carty. With Carty's death Malone might come forward and tell the truth. It wasn't a given but it was worth pursuing. I made a mental note to deal with that.

HQ finally called with a list of Shanahans based in and around the Ranelagh area. There were twelve.

Chapter 37

'You're the coroner?'

'Yes.'

'The man everyone keeps shooting at?'

I forced a smile, but at that moment I'd love to have punched Niamh Shanahan's father on the chin. We found him after ninety frustrating minutes calling on houses in and around the south Dublin suburb of Ranelagh. We met tall Shanahans, small Shanahans, tattooed and bald Shanahans. We even found a Shanahan so camp Reilly did a runner as soon as the man spoke. Finally, just after 5 p.m., we found the Shanahan we were looking for.

'Not everyone.'

'Only a select few?'

I kept my composure. 'A very select few.'

He wasn't put out. 'There's nobody dead here so what do you want?'

Declan Shanahan was a big man, muscular and fit-looking. I put him somewhere in his mid-sixties. He was in gardening clothes of open-necked checked shirt, dirty overalls and clay-covered boots. He had a weeding fork in his right hand. His bushy grey hair was matted with perspiration and he brushed a sweat-stained sleeve across his brow to stop the drips running into his eyes.

'This is a long shot and maybe you'd prefer not to get involved.'

'Get to the point.'

'It's about Patrick Dowling's inquest.'

Shanahan's features hardened. He inspected me closely, paying particular attention to my scarred forehead. He glanced over my shoulder. 'Who's he?'

'My bodyguard.'

'Does he follow you everywhere?'

'Yes.'

'Is he armed?'

Reilly cut through. 'I carry a loaded revolver and there's a sub-machine gun in the car.'

Shanahan looked up and down the road. It was a modest district, a mix of terrace and mock-Georgian houses. 'Don't let the neighbours see it.' He kicked off his boots and left them at the front door. 'I'll give you thirty minutes.' I mumbled my thanks. 'I heard about that attack on Pearse Street. Is that the third or fourth attack?'

'Third.'

'That's the life you choose, Dr . . .?'

'Wilson.' We shook hands. 'And this is Tony Reilly.'

'I can't say I'm pleased to meet either of you. But I did know Patrick. If I can help I will.'

We were ushered into a living room. There was a large sofa, two armchairs, a plasma TV stuck in a corner and a small coffee table with a few tatty magazines on it. The fireplace was a coal-effect version, now covered in dust. There were watercolour scenes on the wall. No refreshments were offered even though I was parched and would have killed for a cold beer.

Reilly and I sat on the sofa while Shanahan stretched his long legs out from one of the armchairs. There were holes in his socks and dirty toenails poked through. He darted suspicious eyes from Reilly to me and then back to Reilly. Finally he dabbed a sleeve at his brow, pulled a wristwatch from his overalls and set it pointedly on the table between us. 'Thirty minutes. After that I'm going back to the garden.'

I got straight to it. 'Tell me what you know about Patrick.'

'In what way? How he got on with his family? How he became involved in drugs? His decline to helpless and wasted addict? Where d'ye want to start?' He pointed at the watch. 'One minute up already.'

'Let's focus on what's important.'

'Shoot.'

'Why did you ask the Dowlings to leave your daughter Niamh alone?'

'I didn't.'

I bottled my surprise. 'That's what I was told.'

'Who said it?'

'Richard Dowling.'

'You're mixing with strange company. Don't believe all you hear.'

I was caught off guard. 'Help me out here.' I didn't want to have to search for clues. 'If the clock's ticking, tell me what I should know.'

Shanahan frowned. 'Niamh was emphatic we didn't speak with the Dowlings. I'd nothing to do with it.'

'I was told Niamh was close to Patrick. Why would she block communication?'

'I never got to the bottom of that myself. And I wasn't pushed to find the reason.' He wriggled his toes and dirt flaked. 'Patrick Dowling was once a decent young man. When he came here we welcomed him. He was battling addiction but we never brought that up. He was getting enough grief in his own house. After a while he stopped calling and, to be honest, we didn't invite him. Niamh fought very hard to help him. She visited every institution his father forced him into. My daughter's a great kid. She values friendship and goes that extra mile to help her pals. Patrick wasn't in her group but she got to know him through her studies. That's why she stuck with him to the end. But the end was so brutal she felt betrayed.'

'Were they romantically involved?'

Shanahan almost laughed. 'You know very little at all, don't you.'

'That's why I'm here.'

Shanahan dragged his legs in tight and hunched forward so he was closer. 'Niamh's commitment to Patrick was professional. Think of it as therapist/patient. They certainly weren't involved romantically.'

'I've seen photographs of them together.'

'So?' A bead of sweat ended its journey from forehead to the tip of Shanahan's nose. He blew it away.

'I put two and two together.'

'And came up with five.' Shanahan was fully engaged now. 'Where were the pictures taken?'

I described the beachfront scene with the white sands and tropical-green sea in the background. Then I pulled the second snap from my pocket and passed it across. 'They seem such a happy couple, delighted to be in one another's company.' Shanahan was smiling as he admired his daughter. Then he frowned as if something clicked in his head.

'Who took this photograph?'

I had a blank moment. This wasn't an angle I'd considered. I looked at Reilly for help but he was inspecting his fingernails.

'I don't know.'

'Mary Dowling used to have three sons. Now she has

two.' He pointed at the photo. 'Here all three are present. One of them used the camera and it obviously wasn't Patrick or Richard.'

I cursed silently. *Why didn't I think of that?*

'And I suspect the same brother took the holiday picture.'

'Seamus?'

'I'd say he was the photographer. His mother bought him a fancy Nikon for his eighteenth birthday and he carried it everywhere.' He studied the photo. 'My daughter seems happy because she's looking at Seamus. She's in love with him. And unless I'm an extraordinary bad judge of character, he's in love with her.'

Then his face twisted, as if he'd tasted something bitter. 'Richard Dowling's a lecherous thug who came on to Niamh. She rejected every advance. She can't stand him.'

Shanahan grinned at my stunned look. 'Am I going too fast? Or is this all new to you?'

I swallowed hard. 'I've heard snippets.'

My deceit was obvious. 'Don't insult my intelligence. You haven't a clue what's going on.' Shanahan checked the watch. 'Your thirty minutes is almost up. But we've barely touched on the first question: what do I know about Patrick Dowling? I know a helluva lot more than I suspect you do. And more than his family would like brought into the open.'

I must have looked as addled as I felt.

'How about a beer?'

Chapter 38

Shanahan's garden was picture-postcard perfect. There was a small lawn, carefully mown with barely a weed. There were flower beds with annuals at the front and evergreen shrubs at the rear. It wasn't a large plot but it had been packed for maximum effect. Yellow sunflowers competed with red and white sweet peas. Red geraniums trailed from terracotta pots. I relaxed with a glass of cold beer. Reilly sipped on lemonade like it was poison.

'Niamh is twenty-five, the same age as Seamus.' We were sitting in wicker chairs on a back patio. The rest of his family were out and it looked as if Shanahan wasn't expecting anyone to return soon. 'They met at Trinity College.'

'What were they studying?'

'Seamus attended the drama department. He was keen to pursue a career in acting.' At least that was consistent with what I'd heard earlier. 'Niamh read psychology.'

'What about Patrick?'

'He'd a degree in history and politics. He stayed on to do masters in politics. All this was driven by his father. Patrick wasn't the least bit interested in the subject. He'd dreams of being a writer but couldn't say that in front of Albert.'

Shanahan took a long draught of beer, licked his lips and sighed. 'Beautiful afternoon, isn't it?'

I mumbled agreement.

'Why couldn't he say that in front of his father?'

'Albert was grooming Patrick for a career in government. He insisted he join the local party organisation, attend meetings and do leaflet drops, door-step constituents. In Albert's mind Patrick would one day lead the country.'

'So he was forced into these studies?'

'Yes. Albert terrorised Patrick and Seamus. But he couldn't touch Richard. Not Mummy's favourite. Mary made sure Richard escaped his father's wrath.'

'He's certainly not from the Dowling side of the family.'

Shanahan crossed and uncrossed his legs. 'Richard's from his mother's connection. He's a scheming, lying, manipulative and dishonest prick.' He finished his beer and inspected the bottom of the glass. 'But he did inherit some traits from his father. He'd use brute force and intimidation to get his way.'

There was a short silence. 'You're being very helpful,' I said. 'Can I share something in confidence?'

Shanahan checked his watch. We'd been with him for nearly an hour. He pulled his chair in tight and bent his head slightly. 'Everything we say is off the record. I don't want lawsuits and I certainly don't want my daughter caught up in this. What's said here stays here. Okay?'

He insisted on a handshake. His grip made me flinch.

'Richard hadn't a kind word to say about his brother. Any idea why?'

Shanahan leaned back in his chair. 'Jealousy? Once upon a time Patrick had looks and charm and plenty of girlfriends. Richard was always ugly and boorish. And he hadn't a friend in the world. Male or female.'

Now my head was full of conflicting information. 'I don't know what to make of this. I'm getting very different versions on Patrick Dowling. What *is* the truth?'

'What truth are you looking for?' Shanahan shielded his eyes from the setting sun. 'How Patrick lived, how he got involved in drugs, how he died? What's your priority?'

'How he died,' I said.

Shanahan looked surprised. 'He killed himself. Isn't that what the autopsy showed?'

'There are uncertainties,' I said.

'Well, I don't want to hear them.'

Shanahan stood, stretched and looked around. 'Like another beer? Another soft drink?'

I said yes, Reilly said no. I could see by his expression that there was only so much lemonade he could handle.

I waited until my glass was topped up and Shanahan settled again.

'Do you know where Patrick got drugs?' I asked.

'Does the name Jonathan Redmond mean anything to you?'

I swallowed hard. 'Yes.'

'Redmond introduced Patrick into the drugs scene at Trinity. The boy was depressed. He loathed the course he was studying and couldn't handle the pressure from his father. According to Niamh, Redmond offered him cannabis to experiment with. "That'll ease your worries." Within a year Patrick had moved on to heroin.' A fat bluebottle buzzed around Shanahan's nose and he swatted at it. The bluebottle did aerobatics and returned like a kamikaze pilot for one last attack. Shanahan knocked it out of the air with the back of his hand. He grinned with the simple satisfaction of ridding one more pest from the world. 'Niamh met Patrick during his first rehab admission. She was studying addiction as part of her psychology course and interviewed him as an in-patient. She followed his progress and kept an eye on him. She also met his brothers around that time.'

'And fell in love with Seamus?'

'Not immediately. But they did date for a while, broke it off and then made up.' Shanahan offered a wry grin that told a thousand insights of a father with children of a marriageable age. 'The usual sweetheart story: making up after breaking up. Missing one another so much that they couldn't bear to be apart. That sort of thing.' He turned to me. 'Real romance, Dr Wilson. Not twisted lust like Richard Dowling might prefer.'

'I'm with you,' I said. And I was. The early months with Sarah were much the same. There were arguments over stupid issues, followed by angry and parting words. Then came tense, anxious days with both of us waiting to see would the other make the first move to patch things up. This was followed by passionate reconciliations and pledges of affection. Great, riotous afternoons in bed, pillow-fighting and making love. There was passion but also romance. And in the end there were two people who believed life was not worth living without the other.

'Would Richard Dowling have known who was supplying Patrick with drugs?'

'Absolutely. Redmond had carved out a middle-class niche of users. Even the dogs in the street knew who the main dealer was.'

'He told me he didn't know.'

'He's lying. I don't know why but he's lying. Everyone knew Redmond was pushing drugs onto Patrick.'

I filed that away. That file was close to overflowing.

'Where's Niamh?'

Shanahan said nothing.

'I know Seamus is in London,' I said.

'Seamus and Niamh are together in London. She's studying forensic psychology and he's at acting school. They've been sharing the same bed for the past few months.'

'I was told he'd only found somewhere to live this week.' I knew immediately I'd been lied to.

'Where'd you hear that?'

'Richard Dowling.'

Shanahan looked away.

The garden was catching shadows from nearby trees. Next door a barbecue was in full swing with glasses tinkling and loud guffaws. The smell of cooked sausages wafted into Shanahan's garden. My stomach rumbled and I realised I hadn't eaten since breakfast. I wondered how Sarah and the children were. I hoped they'd made up for the lost afternoon on Killiney strand.

Right then I wanted to go home and enjoy the remains of the day. I sensed Reilly was itching to flee. His soft drink lay untouched and he was shifting uneasily in his chair. Declan Shanahan, the reluctant host, was becoming more talkative, possibly loosening up with the beer. I was keen to keep him in this mood.

'Did you know about Niamh's relationship with Seamus when Patrick died?'

'Yes.'

'So how could you keep your families apart for ever?'

Shanahan considered the question. 'You need to understand the Dowlings. They're no ordinary breed.'

This was something I'd concluded early on. It was how un-ordinary they were that I wanted to learn.

'Tell me more.'

'Mary Dowling can't stand her husband. Her people can't stomach their son-in-law. They never could. Theirs was a marriage of convenience. Mary's family were builders and developers. They couldn't look at a greenfield site without seeing a factory or housing estate. She brought money to the union; Albert brought political clout and inside information. They fed off each other. Mary's side were leaked re-zoning plans. They bought significant land banks and waited. Once these changed to commercial use they sold on and made a fortune. Some of this was used to keep Albert's war chest full. He never lost his seat in an election. His wealth bought senior positions in each administration. He may not have held the top position but he was never far away.'

Shanahan grinned at my gaping mouth. 'I have this as gospel from my brother. He's a political journalist and has been following Dowling's career for years.'

I dropped the next question real casual-like. 'Do you know if Albert Dowling met up with Redmond, the man supplying Patrick's drugs?'

Shanahan didn't have to think about it. 'Nah.' He looked over. 'Do you mean did he ask Redmond to stop giving him drugs? Or checked how much Patrick owed? That sort of thing?'

I shrugged. 'Anything. I'm just wondering.'

'I doubt it. He's in government. Cabinet ministers shy away from that contact. No matter how innocent the meeting, any media leak would spell the end of a career.'

'You're right,' I said. But I was disappointed. I was hoping for scandal.

Reilly stood and stretched. He wanted away.

I finished the dregs of my beer. I thanked Shanahan for his time, patience and insights.

We shook hands. 'I was told Niamh left because of threats from a drug dealer. Patrick owed money and she was afraid of getting caught up in a revenge attack if he didn't pay up.'

Shanahan opened the front door to let us out. 'Whoever told you that is a liar.'

Chapter 39

I rang Sarah's mobile. Jennifer answered it. They'd stopped to drop off their friends and been invited in. They were having a great time, according to Jennifer. I was sad for myself but pleased everything was going well for my family. I'd learned a lot today and they hadn't lost out. Or, as I considered moodily, they'd been able to enjoy themselves *because* of my absence.

'Hi, Mike.' The phone was finally handed to Sarah.

'How're things?'

'Great. We'd a wonderful time. There wasn't a cloud in the sky and the water was warm. None of the blue lips and chattering teeth we usually get with a seaside picnic.'

'What's happening now?'

'We're with Jennifer's friend. Her mum asked us to stay for supper. I'm grabbing the offer.'

'That's a good idea,' I said. 'You deserve a break.'

'What are you planning?'

'Nothing much,' I said. 'I'll get a take-away, put my feet up and relax.'

'Are you sure?'

'Absolutely. It'll give me time to check paperwork. I'll see you later.'

'Well, if you're okay with that.'

'I am. Talk later. Tell the kids I said hello. Love you.'

The phone went dead. Sarah didn't say she loved me. That left me brooding.

Reilly's shift ended and a different detective drove me home. He looked like a rugby prop forward with broad shoulders, squashed nose and cauliflower ears. He smiled once and all I could see were false teeth. I was too tired to recommend a good dentist. The journey home was in silence. We were shadowed by an armed response team.

I told the prop forward to stop at an Indian take-away. I ordered spicy fish cakes, chicken korma with yoghurt, cashew nuts, almonds and cream. Then basmati rice, poppadoms, aubergines, tomatoes and mango chutney. A feast fit for a king – or a starving coroner. I grabbed a bottle of Chablis from an off-licence.

I sat in the back garden, stuffing myself and drinking too much. I dropped sauce on my shirt, a chicken wing on my trousers and poppadoms on the flower bed. On top of an empty stomach and after four beers I was soon drowsy. An hour later and there was very little wine left. I wandered unsteadily, glass in hand and listening to the evening. Boisterous laughter two doors up. The occasional shout of a child and bark of a dog. Birds chirping. Now a different child crying and complaining about a sore knee. I smiled, relieved I was past that stage with Jennifer and Gregory.

Overhead a flock of swallows zigzagged. I slumped into a garden chair and began to doze. I went indoors in case I fell asleep.

I watched television. The main news bulletin related to Albert Dowling's retirement on health grounds. There were clips of his parliamentary career. One captured the young Dowling grinning after his first election victory. Then a later, more cynical and grey-haired government minister smirking after a poll-topping result. There were replays of Dowling opening hospitals, cutting the ribbon on a new road development, laying the foundation stone on a social-housing project. A recent piece showed him as Minister for Economic Development hosting a forum on job creation. There was a clutch of financial officials in the audience. I recognised Dan Thornton, CEO of Standard and Chartered Bank. He seemed engrossed, hanging off Dowling's every word. The rest of the bulletin related to unemployment, emigration and the falling value of the euro.

There was no mention of my withdrawal from office. That hadn't been released to the media yet. Then the weatherman warned the hot spell would end as a cold front reached the east coast. There was a risk of thunderstorms.

I fell asleep.

I woke with a crick in my neck. It was 10 p.m. and dark. There was no sign of Sarah, Jennifer or Gregory. I thought of ringing to make sure they were okay but dismissed the notion. If anything happened it wouldn't be me looking for them. It would be some detective pounding my door with the news.

I flicked on the lights and staggered to the toilet. I had to grip the wash-hand basin while I had a pee. I was drunk and couldn't give a damn. My mouth was dry and my head was spinning. I could still taste chicken korma. I grinned at myself in the mirror: there was stubble on my beardline; sauce smeared my upper lip. My eyes were bloodshot; my hair was a mess. The gaunt features still held, though not as haunted-looking. The bullet track was healing.

The phone rang but I ignored it. I wasn't sober enough to talk to anyone. It rang out. I made my way upstairs, one careful step at a time; afraid I'd fall and break my neck. I reached the first floor when the phone rang again. I cursed it and ignored it. I lurched around the bed, shedding clothes left, right and centre. Trousers ended up on the laundry basket, my shirt drifted into a corner. Boxers and socks were used to score in an imaginary basketball net. I groped to the shower and turned the water ice cold. Shivering and dripping wet, I dragged a towel around my waist and collapsed onto the bed.

The phone rang for a third time. Surprisingly there was a handset close by, not in Jennifer's room as usual. I stared at it. This time it didn't stop. I was so annoyed I snatched the receiver.

'Yes?' It was a very curt yes.

'Dr Wilson?'

'Yes.'

'This is Jonathan Redmond. I believe you know me.'

I grabbed the side of the bed to steady myself. I panicked, unsure what to say. Could this be a prankster? But the voice was exactly as Sarah had described: *'an educated south Dublin accent'*.

'Why are you ringing me?'

'To warn you. Stop interfering in things that don't concern you.'

'Why?' He obviously hadn't heard of my resignation.

'Because this will be over soon.'

'What'll be over?'

'My business dealings. Then I'll be so far away you need never fear me again.'

'Do you expect me to believe that?'

'I don't care whether you believe or not. I'm merely offering you advice.'

He did sound, as Roche had said, 'a class act'. Calm, controlled and confident.

'Stay away from my affairs.' Now the tone changed. The menace was unmistakable.

'And if I don't?'

There was silence. Redmond was still there. I could hear him breathing. I could almost smell him.

'You won't get away with it. The next time, I will personally kill you.'

I counted to twenty. My mind was a chaos of sounds and images. Gunfire and screams. Jennifer and Gregory clinging to their mother for reassurance after the first attack. Their eyes wide with terror.

'No you won't.' Even though the room was warm I was shivering. I forced my teeth from chattering. 'I've dealt with bigger thugs than you.'

'You're drunk.' The oily drawl was fading.

I ignored the jibe. 'No one tells me how to do my job. Especially not some jumped-up drug dealer.' I surprised myself with this bluster. 'And I know what you did with Patrick Dowling. Someone was in the woods that day. Someone saw everything.' Now was the time to press my advantage. 'And I've the testimony on record.' This was a lie but I had to sow the seeds of doubt in his mind. 'He's still hiding there, just waiting for me to give the word to bring him to safety. So don't bother looking for me, watch your own back.'

'You're a fucking liar.' The snarl was as vicious as a snake bite.

I don't know why I said what I did but the words spilled out before I could stop them. 'Your university education didn't put manners on you, did it?' Then I hung up.

Now I was gasping so much I hardly knew how to

breathe. I slumped to the floor, physically drained. Downstairs I heard the front door open and the noises of Sarah, Jennifer and Gregory in the hallway.

I shouted a quick hello and dragged myself into shape. Then I called Reilly. I knew within minutes the house would be surrounded by a rapid reaction force.

'Hi Mike,' Sarah was in the room. 'This place smells like a brewery. What've you been up to?'

'Nothing.' I burrowed my face into the pillows.

Chapter 40

The weather changed overnight. It started with great plops of rain on the corridor skylight. Soft thumps, like clay, hit the glass. The tempo slowly increased. *Plop, thump, plop, thump, plop, plop, plop, thump, thump, thump, ploppppppppppppppppp.* Soon the skylight was taking the brunt of a downpour.

I lay beside Sarah, awake and watchful. Her soft breathing told me she was asleep, undisturbed by the racket. I prayed no harm would come to her because of my drunken recklessness. I kissed her lightly on the cheek. She didn't stir. The day at the beach had exhausted her.

There was a rumble of thunder in the distance. Seconds later the skies to the west glowed from a bolt of lightning. Then darkness returned. I wrapped myself in a dressing gown and went downstairs. I sat in the shadows of the living room and tracked the storm.

Stair-rod rain drilled against the roof. Beneath the glimmer of street lights I watched the garden foliage droop. Sarah's rose bed was taking a battering. In bare feet I padded the ground floor, checking for suspicious movement. Outside my shadowy protectors were in place. There was a police car in the road with two occupants. Another armed detective stood at the back door, stomping his feet to keep his circulation flowing. He'd squeezed into a recess for cover. Two other officers patrolled the grounds. They wore long coats that glistened in the rain. I wanted to let them shelter in the house but couldn't risk it. If Sarah or the children heard voices and came down to find armed policemen they'd freak out.

I followed the thunderstorm as it passed over the east coast. Then it vented its anger in the Irish Sea. I watched as electrical bursts sparked in its wake. I thought about all that had happened recently and how much my life had changed. And how much more it could change if things went wrong. One slip by my bodyguards and Redmond could be in. One misjudgement or incorrect call on security and I'd be taken out by a bomb or bullet.

I watched until early morning stretched and yawned its way from the horizon. The rain continued. There was a constant gurgle down drain pipes. Small pools were forming in the garden.

How was Hobbs faring in these conditions? I tried to imagine him secure in his watertight hut, rain hopping off the canvas roof, wrapped up in a sleeping bag and lying on his camper bed. The claps of thunder rumbling through the trees, lightning flashes as intense as phosphorous flares. What a place to hide out in. How scary. How spooky. How dangerous.

I was still sitting in the living room at 4.30 a.m. Staring as shade gave way to glimmer and glimmer gave way to light. Between five and six thirty the cloud cover lifted and a weak sun broke through. Puddles rippled in a gentle breeze. The garden shook itself alive and shrubs wobbled away raindrops.

At 7 a.m. the overnight crew left and another unit took over. Now a different set of uniforms patrolled the area. I was surrounded by a small army and wondered how the Irish state's fragile economy could afford such security. And I hoped the judge living opposite wasn't regretting the offer of his front room. He might think a permanent presence was becoming established.

Redmond's final snarl still echoed. At the beginning he'd sounded rational and in control. But there was no mistaking his threat at the end. He'd kill me if I kept interfering in his affairs. But what exactly were his affairs?

And in my drunken rage I'd exposed Hobbs to danger. I'd told Redmond someone was in the woods the day Patrick Dowling died. I'd said he was still hiding there: *'just waiting for me to give the word to bring him to safety'*. The drug baron might go looking.

At seven thirty I showered and dressed. I checked Jennifer and Gregory were asleep. I kissed Sarah's forehead. She was snoring softly. Then I rang Reilly. 'We have to find Hobbs.' I filled him in on the telephone call. 'He's in danger.'

Chapter 41

As I waited for Reilly, I worried. Redmond had rung me nine hours earlier. He was an intelligent man. He'd had ample time to figure out if I was lying. Nine hours to decide there might've been someone else there on the day Patrick Dowling died. Nine hours to discover Dowling's friends and occasional companions. Nine hours to learn about Hobbs, and to know Hobbs had abandoned his usual city haunts. And that he might indeed still be in those woods. By now he'd had three hours of morning light to search. Hobbs's hideaway was deep inside the forest. Maybe Redmond wouldn't find it? I knew he'd search until he was sure.

And his assassins wouldn't come on high-powered motorbikes. There'd be no engine roar to warn they were closing in. If Hobbs was asleep he wouldn't hear Redmond and his henchmen trek through the trees and undergrowth. With the thunderstorm and rain, Hobbs wouldn't know what was coming until the first shot was fired.

Then I worried how Redmond had my updated landline number. It'd been changed after his call was fielded by Sarah: *'say hello to Coroner Wilson'*. Few in the police knew the new number. But everyone in my office did. He'd got it from the spy in the coroner's court.

At 8.30 a.m. Roche and Reilly arrived together. Reilly

was grim-faced, Roche showing barely controlled anger. And why wouldn't she be in a foul temper? I'd screwed up. Why'd I let slip Hobbs was still in the woods, waiting my call? Answer: drunken bravado. John Hobbs, my star witness if I got him into court, had been exposed. I'd practically issued a search and destroy order on him.

Reilly and Roche were well prepared. They both carried handguns, stun guns and Uzi sub-machine guns. They were in wet gear over bullet-proof vests and wearing rubber boots. Roche's features were disguised with black-out camouflage. It hid her cute face. It didn't hide her rage. We avoided eye contact.

I'd already prepared for the journey. I wore a rain jacket over jeans, sweater and security vest. Thick hiking boots chafed my ankles. I carried my work outfit in a black plastic sack. I dumped it in the boot of the unmarked police car.

'It's time to end this.' Roche was edgy. We were moving into dangerous territory. She sat in the back seat with me, her petite frame allowing me ample room.

She passed over the Glock I'd returned after my disastrous beach day, plus a shoulder holster. I slipped it over my head. It fitted neatly under my left arm. I stuck a spare magazine clip into a side pocket.

'Reilly told me about Hobbs and the missing file.' She was staring straight ahead.

I said nothing.

'If Hobbs is alive, this time we take him with us.'

Outside banks of dark grey clouds swirled, collecting for a further downpour. Traffic was heavy as rush hour closed in. I prayed silently. *Don't let there be delays. Don't let Redmond have got there first.*

'Dan Thornton struck a deal with prosecutors,' said Roche. 'He'll go state witness in return for an amnesty from criminal charges.' Thornton was CEO of Standard and Chartered Bank, the financial institution linked to Redmond. The same bank Timothy Cunningham worked in before his sudden death.

'He knows he's facing a long gaol stretch. He wants to cut and run.' A heavy shower suddenly drilled against the windscreen.

'What's he offering?'

'He'll testify on financial irregularity, money laundering, illegal share trading and false accounting.'

The car stopped. We were caught in a tailback. Roche shifted uneasily. There was subdued muttering and cursing. Visibility was now so poor I couldn't decide how far we'd progressed. Then I recognised a petrol station and realised we were still in the outer suburbs. By now we should have been on the R117 to Enniskerry. If we snail-paced like this it would take an hour for what should have been a twenty-minute trip. Reilly slapped the steering wheel in frustration. I chewed the side of my cheek. A taxi cab had skidded off the road and a rescue truck blocked part of our lane. Finally we managed to edge past. I checked the time: it was close to 9 a.m. Redmond could've been and gone, Hobbs could be dead and any hopes I had of finding the truth behind Patrick Dowling's death would've died with him. I glanced out the window. Groups huddled in bus shelters trying to avoid wheel splash. Umbrellas were tossed in the wind. People were hurrying for cover, heads down and collars gripped at the throat. I rang the coroner's court to advise I'd be late. The first inquest was due to start at 3 p.m. I told Joan I wanted to speak with the staff before they left the office. I planned to brief them on my resignation before the media got hold of the story.

Now the rain was in torrents. It was almost impossible

to see through the deluge. Reilly was in third gear, hunched forward and squinting past the wipers. *Swish, swish, swish.* The windscreen was streaked with water marks. We made Aikens Village and the R117 at 9.30 a.m. We should've been less than ten minutes from the forest, but every corner was a skating rink. A horse box behind a Range Rover skidded across our path, forcing Reilly to mount the grass verge. The air was blue from swearing.

'Is there anything we can use immediately?' I engaged Roche to distract myself. *Come on, come on.* It was 9.45 a.m. and we'd barely moved half a mile.

'Redmond's money trail has been disclosed to authorities in Jersey and Spain. His accounts have been frozen for thirty days. He can't touch a red cent. But we have to prove criminal activity. If we don't, the accounts are released and he's free to move the money.'

I was thirsty from last night's booze. I licked my lips for moisture. The chicken korma was repeating.

Roche passed over a sheet of paper. 'You asked for this.' It was a print-out of Albert Dowling's medication, hacked from pharmacy records. I scanned it quickly, then stuffed it into my pocket. My heart raced. I was getting closer to the truth. I could almost feel Patrick Dowling's ghost beside me, urging me on.

Reilly's mobile rang and Roche answered it. She explained who she was and lied why Reilly couldn't take the call. There was an intense conversation. The mobile was snapped shut. Then she turned to me. 'Timothy Cunningham's brother will meet you at your office at one o'clock. He wants to know exactly what's going on. He says he's proof of perjury at that inquest.'

The net was tightening. Whatever Redmond was doing at Cunningham's inquest might become clear.

The rain began to ease and at last we could see the

road clearly. We were stuck behind a tractor on a narrow stretch and couldn't overtake. I pressed the side window open and looked out. A mile ahead was the woodland. I could see the treetops. Then I spotted a field and rusted gates. I recognised the terrain.

'It's about a hundred yards from here.' I was sitting forward, neck craned to see. I tried to moisten my lips with a flick of my tongue. But my mouth was too dry from last night's booze and today's jumpy nerves. The tractor pulled onto a side track.

'Fuck.' Reilly saw the Subaru 4x4 first. It was parked in a narrow lay-by, no more than fifty yards from the start of the forest trail. We cruised behind it and stopped. Reilly called in the number plates. Roche stepped onto the road and looked up and down. There was a steady drizzle. A car sped past, throwing up mud. Roche squinted inside the Subaru. Then Reilly heard from HQ. The plates were false. And Roche noticed the butt of a revolver underneath the passenger seat. She called for backup.

'We may be too late.' Her face was misty damp. She looked anxious.

'We're going in anyway,' I said.

We checked our handguns. Reilly held his Uzi slung around his waist. Roche held hers with the barrel pointing forward. Stun guns were jammed beneath waist bands.

It was decision time. If we saw Redmond would we try to apprehend him? Or would Roche's Uzi go off 'by mistake' and end the thug's life before a word was exchanged?

Or was Redmond waiting for us?

Chapter 42

The trail had been used this morning. Four days earlier it was dusty and dry. Now it was muddy. The leaden skies offered little light but the footprints were still visible. They looked no more than an hour old. The steady drizzle was making them indistinct. Roche examined them, crouching down beside them like an Aboriginal tracker. She crab-stepped backwards and forwards, checking every boot mark. Then she studied the route ahead. The woodland was dense, rain dripping from leaves. A background trickle of a rivulet had been opened up by the downpour. A crow suddenly flew out from the undergrowth, scaring the hell out of us.

I glanced at Reilly. His face was streaked from rain. His wet gear dripped, his boots were muddy. He gripped his Uzi tightly. Our eyes met. He looked worried. I was scared stiff. Whoever walked this way were not hikers. They were killers. And they'd not returned to their 4x4. We would confront them. We might have surprise on our side, but if they saw us first they'd have the advantage. We'd be like target practice, ducks in a fairground shooting range.

Distant foliage rustled. Roche froze. She motioned with her Uzi to get down. We squatted. Reilly shook his straggly crew cut free from damp. A fox padded out from behind a clump of ivy, snuffling the earth. It stopped and stared. It padded backwards, dark eyes never leaving us. It stopped again. It kept staring. None of us moved. My left leg cramped and I shifted the pressure on to the other. The fox nuzzled its snout into the scrub and worked at something. Seconds later it surfaced with a rabbit between its jaws. The rabbit wasn't dead but its final wriggles were weak. The fox shuffled past, checking on us out of the corner of its eye. When it reached a safe distance it hurried into the safety of the woods.

We agreed strategy.

'Keep in contact by mobile,' Roche whispered. 'Put it on vibrate and use only if necessary.' She pointed to the footprints. 'Three sets.' My gut knotted. Hobbs wouldn't stand a chance. 'You know this area,' she was looking at me. 'Where's the hut?'

I looked at Reilly and he looked along the trail. Then he looked back at me. We both squinted into the darkness for a landmark. The forest looked back, inviting us in. Branches sagged from the overnight storm, cobwebs necklaced between twigs. Droplets trembled in their mesh.

I tried to remember the number of paces we'd counted from Hobbs's hideaway to where Patrick Dowling had been found hanging.

'It's further along.' We trekked another tense twenty yards. Each stride was slow and deliberate. Every yard gained brought us closer to the enemy. Roche took up the rear to make sure we weren't being followed. Then Reilly pointed. I stood on my tiptoes. There was fresh undergrowth, more moss and dripping foliage. But there was also the tree with forked branch and snapped bough with toothpick-like stump. We'd reached the clearing.

'Fifty yards from here.'

Now Reilly led the way. I was in the middle, Roche

behind me. I gripped the Glock in my right hand. I patted my side pocket. The spare magazine clip was secure. My face was wet from rain and my clothes dripped. My collar was damp. My bullet-proof vest was making me sweat. Every step was an effort as muck sucked at the soles of my boots. Abruptly the tracks disappeared. 'They went in here,' Roche mouthed. Her camouflage was running like wet mascara. We listened. The only sound was dripping rainwater, cooing wood pigeons and the thumping of my heart. Like a drum pounded by a madman.

Reilly urged us into the trees.

I moved through the shadows and tripped over a wet branch. I fell on my gun hand and sprained the wrist. I nursed it against my chest, silently swearing. I didn't move until the throbbing eased. The deeper I went, the darker it became. The darker it became, the heavier the raindrops. The woodland was a dripping, trickling and rustling terror zone. Roche gestured to the right. Reilly signalled he was edging to the left. I stayed in the middle. Wet cobwebs draped themselves across my raincoat. I heard Roche's boots snapping sticks underfoot. I stopped. I was sweating. My insides were churning. Two more paces and I stopped again. A white butterfly floated by. I looked left and right, forwards and backwards. I saw Reilly, his Uzi at shoulder level. Roche's tiny frame ghosted between trees.

I was startled by an angry shout. Then gunfire. A salvo from a semi-automatic weapon. Crows cawed and flapped skywards twenty yards ahead. Their surprised squawks continued for more than a minute. Then silence.

I stood still. My eyes searched the glade. Trees dripping, drooping branches, wet undergrowth. Scurrying animals. I looked up and saw a grey squirrel jump from branch to branch, as if trying to escape the mayhem below.

I was too frightened to move. Someone with significant firepower was no more than twenty yards away. I desperately tried to get my bearings. But every corner looked the same. I thought I was close to Hobbs's hideaway but couldn't be certain. Then a bough cracked and I saw Reilly ease forward. I darted a glance to the right. No sign of Roche. Suddenly the wood filled with automatic fire. Instinctively I dropped to the ground. I stared at the greenery around me. Moss and fern, spruce shoots, laurel leaves. Beetles crawled over my boots. My breathing came in short rasps. My mouth was so dry I licked rainwater off wet shrubbery.

Then came more angry shouts, the voice I'd heard a minute ago. I couldn't make out the words. I risked a glance forward. Nothing.

I felt for my mobile but it was too deep in my pocket and my fingers were shaking. I couldn't grip it. I tried twice and twice it slipped away.

I started crawling forward over moss-covered branches and along wet ferns and ivy. I squirmed as far as the next tree and waited. I lay on my back and looked up. A beech tree splattered raindrops onto my face. I flicked my tongue to catch the trickle. There was a gentle hum from the wind. It made branches creak. It made me nervous as hell. A shaft of light threw shadows. I listened. There was more crunching of boots. I eased to kneeling position and looked around. There was no sign of Reilly or Roche. *Jesus, what am I doing here? This is madness.* Then my mobile vibrated. I fumbled until I got it. It was Reilly. 'I can see one of them. He's got a handgun.'

The call went dead. One with a handgun and another with a semi-automatic. Where was the third? I crawled on hands and knees towards the next tree. Every yard gained was like a mountain climbed. I was sweating heavily and my ears buzzed from the adrenalin rush. I put one hand in front of the other, and then dragged my knees to support. I kept my head down. I reached the next tree. I rested against it. I was panting. I wanted to be anywhere but here. Then I heard mumblings. I held my breath until my body screamed. I exhaled in slow, short gasps. The mumblings became murmurs. There was movement, twigs crunched underfoot. They were coming closer. I gripped my Glock and prepared. I'd let one go past and wait for the second. When I had two in my sights, I'd shoot. I fiddled with my mobile, trying to warn the others. My fingers were too shaky from fear, my hands too wet from sweat and rain. I drew my knees in tight. The steps came nearer. The murmuring was indistinct but more audible. Then a shape appeared. I looked up. There was a tall man in a soaked grey track-suit carrying a semi-automatic. He swung it in an arc from his hip. He was around six feet, lean and tanned. His hair was stylishly long. I could just about see his eyes. They were suspicious and anxious. My heart stopped. My breathing stopped. My limbs lost all strength. Jonathan Redmond was standing over me. The man who'd tried to have me killed, who'd attacked my wife and children and left them stunned and racked with fear. The gangster who'd warned me off interfering in his affairs. If he looked down he'd see me and finish me off with one press of a trigger. But he didn't look down. I held the Glock in my right hand and pointed it straight at him. My wrist ached and I had to support it at the elbow. Instinct screamed *kill him*. Wisdom cautioned patience. If he turned I'd shoot and run like hell. His side-kick wouldn't know what was happening until it was too late. Redmond murmured something. There was a whispered response. Then he backed away. I heard him move. *Crunch, shuffle, spit, murmur, crunch, shuffle, spit.* I waited five minutes by my watch. I looked. There was no one. I realised my heart hadn't stopped beating. It was like an express train. And my lungs were still working even though they seemed desperately short of oxygen.

My limbs regained strength and I crawled towards the next tree. I wanted a different lookout position. I kept crawling; head down, careful to take short, quick breaths. I crawled like this for maybe three minutes when my fingers dug into something wet and sticky and warm. I stopped, frightened to move. I knew this sensation. I'd felt it before. I sniffed. I'd smelled it before. It was fresh blood. I didn't want to look but had to. In front of me was a body. I swore viciously and silently. They'd got Hobbs. I waited. I listened. I dared not look up. I waited. Then I inched forward. The body was lying face down. I lifted the lifeless head in both hands and turned it towards me. My gut twisted in a knot so tight I almost cried out. In my sweating, shaking and bloodstained hands was the head of the man who'd sat in the court during Patrick Dowling's inquest. The man wearing the stolen press pass. I looked closer. There was a six-inch gash in his throat. A cut so deep the tendons and muscle and blood vessels were exposed. I almost admired the wound. It was neat, deep and fatal. Done by a professional. I rested the head back on the ground. I risked looking up. Nothing. I scanned the forest. Redmond had gone. I couldn't see Reilly or Roche. I could hear the noises of the woods. Rain dropping from above, trees moaning in the wind, the occasional crash as a branch snapped. I sniffed. There was the soft smell of earth and untouched greenery. Natural smells. I sniffed again. Something else flared my nostrils. Something out of place. Something that was not of this woodland. My heart skipped so many beats I was dizzy. I felt a rustle behind and started to turn. A rough hand grabbed me by the hair and snapped my head backwards. I felt cold steel against my throat.

'Don' fuckin' move or yer dead.' John Hobbs had me.

I started to croak my name but the knife cut into my skin. It made me wince. Hobbs grabbed my hair so viciously it tore at the roots. 'Don' move.' I felt the heat off his breath.

Suddenly the woods filled with gunfire. Two short bursts from an Uzi. Three rapid rounds from a handgun. Roars, gurgling and moans. I heard Reilly shout. I heard Roche answer. There was another deafening salvo.

Chapter 43

The forest buzzed with armed police. Sniffer dogs howled and barked. White-suited forensics cordoned off the scene. There were two bodies. Both unidentified but I knew all about them. When Reilly dragged the balaclava off one, there was the Bongos bomber. There was no mistaking the thick scar running from left ear to neck. Nor the blond highlights and big ears with studs. This was the same man who shot up my house less than forty-eight hours later. The other was the bogus crime correspondent at the inquest. Was Redmond's gang being taken apart, one by one?

Hobbs had been up all night, struggling to stop rain seeping through a tear in his canvas hideaway. He hadn't slept properly for days. He'd read of the attack on me. He worried someone would come looking for him. Anyone associated with Patrick Dowling was now fair game. So he created an early-warning system.

'I strung fishin' line from wan tree till another. They linked up. Anythin' higher than a deer broke it. If wan gave it loosened the next, all the way till the hut. I'd empty bottles tied together and hangin' off the twine. When they crashed I knew somewan was comin'.' Hobbs sucked on a cigarette. He was agitated and wound-up. His hands were shaking, his nicotine-stained fingers struggling to hold the butt. His hair was bedraggled, his beard thicker and longer. He'd abandoned his long coat. This was a relief; he stank enough without it. 'Hikers and runners use the trail. Nobody fuckin' uses the woods.'

When the gang turned up he was ready. He heard them stomp and stumble, trip and fall, curse and swear. He told how he sneaked through the gloom, singling out the bogus reporter when he became separated. 'He was an easy target.'

He slit the man's throat with a Bowie knife.

When the others realised what'd happened all hell broke loose. They shot anything that moved. They shot at shadows. They shot into the air and onto the ground. They found Hobbs's shelter and destroyed it. They tried to burn it but it was too wet. Frustrated and angry they scoured the forest. They walked into Reilly and Roche. The Bongos bomber tried to shoot his way to freedom. He didn't make it.

But Redmond got away. He was last seen dodging and weaving between trees towards the foothills. He'd enough ammunition to return fire. He disappeared along a wet ditch leading to dense undergrowth. Roche knew not to risk going after him. She called for support. A helicopter was already scouring the area.

We bundled Hobbs down the muddy path to the car. 'We're taking you somewhere safe.' I forced him into the rear seat. 'You've gotta tell us all you know.' I was excited and jittery. I had a sense of finality. 'You told us to find out why Patrick Dowling ended up in these woods, then you'd fill in the missing links.' I didn't admit my drunken rambling had blown his cover.

Hobbs eyed me warily. 'And yiz know everythin'?'

'Pretty much.' This wasn't true but I hoped it was enough.

'Pretty much means fuck all.'

So I told him about my visit to the Dowling house. The lies I'd heard from Richard Dowling. Declan Shanahan's version. I told him how Standard and Chartered Bank was involved in criminal activity and somehow Patrick Dowling knew something or heard something that wasn't meant for his ears. I named Redmond as the mastermind.

Hobbs slumped into his seat and stared into the distance. He chomped his gums. He scratched. He picked lice from his hair. I didn't give a damn. He was alive.

'You said this is all about money.' I tried to spark a response. 'You were right.'

But Hobbs stayed silent.

Reilly drove at some pace towards Dublin. Roche was making and taking calls. The car was charged with tension. We were coming to the end of an explosively dangerous journey.

We crossed the M50 ring road and made the outer suburbs by 11.30 a.m. Reilly broke three sets of stoplights. The overnight rain had left the roads wet and traffic sluggish. A weak summer sun struggled through grey clouds.

'Did yiz get Redmond?' Hobbs finally spoke. My heart quickened. Now we might finally hear something.

'He escaped.' Roche finished a call. 'He's being hunted like an animal. Every ferry port, airport and border crossing knows of him. He'll be picked up. He can't hide for ever.'

'If he's outta the way I'll tell yiz everythin'.'

I didn't react. But I prayed Hobbs wouldn't renege.

We took diversions along side roads I'd never seen before. I saw buildings that I didn't know existed.

Roche went back to her mobile. Hobbs began to nod

off. The lack of sleep, poor diet and this morning's uproar had exhausted him.

I made a call. Dr Stan Rowe was a senior physician at University Hospital, where I'd worked before being head-hunted to the coroner's court.

'I need a secure room.' I outlined the situation, playing down the drama.

Rowe gave me all the time I needed.

'I've a witness for an inquest. He's been living rough for months. I need him scrubbed up and made presentable.'

'No problem.'

'I also want liver function tests, urea and electrolytes and full blood count. I'd like an abdominal ultrasound, ECG, chest X-ray and CT scan of his brain. I need a detailed cognitive assessment.'

'Why?'

'His evidence is vital. I need to know he's of sound mind. I have to be sure he's got enough self-control to appear in court.'

'Anything else?'

'Give him I/V nutrition with multivitamins. Feed him up. Push fluids. Treat any infection aggressively. Gimme all the help you can. He's my ace card.'

There was a short pause. 'Is he dangerous? Could he be violent towards the staff?'

I looked at Hobbs. He was lying with his head resting on Roche's shoulder. Her rain gear was still wet and dripping and the car was beginning to steam up. Roche was arguing with someone at HQ, oblivious to the situation. And smell. Hobbs looked worn out and pathetic. He mumbled in his sleep, limbs jerking as he fought off some imaginary foe. There'd been too much excitement in his fragile life recently. He'd enjoyed months of solitude before County Coroner Rafferty appeared on the scene. Then Reilly and I confronted him. Today three men wanted to kill him. His world had been turned upside down. I decided he wouldn't cause trouble.

'No.'

'Then it's do-able.'

We were approaching Trinity College from Dame Street. Huddled around the entrance was a buzz of students and summer visitors. We turned into Westmoreland Street and used the car's siren to force our way through the traffic.

'I need the results this evening. I'll call in later.'

'Are we at risk of outsiders looking for him?' Rowe's tone changed. 'I'm not talking about those bearing grapes and flowers.'

'His identity must be kept secret.'

'This is University Hospital, Mike. There are no secrets here.'

'I only need the room for a day or two.'

'I'll put him in an isolation unit.'

We cut sharp right from O'Connell Street, causing a bus to swerve. I could see the frightened face of the driver as he dragged on the steering wheel. Then he was no more than a dot in the rear-view mirror. Minutes later we pulled up at the coroner's court on Store Street. I grabbed the black plastic bag holding my work gear and slipped in through a side entrance. I showered in the bathroom off my office. I checked I looked presentable and decided I was good to go. I spoke with Joan and asked for the staff to meet me in the front office after the last inquest.

'There's a man called Lorcan Cunningham here to see you,' she said. She appeared edgy. 'He says it's important.

Something about it being agreed earlier this morning by phone.'

This had to be Timothy Cunningham's brother.

'Tell him to wait in my room. And could I get sandwiches and coffee?'

Joan scribbled a note and hurried away. She stumbled on the saddle board at the door. That was strange. She'd been in and out of my room many times and never once tripped. What the hell was bugging her?

I called Sarah and outlined what'd happened. She listened without interrupting.

'Every radio station is carrying the story,' she said at the end. 'Everyone knows Redmond is on the run. Thank God this is finally coming to an end.'

Chapter 44

Lorcan Cunningham's head was as smooth as a billiard ball. He'd a long, angular face at odds with his small squat body, and side locks that connected with a short goatee beard. He was in a blue striped shirt, casual jacket and too-tight trousers that barely contained his waistline. I put him in his early forties. He sat opposite me in the room of sighs. 'You're going through a rough time,' he said. His voice was a grating whine.

'I've known better days,' I said.

Then he got straight to the point. 'Why'd the police call me?'

'I wanted to speak with you.'

'About what?'

'I've concerns about your late brother's inquest.'

Now anger broke through. 'Did you make a mistake? You decided Tim committed suicide. You weren't interested in any other verdict. What's changed your mind?'

'I'm not getting into an argument,' I came back firmly. 'This is information-sharing.'

He eyed me suspiciously. 'What information?'

That's when I started gambling. And even though I didn't know it then I'd gamble the rest of the day.

'I'm offering you background knowledge. In return I want you to tell me what you know.'

Cunningham shifted in his seat to make himself

comfortable. He stroked his beard, waiting for me to elaborate.

There was a knock on the door and Joan brought in a tray of sandwiches and mugs of coffee. I was starving. I offered Cunningham coffee but he declined. He wasn't interested in a cheese-and-ham delight either. Great. I'd a belly screaming to be filled.

Reilly had abandoned me when we reached the court buildings. He sped off with Hobbs to University Hospital. I prayed Dr Stan Rowe would make him presentable, and give him back to me in a fit state. DI Roche had grabbed a lift from a passing patrol car and headed to HQ. From there she would direct the search for Redmond.

'What've you got?' Cunningham pressed.

I wondered how to reply. The uncertainties were based on the missing dossier. Plus Redmond's presence at the inquest. But I'd nothing solid to offer. Cunningham said he'd been doing his own detective work. He believed someone had committed perjury. How would I prise that from him?

I played my only card. I pushed a photo of Jonathan Redmond across the table. 'Do you know that man?'

Cunningham studied the picture. 'No.' Emphatic, unambiguous. No 'maybe's or 'if's or 'it's possible's.

'But do you recognise him?'

'Yes. He was in the gallery during Tim's inquest. I assumed he was someone from the insurance company. They're dragging their heels paying out on Tim's life policy.'

If only it was that simple. I told Cunningham about Redmond. How he was behind the current murder campaign directed at me. I offered snippets about his involvement in the narcotics trade. Finally I hinted at his links with Standard and Chartered, the bank his brother worked in up to his death.

Cunningham listened closely. He stroked his beard, scratched his chin and rubbed at his eyes. His eyes darted as each revelation was absorbed. By the end there was less aggression and more brooding.

'Why would he sit in on your brother's inquest?'

Cunningham said nothing. The disclosure about Redmond had thrown him.

A thought crossed my mind and I asked Arthur O'Leary to come in. O'Leary was in charge of jury selection but helped out with office work during slack moments. He was tall and seriously overweight with marked nasal tone and poor eyesight.

He stuck his big head around the door. 'Yes?'

'Would you get this file from the basement?' I passed him the ID. I watched O'Leary for any reaction. He peered at the number through his thick-lens glasses, squinting at it twice to be sure. 'Okay,' he said as he left. There wasn't a hint of uncertainty.

I hadn't had time to follow staff behaviour. I knew there were on-going background checks. So far nothing had surfaced. Then I recalled how strange Joan had been earlier. Avoiding eye contact, tripping over a saddle board. This while Cunningham waited for me. She must have known who he was and why he was here. Had his presence unnerved her? Was she the mole? Was that how Redmond learned my new landline number? As my PA, Joan was notified of all changes. Now I'd more issues to contend with. It was almost impossible to focus on one.

'Give me a minute while your brother's file is brought up.' I started into a second sandwich and toyed with the rest to see which wouldn't give me indigestion. There was fruit and yoghurt. I'd keep that to the end. 'Tell me what you know,' I mumbled through bread crumbs.

Cunningham leaned forward and rested his elbows on

the desk. He held my gaze. 'When Tim died the police decided he'd committed suicide. They weren't interested in other possibilities. I told them about his phobia of water and pleaded with them to re-think. They dismissed that as nonsense. But it wasn't nonsense, it was true.' The whine was grating on me even more.

He reminded me of his brother's childhood accident when he'd nearly drowned. That had precipitated his fear.

'I told them my family weren't happy and we'd make our own inquiries. They warned us not to contact witnesses until after the inquest.' Now he was scowling. 'In this court I was sure we'd get a proper hearing. But that didn't happen. The inquest was rushed, the witnesses barely challenged. The officer in charge of the case didn't even turn up. The verdict was agreed inside ten minutes.'

The room was becoming stuffy and I opened a window. It momentarily spared me the other man's angry glare. Dublin street noises filtered in. Car horns, the hum of tram tracks, the growl of bus engines, and the usual amount of street language, mostly swearing.

'I didn't accept the verdict. So I did my own checking.' He pulled a tattered notebook from a side pocket. The inside pages were covered in scribbles.

'Three people gave depositions that day.' He turned the pages until he found what he wanted. 'Two worked with Tim in Standard and Chartered. I spoke with them afterwards. They were cagey. They didn't give much away. But they stuck with their stories. Tim was worried about bank practices.'

I bit into another sandwich. 'Go on.'

'He'd an acquaintance in the State Irish Bank called Malone.'

I paused mid-chew. 'What's Malone's first name?'

'Harold. He's usually called Harry.'

I almost choked. I grabbed a mug of coffee and knocked it back in two gulps.

Cunningham looked at me. 'Are you okay?'

I dabbed at my lips. I put my snack down and pushed the plate to one side. My mind was in free-fall again. There was a Harry Malone, the friend of Patrick Dowling. He was supposed to offer testimony at the inquest. But he'd retracted at the last minute, almost certainly under duress. There couldn't possibly be two different Harry Malones involved?

'One moment.' I rifled through my briefcase. In the same side I'd stuck the Glock handgun I found the Dowling dossier and paperwork relating to Malone. Name, address and a work contact number. I hauled out the telephone directory, ripped through it until I found the State Irish Bank entry. The numbers matched. It *was* the same Harry Malone. What the hell did Malone have to do with Timothy Cunningham's inquest?

'Go on.' I forced the excitement out of my voice. Was more about to unravel that would make sense of the Dowling mystery? Or was another puzzle surfacing? The death of Timothy Cunningham?

'I tried to talk directly with Malone but he refused. I finally managed to get through to him by phone. He said he'd never heard of Tim.'

'And?'

'He was lying through his teeth. After the inquest I checked Tim's mobile phone. He used it to record meetings and appointments. Visits to the dentist and doctor, things like that.'

'Ahuh.'

'I found Malone's work and mobile numbers in his contacts list. And I discovered a meeting with Malone. Three days before he died.'

He let that sink in.

'There was another entry,' he went on. 'The day before Tim drowned he'd an hour-long talk with Dan Thornton, CEO of Standard and Chartered Bank. I tried to get in contact with Thornton but was fobbed off. I rang countless times and left messages. He never returned the calls. I wrote to him and didn't get a reply. Finally I sent a letter by registered post.'

He paused for breath. And to control his temper.

'Did that trigger a response?'

'A week later a bank lawyer rang me. He offered condolences on behalf of Thornton. But, he said, Standard and Chartered was going through a crisis. As were all the other Irish banks. Mr Thornton didn't have time to meet but was sure he'd arrange something at a later date.'

My hunger disappeared. I was struggling to understand how this was connected to the Dowling case.

There was a knock on the door. O'Leary was back, clutching the Cunningham folder. His glasses were shoved back on his head. The lenses looked damp. *Now when and how was that dossier put back?* I wondered. *Did the one who took it realise I was looking for it? And knew that I knew it'd gone missing?* O'Leary set it in front of me and left without a word.

'He's got big feet.' Cunningham was inspecting mud on the carpet from O'Leary's shoes. The footprints did look large, but O'Leary was a big man.

I sifted through the file, desperate to see if any documents were missing, and not alert Cunningham that his brother's dossier had been taken from the court. Probably for criminal purposes. Everything seemed in order.

'Read the deposition from Matt Dillon,' Cunningham said.

'Who's he?' I flicked through pages of typed script.

'The man who said he saw Tim jump into the canal. Dillon claimed he went to help but couldn't. He rang the fire brigade and police.' The whine was now heavy with sarcasm.

'Got it.' I scanned the deposition. 'You think Dillon perjured himself?'

'Yes.'

'In what way?'

'Tim walked out of the pub around five past nine that evening. I confirmed that with those who were with him. It's a fifteen-minute walk from the pub to the end of the nearby tow bridge.'

'How do you know?'

He stroked his goatee. 'I timed myself walking that exact route.'

I studied the toxicology report. Timothy Cunningham's blood alcohol level was low. There were no drugs in his system.

'What's your point?'

'Dillon made the ambulance and police calls at nine fifty-five p.m. I know that from their official records. That's a thirty-minute gap.'

'Maybe he was trying to rescue your brother?' I was challenging Cunningham's argument to make sure he was on solid ground.

'Not a chance.'

'Why?'

'I found out he'd been in an accident three weeks before. He was on crutches that day. He couldn't have helped Tim even if he'd wanted to.'

'What're you suggesting?'

'He lied under oath.'

'Why? What was in it for him?'

'I don't know. I can't get hold of Dillon. He's disappeared.'

There was a suspicious lull. I massaged my temples, as if that would help me think better.

I broke the silence. 'How can he just disappear?'

'If people want you to disappear it can be arranged.'

I lifted the phone. 'I'll have this checked.' I started dialling.

Cunningham reached across and stopped me. 'Don't bother. No one will find him. He's gone. Even his family don't know where he is.' Without looking I put the phone back on its cradle, missed and the handpiece fell to the floor. The plastic casing cracked and the cable became loose. I lifted it and checked for a dialling tone. It was dead. I made a mental note to have the set replaced.

I picked another sandwich and started eating. It tasted awful but I didn't give a damn. I nodded to Cunningham to go on.

'Matt Dillon worked at Standard and Chartered for over twenty years,' Cunningham continued. 'He joined when he was eighteen. He became the institution's trouble shooter.' Dillon was being spoken of in the past tense. 'He handled the dirty work. He chased bad loans and investigated staff suspected of dipping into the till. He audited overseas branches. He was the heavy hitter who sacked employees. He was hated in-house. And was very close to the CEO, Dan Thornton.'

I interrupted. 'Thornton's been arrested.'

'I heard that.' Cunningham didn't seem surprised. 'I'm only beginning to understand this myself,' he went on. 'In financial circles if you ask the right people the right questions they'll give you a hint of an answer. It's rarely a direct reply like "yes" or "no", usually it's a "maybe" or "that could be correct". Vague crap like that.'

'So what've you learned?'

'There was something strange going on at Standard and Chartered. I don't know what but I'd guess it wasn't legal.'

My addled brain was swamped with this new information. But I told Lorcan what I learned at the security briefing. Standard and Chartered was under scrutiny by the Criminal Assets Board and the Fraud Squad. CEO Dan Thornton was implicated in money laundering, crooked accounting and falsifying bank records. He'd cut a deal with the state: immunity from prosecution in return for the truth. Cunningham nodded throughout. I was confirming his suspicions.

'Dillon associated with Richard Dowling,' he added. 'Son of Albert Dowling, our newly retired cabinet minister.'

'And Albert Dowling's linked to Jonathan Redmond,' I added for good measure.

Cunningham's eyebrows arched. I reminded him. 'The drug dealer who sat through your brother's inquest.'

We stared at one another. We were both stunned. Cunningham checked his watch. It was a few minutes before 2 p.m.

'My brother didn't commit suicide.' He stated this as fact. 'Somebody killed him. And whoever did it was trying to protect that rogue bank.'

He stood, adjusted his shirt where it was riding up at the back and stared straight at me. 'Tell your police friends they have a helluva lot more work to do.'

Chapter 45

I'd gambled with Cunningham to see what I might hear. I was expecting snippets, maybe the occasional nugget. Instead I was swamped with new revelations. The inquest of Timothy Cunningham had links to the death of Patrick Dowling. How, I didn't know. But the same names kept surfacing. Jonathan Redmond: drug dealer with links to Standard and Chartered Bank. Harry Malone: friend of Patrick Dowling and reluctant witness, employee of State Irish Bank, and liar, if both County Coroner Harold Rafferty and Lorcan Cunningham were correct. Then came Dan Thornton, CEO of Standard and Chartered Bank and now implicated in money laundering, crooked accounting and falsifying bank records. Finally there was Albert Dowling: retired government minister with possible connections to both Redmond and Thornton.

It was time to pull this together. It was time to hold Patrick Dowling's inquest and hear the truth. It was time to gamble again.

I picked up the phone. I forgot the handset was dead. I used my mobile.

First I called Charles McGrath, lawyer to the Dowling family. 'Tell your clients I'm reconvening Patrick's inquest for Wednesday at 10 a.m.' I told him I meant this Wednesday, two days away. McGrath complained at the

short notice but I silenced him. 'I know what happened.'
I hung up. I was gambling. I *didn't* know what'd
happened. I was praying Hobbs would tell me later. But
this would give McGrath something to think about.

Then I called Fred Hodgins, lawyer for Harry Malone.
I explained I was recalling the Dowling inquest. There
was no reaction. 'Tell Malone fresh information's come
to light. Tell him I want him here to offer his deposition.
And tell him it'll be in his interest to tell the truth.'
Now Hodgins was all over me. What exactly did I
mean? Was I suggesting his client was in trouble?
I listened impatiently. Hodgins was working up a right
lather so I cut to the chase. 'Get him here on Wednesday
or I'll issue a subpoena.' I hung up. That was another
major gamble.

Next I contacted Gerard Canny, the pathologist who'd
conducted the autopsy. I asked if he'd turn up in case
his results were challenged again. Canny listened politely,
agreed to attend but warned that he wasn't changing his
mind. 'Patrick Dowling committed suicide.'

I called Reilly. He was on his way back from University
Hospital. Hobbs had been taken from him by Stan Rowe
personally. Rowe had looked Hobbs up and down, shook
his head and advised Reilly not to return before 7 p.m.
'It'll take that long just to clean him.' I told Reilly about
the conversation with Lorcan Cunningham. He murmured
his surprise. Then he came back with positive news.
Hobbs's military record was good. Honourable discharge,
good service history. Maybe a bit fond of the bottle when
off duty but nothing that was an issue while in uniform.
That was a relief.

I rang DI Roche and told her what I'd learned and
what plans I'd set in motion. She worried about Hobbs.
She worried about Malone. She worried about rushing

proceedings. I told her to stop worrying and leave the decisions to me. 'Anything new on Redmond?'

'He hijacked a car about a mile from that woodland. A farmer was checking stock when Redmond grabbed him from behind. He forced him into the boot of his Saab and drove off. It was found abandoned on a back road near Enniskerry. There's a report of a Honda Civic stolen from a car park in the village. Someone fitting Redmond's description was seen speeding away. He headed towards the motorway. If he reached that he could be anywhere. My feeling is he's going to try and leave the country.'

Now it was my turn to worry. And gamble again. I gambled Redmond wouldn't risk another attack on me or my family.

Then I heard the afternoon inquests. An unexpected hospital death during a routine operation. A fatality in a light aeroplane crash. A nursing home bereavement caused by incorrect prescribing. A drowning.

I listened as depositions were read out, expert witness opinions offered, police paperwork confirmed. I offered my sympathies to the bereaved. I made recommendations about anaesthetic equipment maintenance, correct prescribing patterns and the wisdom of holding an aerobatic display in a built-up area. I pleaded for better safety guides for small-craft users. My words were noted, advice recorded and verdicts decided. Ghosts came and went.

At the end of it all I was exhausted. And the hard work was only beginning. At 5.30 p.m. I sat in the room of sighs and prepared for my meeting with Hobbs. I filled my briefcase with paperwork and photographs of the Dowling inquest: crime scene and autopsy pictures plus shots of everyone involved in his life and death. Where I couldn't get direct images I used newspaper clippings. I had to be sure Hobbs's account matched the investigation record. And I wanted material to jog his memory. Finally I moved the Glock pistol to a side pocket.

The Cunningham dossier was still on my desk. I decided to take it to the basement. I found the keys in Joan's in-tray. There was mud on the three rows of stone steps leading to the chamber. The air didn't seem as stale and musty. I couldn't figure that out. The iron-studded door opened easily. The low-watt bulb didn't offer much light, but enough to allow me to keep an eye on the dirt. I went further. There was still mildew in the air, but not as much as before. Last time it'd caught in my throat, making me cough. I worried as I felt my way along the gloomy twists and turns. *Something's different. But what?* I couldn't understand. My pulse was racing, just like it'd done all morning. I'd have a heart attack if this constant stress didn't ease up. Finally, I found the cabinet where the Cunningham file had been stored, removed and put back. The footprints faced straight at it. I replaced the folder. Then I realised the tracks went as far as the last wall. This was granite-built. A lintel shouldered boulders to the ceiling. Underneath was a heavy oak door studded with metal. It hadn't been opened in years. The footprints stopped at the door. And others came from directly outside. This was now a building site where the old city morgue once stood. I pushed the door. It held firm. I pushed it again, only harder. It gave way. Slightly. One more shove and it opened, throwing daylight and a gentle breeze into the cellar. I studied the deserted site. There were mounds of damp rubble, mainly red brick and concrete; abandoned block slabs, old roof tiles, shattered and jagged, and rows of rusting pipes. A yellow JCB digger, idle, wheels caked in reddish muck, windscreen streaked in grime. The sun struggled to get through. A breeze blew plastic bags and litter around the plot, creating little whirlwinds. A police siren sounded in the distance. Seagulls squawked as they swooped overhead. I stepped further and looked up and down. The plot was surrounded on two sides by high buildings, creating a wind tunnel. Any open door would catch a significant gust. Hoarding surrounded the zone. But at one side a gap had been forced. Now I knew why the basement wasn't so musty. Why the smell of mildew didn't spark coughing. Someone was using the entrance often enough to allow stagnant air out and fresh air in. Last night's heavy rain had turned the plot into mire. Anyone walking through it would catch red grit on their shoes. I stepped back, got down on my hunkers and inspected the inside footprints. They'd a reddish tinge. I rubbed some between forefinger and thumb. It was grit, not soil. I smelled it. It wasn't earth mud. The footprints in my office and along the basement were from large shoes. The only court employee with feet that big was Arthur O'Leary. He was using the old door to get in and out. There was no logical reason for that, other than gaining access to records when he wanted. And unseen. And gaining access to the chambers. Unseen. But his poor eyesight gave him away. He didn't realise he was leaving a footprint trail.

I had the mole.

How would I deal with him?

At 6 p.m. the staff waited in the front office. Aoife, Eleanor and Mary, usually full of gossip and scandal and mischief, now they were sombre and subdued. Joan stood with her arms held anxiously at her side. She was in navy skirt and clinging white blouse. Tears welled in her eyes.

I guessed she knew what I was going to say. Larry Naughton, the night watchman, was there also. Paunchy, weary and wrinkled he seemed out of place in daytime. He sat on the side of a desk, waiting and watchful. Then came my mole, the jury recruiter Arthur O'Leary. He was chewing gum. He checked his watch as if he'd an appointment elsewhere.

I kept the announcement short. 'Before you hear from the press I want you to know I've handed in my resignation.'

I glanced around. There was little response. This was expected, maybe even hoped for. I suddenly realised the past eleven days had taken its toll on the staff. They must have felt as much under threat as I did. I made a few comments about the difficult working conditions we'd experienced recently. I stressed how important their support had been throughout. Looks were exchanged. Relief? Sadness? I couldn't decide.

'Thank you all.' I shook each one by the hand. Joan couldn't resist pecking me on the cheek. Then I faced O'Leary. 'Thanks for your loyalty.'

'No problem, Dr Wilson.' He avoided eye contact. 'I wish you a safe and happy retirement.' Not just a happy retirement, but a *safe* and happy retirement. He seemed to be warning me. *It's not over yet.*

They clapped me out of the building. Even O'Leary. There was a clutch of journalists and photographers waiting. Camera shutters whirred, questions were barked. I held my briefcase close to my chest and forced a way through. I squeezed into the rear of Reilly's car and told him what I'd discovered in the basement. He pulled out and circled the narrow streets. Three minutes later we were parked at the far side of the court entrance. Most of the reporters had gone with only a few stragglers hanging about, gossiping and smoking. Minutes later O'Leary hurried from the building. He hailed a passing cab and disappeared into the evening traffic.

Reilly made a call to HQ. Then we drove towards University Hospital.

Chapter 46

Dr Stan Rowe, chief physician at University Hospital, greeted me at the street entrance. It was 7.30 p.m. Rowe was a giraffe of a man: long, loping and spindly legs, long and thin neck with permanently pursed lips. He wore green scrubs under a white coat with a stethoscope hanging out of a side pocket. The other pocket was crammed with pens and paperwork. He was under pressure, checking his pager as he hurried us along the corridors. Security staff patrolled the walkways, directing the lost, bewildered and sick. Medics huddled in corners discussing patients. Everyone seemed to be frowning.

Rowe scampered up the stairs rather than wait for the elevator. He zigzagged past groups of people. My brief-case weighed me down and I struggled to keep up. We finally made the top floor. It was bustling. Nurses rushed from ward to ward. Orderlies ferried patients in wheelchairs. Some had drip infusions; others breathed through oxygen masks.

'Hobbs is in reasonable shape considering his lifestyle,' Rowe began. 'The world hasn't treated him kindly and he's let himself go. He's drinking heavily and his diet is poor.'

I listened but I was praying. *Don't give me bad news.*

He ran a finger along a set of lab results. 'His liver

enzymes are all over the place from too much booze. But he's not a consistent drinker. He gets drunk when there's enough money. In between he eats what he can get hold of. That should protect him from withdrawal psychosis.' In other words, Hobbs was unlikely to go crazy because his booze supply had been cut off.

Nearby an elevator pinged. An elderly woman on a trolley was wheeled out. She had tubes going in both arms and another tube running down her left leg.

'Anything else I should know?'

Rowe sifted through the reports. 'His renal function is impaired so we gave him a litre of fluids. A full blood count was reasonable. Toxicology is clear for substance abuse. ECG and chest X-ray are normal apart from old infective scarring in one lung. An abdominal ultrasound shows liver enlargement with fatty infiltration. A CT scan of the brain showed white matter atrophy and ventricular enlargement. This reflects alcohol abuse. There are also healed skull fractures. However, the findings are compatible with normal cognitive function.'

He noticed Reilly's puzzled look. 'The tests mean nothing if the patient's ga-ga. Hobbs isn't ga-ga. He's just another unfortunate brought down by this recession.'

This was sounding good. Along with his clean army record Hobbs was shaping up to be an ace witness.

'I asked one of the nurses to keep an eye on him. She's experienced and astute.' He paused to inspect a message on his pager. 'She said he was talkative and responsive. He told her about his years in the army, trips overseas, marriage that went south because of long absences. He doesn't have children and he's too proud to contact any of his family. He's ashamed how low he's fallen.'

'That reflects insight and a working mind,' I suggested.

'It does. But when she pushed further he backed off. She believes something's troubling him.'

'What's the bottom line?' Was Hobbs sane enough to be presented as a credible witness?

Rowe didn't hesitate. 'He's good, Mike. I'm surprised how well he's holding up considering his lifestyle.' The pager shrilled again. Rowe scowled. 'I've gotta go. Someone's having a heart attack.' He handed me a file with the name JOHN HOBBS written in felt tip across the top. There was also a hospital ID number. 'He's all yours. Scrubbed and cleaned and in fresh clothes. Room twenty-two on this floor.'

He started to hurry and then stopped. He gave me a long, hard look. 'I'm hearing a lot of bad things about a criminal called Redmond. They say he's behind these attacks. And he's on the run.'

'You know as much as I do, Stan. I'm not hearing anything different.'

'Keep your head down, Mike.' He checked his pager. Then he was gone.

I noticed Reilly was pale and uneasy. 'You don't like this place, do you?'

He dabbed at his forehead. 'I hate it.'

I would have smiled if I wasn't so uptight. Reilly didn't much care for any territory I worked: the coroner's court gave him the creeps and he hated hospitals, but these corridors and noises and smells were familiar to me. I was once senior pathologist and king of the basement jungle. When I growled, the other animals paid attention.

We headed towards room twenty-two on a level reserved for infectious diseases. Reilly darted nervous glances into the wards. Gaunt faces stared back. Food lay untouched, not from distaste but lack of appetite. Staff wore masks and protective gloves. The smell of antiseptic made my eyes smart.

'Don't drag this out.' Sweat beaded Reilly's brow. He parked a chair in front of the door.

Chapter 47

The man in room twenty-two bore little resemblance to the John Hobbs of Enniskerry woods. The stench of living rough had been scrubbed away. Gone too were the dirty locks and dishevelled mane. His hair had been cut to a neat side parting and slicked down with gel. He was shaved and his face scrubbed clean. He certainly couldn't have been described as striking but at least he looked half decent. The giveaway was his wizened skin and tobacco-stained fingers. They hinted at another, and rougher, existence. But his eyes were alert and suspicious.

The hospital had supplied a pair of denims that hung loose at his waist and they were short at his ankles. He was in a freshly laundered T-shirt with a lion logo on the back. He was wearing white runners that'd seen better days and looked too tight for him. The laces were undone.

The room was sparse with a single chair, small table, locker and bed. The walls and ceiling were painted a clinical grey, the towels and bed linen were a faded white.

I offered a hand. He didn't shake it.

'Will ye get me a fag before I lose me head?'

'You can't smoke here.' I tried not to sound too preachy. 'If I get you one then smoke it out the window.'

'If I don' get wan soon I'll jump out the fuckin' window.'

I picked up the internal phone and spoke with the charge nurse. After an argument she eventually relented.

A pack of Benson & Hedges would be passed inside. They'd come from her own handbag.

Minutes later Hobbs was leaning out the window and drawing on his first cigarette of the evening. It sparked a bout of convulsive coughing. He spat plugs of phlegm into the night air.

He admired the sunset and flickering city lights. A far-off radio mast winked a red beacon. A wail of ambulance klaxons drifted upwards. As Hobbs smoked I inspected him. I knew he was sixty-three but he looked ten years older. He was around six feet but stooped. He was painfully thin. His worn, stained and stinking forest overcoat had hidden his frailty. There were folds of grime at the back of his neck. There were scars at the side of his newly exposed hairline. He burned the cigarette to the end and flicked the butt away.

'Hows abou' a few beers?'

This was becoming hard work. Keeping Hobbs happy might break every hospital rule there was. Next he'd be looking for a hooker.

'I need to hear everything first,' I said. 'I can keep you in fags and booze tonight. But it can't go on for ever.'

Hobbs scowled. I ignored his annoyance.

'Tell me about Patrick Dowling.' I needed more than what he'd offered the first time.

Hobbs tapped at the cigarette pack. He took one out, started to light it and then stopped.

'Paddy was thrown outta his house God knows how many times.'

'Go on.'

'He was a serious addict. When he'd enough gear he'd shoot up under a bridge where I hung out. We talked for hours. I kinda protected him. Somebody had to. He'd have got his head kicked in if he looked cross-eyed at the others.'

'Where'd he get money to buy drugs?' I'd asked this before and didn't get an answer.

'He didn' need money. He was well supplied.'

This was hard to believe. 'Why would someone just give him drugs?'

'He was bein' used. He was a government minister's son. As long as Paddy was on a lead the minister wasn' far behind.'

I sat on the side of the bed.

'He was nothin' more than a messenger.' Just what DI Roche believed from the beginning.

'Where were the messages going?'

Hobbs inspected his fingers. He chewed at the stumps of nails.

'To Noel Carty?'

'That fucker.' Hobbs's face twisted with contempt. 'He was wan mean bastard. I was delighta to hear he'd got killed.'

'So it was Carty?'

'Carty was only the muscle. Redmond pulled the strings.'

Hobbs's face clouded. I sensed a crisis. I held my breath, wondering what was coming.

'Paddy didn' die alone. There was others there that day.'

I let my breath out slowly. I coughed to hide my surprise. I was tantalisingly close to the answers I'd wanted to hear. But I needed to know why Hobbs was prepared to talk now. I'd others to convince.

'Why didn't you come forward with this earlier? His death was widely reported. If you saw something why didn't you tell the police?'

'I wanna stay alive. I didn' want to be dragged inta this. The bastards involved are vicious.' Hobbs paced the narrow floor, touching the walls. Back and forth, back and forth. 'Ye seen what happened. That's the sort I'm talkin' about.'

Hobbs inspected the ceiling. He lit another cigarette and blew the smoke into my face. He knew this would drift outside and soon some nurse would pound the doors wanting to know what was going on. I kept my cool. It was going to be another long day but I was in no mood to rush. The prize was too great.

He ground the butt to ash, went over to the window and looked out. When he turned again his voice had changed. He was angry. 'People think vagrants are dirt beneath their feet. They say stuff in front of us they shouldn'. Because we're in the gutter they think we don' understand. Or we're so fuckin' useless it makes no difference.'

He searched for another cigarette.

'But we see and hear a lot. Ye'd be surprised how news spreads. We know the dangerous areas, where the junkies are hangin' out, where the dealers are sellin'. We know which pubs are gonna be raided n' the brothels gonna be busted. We look like sewer rats. But we're not. We hear a lotta scandal.'

'What'd you hear?'

'Redmond has a politician n' a bank in his pocket.'

The story was stacking up.

'He's desperate to cut n' run.'

The story was stacking up even more.

'Was he involved in Patrick Dowling's death?'

The answer wasn't straight. 'D'ye want proof?'

'Yes.'

'Here's somethin' to think about, Mister Coroner.' The wizened features creased, the eyes hardened. 'Paddy wasn' the only wan to die in that forest.'

* * *

I allowed Hobbs another cigarette. I even opened the pack and struck a match to light it. My hands were shaking, his remarkably sure considering the circumstances.

I sat on the end of the bed and took a Dictaphone out of my briefcase. I checked I'd spare tapes. I dragged the narrow table between us. I set the recorder on top. Hobbs eased himself into the chair. He smoked and watched.

I produced a clutch of photographs. They were police files, taken when Dowling's body was discovered. There were different angles of the scene and surrounding forest.

Separately I set out fourteen other pictures, ten glossy and four newspaper clippings. Some I put on the window-sill, others on top of a radiator. By the time I'd finished there was a significant gallery.

Hobbs watched on. He picked up a photo I'd dropped. He scanned the face. He scowled.

I was a bag of nerves, frightened everything might yet come apart. Would Hobbs freeze at the last minute and clam up?

'Who was there that day?'

'What abou' tha' beer?'

I held my temper. My nerves were in shreds, my legs like jelly and my stomach rumbling. I felt weak. I knew I'd have to move Hobbs. Word would spread about the vagrant in the isolation room looking for cigarettes and beer. Stan Rowe's reputation would be compromised. 'I'll arrange for a six pack when I can.' I knew this would barely slake Hobbs's thirst.

The room was oppressively hot despite the open window and I wished I could get fresh air. I wondered how Reilly was coping in the corridor. I hoped he hadn't bolted. Or fainted.

Finally Hobbs went through the collection. 'Ye wanna know who was there when Paddy died?'

'Yes.'

He inspected each one carefully. 'That wan.' A stained finger pointed. 'That wan.' I blanked my shock. Then he tore a newspaper clipping in two, crumpled one of the halves and set the other in front of me. 'And him.'

I slipped the group into a file. Then I pressed the record button on the cassette. 'My name is Dr Michael Wilson, Dublin City Coroner.' I noted the time, day and date. 'This deposition relates to the inquest of Patrick Dowling.' I added the file number. I read into the record who Hobbs was, where he'd been discovered, how he'd ended up in University Hospital. For good measure I added the floor level and room number. I added basic medical details with Dr Stan Rowe identified as attending consultant. I referred to a second investigation that would confirm Hobbs's power of recall.

Hobbs chewed on his nails, crossed and uncrossed his legs, cleared his throat, inspected the floor. He looked like an impatient visitor in a doctor's waiting room.

'John Hobbs has identified three individuals he claims were present when Patrick Dowling died.' I read the names into the record. I switched the cassette off. I prepared fresh tapes.

'I'm starting,' I said.

Hobbs nodded.

I pushed the recorder forward. 'Tell me what you saw on 29 November 2009.'

Chapter 48

Hobbs finished at 9 p.m. Twice I stopped him to make sure he understood the significance of his testimony. He smoked his way through the exchanges. At one stage he became angry. 'D'ye wanna know wha' happened?'

'Yes.'

'Then shut up n' listen.'

As his memory unlocked the words tumbled in a torrent of rage and hunger for revenge. By the end he was worn out, like a gladiator who'd fought to a standstill.

I used four tapes. I slipped them into my briefcase and went outside.

Hobbs shouted after me. 'Gimme cigarettes n' a few beers.'

Reilly hadn't bolted or fainted. But he still looked uneasy. I briefed him on what I'd just heard.

'This is a police issue now,' I said.

'Not until it's revealed in open court.' I wasn't being let off the hook.

I set out my plan. 'I'm re-calling the inquest for Wednesday. It's short notice but I don't know how long I can keep Hobbs sober. We need him there as soon as possible.'

I rang Roche.

'I know everything,' I said.

'Run it by me.'

I spent the next fifteen minutes going over Hobbs's account.

'Tell me those names again.'

I did.

'He's sure he knows where this body is?'

'Yes.'

Roche couldn't contain her excitement. 'We're in business.'

'This is pretty brutal stuff,' I said. 'I'm stunned with what I heard.'

'So am I. But will Hobbs repeat it all in the witness box?'

'Leave that to me,' I said. Then I outlined my worries about his demands for booze and cigarettes. 'He can't stay here.'

'We'll take him to the judge's house opposite you. There's an army of security there.'

'What about the judge?'

'We'll put him up in a fancy hotel until it's all over. He'll have a ball.'

I hoped she was right. I doubted I'd have many friendly neighbours the way things were going.

'None of these people should be allowed to leave the country,' I said.

'They're under surveillance. They'll be stopped if they try.'

'I'll conduct the questioning,' I said. 'I'll get the best out of him.'

'That's your call.'

'And what happens after that is your call.'

'Leave the police work to me, Dr Wilson. I'll deal with whatever happens afterwards.'

Suddenly I felt quite happy.

Roche told me she was trying to find Arthur O'Leary. So far, the traitor hadn't been traced. He wasn't in his apartment, nor in any of his usual watering holes, according to friends who knew him. He'd gone to ground.

'Any news on Redmond?' I asked.

'No. But he can't run for ever.'

He can't, I thought. But I was uneasy. He was still at large.

I checked the Glock was still in my briefcase.

Reilly and I had coffee in the canteen. I wanted to thank Stan Rowe but he wasn't available. He'd been called to yet another emergency and couldn't be disturbed.

We discussed the day's events. So much had happened, so much was happening and so much would happen we were struggling to take it all in.

'I think I'll quit protection duty,' Reilly announced.

'Why?'

'It's too bloody risky. I've haven't fired a shot in anger for years. Since you came on the scene I can't keep up with the excitement.' He was grinning but it was forced. We were both exhausted. And we'd both had enough so-called 'excitement' to last a lifetime.

'I better go,' I said.

Reilly took the coast road towards Glasthule, past the Booterstown marsh bird sanctuary and along Blackrock and Dunlaoghaire sea fronts. Lights bobbed on boats in the darkness of the bay. The Howth Head lighthouse flashed its beacon into the shadows. There was a tang of sea salt in the air. Small groups wandered the strands, enjoying the late-evening warmth. Crowds gathered outside pubs. Life looked good. I wanted to be at home with my family and as soon as possible. I'd had enough of death.

But I knew as soon as I crossed the front door something wasn't right. Not some other danger, but a domestic crisis. Jennifer and Gregory were in the television room with the volume up. It was a warning: stay away. Sarah hovered about upstairs, ignoring my hellos.

I fixed an omelette with tomatoes and mushrooms and rounds of toast and drank mugs of strong tea, all on my own in the kitchen. Then I sensed movement. The television had been turned off. I heard whispered instructions, padded footsteps as Jennifer crossed the landing to Sarah's room. I heard Gregory shout and shushed. Then I heard sobs and doors closing. *What's going on?* I was too frightened to ask and went outside to clear my head. It was dark. The moon was part shaded by cloud. Street lights offered an amber glow. Now there was a gentle breeze with the hint of more rain to come. Somewhere a dog barked and another replied. As I wandered through the garden I spotted Sarah staring at me through the living-room window. Even in the dim light I could see she was unsettled, puzzled almost.

I went into the study. Soon afterwards, Sarah walked in and sat down. She glanced at the paperwork, picked up a deposition and started reading. Then, as if bored with it, she put it to one side. She faced me.

'Hi Michael.'

'Hi Sarah.' I knew no good was going to come out of this conversation. This was another Michael moment.

'I've been following the news reports.'

'And?'

'Redmond's still on the run.'

'He'll be caught.' Even as I said that I knew I didn't sound convincing.

'Five days ago you told me this would be over.' Sarah looked tired and drawn. Her skin was unhealthily pale, her eyes sunk in her head. Her hands shook and I sensed her struggle to control them. 'While he's on the loose none of us are safe.'

'Our home is well protected,' I argued.

'Indeed it is,' she conceded. 'If we spend the rest of our lives here and never venture outside we'd be very safe. That's not what I'm talking about.'

'No.'

'I can't live like this, Michael. Nor will I allow my children to live this way. It's absurd having armed policemen skulking around the garden.'

I started to say something but was silenced by a furious look.

'Jennifer received a string of texts from friends. They're not allowed to meet up with her. Gregory wanted to play tip rugby but the team wouldn't let him near the pitch.'

That was brutal and cruel. But I understood the other parents' concerns. The airways were full of news about Redmond. His violent criminal record was being dissected and analysed on every channel.

Sarah dragged a stray hair from her eyes. 'I've made a decision.'

I didn't want to hear what was coming.

'We're leaving. I've spoken with Jennifer and Gregory. They're heartbroken but relieved. They're not sleeping properly. They're having nightmares. Their friends are mocking them.'

I looked at her but she avoided eye contact.

'I want you to come with us. I want you to accept this fight has gone on long enough. No one could fault your effort. No one could fault you quitting to stay alive. You're a doctor and a civil servant, Michael. You shouldn't have to carry a gun.'

My wound throbbed and I massaged the skin around

313

it. 'There's less than four weeks before my resignation kicks in. Until then I'm Dublin City Coroner.'

She came back in an angry flash. 'Are you coming with us or not?'

I needed time to think. 'What're you planning?'

'My brother Trevor has an apartment in London. He rarely uses it and it's free.'

Trevor was a fifty-three-year-old IT consultant living in New York. Trevor was also a high-flyer who travelled the world. He'd corporate apartments in Paris, London and Sydney. He was very well off and confidently fluent in French and German – even his bloody English was BBC perfect. Trevor was always in control. I, by contrast, wasn't so well off and spoke only one language. My Ulster drawl compared poorly with Trevor's linguistics. And I carried a mountain of emotional baggage. Trevor didn't, of course. Something Sarah occasionally pointed out to me when we'd a row. 'I'm moving there with Jennifer and Gregory until this is finished. If that takes a week, a month, a year or the rest of my life, I don't care. I will not live in constant fear.'

My mind was reeling. But I was determined. 'I won't quit until this is over.'

Sarah's features collapsed. Her eyes brimmed with tears. She wasn't expecting resistance. She'd presented a logical argument for which there was no sensible defence. How could I not see its wisdom? Now her whole body shook and her face streaked with tears. She searched for a tissue, finally using the sleeve of her blouse to wipe her nose. I reached across but was brushed away. 'Leave me, Michael. I can't bear to hold you. I love you so much I can't think what life would be like without you.'

She stood up and squeezed my shoulder. 'I've booked

four tickets out of Dublin on Friday morning. If you change your mind come with us.'

She closed the door behind her.

I was left staring at depositions on death.

At midnight I crept up to the spare room, undressed to boxer shorts and hauled myself in between cool sheets. I set my watch alarm to waken me two hours later. I dragged a pillow behind my head and closed my eyes.

The door opened and Jennifer came in. She shoved me over and climbed in beside me. She was crying.

'Daddy, please come with us.'

I swallowed hard. There was a lump in my throat. 'I'll follow you.'

'Stop lying.'

I was taken aback. What could I say that wouldn't worsen the situation?

'Mum's worried sick.'

I craned my neck to see my daughter better.

'I know. I'm so sorry I've brought all this on our heads.'

'She can't believe you're going to stay here.'

I mumbled something about running away wouldn't solve anything. Jennifer came back with a verbal upper cut. 'You're a big man with an exaggerated sense of your own self-importance. You think no one could be as good a coroner as you. No one else can solve the Dowling mystery.' She pulled my chin around so she could see me eye to eye. 'We don't care about the Dowling mystery. We just want to stay alive.'

She climbed out of the bed.

'If you get killed I'll never forgive you.'

Chapter 49

At 2 a.m. my watch alarm sounded. I killed it dead. I sneaked downstairs to my study, switched on the lights and locked the door. I removed the cassettes containing Hobbs's testimony with the questions and answers that flew between us. Each exchange, no matter how heated and angry, was vital.

I flicked on my PC, set the Dictaphone on the desk and checked for sound quality. It was perfect. Hobbs's voice was occasionally indistinct and muffled but never sufficient to misunderstand. My voice, as I listened, was clear and precise.

I opened a Microsoft Word document and typed a heading: 'Oral deposition of John Hobbs'. I added the date and time and location. I leaned back in my chair, cracked my knuckles and arched my back for comfort. I glanced at my watch: it was 2.15 a.m. There were four tapes to get through. Ordinarily, this would be done at the office by one of the staff. But I didn't want anyone to hear what I'd heard earlier. I was going to transcribe everything myself.

I rewound the first tape, set my fingers on the keyboard and turned the Dictaphone on. I heard my voice. *'Tell me what you saw on 29 November 2009.'* I heard Hobbs clear his throat. *'They was waitin' for Paddy.'*

I started typing.

I kept typing.

I stopped, rewound and started when the words spilled too fast.

At 2.45 a.m. there was a knock on the door. I wondered whether to open it. It might be Sarah with a last effort to change my mind. Or Gregory having a nightmare. Or Jennifer, feeling unwell.

'Who's that?'

There was a mumble. I couldn't distinguish the voice. 'I'm busy. Is it important?' Through the light under the door I saw a shadow. 'Is that you, Sarah?' The shadow moved away, paused and came back but then stopped again. I waited for a minute, frustrated at the interruption. I unlocked the study door. Whoever was there had gone. I went to the foot of the stairs and looked up. Nothing. I took a tentative step higher and craned my neck to see if there were lights in any of the rooms. Gregory's door was shut and dark. Jennifer's door was slightly ajar but no more than usual. Her bedside lamp was off. The spare room was open but unlit. I took another step towards the master bedroom, and as I looked the light under the door went out. Sarah had come looking and I'd made it so unpleasant she fled rather than wait. I was racked with guilt and wanted to creep into the room, snuggle up beside her and hold her in my arms.

But I couldn't. Hobbs's words had to be protected. Tapes could be destroyed, memories might fail. But the transcript would capture his testimony for ever. This story *had* to be told.

I went back to the study and locked the door. I scanned what I'd just written and pressed the Dictaphone. *'Paddy was shakin' with fear.'*

I started typing again.

I kept typing.

I typed even though my fingers ached.

I missed an important exchange and rewound the tape. Then I pummelled the keyboard once more.

I finished the first two tapes in an hour. I saved the text to the hard drive and a memory stick. I was tired and sore and had a headache. I padded to the kitchen and made a pot of coffee. Then, my mind addled with the images of what I'd just heard, I prowled the area. Outside my security team was more obvious than usual. I stood on tiptoes and squinted into the shadows. On the other side of the road the judge's house bristled with police. A white van with FORENSIC SQUAD in bold letters was pulling up. White boiler-suited specialists climbed out and began talking with the duty officers. Cigarettes lit up. Conversation was exchanged.

I went back to the PC and turned on the cassette tape. This time my voice came through. *'There's absolutely no doubt about that?'* Hobbs answered no. He was so emphatic he barked it a second time. I typed the words as they spun from the reel. I realised my clothes were damp from sweat but I couldn't go upstairs to change. I saved more text to the hard drive and memory stick. I flicked out the second tape, clicked in the third, rewound and pressed the ON button. Hobbs's voice was clear. *'There was shoutin' n' roarin'. It was like a fuckin' madhouse. Nobody seemed to know what was happenin'.'*

I groaned at the thought of more work but soon my fingers were dancing along the keyboard as if they'd a mind of their own. And even though I was hearing the tale for the second time my stomach churned. Hobbs's recall was astounding, considering all he'd been through. I offered a silent thank you to Stan Rowe and his staff at University Hospital. The bedraggled, dishevelled and embittered Hobbs, unemployed and insolvent ex-serviceman, had been turned around.

I must have dozed. My mobile sounded and I awoke, startled and alarmed. It was Roche.

'Yes?' The PC glowed in front of me, neat rows of horror text waiting to be continued. The cassette had come to the end of the third spool. It was 4.20 a.m. 'What's happening?'

'Hobbs is being taken to the woods. It shouldn't take more than forty minutes to get there. Rain is forecast and they want to dig immediately.'

'Okay.'

'I'll let you know if they find anything.'

The line went dead.

I slipped the final cassette into the recorder and pressed the ON button. The tape whirred and now Hobbs could be heard sobbing. I remembered that emotional point. The story was coming to an end. I checked my watch. It was 4.25 a.m.

I started typing.

I typed like a man possessed, which I was at that moment. I typed even though my head was splitting and my neck muscles ached and my back protested for relief. I typed through Hobbs's tears and my shouts and his shouts back and my curses and his swearing. I recorded every word, good, bad and appalling. At one point Hobbs could clearly be heard sobbing. He blamed himself for not intervening. I was still typing as dawn broke. Hobbs's distress was overflowing. *'I shoulda done somethin'. I shouldna have left him like tha'.'*

I was walking the floor to ease leg cramps when my mobile shrilled again. I was so distracted I almost let it ring out. In time I heard the tone.

'Yes?'

'Hobbs was right.' It was Roche. 'There's a grave with a body in it.' She hung up before I could get a word in.

I was numb. I was exhausted. I was elated. I'd gambled with Hobbs and it'd paid off. So far.

I started typing again.

And kept typing.

Until John Hobbs had nothing more to say and I'd nothing more to ask.

I saved the text to the hard drive and the memory stick. I sent an encrypted copy to my coroner's court email address.

I rested my head on the desk and fell asleep.

Chapter 50

Around 7 a.m. I woke up again. I was damp with perspiration. My body hurt. My legs cramped. I'd a headache. Soft yellow daylight flooded the room. Outside I saw a ginger cat on the prowl. Magpies strutted. Flower buds unwrapped to look for the sun. A fat bumblebee bounced off the window pane. Twice. I sneaked upstairs to the clothes cupboard and found a fresh change. I checked the rooms. Jennifer was asleep. I wanted to kiss her on the forehead but didn't dare disturb her and start another confrontation. Sarah's door was shut. I wouldn't risk wakening her. If she was asleep.

Sarah was right, I *had* changed. I was consumed by the Dowling case, almost to the point of ignoring everything else. Almost, but not totally. I couldn't walk away from the final moments of the inquiry and flee to London. Not after what I'd heard from Hobbs. Not after what I now knew happened to the twenty-eight-year-old drug addict and son of a senior government minister. This wasn't Ulster stubbornness as Sarah believed. This was obligation. My predecessor, retired coroner Paul Crossan, warned me about this. *'Your responsibility is to the dead of Dublin and no one else. Think of inquests as their final court of appeal. Never again will the deceased's final hours be so carefully examined.'* I owed Patrick Dowling his day in court. My family was safe, our house protected. The inquest would be heard. With Dr Michael Wilson on the bench. I looked into Gregory's room but he wasn't in bed. For a moment my stomach flipped. A thousand murderous images flashed. Had Redmond penetrated the defences and taken my boy? Then I heard the television downstairs. He must've woken early and gone there without saying hello.

In the ground-floor bathroom I shaved, showered and dressed. I snacked on four bowls of cereal, then called the security detail and asked to be taken to work. 'Give us five minutes,' they said.

I went to the study and collected my briefcase. I took out every item and set them on the desk. Meticulously I went through the material. The four tapes used to record Hobbs's deposition. CHECK. Typed pages of transcript. CHECK. The memory stick with the Microsoft Word document saved. CHECK. I inspected the outbox on my PC. The encrypted email had been sent. CHECK. Glock handgun with spare magazine clip. CHECK. I was ready for the day. But the noise from the television distracted me. I went to investigate.

Gregory was lying on a sofa watching an episode of *The Simpsons*. He was curled up inside his duvet, head resting on cushions, just as I liked to do at his age. The curtains were drawn and the room was in darkness apart from the glow of the television.

'Hi Greg.'

He didn't answer.

I was in a rush but knew I couldn't walk away. I squeezed beside him. On screen Homer was downing a pitcher of Duff beer. Bart was shooting pebbles with a catapult. The family pet was like a rabid dog, foaming at the mouth. I wanted to stay and see what happened. But my son was in no mood to engage.

'What's wrong?'

'Nothing.'

'Come on, something's bothering you.' Homer was being chased up a tree by a pack of snarling mongrels. This usually had Greg belly laughing. Instead he was silent and unresponsive.

A foot kicked at me for space and I inched away, smarting at the rejection. 'There's nothing wrong. Leave me alone.'

I watched him out the corner of an eye. He was frowning, his face puckered and forehead creased. An expression I carried for years. He was a Wilson if ever I saw one. For some reason I can't explain, a distant memory flashed. When Gregory was five he spiked a temperature; he hallucinated, he saw spiders. Flushed and shivering, birthmark glowing, he clung to Sarah. We tried to cool him. The visions became more frightening.

Jennifer, then nine, heard the fuss and came running to help. 'What's happening?' She was in pyjamas and clutching her favourite teddy bear. Hair bedraggled, face scrunched in concern, she went to Gregory to console him.

Gregory looked at his sister and saw a monster. He thrashed with fists and feet. Sarah struggled to restrain him. His glazed eyes searched for his mother's face. He twisted and looked straight at her. Then his body went limp. 'Where's my real mummy?'

It was like a kick in the stomach for Sarah. 'Do something, Mike,' she sobbed.

I turned the shower to cold. I stripped to my boxers and grabbed Gregory. I held him against my chest underneath the freezing jet. I padded in a circle. He screamed until my ears buzzed. He wriggled and wormed but I held tight. We were like mismatched wrestlers in a hailstorm.

Finally his delirium eased. Gregory was still hollering

but not from fear. He reached for Sarah. She was no longer an ogre. He'd got his real mummy back.

I came out of the shower, teeth chattering and dripping. We climbed into the same bed. Within minutes Jennifer and Gregory were asleep. Then Sarah dozed. This left me squashed into a corner, one foot on the ground to stop myself falling out.

Where's my real mummy? Gregory's words echoed. His real mummy was beside him. I'd spent my teenage years asking that same question. I knew terrorists had taken her from me, but it didn't stop me searching for her spirit. There were evenings, dark and desolate evenings, when I sat by my parents' grave. It was my first port of call during school holidays. I huddled against the headstone, arms wrapped round my body for heat. The grave to the left held a young boy killed in an accident. The one to the right had three bodies from the same family who'd passed away within twenty years of one another. A church with a tall spire overshadowed the plot. In the distance were hills of corn and barley. I spoke quietly, as if they were beside me. I explained how I felt, how much I missed them, why I was so lonely, why I hated the world. Long, rambling conversations choked with emotion and anguish and a sense of loss. And hatred for the killers, Dermot McKeever and Morgan Cusack, who'd come to take my life but instead made off with my soul.

Now, as I sat on the couch, I sensed a gulf between Gregory and me. He was closer to his mother and I was jealous of that. I recognised it was natural but it still troubled me. I could never have such a relationship.

'When this is over we'll talk,' I said. 'You're too angry to hear what I might say and I don't want to upset you.' I ruffled his hair. He dismissed me with an angry flick of the wrist.

Chapter 51

The rest of that day, Tuesday 15 June, was a haze. Details on the hunt for Redmond occupied most airtime. His middle-class background, university education and drug-trafficking career was unfolded to an astounded and enraged public. His involvement in the assassination of County Coroner Harold Rafferty was decided. Senior lawyers warned of trial by media. This would prejudice a criminal court case, if he was apprehended. I knew that was a big *if*. Roche had warned of this. *'If we get sight of Redmond we'll try and detain him.'*

I'd asked what she meant.

'We won't be too careful,' she'd said. *'A gun could go off by mistake.'*

Updates continued throughout the day. Redmond's henchmen were named. The two killed in the forest were ex-paramilitary thugs. Their loss was no loss. Later, another man and two women, one-time Redmond associates, were detained at a terraced dwelling in Rathmines. The house held a small arsenal of weapons ranging from handguns and grenades to sub-machine guns. Television crews filmed the haul. That he was now using old contacts suggested desperation. Security pundits concluded Redmond's empire had collapsed.

At noon the government moved on the Standard and Chartered Bank. Its assets were seized and the institution declared criminally corrupt. The press was informed CEO Dan Thornton was 'assisting an inquiry into malpractice at the institution'. Offshore branches were targeted by local authorities. Redmond's accounts in Jersey and Spain were ring-fenced and access was denied. To recover the money he would have to prove it was not the profit of unlawful enterprise. This would be extremely difficult for him. An international warrant for his arrest had been issued.

While all this was going on I conducted inquests in the chamber of ghosts. Before I started I placed one copy of the Dowling inquest in the safe. I slipped the Glock pistol and spare magazine clip into the front drawer of my desk. Then I was ready for my daily diet of heartache and suffering. My personal crises mattered little. Others waited for closure on their loved ones. And the dead of Dublin were a never-ending line.

'He was a chronic alcoholic, Coroner. He borrowed, stole or mugged to get money for drink. It was pathetic. He was a big man too, over six feet and around fifteen stone in his prime. He was close to his fortieth birthday and weighed less than seven stone when he threw himself into the Liffey. He'd had enough, there was no fight left. Is it any wonder he was swept out to sea? I'm surprised he was found again. The birds and rats wouldn't have had much to pick on.'

After the final hearing I went back to my office to complete paperwork. I slumped at my desk, exhausted and drained. Soon this would end. Soon I would be at peace with my family. I could relax. Relax? That was a word I hardly understood any more.

Then, with nothing better to do, I rustled through the drawer. The Glock was missing. I didn't move. I racked my brains. *Are you sure you put it there? Yes. Maybe Reilly took it. Maybe he thought I'd be distracted with court work and would leave it somewhere stupid.* I rang him on my mobile. His phone rang out. I left a voice message. I went back over every possibility. How could the handgun have been moved? Nothing sprang to mind. I sat there, wondering and worrying. Then I noticed the cracked receiver had been replaced. In front of me was a new unit, same colour but with a hands-free answering facility. I could press a button and speak to the caller.

Something wasn't right. I hadn't told anyone about the faulty unit. So why'd it been changed? My office was a sanctuary. Staff knew not to disturb it to avoid accidentally misplacing documents on my desk. Now a handgun was astray. I stood up, my mind racing and disbelieving. I leaned over the desk and spotted a hint of dirt. It was tinged red. It wasn't there when I started proceedings. I was certain of that. I'd been around the room five or six times. I wouldn't have missed it. I checked the outside corridor. Rust-coloured smudges to and from the basement. Someone had walked the building site to get into the court buildings. Unnoticed. And brought a new phone.

I asked at the front office. 'Did Arthur O'Leary turn up today?'

Aoife stopped typing. Her chubby face scrunched as she racked her brains. 'I think I saw him an hour ago. Let me check.'

Within minutes it was confirmed. O'Leary'd been spotted. Everyone was so busy with the inquest and fielding media queries no one paid attention. He said he was unwell and couldn't stay. No one remembered when he arrived or when he left. But his poor eyesight meant that he hadn't seen the mud that had betrayed his intentions.

'Is anything wrong?' Aoife looked frightened. 'Not more trouble?'

'Not really.' I gripped her elbow. She pulled away and looked at me, puzzled and unsure. I tried to reassure her but the words wouldn't come. I told everyone to stay away from my room. I rushed through the building: *get out immediately!*

I called the bomb squad.

Fifteen minutes later the Dublin City Coroner's Court was empty. Only its ghosts remained.

Two hours later I watched an explosives expert dismantle the new phone. Inside was a small amount of Semtex – enough to kill – and a pre-recorded message. Redmond's educated south Dublin drawl almost stopped my heart.

'I warned you to stay away from my affairs, Dr Wilson. I said if you didn't I'd kill you. And I'm going to. Now.'

It lasted eight seconds.

The first few seconds I'd be surprised and wonder what was going on. It'd probably take another four seconds to understand the significance of the words. By the time my brain clicked so too would the trip device. Just as I realised what was happening the Semtex would've exploded. And Redmond would've won.

Chapter 52

I took control immediately. I ordered my family moved to safety. Then I demanded another handgun for protection. Redmond's determination to kill me scared the hell out of me. Not just for my own sake but especially for the sake of my family, Sarah, Jennifer and Gregory. Roche arranged for their transfer to police HQ and a secure apartment used in the state's witness protection programme. I spoke briefly to Sarah. Initially she was stunned and speechless. Then, as she grasped the significance of what'd happened, she begged me to quit and leave the country with her. But our conversation was cut short. In the background I heard police take over and hurry them away. Later I was told of everyone's distress and fear. This time my family weren't moving to the familiar setting of Auntie Carol's house. Now they'd been taken to the heart of the state's security centre. I heard there were tears, white-faced terror and complete disbelief.

I spent that evening on my own at home. I found enough bread, eggs and bacon to rustle up supper. I paced the floor. Tomorrow Patrick Dowling's inquest would finish. And all hell would break loose. For others, but also for me. My greatest fear was how this might have alienated me from my family, and how I would make it up when everything was finally over. I urged the morning forward. Eventually exhaustion took its toll and I slumped into a deep sleep.

On Wednesday 16 June the radio alarm woke me at 6.30 a.m. I lay in bed and inspected the ceiling for maybe ten minutes, deep in thought. I prayed to my dead parents for the strength to see the inquest through. I asked their spirits to stand beside me at the coroner's bench and help see me cope with the hell that'd be revealed later. When I finally got out of bed I felt strangely at ease, not in the least bit nervous or excited. This was my day.

I snacked on leftovers, showered and prepared paperwork.

At 7.50 a.m. I inspected myself in the hall mirror. I was wearing a red-striped tie on a white shirt under a navy single-breasted suit. My shoes were freshly polished, my socks new. I'd a clean handkerchief in a trouser pocket. My hair was combed to a tousled order. I thought I looked good, if a little underweight. My face had lost its haunted expression; my shoulders were strong and not slumped. My eyes had a glinting determination. The wound on my forehead was now just a rough track. I was calm and unruffled; almost too at ease considering what was ahead. But I took no chances. Roche had arranged another Glock pistol for me. I carried it in my briefcase. Then I decided to do the opposite to what was expected.

'I'm not going to be driven to court,' I told Reilly. He'd had his hair cut: tight crew-cut style again. He was in denims and T-shirt. The designer wardrobe had been abandoned in place of comfort.

'Why not?' He eyed me suspiciously.

'This is Redmond's last chance to stop this inquest. I'm not going to be an easy target in a traffic queue. Let's do it differently.'

And we did.

Two unmarked squad cars pulled away from the road within minutes of one another. Inside two officers were dressed in office attire: shirts, suits and ties. Both carried briefcases. They could've passed as Dr Michael Wilson to potential assassins.

I walked briskly to the local Dart station. There was a light cloud cover with patches of blue struggling to break through. It was warm but a cooling sea breeze kept me comfortable. I called my PA, Joan, on my mobile.

'Is everything organised?'

'Yes.'

She started to say something but I interrupted her. 'Jury selected and ready to start at 10 a.m.?'

'Yes.'

'Have the lawyers confirmed they'll attend?'

'Yes.'

This included Charles McGrath, advisor to the Dowling family. He'd been there at the start of the inquest five days previously. I wondered what approach he'd adopt today.

Joan tried again to say something. I was off before she could get a word in.

'What about Harry Malone?'

'I spoke with his lawyer and he assured me Malone will turn up.'

I rounded a corner and bumped into a jogger. *Oomph.* He winded me. I almost dropped my briefcase but recovered. The jogger swore at me but I ignored him. I slipped on a pair of dark glasses against the glare and picked up the conversation.

'Have we a section for journalists?'

'Twenty agreed on first-come first-in basis.'

I stopped at a zebra crossing. There was a steady stream

of commuter traffic inching its way towards the city centre. In front seats men were shaving and women were applying make-up. I nipped in between a lorry and a panel van.

'Has Hobbs arrived?' This was a major concern. Hobbs was surrounded by police. His cigarette quota was unlimited but his alcohol intake restricted. He wouldn't like that one bit.

'His minder says he's sober and anxious to get this over and done with.'

'Great.'

I'd arranged for an army charity to contact him. I was hoping for a rehabilitation programme to sort out his life. But quietly I didn't believe he'd welcome outside interference. And there was the issue of the man he'd killed in the woods. That demanded investigation and a decision on prosecution. I was sure Roche would contrive some way to keep Hobbs out of the courts.

'The street's teeming with reporters and TV crews. I've brought in extra security.'

'Thanks. It'll be a bit of a circus but we'll get through.'

Finally Joan got to tell her news. 'Albert Dowling won't be coming.'

'What?' I stopped in my tracks. Another jogger almost bumped into me. I glanced around. Was there a race on? Some sort of contest drawing joggers onto these usually quiet streets? I couldn't spot anything.

'He's had a nervous breakdown. He was admitted to a psychiatric unit last night. He's under sedation.'

Suddenly I began to have doubts. Had Redmond outwitted me again? Was something new being plotted? Or was Albert Dowling preparing his defence for another court of law? A plea of insanity?

'We'll go ahead without him,' I said.

I didn't have to wait long for a train. At 8.15 a.m. I sat at a window seat and pretended to admire the coast-line. My right hand was inside my briefcase. I gripped the Glock, finger on the trigger. I knew that sitting opposite me the two workmen in boiler suits with bogus logo were armed police. They argued over soccer results, women and the price of beer in downtown Dublin. I almost believed them. I knew also that in the adjoining carriage eight more armed officers were studying incoming passengers. They moved through the train, assessing commuters.

We made good time, the change-overs at stops were quick and efficient. At 8.40 a.m. I alighted at Connolly Station and followed the crowds along interlinking tunnels and concrete steps. No one paid the slightest attention to me. Or my boiler-suited bodyguards.

From the top of the escalator that dropped onto Amiens Street, I could see a horde of newshounds milling around Store Street corner, leading to the coroner's court. On ground level I zigzagged past traffic backed up to the quays. A break in cloud cover threw early morning sun onto the steel and glass buildings of the International Financial Centre. The growl of the city rumbled in the background. I drew myself in tight as a cyclist hurried past, a wing-mirror clipping my briefcase. Then I took a deep breath, buried my chin on my chest and pushed through the media pack. Cameras were trained on me, microphones shoved in my face. A barrage of questions was shouted. I ignored them.

I finally made it inside.

Joan greeted me with a mug of coffee and whispered encouragement. She was dressed as if determined to make a fashion statement. Black skirt, off-white almost see-through linen blouse and white headband to hold back her dark hair. In the typing pool there was none of the usual banter. Only the constant ringing of phones and garbled answers as staff struggled to cope with the press.

I glanced inside the chamber. I spotted Mary Dowling. She was fingering her rosary beads and praying. Richard Dowling stared ahead, his unpleasant features tight and tense. There was a cluster of journalists. I summoned the lawyers for a pre-inquest conference.

Chapter 53

The room of sighs isn't big, maybe thirty foot long and twenty deep. A desk and bookshelves make it smaller. There's a swivel chair for me and two soft seats for visitors. The ceiling is painted white but seriously needs freshening up. The walls are beige and cluttered with photos of previous coroners.

At 9.30 a.m. it was jammed.

Charles McGrath was waiting. He was wearing a three-piece suit, crisp white shirt and trademark bow tie. Today it was blue with white polka dots. Fred Hodgins, the lawyer for Harry Malone, paced nervously. He was a few inches off six feet, chunky with thick glasses and in a sombre suit. DI Roche and Reilly huddled in a corner. Roche was in open-neck mid-blue shirt and navy trousers. Her tea-cosy hairstyle was back in place and the scar on her forehead covered with make-up. Her eyes darted from face to face, as if trying to memorise everyone. Reilly was still in his casual gear of denims and T-shirt. Detective Jack Matthews stood awkwardly in another recess; he was in official uniform. Matthews was the officer who'd been grilled by me on the opening day of the inquest. Then he'd conceded he wasn't sure Patrick Dowling had committed suicide; that there might have been someone else with him when he died. He

335

couldn't explain why a bottle of whiskey found in the abandoned BMW was free from fingerprints.

'This is a coroner's court, not a court of law,' I said. 'I'm conducting an inquest, not a criminal trial.'

I waited for that to be understood.

'My job is to decide the cause of death of Patrick Dowling. Whatever else is revealed here today is none of my business.' Which wasn't strictly true. It shouldn't have been my business but a certain drug dealer had very much made it my business.

'I still have reservations about the autopsy and will deal with the questioning. I have not engaged counsel to represent the state.'

The lawyers exchanged glances. *Not a wise decision, Dr Wilson.*

I threw out another surprise. 'The police have a strong interest in the evidence.'

The lawyers eyed the policemen; the policemen eyed the lawyers.

'Unlike in most suicide inquests, today we have an eyewitness.'

The room was unpleasantly hot and I loosened the top button on my shirt. McGrath unclasped his bow tie and ran a finger around his fleshy neck.

I told McGrath and Hodgins about Hobbs. How he came to be in the woods, his vagrant and alcohol-soaked lifestyle and delay in coming forward. I explained his stay in University Hospital, scans and lab results and medical conclusion.

'Hobbs's recall is clear. He saw someone else die in the same clearing Dowling was found in.'

McGrath swore softly.

I flapped a six-page fax I'd received minutes earlier from the State Pathology Unit.

'Forensic archaeologists searched the area yesterday and discovered a shallow grave with a male body. It may have been there for some time, possibly a month.'

Two lawyers looked like they wished they were a hundred miles away.

'I mention this only to prove Hobbs's reliability. His recall of the other event has been confirmed. Therefore what he says happened to Dowling can be considered accurate.'

I targeted McGrath and Hodgins. 'Please advise your clients the truth will come out today. One way or another.'

Then I focused on Hodgins. 'Harry Malone altered his testimony under duress. Tell him it's in his interest to give an honest account.'

'I've discussed this with him,' said Hodgins. 'I'm proposing immunity from criminal charges in return for full cooperation.'

I looked to Roche and she shrugged.

'That's not for me to decide,' I said. 'But I suspect he'll get a sympathetic hearing.'

Hodgins took this as given. He wrote a note to himself.

I went on. 'The jury is being briefed on previous testimony. They know about our eyewitness, his background and lifestyle. They know he's medically cleared to offer testimony.'

McGrath fanned himself with an A4 pad. He looked uncomfortably hot and uncomfortably worried.

'The forensic pathologist is not budging on the autopsy result. He believes Dowling committed suicide.'

Chapter 54

'Patrick didn't want to die.'

Harry Malone was twenty-nine; around six foot three with rugged features. He was in a casual jacket, open-neck shirt and beige trousers. His sandy-coloured hair was cut in a V at the back. He first outlined how he met Dowling at school rugby competitions. The friendship was forged during sports bonding sessions. They went on trips abroad, inter-railed Europe and mixed socially. He kept up that relationship to the end.

'But he was dying. A diseased and wasted drug addict.' Malone's voice was unemotional and even. Maybe he'd been practising his lines. Or maybe he was just glad to be unburdening his soul. Whatever, he seemed determined to maintain his composure. He stood straight and faced forward, occasionally glancing towards me.

I listened to him from the top bench. To my right was the dark mahogany witness box where Malone stood. To the left was the jury. This was a new group of three men and six women ranging from early twenties to mid-forties. Sitting at the wide desk separating the jury from the witness box were Fred Hodgins and Charles McGrath. Mary Dowling was squeezed into a corner of the visitors' gallery. She was wearing a linen jacket over a green blouse. Her hair was drawn back and held in a clasp. Her face was a mask of make-up.

Beside her in jeans and open-neck shirt sat a sombre-looking Richard Dowling. Then my bodyguard Tony Reilly and DI Pamela Roche pushed together at the back of the room, as if on a date. But they certainly weren't holding hands. The rest of the space was taken up by journalists. Notepads, cassette recorders and mobile phones were at the ready. The chamber was warm and staff had opened windows. Trams, buses and cars trilled, blared and beeped their way along the streets outside.

'How did he get the drugs?' I knew Hobbs's explanation for this. I wanted to hear what Malone might offer.

'From a dealer called Jonathan Redmond.'

Redmond's name entered the public record for the first time.

'How did he pay for them?'

'He didn't. Redmond gave him all he wanted.' Hobbs's account was supported.

'Why would a drug dealer give free supplies? That doesn't make sense.'

I'd one eye on the gallery. Mary Dowling was praying. Richard Dowling's ugly and pockmarked features were twisted in rage.

'Redmond was using Standard and Chartered Bank to launder money. Patrick was a go-between. He passed messages from Redmond to his contact in the bank. There were no fax, email, telephone or paper instructions.' DI Roche's suspicions were now confirmed. That was what she'd offered when we met in Bongos café. Before the windows came in on top of us.

The jury was engrossed. They were being offered an in-depth account of one drug dealer's *modus operandi*.

'How do you know this?'

'Patrick told me.'

'Why was he acting as a go-between?'

'Redmond targeted Patrick at university. He knew his father was a government minister so he plied Patrick with drugs. Redmond didn't sell heroin but he made sure Patrick had a regular supply. Once Patrick was addicted, Redmond called Albert Dowling. He knew the minister's dubious reputation. The two agreed a business deal: Redmond would pay for a link to the cabinet table. And he'd keep Patrick safe.'

McGrath's jaw dropped. The jury looked stunned. The journalists couldn't believe their luck. Some scribbled furiously, others held up Dictaphones to catch the exchanges.

'How could this help him?'

'Redmond now had an inside track on state security. He knew when it was safe to move drugs. He learned how to launder profits though bogus accounts.'

'Are you saying Albert Dowling passed confidential details to Redmond using his son as the go-between?'

'Yes.'

This caused another stir.

I continued. 'Why did Patrick discuss this with you?'

'He was being pulled between Redmond and his family. He needed to share his problems with someone.'

'Was there anyone else he confided in?'

Malone coughed into a fist. 'Stephen Brady, a reporter with the *Evening Herald*, knew. Stephen shielded him from a lot of unpleasant publicity.'

'Why?'

'I think Brady off-loaded material to other journalists. In return they left Patrick alone.'

'Had Brady another agenda?'

Malone looked puzzled.

I explained my logic. 'Might Brady have realised he'd

a major scoop? By protecting Patrick from the worst of the press he kept the story to himself?'

Malone considered this. If it was something he knew he was putting on a show of ignorance. I looked towards the editor of the *Evening Herald*. He'd a half grin. This was probably true.

'That's possible.'

I scribbled a note in the file. Mainly to give me time to plan strategy.

'Did Patrick talk about this with anyone else?'

'He'd a drug-addiction counsellor called Niamh Shanahan. She exhausted herself trying to help. But Patrick kept drifting to his old habits. One day she lost her temper and challenged him. So he poured his heart out.'

Charles McGrath shifted in his chair. The inquest was drawing his clients into hazardous territory. He looked unsure, throwing worrying glances towards the visitors' gallery. By contrast, Hodgins sat still, chin resting on upturned palms. His face betrayed no emotion. I suspected he'd gone over the evidence with Malone. He knew what was coming.

'What was going on?'

'Drugs were the only buffer Patrick had between insanity and a nightmare existence. Heroin, cocaine, uppers and downers: he used them all. Once Shanahan knew the full story she realised Patrick was in danger. And by telling her everything, she knew she was in danger. That's why Stephen Brady was murdered. He knew too much.' Now I knew why Niamh Shanahan fled. And why she blocked communication with the Dowlings. Her knowledge was a liability. She had to create distance and anonymity.

'Did something else make Patrick's existence much worse?'

'Yes. His father double-crossed Redmond.'

There was a ripple of surprise. I looked to the gallery. Mary Dowling was still praying. Her cosmetic mask hadn't cracked yet. Richard Dowling was making excuses to leave but Roche blocked his exit. She directed him to return to his seat.

'The family made a lot of money during the building boom. They used it to buy more land and property. But they were greedy. They wanted more. They were as addicted to cash as Patrick was to drugs. Albert Dowling knew of government plans to develop a derelict site along the docklands. He decided to buy it. But he didn't have enough capital to show up front. Dowling was close to Dan Thornton, CEO of Standard and Chartered Bank. The bank was laundering Redmond's drug profits. Thornton moved five million euros of this into Albert Dowling's account. Dowling added three million of personal funds to secure the plot outright. It also inflated the value. The idea was to sell at the peak of the market, repay Redmond and pocket the balance. It was all going to plan until the economy collapsed. Land values plummeted, especially in the docklands. Dowling tried desperately to sell but no one was buying. He lost a fortune. And owed five million to Redmond.'

There was frenzied excitement in the chamber. Texts began flying to editors. Among the jurors there was astonished whispering. One woman craned her neck to get a better look at the Dowlings. She shook her head in disgust.

'How do you know this?'

'A man called Timothy Cunningham worked in Standard and Chartered. He spotted the money transfers. At the time I worked with State Irish Bank. I specialised in international trading. He came to me for advice.'

'Why?'

'Because he knew we were doing much the same.'

'Lending money to special clients to inflate land prices?'

'Yes.'

'And hoping they'd sell, make a killing and repay your bank with interest?'

'Yes.'

More excitement in the room. Ties were shed, shirt collars opened. Next day's headlines were changing faster than they could be planned.

'What'd you say to Cunningham?'

'I advised him to keep everything in-house. I said talk with your boss. Avoid scandal. If word gets out it'll trigger a collapse in the financial services industry.'

'Did he go to his boss?'

'Yes.'

'How did Thornton react?'

Malone didn't answer. Now his composure began to slip. He gripped the sides of the witness box to steady himself.

'I never found out. Cunningham committed suicide a day after the meeting.'

The chamber fell silent. It was almost as if the outside traffic had stopped to listen.

'Didn't you consider that suspicious? Didn't it seem strange that Cunningham would kill himself so soon after disclosing massive fraud to his CEO?'

'I didn't believe he committed suicide. I was convinced he'd been murdered. And I was sure I'd be next if I opened my mouth. There were dodgy practices in our division. I trusted no one. If I called in the police a lot of dirt would come out.' Malone's excuses for staying silent sounded pathetic. And personally damaging. I wondered if this was the real reason he'd been reluctant to give evidence.

He went on. 'And I knew Redmond's reputation. I knew there'd be war when he found out.'

'What happened next?'

'Patrick was found dead.' Malone's brow began beading with sweat. 'The Dowlings panicked. Questions were asked about his links with drug dealers. Albert Dowling went to pieces. He couldn't handle the pressure so the family drugged him.'

Charles McGrath was on his feet, flustered and agitated. This was going very wrong for him. 'Coroner, I must object. These are disgraceful allegations.' He opened his waistcoat, undid his bow tie and the top button on his shirt. He flapped at the gap with a page. 'I demand a recess to confer with my clients.'

'This is an inquest, not a criminal trial, Mr McGrath. We discussed this earlier. You may consult with your clients later.'

I turned to Malone. 'What do you mean "drugged him"?'

'With tranquillisers and anti-depressants.'

This was correct. In front of me was the pharmacy print-out of prescription medicines Albert Dowling had been taking for some time. I had asked Reilly to get one of his hacks to access Dowling's pharmacy's records and they had come through for me. High-dose anti-depressants and major tranquillisers.

'They started rumours he'd Alzheimer's disease to cover up the side effects. It kept Albert out of the way while Mary and Richard decided how to deal with the crisis.'

'That's what they considered Patrick's death,' I asked, 'a crisis?'

'Yes. Patrick the go-between was now Patrick the problem.'

There was subdued muttering in the gallery. Two reporters edged away from the Dowlings as if they might be contagious.

'Do you know what happened to Patrick the day he died?'

'I wasn't with him at the end. But I know who was there when I left.'

Throughout these exchanges Malone's lawyer stayed silent. He knew his client's only hope was to tell the truth, no matter how damaging that was to his career.

I called a ten-minute recess.

Chapter 55

In my office I sipped on a coffee and thought over what I'd just learned.

Mary and Richard Dowling were liars. Declan Shanahan, Niamh Shanahan's father, warned Richard Dowling wasn't to be trusted. And he was right. Dowling slipped up with simple errors. For example, he claimed his brother Seamus was looking for accommodation when in fact he'd been living with his lover for months. Then he was evasive when I asked who supplied Patrick with drugs. But according to Declan Shanahan, *'even the dogs in the street knew who the dealer was'*.

If he missed with the small details he was careful with the big stuff. His family had used laundered drugs profits to buy land to make a quick buck. The popular expression at the time was 'flipping' land in a rising market. Buy a site but do nothing with it. Don't even let a cow graze on it. Hold on for twelve months, then sell and pocket the windfall profit. Many did exactly the same. They thought they were financial wizards. Almost to a man (and it was a male-dominated practice) they ended up in serious debt. Ireland's property and banking collapse was spectacular. And now we knew it involved the criminal underworld as well. Jonathan Redmond was planning to quit narcotics. He needed the money he'd sifted away. But Albert Dowling had his hand in

Redmond's pocket, grabbing more than just small change.

I was taken aback how Harry Malone turned a blind eye to such profiteering. Ireland's banks were collectively guilty of incompetence, fraud and cover up. Greed was the driving motive. After greed galloped corruption. Timothy Cunningham was probably murdered because he tried to blow the whistle on his institution's schemes.

I rang Roche. There'd been no attack on either decoy convoy. There were no sightings of Redmond or O'Leary. She told me to keep my Glock at the ready. There was a tap on the door. Charles McGrath wanted a word.

'I've advised the Dowlings not to take any further part in this inquest. Wild and disgraceful allegations are surfacing.'

I sighed. I was worn out by all that'd happened to me over the previous weeks. I was exhausted by the fight to survive and hold my family together. I was mentally drained trying to resolve the cause of Patrick Dowling's death. I was fed up with the Dowling family and their lying. I was in no mood to indulge them. 'They can deny these allegations another day and in another court. They can surround themselves with lawyers. They can surround themselves with barbed wire for all I care.' I let that sink in. 'But here, I'm in control. This inquest goes ahead with or without them.' McGrath started to say something but I cut him short. 'If they step outside they'll be arrested.' I wasn't sure Roche would move so fast but suspected she was itching to stage a grand finale. 'The building's surrounded by journalists. It wouldn't look good to see your clients handcuffed in front of the cameras.'

McGrath started up about their rights again. I told him I wasn't interested. I reminded him my responsibility was to Patrick Dowling only. And on that issue I wasn't budging.

'Then let's get this over with.' He stomped out in a rage.

I ordered the court recalled. I heard the shuffling and mumbling of the jury as they were taken from their room. I wondered what they'd discussed. Such scandal had unfolded. Would they ever forget this day? But worse was to come. John Hobbs's evidence was shocking. Would those involved admit their involvement? Or would they brazenly clam up? I was too tired to think, too tired to worry any more. It was time to finish this. Tomorrow, Thursday, was my last day as coroner. On Friday I'd go to London with Sarah, Jennifer and Gregory. We'd find peace and privacy. It'd give us time to re-think our futures, and put the past behind us. I took a deep breath and let it out slowly. I flicked my swivel chair and left it spinning. I straightened my tie, uncurled a corner of my collar where it was riding up. I offered yet another prayer to my dead parents for support. Then I opened the door leading to the chamber of ghosts.

Chapter 56

Inside the room buzzed with anticipation. I spotted Gerard Canny, the forensic pathologist who'd conducted the autopsy. He'd squeezed his tall frame into a space reserved for officials.

Six new uniformed police officers were now in the chamber. They were big, burly men with frowning no-nonsense expressions, a 'we're here to do business' look about them. They'd pushed themselves into the already crowded public gallery, forcing a significant crush. Those nearest to them scowled their discomfort. Fred Hodgins and Charles McGrath were seated at their desk between the jury and the witness box. McGrath was probably the most unfortunate lawyer in the country at that moment. His jacket was off, his waistcoat open to display his prominent belly. He'd dispensed with his bow tie and was fanning paperwork against his face. Hodgins was shining his glasses on the end of his tie. He hadn't spoken or interrupted during his client's deposition. He'd his own agenda of another day in another courtroom. Then he'd have a helluva job representing Malone.

In the visitors' gallery the huddle of journalists waited impatiently. Beside them, Mary Dowling had stopped praying. She sat motionless and mute. But the mask was slipping. I noticed smudged mascara and streaked concealer. Richard Dowling inspected the floor.

Malone returned to the witness box. This time he seemed less composed, nervous even.

'Go back to the twenty-ninth of November last year,' I said. 'Why were you with Dowling?'

Malone cleared his throat. 'He rang me around ten that morning. He was rambling and disturbed. He'd been told to meet a drug dealer called Noel Carty. He hated Carty and was afraid of him.'

'Why?'

'Carty was a nasty piece of work and used to string Patrick along. For his own amusement he'd make arrangements to meet and not turn up. Or he'd insist on being paid, even though he knew he wasn't supposed to be collecting.'

'But why was Patrick so worried about this meeting?'

'It came out of the blue. And Carty didn't do social calls.'

'What happened?'

'Patrick asked me to go with him for support. I told him I wasn't getting involved. "I just need somebody I can trust," he said. "I don't know what this bastard wants." He was very uptight. He'd taken some type of speed. His hands were shaking so much I drove.'

I noticed Roche direct one of the big police officers to the exit. He checked the lock was secure.

'We made it to a car park beside a pub in Stepaside around eleven o'clock. The block was deserted. It was starting to rain.'

Stepaside was once a hamlet on Dublin's southern fringes. During the building boom the sleepy village was transformed into a dormitory town for Dublin

350

commuters. It was also close to Enniskerry parish and the woodland where Patrick Dowling was found.

'What happened there?'

'Carty was in a Range Rover with tinted windows. He called Patrick inside.'

Suspicious looks were exchanged between jurors. The Dowlings slumped deeper into the benches. Charles McGrath was scribbling furiously. His body language screamed rage.

'How long did Patrick stay inside the Range Rover?'

'About five minutes.'

'What happened then?'

'He got out. But he was staggering and looked shocked. I went to help. He was carrying a bag of heroin and cocaine with needles and syringes.'

Malone asked for a glass of water.

He waited until it was handed to him to deliver the punchline. 'He also had a gun.'

Charles McGrath nearly fell out of his chair. His eyes were out on stalks of disbelief.

'Did he have this before he went into the Range Rover?'

Malone sipped on the water. 'No.'

'You're sure of that?'

'He never used a gun in his life.'

'Why did Carty give him the gun?'

'Because he said he'd need it.'

The drum of street traffic was now overshadowed by the drill of rain as a cloudburst swept across the city.

'Why?'

'To kill his father.'

There was a gasp from the press corps. One of the jurors jolted forward, eyes bulging.

I looked towards Mary Dowling. For a split second

our eyes locked. Pure hate hit me square on. Then she turned away.

'Why?'

'Redmond had found out about the money. He wanted revenge. And he wanted Patrick to do the shooting.'

'What did Patrick do?'

'He threw the gun into bushes and jumped on Carty. They started fighting. It was no contest. Carty could've killed him if he'd wanted. I tried to stop them but Patrick kept going back for more. He jumped on Carty's back and tried to punch him. Carty just knocked him to the ground. Patrick was bleeding and raging and shouting.'

The chamber fell silent. Even the journalists stopped taking notes.

'Then Carty shouted, "it's ye or yer crooked oul fella. Redmond wants wan of youse dead!"'

Malone cleared his throat and sipped on water. 'Then he pushed Patrick into the BMW. I saw Carty throw a few punches to stop him shouting.'

This was consistent with autopsy and police findings. Especially how Carty's bloodstained fingerprint came to be on the BMW dashboard.

'What did you do then?'

'I rang Richard and told him what was going on.' Heads swivelled towards the visitors' gallery. Richard Dowling stared straight ahead. His face was a ghastly grey, his cheeks sucked in. His eyes were as blank as a corpse.

'How did he respond?'

Malone took a deep breath. 'He told me to give Patrick heroin. He said he'd come and sort everything out.'

'Did you do that?'

'I had to. Patrick was shaking so much he couldn't find a vein.'

There was a burst of activity in the gallery. Mary Dowling was trying to stand. Richard Dowling dragged her back down. There were angry exchanges. Charles McGrath leapt from his seat.

'Is everything all right, Mr McGrath?' I asked politely. The lawyer forced a poker face. 'Yes, Coroner.' There was short but intense conversation. 'My clients need clarification on an issue.'

'Can we proceed?'

'Yes, Coroner.'

'Thank you.' I couldn't have been nicer.

I continued. 'What time did Richard Dowling make it to the car park?'

'Around midday.'

'Was he on his own?'

'His mother was with him.'

'Was Patrick relieved to see them?'

'He didn't even know they were there. He was totally spaced out.'

'What happened then?'

'I hung around for a while. It was raining and I was getting soaked. Richard found the gun and held on to it. After that he was on his mobile most of the time.'

'Didn't either check Patrick was okay?'

'No. They were too agitated. Mary ran across the road to a supermarket and came back with a bottle of whiskey. She took a swig to calm her nerves.'

I glanced towards Jack Matthews. So that's where the bottle of Jameson's whiskey came from.

'I tried to clean Patrick. There was blood on his hands and wrists and clothes. Finally I flagged a cab and left.'

'When Patrick was found dead the next day were you surprised?'

'Yes.'

'Did you think he'd killed himself?'

Now it was Malone's turn to ratchet up the tension. He delayed until the very walls began to moan. 'No. Even though he was dying he was scared of the end.'

Chapter 57

John Hobbs's entrance took even me by surprise. He was in an Oxfam hand-out, black, pinstriped suit, dark-blue shirt and cream-coloured tie. Apart from the fact it hung off his bony frame he looked quite respectable. He was escorted by two uniformed detectives, burly men shepherding him by the elbows. Hobbs stopped at the visitors' gallery and eyeballed the Dowlings. Then he made his way to the witness box. McGrath drew his clients together. There was an agitated discussion. Mary Dowling's rosary-beaded fingers gripped the lawyer's shirt. Richard Dowling was trying to whisper but was shushed. I overheard 'say nothing'. Then McGrath hurried to his seat.

As Hobbs took the oath the jury watched intently. Gerard Canny, the forensic pathologist, was sifting through a file, one eye on me and the other on his notes.

In the witness box Hobbs looked uncomfortable. He tugged at the lapels of his jacket and scratched where the shirt collar rubbed his neck. He seemed annoyed, as if anxious to get back on the streets and buy a drink.

I started the questions. 'How come you were in that woodland on the twenty-ninth of November 2009?'

'I'd been livin' rough there for months so I knew the territory. And I knew every sound. When I heard gunfire I went lookin'.' Hobbs faced straight ahead, as if addressing the wall.

'What'd you see?' His deposition was in front of me and I knew the answer.

'It was rainin'. The wind was blowin' leaves n' branches all over the place. I was wearin' oilskins and tryin' to dodge fallin' branches. With the moanin' n' creakin' of the trees it took me a while to track the shooter.'

'Who was there?'

'Two men.' He flashed two fingers.

'Did you know them?'

'Yes.'

'Who were they?'

'Noel Carty n' Richard Dowlin'.'

The court was so still I could hear the patter of rainfall on the windows.

'How can you be so sure?'

'I'd seen them before.'

'Where?'

'Carty was a scumbag drug dealer. Everywan on the streets knew him. We avoided the bastard. We'd an early warnin' system when he was seen around.'

'Where had you seen Richard Dowling before?'

'I was with Paddy wan night when he dragged him out of the gutter.'

'What was he doing in the gutter?'

'Lyin'.'

It was a stupid question. I got what I asked for.

'Who was carrying the gun?'

'Carty.'

'Who was he shooting at?'

'Nobody. It was target practice. He was aimin' at anythin' that took his eye.'

'What happened to the spent shells?'

'He counted every round n' picked up the casin's.'

That explained the absence of cartridge shells.

'What was Richard Dowling doing?'

'Tyin' a hangman's noose.'

McGrath was out of his seat. 'I'm sorry, Coroner, but this cannot go on. You say this is not a criminal trial. I've never attended an inquest where such evidence was offered without the chance of rebuttal.'

Hobbs glanced towards the jury. They were locked onto him.

'Mr McGrath,' I said, 'I too have never held an inquest where such evidence surfaced. But we're going to hear it whether you or your clients like it or not.'

I pressed ahead. 'What do you mean by that?'

Hobbs dragged his tie free and opened the top button on his shirt. 'Richard Dowlin' had a rope knotted in a noose thrown over a branch. The other end was tied to the tree trunk.'

Charles McGrath was on his feet again but I stopped him with a glare.

'The noose swung in the air. Underneath it was a bar stool and stepladder.'

There was a gasp of astonishment.

'Can I be clear on this?' I asked. 'You saw a hangman's noose, a bar stool and a small stepladder. That's a very exact set-up.'

'Oh, they knew wha' they were doin'.'

'What time was this?'

'It was getting' shadowy in the woods but still brigh' enough. I'd say it was about three o'clock. The wind was easin' n' the rain had stopped by the time they were ready.'

'Ready for what?'

Chapter 58

The official account of Patrick Dowling's discovery on 30 November 2009 was being confirmed.

'A search party found Dowling's locked BMW nudged into a gateway beside a corn field. It was parked awkwardly, as if abandoned in a hurry. Inside was the detritus of drug abuse. Needles and syringes, foil packets of heroin and opened packets of cocaine. A bottle of Jameson's whiskey, one-quarter full, was jammed into the glove compartment. The upholstery stank of spilled spirits. The car keys were lying in a culvert close to the vehicle.

Less than an hour later the searchers came upon the missing man. His body was hanging by the neck from a rope around the branch of a tree in a clearing. The glade was no more than twenty yards in from a hiking trail. He'd been dead at least twenty-four hours. Lying to the side of the dangling feet was a bar stool. His footprints were later lifted from the seat. That November was cold and blustery. Strong winds and heavy showers had denuded most trees. On the day conditions were poor, the air damp with heavy cloud cover. The terrain was covered in fallen leaves and twigs.'

The final piece of the jigsaw was slipping into place.

'What happened then?' I asked.

'Carty n' Dowlin' were waitin'. They were shoutin' inta their phones. Carty kept loadin' and shootin'.'

'How close were you to them?'

Hobbs made a quick calculation. 'As close as I am to ye.' Ten feet.

'How did you hide yourself?'

'There was plenty of scrub in that woodland. I burrowed into that.'

'Could you hear what they were saying?'

'There was some row about missin' money. Carty said somethin' to Dowlin'.'

'Did you hear this?'

'Nah. They were too far away.'

'Did you hear any of Richard Dowling's conversation?'

'Only snatches. He was tellin' somebody till wait.'

'Have you any idea who he was talking to?'

'Nah.'

I flicked through paperwork. The jury hadn't exchanged a word. There was a sense of dread in the chamber. It was as if no one wanted to hear the rest.

'What happened then?'

'Two people came up the path.' Another two fingers were flashed.

There was a flurry of activity in the visitors' gallery. Charles McGrath moved swiftly to calm nerves. Mary Dowling was half standing, half leaning against the wall. She looked bemused, as if living a nightmare and trying to wake up. Eventually she slumped back onto the bench. The mask had finally slipped. And the face behind it was raw with fear.

I took a deep breath. I knew what was coming. 'Who were they?'

'Paddy n' his mother.'

Someone groaned.

'You're sure it was his mother?'

'I'd seen her before so I knew what she looked like.'

'Where?'

'She was in a car wan night lookin' for Paddy. He was in a coma under Baggot Street Bridge. She directed everythin'. I lifted him into the back seat beside her. She never said a word, not even thanks.' His voice hardened. 'She looked at me as if I was dirt.'

One juror buried her head in her hands.

'What was Mary Dowling doing?'

'Prayin' n' drinkin' whiskey.' Nobody laughed. This was becoming worse. 'She'd a pair of rosary beads in wan hand n' a bottle of whiskey in the other.'

'What happened when she saw the rope?'

'She started cryin'. She'd Paddy by the arm, haulin' him after her.'

'What did the others do?'

'Richard tried calmin' her. They were so close I heard every word. He said "Redmond knows everythin'."'

'What was Carty doing?'

'Keepin' an eye on the path.'

'Did you try and get away?'

'I was too scared to move.'

'So you saw and heard everything?'

'I seen everythin' but I didn't hear everythin'.'

'Was the storm still blowing?'

'The rain was easin' but they were all soaked. Paddy was walkin' in a circle, mumblin' till hisself. Every stitch he wore was wringin' wet. His mother was almost covered in mud from head till toe. She looked like a rag doll. Richard was tryin' to keep his phone dry. That's all he was worried about, keepin' his fuckin' phone dry. Carty was as uptight as bejaysus.'

'What happened?'

'Paddy was totally gone. He couldna known what was goin' on.'

Mary Dowling began praying loudly. Her eyes were

360

closed, her lips were moving. Richard Dowling had both hands over his ears as if to drown out the world.

'What happened then?'

'Paddy n' Richard started arguin'. Richard called him every scum name under the sun.'

'Did he hit him?'

'No. It was all verbals. Paddy wasn' fit to be on the earth, he was a useless addict, that sort of shit. Paddy threw a punch n' hit him on the chin. Carty pulled them apart.'

Forensic pathologist Canny nodded. This fitted in with his autopsy report. Two separate fist fights had been possible that day. We now knew what happened, where it happened. And who was involved.

'Carty grabbed Paddy by the scruff of the neck. He kicked n' dragged him across the ground n' dropped him beside the stepladder. He shouted at him to get up on the stool.'

'Did he do that?'

'He had til.'

'Why?'

'Carty had the gun agin his mother's head.'

The court was in shocked silence.

'I still don' think Paddy knew what was happenin'. He slipped twice tryin' to even put a foot on the bloody ladder. Carty roared at him n' shoved him back. He made Paddy get up on the ladder, onto the stool n' pull the rope aroun' his neck. Paddy was cryin' all the time. It was a strange cry, like a child watchin' a scary film n' too frightened to run away.'

One of the female jurors was holding back tears.

Hobbs paused to sip on water. I looked around the room. The Dowlings were crumbling. They huddled deeper into their seats. Pale, anxious and fearful. They knew what was coming.

'Richard Dowlin' was on his mobile. He was shoutin' about money. Where could he get money? How soon could he get money? That's all he was interested in. Money.'

Here were the dynamics laid bare. Redmond's contract on Albert Dowling was being bought. But the Dowlings had to find the funds. If not, one of them had to surrender their life. And at that point Patrick was standing on a makeshift gallows with a noose around his neck while his mother was on her knees in a muddy clearing with a gun at her head.

'There was dreadful screamin' n' cursin'. Paddy was roarin' cryin', his mother pleadin' for her life n' Paddy's life. It was a fuckin' nightmare.'

Nobody was bothered about Hobbs's language. They were so shocked at what they were hearing they couldn't have cared less.

'Carty had Mary Dowlin' by the hair, shoutin' at her. "It's ye or him."'

Hobbs's eyes were now red-rimmed, his voice choking.

'None of them was watchin' Paddy.' He paused. 'But I was.'

There was a split second of dazed silence, then Hobbs went on.

'He reached up.' Hobbs lifted his hands and made a climbing movement. 'There was slack in the rope n' he gripped it tightly. The rope went taut.'

Hobbs kept his hands in the air.

'The rest were still arguin' n' yellin'. Carty had Mary Dowlin' forced onto the ground. He'd his heel on the back of her neck. Her face was twisted in the muck.'

I caught Roche's gaze. She shook her head in disbelief.

'Paddy tipped the bar stool with the heel of his shoe. It fell over. He held on till the rope. I dunno where he found the strength. He dangled in the air for mebbe twenty seconds. Then he shouted.'

Hobbs took another sip of water. When he spoke again it was a mumble.

'None of us heard that,' I said. 'What did he shout?'

Hobbs glared at the visitors' gallery. *'Jesus help me.'*

The room was silent. Only traffic noise broke through.

'Then he let go. He dropped about two feet before the rope caught him. Sure he was only inches from the ground.'

McGrath buried his head in his hands and rocked back and forth. Gerard Canny stared at the floor. Not one of the journalists moved.

Chapter 59

I asked McGrath if he wanted to challenge Hobbs's testimony. He refused. I asked the Dowlings if they wanted to challenge Hobbs's testimony. They ignored me. McGrath buttoned his waistcoat and re-fastened his bow tie. 'These outrageous allegations will be dealt with in another court, Coroner.' He forced an air of indignation, but his heart wasn't in it.

'That's up to you,' I said.

He muttered something but I wasn't listening. I'd an idea of his tactics. Hobbs might never turn up again. If he did he mightn't be in such a good state. Then his words would be aggressively challenged. That could tax him to breaking point. But today he'd done everything I'd asked. The truth had finally come out. He was rushed out a side door and back to the judge's house.

I addressed the jury, explaining that their task was to agree a cause of death. I went over the issues. Patrick Dowling had surely ended his own life, as described by Hobbs. But was that suicide? He'd been forced up a ladder almost at gunpoint. The noose had been prepared by his brother. That could not be premeditation. He was under enormous pressure. He'd been ordered to murder his father. Then a gun was put to his mother's head. 'It's you or her', an either/or decision. One life had to be taken. Was Patrick's gesture an act of supreme courage to protect his mother? Or was his mind so confused from drugs and the emotional turmoil going on around him that he didn't know what was going on?

I explained the limitations of a forensic post-mortem. The pathologist can dissect and examine the body, but there is no such thing as a psychological post-mortem. No matter how carefully the brain is inspected no thoughts or emotions are revealed.

'We'll never know what was going through his mind.'

The jury left to confer. I asked the journalists to leave the chamber and wait until a verdict was reached.

When the last one shuffled out the police took over. Roche arrested Mary and Richard Dowling. They were advised of their rights and charges read out. McGrath shepherded them from the chamber.

'Heads up, eyes forward, answer no questions,' I heard him shout. 'Brazen it out.' Which was pretty good advice, considering the circumstances.

While I waited I went back over everything that'd been revealed. The clean bottle of whiskey now made sense. Richard Dowling probably jammed it in Patrick's car, first making sure no prints or smudges were left. He may have encouraged his brother to drink to dull his thinking. At autopsy Patrick's blood alcohol level was low, suggesting some intake. Patrick Dowling didn't make his own way to the woodland clearing in a drug-induced stupor. I'd my doubts about that after reading the file for the first time. Now we knew he'd been driven there by his mother. Nor did he tie a rope to a tree and fashion it in a noose. His brother had that ready even before he arrived. And he didn't climb up a bar stool on his own. There was a stepladder to help him.

Hobbs told me what happened afterwards. Carty grabbed the stepladder and ran like hell to get away.

Mary Dowling prayed beside her dead son as his body swung from the end of a rope. Richard Dowling spent over an hour dragging branches over the muddy plot to disguise the footprints. He collected fallen leaves and twigs and threw them into the clearing. By the end it was raining heavily again. By nightfall the death scene was pretty much as the search squad found it the next day. No one could have known what really happened.

Hobbs wept as he watched his friend's body hang.

'I shoulda done somethin'. I shouldna left him like that.'

Chapter 60

'Patrick Dowling took his own life to save his mother. It was an act of extraordinary bravery.'

The jury returned before 1 p.m. They were red-eyed, distressed and angry. The three men and six women had endured two hours of gruelling testimony. At first they were intrigued as they heard how Jonathan Redmond laundered money through a respectable bank. Then intrigue turned to astonishment as the rest of the tale unfolded. Albert Dowling, a senior government minister and father of the deceased, passed classified information to Redmond to enable him to shift narcotics securely, using his son as the go-between. Then Dowling, with the help of the crooked CEO of Standard and Chartered Bank, dipped into Redmond's secret account. However, the plan to buy land and sell it on in a rapidly rising market went seriously wrong when the economy collapsed. What seemed like a clever ruse turned into a nightmare of debt. And revenge. One man had to die. The most vulnerable in the Dowling family was sacrificed to appease the wrath of a wronged drug dealer. By the end the jurors were overwrought, exhausted and disbelieving. But they were able to make a decision. As they filed into the pews, they looked for the Dowlings, surprised to see they'd left. Only a huddle of journalists remained, gloating and exultant.

'The verdict is suicide.'

Forensic pathologist Gerard Canny closed his file, glanced up at me and offered a rueful smile. *I was right*, he seemed to say.

I thanked the jury. I explained I'd never heard such appalling depositions in the coroner's court before. I apologised for any upset. Anguish, dismay, disbelief and shock were etched on their faces.

I asked for the court to be cleared. There were mutterings, mumblings and soft curses as jurors and journalists filed out separately. Mobile phones were turned on. Calls and texts began to fly. Soon the world would hear what'd happened in the Dublin City Coroner's Court. The shuffling of feet and moving of chairs died away. The murmur of conversation faded. Alone, I sat. I rested my chin on upturned palms. I sighed, a deep and exhausted sigh. I was drained, physically and emotionally. Tracking County Coroner Harold Rafferty's footsteps I'd eventually unearthed the truth behind Patrick Dowling's death. But at some cost: attempts on my life; being armed to protect myself; forced to live with a constant security presence; alienation from my family; resigning my post of coroner. At that moment I wondered whether it had been worth it. I was on the highest bench and could see every corner of the chamber; the mahogany witness box; the dark wooden benches where families gathered to hear the account of their loved one's final hours, stained with sweat and tears. To my left the jury benches, worn and scratched. Then a table in the middle for lawyers. Now there was no scribbling of pen or click of tape recorder. No weeping or stifled sobs.

I waited and listened. I heard only the background growl of inner-city Dublin: car horns, the hum of tram tracks; trains screeching to a halt in nearby Connolly Station; the rumbling of lorries, street cries, seagulls squawking.

Outside the phones rang incessantly. I heard Joan calling Aoife. A door banged. Aoife called back.

Redmond's empire had surely collapsed. He'd be shunned in underworld circles, considered too dangerous to associate with. And he had enemies. There'd be plenty of other gangsters hungry to muscle in on his lucrative territory. Already there'd been major drug and weapon finds as police searched for him in all known drug-dealing haunts. He'd become bad for business. And in his world, that was a serious offence. He'd soon be betrayed to take the heat off the usual mob.

So, I wondered, *how will he react?* The answer was simple. He wouldn't rest until he'd killed me. I'd refused to buckle. I'd dug too deep and exposed everything. Revenge would be his sole driving force. It was me against him; him against me. This time I wanted to deal with him on my terms. But first I had to find him. I was confident of one link: Arthur O'Leary. His close-up vision might be poor but he'd good long sight. He'd watch the building, waiting for me to leave. Then he'd alert Redmond. And Redmond would come hunting.

I left the empty and silent court chamber. Outside the corridors milled with people. Cameras whirred, flashes lit up dark corners. Journalists were gathered at the front office, jostling for position and shouting for inquest transcripts. Jurors were targeted for comments and opinions. Phones rang unanswered. The security squad was struggling to keep control and usher the mob outside. I heard Joan's shrill voice rebuke someone for violating the sanctity of the office. Then Aoife demanded no photographs be taken of the chamber. A flash glowed anyway, enraging

369

her further. Control turned to frustrated anger. I heard curses I hadn't heard for years.

I escaped the melee through the rear stairs and made my way to the top of the building. Here was a turret room, an attic space with windows looking south, east and west. It was no more than twenty foot square, musty and cluttered with old typewriters, faulty dictation machines and stacking chairs. I occasionally used it to escape the madness and sadness of the ground floor.

The turret had restricted views of the city. Immediately south was Busaras, the central transport depot. I watched buses pull out to destinations as far away as Derry, Galway, Letterkenny and Waterford. Eastwards was the International Financial Centre, the first phase of the Dublin dockland regeneration programme. One hundred yards north of that was Connolly Station. Mainline and local Dart trains crossed its tracks. Lower, on the main road, Luas trams trilled their way eastwards to stops at the Four Courts, Goldenbridge, Kylemore, Belgard and finally Tallaght. To the west was Store Street police station, the busiest law-enforcement unit in the land. The afternoon was now overcast and gloomy. Heavy rain clouds were forming. I watched groups huddle on the street. Somewhere among them waited Arthur O'Leary. I was sure of that.

I sat and waited. I inspected my 9mm Glock pistol, checking the magazine was snugly connected. It had a seventeen-round capacity, more than enough for what I planned. The gun was a low-weight, high-capacity weapon and easily concealed. I could move anywhere without causing alarm.

I glanced at my watch. It was 2.30 p.m., a little over an hour since the final verdict. I pulled a chair closer to the south-facing window. Below, on Store Street, was the front door of the coroner's office. Even a sneaked getaway through the side door still routed onto Store Street. As far as O'Leary was concerned, no matter how I left the building, I'd end up there. And as soon as I appeared he'd relay that message to Redmond.

I leaned back on the chair and rested my feet on the window ledge. I rocked back and forth, waiting. Silently, quietly, patiently. My mobile rang. It was Roche. 'Where are you?'

'Still at the office.'

She seemed reassured.

Then Reilly called. 'When're you leaving? I'm outside waiting.'

'I'll let you know.'

But I didn't want anyone interfering. I was considering tactics.

I rocked back and forth, Glock gripped firmly in my right hand. My mind drifted to the faces of the men who'd killed my parents, Dermot McKeever and Morgan Cusack. Twenty-nine-year-old McKeever was a six-foot, beefy, west Belfast refugee who'd fled across the border to County Louth. He only ever returned in the dead of night to terrorise. Thirty-year-old Cusack was a rat-faced whippet from south Armagh and the brains behind many operations. He'd been interned without trial for three years at the start of the Northern Ireland troubles. In prison he learned how to make bombs, use heavy-duty artillery and hate with an intensity that frightened even his own side. I learned much later he'd done the shooting when they attacked my house.

How many times had I fantasised about confronting them? Hundreds. No, more than hundreds. Thousands. And each time the scenario began and ended the same way. I'd still be twelve, the age I was the night they

371

came to kill. I'd spot McKeever and Cusack sitting on a seat at the side of some country road, sporting thick moustaches and heavy beards, the fashion among terrorists around then. They'd be talking and laughing. Enjoying life. I'd walk up to them and calmly stand in front. Left hand in a side pocket, the right hand behind my back gripping the old Glock pistol my father gave to me.

In my dream I'd watch their puzzled faces. 'Who're you?'

I'd always respond with the same words. 'Michael Wilson. Does that mean anything?'

They'd shake their heads, no. Sure what was one survivor to them? They'd murdered so many, how could they recall the faces of those that got away? Then slowly and deliberately I'd hold the Glock in both hands, pointing forwards. 'It'll mean a lot now.'

In this dream I always shot McKeever first. One round between the eyes. I did this so that before he died, Cusack would know gut-churning, heart-stopping fear. As I'd done. Then Cusack would get his comeuppance. Also between the eyes.

Now, in the turret of the Dublin City Coroner's Court, as once more I came to the end of that violent and brutal fantasy, something distracted me. A cloudburst was sweeping the streets. Pedestrians fled for shelter. Those queuing for buses huddled underneath awnings. The emptying streets left one man standing out. He was in a grey tracksuit top and bottoms with a grey hoodie to hide his face. He was tall and seriously overweight. And he was trying to clean his glasses. I stood and watched, my heart thumping like the beat of a drum. A gust of wind blew the hoodie onto his shoulders. My chest gripped in a vice of adrenalin. It was O'Leary. He was talking into a mobile phone. Redmond couldn't be far away.

I pulled off my red-striped tie and opened the top three buttons on my white shirt. I ruffled my hair to a dishevelled state. I draped my navy single-breasted jacket over my left arm. Then, Glock handgun gripped firmly in my right hand, I hid it in under the jacket folds. I walked quietly downstairs. The worst of the bedlam had subsided. A few journalists were gathered at the front door giving direct-to-air reports. Anyone with an opinion was being interviewed. There was only a handful hanging about inside, still badgering my staff for information. Phones were ringing and being answered. There were no loud rebukes. I didn't see Joan or Aoife or any other familiar face. No one noticed me take the basement keys. No one paid any attention as I reached the granite steps leading to the underground storage chamber. I unlocked the iron-studded door. I didn't need the low-watt bulb; I knew exactly where I was going. I went around one corner, sniffing mildew. It didn't make me cough. I felt my way along more shadowy twists and turns. Jacket draped over left arm, Glock held firmly under its folds. Past large steel cabinets jammed against the walls, filled with the files of Dublin's dead. Row after row of inquests.

Finally I reached the outer heavy oak door. On the other side was the building site. It would be wet. Red earth would ruin my shoes. And I'd cleaned them especially for today's inquest. I pushed the door. It gave way, slowly, reluctantly. Its ancient hinges had seen some action over the past weeks. I stepped into the open air. There was a hint of rain, a mist in the breeze. I studied the deserted site. Same mounds of rubble, red brick and concrete. Same block slabs. Same roof tiles, shattered and jagged. And rows of rusting pipes. The yellow JCB digger was gone. Someone must have driven it away this morning. Dark cloud covered the city skyline. I sensed static in the atmosphere. An electrical storm was brewing. A green plastic bag, blowing in the wind, wrapped itself around my right leg. I kicked it loose. It tumbled along the red earth. I pushed the door closed behind me. I stood and watched. A rat, big, brown and fat, scuttled along the side of the building. I followed it. The rat stopped, its front paws scraping the red clay. I couldn't take my eyes off it. Long, thin tail, ugly brown and scabby coat, narrow and pointed snout. It turned towards me. Motionless, unafraid and resolute that rat fixed on me. I stared back. The rat didn't flinch. Finally I forced a scowl so angry the rat bolted. I made for the gap in the hoarding at the back of the site.

Chapter 61

O'Leary was on the move. I'd circled the area twice, finally spotting him at the corner of Amiens Street. He was hurrying, mobile to ear. I followed at a distance, about twenty yards behind. The traffic was heavy, a snarling line edging towards the city centre. A stoplight was flicking too quickly from red to green and missing amber, adding to the confusion. Drivers seethed. Horns blared. Exhaust fumes billowed. Mini-whirlwinds shifted litter. O'Leary turned right along Custom House Quay. He darted a glance over his shoulder. I pretended great interest in a flyer stuck on an electricity pole. There was a free concert in one of Dublin's pubs tonight. Traditional Irish music, singing and dancing. It sounded inviting. I wouldn't be going. I'd other things on my mind.

The roads were wet and a breeze was picking up. People rushed to avoid the oncoming storm. Heads down, jacket collars up. Except me. I strode purposefully, my right hand clutching the Glock pistol inside the folds of my jacket. It was still draped over my left arm, pulled tight against my chest. My shirt was open at the top, my hair tossed and unkempt. My shoes were caked with building-site mud. I looked a sight and knew it. But I didn't care. I could see O'Leary and he couldn't see me. He'd lead me to Redmond.

O'Leary waited for a gap in traffic and hurried south. He crossed Butt Bridge onto Tara Street. I tracked him, zigzagging between a van and a sand lorry to keep him in sight. I darted in front of a green Ford Focus. The driver jammed the brakes, honked and shook an angry fist. I ignored her. But I was unsettled. Green was my unlucky colour. Was this an omen? I forced that out of my head. For such a big man O'Leary was moving faster than I could keep up with. Then I lost him. I pushed people out of the way, mumbling apologies. I had to find O'Leary. He'd gone. I chewed the inside of my cheek until it bled. I was getting desperate. Where was he? He was my only link to Redmond. I stood on tiptoes. Nowhere.

Then a horrible thought struck me. Someone had picked him up. He could be anywhere. I climbed onto black railings that circled the Customs House building. Now I could see heads bobbing, cyclists, vans, cars, trucks and lorries. I saw vagrants begging, hawkers selling trash jewellery, seagulls flapping away from the oncoming downpour. But I couldn't see O'Leary.

The cloud cover was now ominously dark, almost navy-black. To the south lightning flashed. Seconds later came a rumble of thunder. I smelled rain. I jumped down and ran towards Tara Street. I almost caused an accident dodging through a line of coaches. More horns sounded. A sudden gust blew grit into my eyes. I stopped. I couldn't rub them without revealing my gun. I blinked and blinked until enough tears washed the dirt away. I'd lost time. There was another flash of lightning. Followed by thunder. The storm was closing in. Raindrops, big and fat, plopped from the sky. I pushed on. Mouth now dry, gut now knotted. Around me umbrellas snapped into action. Most people had their heads bowed against the elements. I seemed to be the only one straining to see ahead. Still no sign of O'Leary.

I sprinted across Butt Bridge onto Tara Street, breathless and sweating. I skidded on wet pavement and almost fell on my face. A toddler clutching his mother's hand laughed out loud. Then I took off again, clumsily trying to hide the Glock. I was going against the traffic flow that'd taken me to the coroner's court five days previously. The day Redmond tried to have me killed. The day a contrived van breakdown stalled my security detail, triggering a shoot-out on Pearse Street. The same street I now turned into.

And almost collided with O'Leary. He was outside a public house, one finger in his left ear, shouting into a mobile phone. He'd his back to me, hopping from one foot to the other. Frantic. His hoodie was soaked, his hair matted. I stepped well back and stood in a shop front. Watched. Waited. O'Leary looked up and down Pearse Street. Then he glanced back along Tara Street. I pulled myself in deeper. He hadn't seen me. He dragged the top of his hoodie over his head but the wind blew it back. Then he hailed someone, beckoning to go into the pub.

I waited to a count of ninety. I went to the swing doors of the hostelry and squinted through a gap. O'Leary was sitting on a bar stool, wiping the lenses on his glasses. Beside him was a tall man in blue denims and white T-shirt. He'd a cheap plastic raincoat draped round his shoulders. Slim build, high cheekbones, handsome face with about two days' growth of moustache and beard. Bald head. The two were having an intense conversation, heads together.

I stepped aside to allow a customer in, coughing as if I was only there to catch my breath. The rain was getting heavier, bouncing off the pavements. The only noise I heard was the downpour on rooftops. And the pounding

377

of my heart. I thought my rib cage would explode. I chewed the inside of my cheek so hard pain seared along my cheekbone. The Redmond I knew had a fine head of hair. I'd seen that myself two days earlier when he stood over me in the woods. I glanced inside again. The two were on the move and coming towards me. I dodged out of the way and hid behind a parked lorry. I stepped into a puddle of water. My shoes and socks were soaked. I didn't care. I couldn't move. The public house doors swung open. O'Leary came out first. He checked up and down. A slight gesture waved the stranger to follow.

'Is everything okay?' The words were almost swallowed up in a squall of hail and wind. But I caught a very definite accent. *Educated south Dublin drawl*, as Sarah described it. Was it Redmond? The shaven head was too pale. There were cuts and nicks and blood spots above the ears, on the crown and temple. Whoever it was he'd been in one helluva hurry to change his appearance. But the bald head and facial hair didn't fool me. I pulled the Glock free. I waited until I was absolutely certain I'd the right man in my sights. The rain was now stair-rod heavy. I was soaked to the skin. My hair dripped rivulets onto my face. I blew them away. I blinked repeatedly. I had to focus on the final act. And I had to shoot straight.

'We've gotta get away from here.' It was Redmond. Those six words clinched it. He could hide his appearance but he couldn't change his accent. The street went halogen white from lightning. I counted. One, two, three, four, five, six. Now a deafening clap of thunder. It shook the ground. O'Leary was trying to hail a taxi. Redmond dragged his raincoat over his head, clutching it at the throat. I heard him swear. Six seconds after the next lightning flash there'd be another peal of thunder. That's when I'd make my move. Suddenly lightning flooded the sky an intense grey. The streetscape froze. I started counting down.

Six: a taxi pulled over.

Five: O'Leary reached for the rear door.

Four: he dropped his glasses. He swore as he fumbled on the wet road. I heard the cab driver shouting at him to get in.

Three: Redmond pushed O'Leary, forcing the big man into the back seat. Rain drilled off the car roof, like a relentless drumbeat.

Two: 'Redmond!' I shouted. Out the corner of my eye I noticed the cab driver. The windscreen wipers were swishing at full speed and he'd twisted his neck to see me better.

One: Redmond turned, as if in slow motion. I'd dropped my jacket and was holding the Glock in both hands. I was soaked through. My hair was bedraggled and straggling. My shirt stuck to my chest, my trousers were like drainpipes. My shoes were sponges. The drumbeat in my chest got louder.

Zero: the ground shook from a roll of thunder that almost popped my eardrums. And in that second of nerve-jarring commotion it was as if the world stopped. Redmond stared at me, slack-jawed and stunned. As the rumbling died away I shouted again.

'It's good to meet you.'

Chapter 62

I stood in that filthy, rainswept street, sodden and dishevelled. My heart wasn't pounding now; my mouth wasn't dry or bloody. No more than three feet from me stood my tormentor. Stunned, disbelieving and impotent, as if frozen in time. Our eyes met and I saw hatred. It was time to end it all. I raised the Glock towards Redmond's chest and braced for the recoil. Two quick rounds to the heart and lungs, that'd take him out immediately. If he moved after that I'd keep firing.

But I'd been followed.

There was a screech of brakes as a van pulled in front of the taxi. A side panel crashed open and six armed and balaclava-clad men jumped out. From behind strong arms grabbed me by the chest, wrestling me to the ground. A baton knocked the Glock from my hand. My head bounced off the tarmac, momentarily stunning me. Dirty water splashed on my face and I tasted oil. I spat, coughed and spat again. The taste of oil lingered. I heard shouts and curses, the scuffing of feet, glass shattering. Then a muffled gunshot. Someone moaned. Then another muffled gunshot. I heard O'Leary screaming 'Don't shoot, don't shoot!' There was a thud, like fist against jaw. O'Leary stopped screaming.

I was lying in a dirty puddle. Whoever had me in this bear hug was strong as an ox. I didn't struggle. I hoped he wouldn't crack my ribs. I looked up, blinking at the downpour. Another flash of lightning left orange, red and amber haloes in my vision. Seconds later thunder shook the ground. 'Don't move.' The bear hug eased. It wasn't an issue. I hadn't the strength to move. I opened my mouth and caught raindrops. Then I heard more angry shouts, 'Get down, get down, don't fucking move!' From my worm's-eye view I could see the taxi driver face down, arms and legs spread out. Rain drilled off the road beside him. There was a handgun pointing at his head. I wanted to cry out he was innocent. But the words wouldn't come.

Then I heard another gunshot. This time loud and distinct. I closed my eyes. When I opened them the taxi driver was still alive. Then there were more shouts. I recognised the Munster voice of DI Roche, now screaming: 'Get Wilson away!' Two shadowy figures swarmed over me. The bear hug was released and I was manhandled into the van. Waiting there was my bodyguard, Tony Reilly. His tight grey crew cut was covered by a black balaclava pulled up at the front. He was dressed in black: black T-shirt, black tracksuit top and bottoms and black runners. He reached out and dragged me inside, then forced me onto the floor. 'Go!' he shouted. The van scorched off with a squeal of tyres.

I struggled to a sitting position. In the rear of the van were narrow bucket seats with overhead leather straps. There was a steel container bolted to the floor. It was open. Inside were spare firearms, stun grenades and ammunition. As we sped through Dublin's streets I slid from one side to the other. Reilly heaved me into a seat and jammed my right hand into a strap. He looked at me, head shaking in disbelief. And what a sight he saw. I was soaked to the skin; my hair was like a field of corn after a hurricane. My shirt was filthy from mud and oil and sweat. My trousers, shoes and socks were soaked from dirty water. My face was streaked in grime, sweat and dirt.

Finally I spoke. 'Is it over?'

Reilly flicked his mobile phone open and spoke to someone. The conversation was short and agitated. Then he closed it and bit on his knuckles. He glanced at me. 'Yes. Redmond's dead.'

I felt my insides churn. I gasped for air. I took deep breaths, in and out, in and out, to keep myself from sinking into darkness. The van rounded a corner and I banged my head on the panelling.

'Slow down!' Reilly shouted.

The driver muttered a 'fuck off'.

'What happened?'

Reilly fiddled with his phone. The van went over a ramp and we were thrown around. My wrist twisted in the leather grip making me wince.

'What happened?' I pressed.

'Our orders were to arrest him. But Redmond wouldn't give up. He fired at us and we fired back.'

But I hadn't heard anyone shouting at Redmond as if to arrest him. He wasn't even carrying a gun. He'd an 'accident', as Roche warned. 'We won't be too careful. A gun could go off by mistake.' I imagined what'd happened: two quick rounds would kill him. Then a rogue gun, probably taken in one of the recent arms finds, would be forced into his lifeless fingers. Then another hand would take over, discharging a bullet into the taxi roof. And later the story would be recalled in reverse. Redmond was challenged; Redmond tried to shoot his way free; Redmond got shot. Twice.

We rounded another corner. I began to slump from

exhaustion. I forced my heels against the steel cabinet for support.

'Where's Sarah and the kids?'

Reilly's wizened features relaxed. 'They're good. We're taking them home.'

I leaned back. I heard rain drilling on the roof; I saw lightning flashes and heard thunder rumble. The storm was still overhead. Then the banging and rattling of the journey drowned all sounds. I closed my eyes.

Chapter 63

But it still wasn't over. Not for me and many others.

The inquest was reported nationally and internationally. Albert Dowling might have hoped for shelter in a secure psychiatric unit but was tracked down. The hospital was besieged by reporters and television crews. His treating psychiatrist gave a short press briefing: due to doctor–patient confidentiality he was restricted in what he could offer. His patient was undergoing a number of tests. Dowling was heavily sedated. Updates might be offered, depending on progress.

Then a British tabloid identified a second cabinet minister suspected of criminal association. He denied all, but resigned to give himself time to clear his name. Everyone knew he was a crook. No one expected his name to be cleared. The administration went into meltdown and surrendered. A general election was called.

'This mumbling, bumbling, incompetent and dishonest government has finally gone. Good riddance.' That's how one broadsheet editorial called it. The others were savage: 'Crooks!', 'Thank God They've Gone', 'Reject These Thugs'. Political observers predicted an opposition landslide victory. The same opposition offered 'new, dynamic and transforming' policies when in power. As a stunned electorate struggled to come to terms with this, another scandal erupted. Dublin's Evening Herald ran an exclusive, based on recovered notes held by their murdered crime correspondent, Stephen Brady. Most was a re-hash of what was already known. Brady had got hold of Redmond's A-list clients. This was published in a three-page exclusive. With photographs. There was public fury. Redmond's clientele included lawyers, doctors and media stars. *'They snorted enough white powder to allow Redmond to live like a king. And kill at will.'* Quote, unquote.

This triggered a national sense of shame. Role models were tumbling like nine-pins. The Roman Catholic Church was already reeling from child sex abuse scandals. Lawyers appeared regularly in court on charges of fraud and corruption. Doctors were considered the last bastion of decency and morality. When prominent surgeons and physicians were found to be dope heads it was almost like the end of civilisation. Media idols were somehow exempt from criticism. They were expected to behave like fools.

As the days progressed other details emerged. Noel Carty was thrown off the apartment roof by Redmond. Analysts believed Carty knew too much and had become a liability in Redmond's planned life of untroubled retirement.

The body in the shallow grave was eventually identified as Matt Dillon, the Standard and Chartered Bank troubleshooter. Dillon was in collusion with Richard Dowling to shore up the bank's secrets and stop leaks about the Redmond–Dowling connection. Piecing together strands of fact and lacing this with liberal doses of conjecture, reporters decided Dillon murdered Timothy Cunningham. Cunningham had already contacted Stephen Brady about his bank's corrupt activities. When Brady started making inquiries it was decided Cunningham had to be silenced. Dillon probably pushed

Cunningham into the canal. With his phobia of deep water he didn't stand a chance. But Mr Fixit Dillon also ran into trouble: when Redmond realised how much was missing from his finances he made his own inquiries. In his own way. He turned up at Timothy Cunningham's inquest to hear the official version. Then he bribed Arthur O'Leary to act as informant within the coroner's court. Cunningham's inquest file was removed (it was impossible to know for how long). Not long afterwards Matt Dillon disappeared. Autopsy showed he'd been tortured before being shot. Hearing shouts and gunfire John Hobbs spotted two men digging a trench. His woodland bolt-hole was also Carty's killing ground.

As more information became known, Standard and Chartered's CEO, Dan Thornton, was called in for further questioning. It was believed he'd ordered Timothy Cunningham's murder. His immunity from prosecution was revoked. New charges were drawn up.

Hobbs went off the radar. After the inquest an army charity moved him into a hostel. But when police kept badgering him for information and statements he did a runner. DI Roche eventually tracked his whereabouts. He was needed for another day in another court.

Roche was promoted to front an anti-racketeering unit. I heard that Danuta, her beautiful Polish doctor lover, was less than pleased with her partner's sudden rise to prominence. Their relationship came under intense media scrutiny. Danuta fled to Warsaw to escape the paparazzi; Roche hid out in a cottage on the west coast. Neither was seen again in public for some time.

Tony Reilly resigned from protection duty. When I spoke with him he told me he'd been moved to a desk job at police HQ. Strangely he seemed quite happy with the transfer. I always considered him a bit of an action man and thought he'd soon get bored. Nonetheless, he was certainly relieved to be finished with me.

Arthur O'Leary, the traitor in the coroner's court, was charged with a number of offences and refused bail awaiting trial. By contrast, the mole within the police was never identified. Everyone suspected Alan Hutchins. He was the senior officer who'd called an abrupt end to the Dowling investigation. But there wasn't enough to pin him down. He was sidelined within the force and treated like a pariah. He eventually resigned. Still, no one was brought to justice.

Looking back I should've known Albert Dowling's descent from bully-boy minister to feeble and addled husband was a smokescreen. The decline was too soon and dramatic. In my own defence there was so much else going on it took time to grasp that tactic. Mary and Richard Dowling were released on bail. Their passports were confiscated and they were put under twenty-four hour surveillance. It was more or less house arrest. The mob bayed so loudly the judiciary promised an early trial.

Seamus Dowling and his lover Niamh Shanahan fled London to escape the media chase. They made their way to Amsterdam and then disappeared. I'm sure Declan Shanahan, the girl's father, knows where they are. I'm also sure he won't tell anyone.

Chapter 64

But what about me? And my wife and children? Did we come together again? Yes, but with great difficulty. Sarah didn't leave for London. She didn't seek refuge in high-flying brother Trevor's fancy apartment. With Redmond dead the threat to our lives ended. The security that had enveloped us disappeared within hours. The judge was taken from his fancy hotel back to Glasthule. I heard he wasn't a bit pleased. But our home had changed. It now seemed like a hotel with vaguely familiar guests, desperate not to meet one another. We were overly polite. Excuse me, sorry about that, my mistake. Good morning, Michael. Good night, Michael. I'm going shopping, Michael. Will you be here for dinner? Yes? Anything you'd like especially? Sarah treated me like a lodger. Jennifer and Gregory left early each morning and returned home late most evenings. Now that they were no longer considered dangerous companions, they'd re-connected with friends. Indeed they were sought after by other parents, desperate to hear the inside track on everything. This sort of hot gossip didn't come round very often. Sarah too found time to have coffee with girlfriends, visit relatives, whatever.

How did I feel? To be honest I was still in a state of shock. Then I was swamped by self-recrimination. Especially as I watched my family treat me like some houseguest. I couldn't sleep properly, tossing and turning in the spare room. Each day I awoke feeling emotionally drained and physically exhausted. And each sleepless night I went over events. Did I *have* to behave as I did? With hindsight, that great gift, did I *have* to become so involved in the search for the truth behind Patrick Dowling's death? Surely that was a police inquiry? But the inquest file was riddled with faults. I couldn't have let that go unchallenged. And didn't. As DI Roche said when we first met, I owed it to County Coroner Harold Rafferty. To finish the mission he'd set out on. And I owed it to Patrick Dowling. Who else was going to stand up for him? After a while I stopped torturing myself with why, what if, maybe etc. What happened happened; the clock couldn't be turned back.

There was a public clamour for me to stay on as Dublin City Coroner. Somebody even started a petition. There were thousands of signatures, from all over the country. I was touched by the show of affection and support. I promised nothing. I declined media interviews. I became a recluse. The state hurriedly moved a coroner from the north-east to look after Dublin's ghosts.

Ten days later and after yet another disturbed night, I slipped out of the house. Before I left I tiptoed around the first floor, checking on everyone. Sarah was asleep and beautiful as ever, her long blonde hair fanned over the pillows. Gregory was lying almost upside down in his bed, pillows scattered on the floor. Looking down on him a new Chelsea poster, this time Frank Lampard kissing his badge. I brushed my fingertips against Gregory's forehead and he wrinkled his nose. I stared at him for maybe three minutes. All I could see was myself at the same age. He *was* looking more and more like me. Jennifer was curled in a ball, arms clutching her favourite teddy. I squinted for a better look. There was Sarah Ross at fifteen, I was sure of that. She was the image of her mother. Was it any wonder they had so many secret chats?

I scribbled a note for Sarah and left it on the kitchen table: *'Gone for a long drive to sort my head out. Love, Mike'*.

The radio clock ticked to 6.30 a.m. as I eased my five-year-old Saab onto the road. I drove slowly until I was well away from the house. Then I opened the engine up and headed for the M50 ring road around Dublin. I headed northwards. Traffic was light and I made good time. Two hours later I was across the border in county Tyrone and in the area where I grew up. I took a left off the main road and cut through narrow country lanes; stopping at familiar signposts, negotiating familiar and dangerous bends. There was high cloud cover with a weak sun. It was humid. The air smelled of fertiliser and manure. Fresh hedge cuttings lay in clumps. A black sheepdog gave chase for about a hundred yards, barking and snapping. I followed his annoyance in the rear-view mirror until he lost interest.

Around 9.30 a.m. I stood beside my parents' grave. The area was deserted. The church with its tall spire towered over the cemetery. In the strengthening light it cast long shadows. The far-off hills had been harvested and only corn stubble remained. Rooks cawed, cows lowed, sheep bleated, dogs barked. There was a gentle breeze. I scraped moss from the headstone and picked weeds from grass covering the plot. I noticed fresh disturbance in the grave to the left. Last time I'd been here it held one body, a young boy killed in an accident. Now there was a recent addition. I squinted at the letters chiselled on the granite headstone. His sister had joined him a month ago. GONE TO THE LORD. Nothing else offered by way of explanation. I checked to my right.

Still the same three souls from the same family, buried within twenty years of one another.

I spoke quietly to Mum and Dad. I told them what'd happened. 'I know you know all this. Didn't I pray to you for support? Thanks for helping me get through that hell.' Then I explained how I felt now, how my heart was broken. I was a stranger in my own house, to my wife and children.

I admitted I still felt hatred for their killers, McKeever and Cusack. I apologised: 'You didn't rear me to hate.' Finally I stopped and listened. And listened. And thought. And listened. Only the rooks, cows, dogs and the sheep showed life. The graveyard held only the dead. Then my mobile rang. I checked the ID: it was Sarah. I let it ring out and listened to her voicemail message. *'Where are you, Mike? Please ring me. I love you.'* I re-played the message. Sarah had used the affectionate Mike, not the disdainful Michael. She said she loved me. I sent a quick text, *'home @ 2.'*

It was time to join the living again. I remembered Jennifer's telling-off: 'Dad, you spend too much time with the dead. Someday you'll wise up and realise that the living are important too.' I *had* wised up and knew what was important.

I drove back to Dublin, stopping once for sandwiches and coffee. I made Glasthule in the early afternoon. In a nearby florist I bought the biggest bunch of red roses I could find. When I pulled into our street Sarah was pacing the pavement.

'Where've you been?' She was distraught, her face pale and drawn. Her eyes were red and swollen. She was dressed in an old tracksuit top and bottom and her hair looked a mess. Mussed and unkempt. 'After all that's happened how can you just suddenly disappear? I was worried sick what you might do.'

I handed the flowers over. She inspected them and sniffed their perfume.

'Hi, Sarah Ross,' I said.

She looked me up and down. Her distress was easing but her chest still heaved with fright.

'Hi, Dr Wilson.' There was the hint of a smile. But only a hint.

I glanced up and down the road. I saw parked cars, a delivery van and a motorbike courier. That didn't frighten me. I was past caring about motorbike assassins. A cyclist cruised past. A middle-aged lady in denims and too-small T-shirt strode briskly towards us. She was listening to music on an iPod while straining to control a large dog. I waited until she'd rounded the bend.

'I love you, Sarah. I can't live without you and I can't live without my children. Can we put all that's happened behind us and start afresh?'

Sarah was crying into the bouquet. I reached across and wiped her tears away.

'Would you marry me again? After all we've been through, would you still say yes?'

Sarah blinked the wetness free and put on a great show of considering this. Finally, 'Are you asking, Dr Wilson?'

'I am, Miss Ross. Will you marry me?' I leaned down and kissed her. It was pure nectar. Soft lips, her tongue searching for mine. The flowers slipped to the pavement as she wrapped her arms around me. I bathed in her softness, relished the smell off her skin. I kissed away fresh tears. We broke free, seeing one another for the first time after a dreadful period.

Sarah reached up and took my head in her hands. She drew me closer. 'Yes, I will.'